THE
CHINA
FRONT

Anastasia,
Good luck with your
writing!

THE
CHINA
FRONT

BY
D. ORION ENKING

Perma
PUBLISHING

Printed in the United States of America

First Printing, 2020

ISBN 978-1-7351170-0-3

Perma Publishing
1714 Franklin St, #100456
Oakland, CA 94612
www.PermaPublishing.com

Edited by Molly Enking
Cover design by Alexander Paul

Cover image created with the use of: "Around Trinity Place (41761010471).jpg" from Wikimedia Commons / Tom Winckels (CC BY 3.0) and "Beijing Imperial Palace At Night (165363861).jpeg" from Wikimedia Commons / Billie Grace Ward (CC BY 2.0).

To my parents, Kathy and Patrick,
for always believing in me and giving me the space and
encouragement to become who I am.

ACKNOWLEDGMENTS

First I have to thank my sister, Molly, who also has the fitting and unnerving (for me) role of being my editor. I've always said that she's a better writer than me, and I hope she someday gets around to writing her own book. Her sharp eye, wit and brutal honesty were essential in getting through multiple iterations of this book.

This book was inspired in part from conversations with my friends Huishan Lian and James Barnard, both of whom suggested I should turn my ideas and experiences into a novel instead of following the well-worn path of memoirs written about being a foreigner in China. James is also part of my "Goals Check-In" group, along with Charles Becker and Anthony Singleterry, all of whom taught English with me in China, and all of whom read earlier parts of this story, gave me invaluable feedback, and encouraged me to keep at it.

I also want to thank the other trial readers of earlier drafts, including my good friends Riley Rowland, John Hoopes, Weiyi Zheng, and my cousin Katie Mickschl.

Finally, teachers never get enough credit in this world, and so I need to acknowledge two of the most influential teachers from my childhood: Tom McKibben, who encouraged my early creativity and inspired me to protect the environment, and Hank Ogilby, whose global politics class was the fork in the road that led me to eventually travel and live abroad.

CONTENTS

AUTHOR'S NOTE

There is a lot of speculation surrounding the concept of geoengineering, much of which lacks any basis in science or fact. But the idea of solar geoengineering is very real and very attainable, and it could have monumental consequences for our planet and world geopolitics.

While this book is a work of fiction, it attempts to separate the fact from the fiction when it comes to geoengineering and weather control. The information uncovered by the protagonist is based on real science and technology, some of which are viable today.

CHAPTER 1:

THE CENTER IN THE MIDDLE OF NOWHERE

Andrew Oxley was not a spy. Not really. So how in the world had he imagined they'd be able to break into a top-secret Chinese government facility?

They bounced up and down over the dirt road in the jeep they'd stolen ten hours earlier on the outskirts of Beijing. Looking out the windows, all Andrew could see was the vast expanse of the Mongolian-Manchurian steppe stretched out before them. The nearly flat plain was blanketed in nothing but tall, thin grasses, swaying slowly in the chilling fall winds sweeping down from Siberia. Nothing, except for a single rectangular building that had appeared on the horizon minutes earlier. It imposed on the grasslands like an expansive sore disrupting otherwise smooth skin. The sun was just beginning to rise behind the building, casting it in a long shadow.

Charlie Wu was driving, his normally candle flame-shaped black hair blowing every which way. Today in place of his normally fashionable appearance he'd covered his slim frame in a cheap collared shirt and faux leather jacket—the typical garb of the average Chinese handler. Only a few years older than Andrew, Charlie still had the restless energy of a teenager. He was trying, with one hand, to light a cigarette clutched in his teeth while using the other hand to protect the cigarette from being blown out by wind from the open window. Only his knee was steering, just barely keeping the vehicle from careening off the dirt road.

Andrew thought for a moment about telling Charlie to cut it out, but then he thought better of it. Charlie had risked a lot to help him. And they were all tired. Andrew hoped it would all be worth it. With any luck, the building in front of them would contain the answers he'd been seeking for months. And once they revealed its secrets, the world would change.

To his right, Mazken was somehow managing to sit quite still, a blank expression on his face, earbuds tucked neatly into his ears. The rising sun was reflecting off of his entirely shaven head, sending a faint beam of light toward the front window. Andrew imagined Charlie using the glare to light his cigarette. Mazken had changed out of his usual T-shirt and jeans into a black suit that made his six-foot-two figure look even more intimidating than usual. Mazken was risking a lot too, but it was different somehow. Mazken seemed to live for these kinds of things.

Mazken turned to examine Andrew. Then he grinned and took the earbuds out. "We must be getting close, huh, mate?"

Andrew realized Mazken must have sensed him tensing up as the building had come into view. He nodded.

"So which do you think is the most convincing Russian body-guard glare?" he asked, making a flat expression that Andrew thought made him look slightly stoned, then widening his eyes and twisting his upper lip into a gnarled shape that made him look like some sort of Halloween ghoul.

"Definitely the second one," Andrew hoped Mazken was just messing around. Neither look seemed convincing.

"Oh no."

"What is it, Charlie?"

"I see tanks. I knew this is a bad idea."

Mazken climbed to the space between the two front seats and peered out the front window. "Those aren't tanks mate, those are just big trucks."

"Whatever. Point is, this place is too heavily guarded.

How we ever going to get in?"

"The plan will work, Charlie," Andrew said, maybe as much for himself as for Charlie. "I'm sure Mazken and I can pass as Russians."

"Ha, sorry Drew, you don't look like Russian executive."

"It's all about how he presents himself, mate. If Drew thinks, walks, and talks like a Russian executive, then he'll look like one."

Charlie smirked, "How is he going to do that? He's never even been to Russia!"

"Neither have you. Neither have most Chinese."

"But we don't know about these ones. There could be high up government agents that travel there all the time."

"You know, you're not making this any easier on Drew here mate."

"None of that matters as long as Mazken plays a convincing bodyguard," said Andrew, again trying to reassure himself.

"Uh, mute bodyguard," Mazken reminded him. "I don't speak a word of Russian."

"Well then, it's a good thing I took some in college. But meetings like this always happen in English anyway… right?"

There was a long pause. They looked at each other.

"It is too dangerous. I say we sneak in back."

"In back where? The place has probably got soldiers everywhere."

"And then once we get in," Mazken chimed in, "how are we going to get any documents that prove what they're up to?"

"You leave it to me. You know I can hack any computer," Charlie grinned.

"As much as I believe it mate, we have more collective experience in people-hacking."

People-hacking. That was a good way to put it. That's what he'd been learning from Mazken and Charlie over the past few months. And that was how Andrew had gotten his hands on the information that had led them here. But that information had come at a high price. And who would be the next casualty of his recklessness? Andrew shook his head, trying to banish those thoughts. There was really nothing he could have done differently. And anyway, he couldn't afford to dwell on that now.

The building was coming closer into view. He could see that next to the building stretched a large runway, with five airplanes parked on it. The planes looked very strange. Their bodies seemed roughly the size of large passenger jets, but they had the shape of stealth bombers. The wings were also far longer than either type of plane, making them look somewhat like high-altitude spy planes.

"What's the matter, Drew?" Mazken was looking at him again.

"I thought maybe those files had been wrong about the airplanes spreading chemicals in the stratosphere. But there they are. This wasn't what I was expecting at all."

"Well if you already know what is out here, why we have to come all this way?" Charlie complained.

Andrew ignored him and continued to look ahead. The entire facility was surrounded by a barbed-wire fence, but there was a gate dead ahead of them, with what looked like several armed soldiers. Andrew took a deep breath.

"What if they see this Russian guy before?" Charlie continued. "They will know Andrew is not him."

"Come on Charlie, you know all white guys look the same to Chinese people."

Charlie finally grinned. "I never said it."

"I had my… organization do some research on this guy. They didn't find a record of him coming to China before."

Charlie twitched.

"See mate?" Mazken laughed, pounding Charlie on the back. "There's nothing to worry about. This is going to be a bloody good time."

"Oh noooo," Charlie moaned, his face turning pale.

Andrew looked ahead and saw at least half a dozen armed soldiers running out of the gate in front of them, and lining up in front of the gate with machine guns pointed in their direction.

"Don't stop until we reach them, Charlie," Andrew warned. "We don't want them to see us hesitate." Andrew turned to Mazken. "Still think this is going to be a good time?"

Mazken was frowning now. But then he shrugged. "At least they haven't started firing yet."

Charlie began to slow the jeep, finally coming to a stop about 20 feet from the soldiers. Andrew suddenly realized he was squeezing the seat in front of him so hard that the blood was draining from his fingers.

"You've got this Charlie. Mazken and I better stay in here, like nothing is wrong."

Charlie rolled his eyes and mumbled something under his breath, then stuck his head out of the car and yelled at the soldiers in Chinese.

"Qing gei e luo si youqi gongsi de Ivanovich xian sheng rang yi xia lu." *Kindly move out of the way for Mr. Ivanovich from Russia Oil and Gas.* Andrew saw that Charlie's leg was trembling, but Andrew noted that he managed to keep the top half of his body still and confident.

The soldiers didn't move for a moment. A few of them looked at each other. Then one of them shouted back at Charlie, "Suo you ren xia lai, ba shuang shou ju guo tou ding." *Everyone in that vehicle must get out and put your hands above your head.*

Charlie turned back to Andrew and Mazken, "He said, everyone in that vehicle must get…"

"We understood what he said, Charlie," Andrew cut in.

"I know you two understand Chinese," Charlie shot back, "But now you are Russian executive, remember? So I have to at least pretend to translate."

"Kuai, Kuai!" *Hurry up*, yelled the same soldier.

Andrew let Mazken and Charlie get out first, then he stepped out next to Mazken and slowly raised his hands in the air. A few of the soldiers approached them slowly and began patting them down.

"*You are making a big mistake,*" Charlie continued. "*Mr. Ivanovich has come a long way and does not wish to be held up,"*

"What is this? Who are you?" The man acted like he hadn't understood anything Charlie had said.

"As I said, this is Executive Vice President Ivan Ivanovich from Russia Oil and Gas. He has a scheduled visit to the facility today."

The man looked at Andrew, who was dressed in a suit, and Mazken, who was glaring at him with a scowl on his face.

"No one informed us about this."

"And who would have informed you about Mr. Ivanovich's visit?"

"The center director, Dr. Stone."

"Well, then I suggest you call Dr. Stone and tell him to come down here."

The soldier hesitated for a moment, then pulled out a radio, turned around, and began walking back toward the gate, mumbling something into the radio. Nice going, Charlie, thought Andrew. The soldiers seemed to relax, so he slowly began putting his hands down. But one of the soldiers turned his gun directly at him: "Bie dong!" *Don't move.*

Andrew heard a reply shouted back at the soldier through the radio. It sounded like someone on the other end was not happy. The soldier responded, matching the whining tone of the person on the other end. Andrew held his breath.

Finally, the soldier turned back to them and shouted, *"Please wait a moment, Dr. Stone will be out here shortly."* Andrew slowly let his breath out.

"Now for the real test," mumbled Mazken. "Let's see if this Dr. Stone is a Mao or a Zhou."

"Do you mean alpha or beta?" Charlie asked.

"Just trying to add some Chinese characteristics to my English, you know mate?"

"Shut up, you two," Andrew hissed.

A few minutes later, they saw a figure walking toward them from the main building, flanked by more soldiers.

"Oh," Mazken smirked, "definitely a Zhou. This is going to be no problemo."

"How can you tell?"

"Just look at the man."

Andrew saw that the man was short, with large glasses and a balding head. He wore a flowing white lab coat over a striped button-down shirt and dress slacks. Andrew thought he knew what Mazken meant.

Dr. Stone stopped in front of them and looked Andrew up and down. Then he turned to Mazken, who glared at him. He flinched a little and turned to Charlie.

"*To be honest, we were not expecting Mr. Ivanovich until tomorrow.*

"*Well as you can see, he's here today, and he's getting impatient,*" Charlie said.

Dr. Stone looked at Andrew again and narrowed his eyes. "*He is far too young to be Mr. Ivanovich. I've seen his pictures.*"

Andrew's mind froze. He'd seen his pictures after all. They were screwed.

"*You're lucky he didn't understand what you said about his age...*" But Charlie was cut off.

"*Enough! Arrest them.*" Andrew could see a triumphant look in Dr. Stone's eyes. Had he been expecting this?

The soldiers all stiffened their stances and cocked their guns.

"*On the ground, now!*"

"*Now hold on a minute, what do you think...*"

A gunshot went off. All three of them ducked. Andrew braced himself for pain or screams, but it didn't seem like anyone had been hit. Six of the soldiers ran forward and grabbed each of them by the arms. Andrew looked at Charlie, who stared back at him. He was out of ideas. And anyone that could help them was hundreds of miles away.

And then, Andrew's dread turned to ice-cold fear as he realized that his former boss, Lao Cheng, who he'd been spying on for months, would likely be informed of his capture. Falling into the hands of Lao Cheng, one of the most powerful men in China, would likely mean torture of the worst kind. He'd eventually die a prisoner, and the world would never know about the Chinese plan to manipulate the climate.

CHAPTER 2:

THE GRADUATE

Five months earlier...

It was far too hot for a spring day in Boston, but Andrew was more concerned with the man in the grey tuxedo and cowboy hat, looking in his direction. Even though Andrew had grown used to being watched, that didn't stop the chills from rolling through his body. And usually, the men watching him were more inconspicuous.

"I think we should go inside until the ceremony starts," he said to his mother. It was his graduation day, and his family was gathered around him on the academic quad of Tufts University. His mother Abigail Oxley was in the middle of their group, using one hand to tighten the tie Andrew's brother Matthias was wearing, while supporting her father, Major Joseph O'Brien, with her other.

"Why in God's name would we do that? We're going to have a hard enough time finding seats together as it is." With a shove to match the strength of her resolve, she managed to stretch her arm up to Matthias's neck, and then finally let go.

"This thing is restrictive, Mom."

"I don't want to hear any more complaining Mattie. I know you've never put a tie on properly in your life, but for your information, they're meant to be worn that way." Matthias had inherited the tall, lanky Oxley genes so that their short, pear-shaped mother could barely reach his neck. Andrew by contrast had stopped growing when he'd reached five-foot-eight, but he had a lean build, which he attributed to practicing martial arts.

Andrew looked around to see if anyone else in the crowd was looking at him. It had all started about a year ago when he noticed a man in a suit reading a newspaper on a bench outside his dorm – something that seemed out of place for a college campus. After that he'd begun to notice them here and there. From then on they were always dressed in plain clothes, but they still looked out of place. He knew they were neither professors nor parents, and each one seemed to take just a little too much interest in him.

"What are you looking at, Drew?"

His sixteen-year-old sister Rose had turned her astute eyes on Andrew. He knew she could read even the smallest hint of an expression on his face and interpret how he was feeling. She had inherited her keen observation powers from their mother.

"We should avoid being outside for too long. It's going to be unnaturally hot today." He looked over at their mother. "I'm worried about Grandpa."

"What's that my boy? Did I hear you say you're worried about me? There's no need for that, now. Your grandpa can take care of himself."

"Why so worried?" Rose pressed him. "You don't still believe in those conspiracies about the government controlling the weather, do you?"

"Conspiracy? Nonsense, my dear girl. Haven't you noticed all those white streaks in the sky lately? Chemtrails, they call 'em. They weren't there when I was young." He lowered his voice. "It's the government spraying chemicals to change the climate."

At his grandfather's mention, Andrew glanced up. Sure enough, there were several white streaks crisscrossing the sky already that day.

"You too, Grandpa? Where do you read this stuff?" asked

Rose, raising her eyebrows.

"Oh, everyone knows about it. It's science," he said, waving his hand in the air. "It goes all the way back to 'Nam. Our guys sprayed chemicals into the air over the Vietcong to make it rain on their trails. And it worked like magic. I'm sure that played a big role in their defeat."

"But we didn't defeat them, Grandpa. They won that war."

"Like hell they did."

"Watch your language now, Dad," Abigail intervened.

"You didn't answer my question, Drew."

Andrew knew Rose wouldn't let him off the hook. "How do you know it's not true, Rose? All this extreme weather can't just be explained by global warming."

"The only reason you believe that is because of whatever Dad said to you."

Andrew stiffened at the mention of their father. His mother looked over at Rose too and frowned.

"So what if it is? I'm telling you, he knew something. You weren't there to see that look on his face."

"I know, I know, I was too young, blah blah blah."

"All right you three, no more conspiracies, we need to get a family photo and then find some seats. Mattie, your tie is loose again. I told you not to play with it."

"There's no way I'm keeping this thing on all day."

"Now you listen to your mother, young man," Grandpa Joe chimed in. "When I was in 'Nam we had to wear a lot more gear than that while we were out in the blazing sun all day."

"Mom, will you fix my braid? The left one is coming out."

"Don't you think it's time you stopped wearing your hair that way, dear?"

Andrew knew it would be impossible for anyone but their mother to herd the family anywhere. Despite his more immediate concern of the man in the tuxedo, he was genuinely concerned about the heat. He'd spent enough time studying the weather over the past several years that he was sure something unnatural was happening. He just wasn't sure what – or maybe, *who* – was causing it. It wasn't that he didn't believe in global warming. But he was convinced that someone was purposely magnifying its intensity. He recalled again what his father had said to him on their sailboat twelve years ago, as they'd raced toward the safety of land. *This hurricane is manmade.* He knew his father had kept a lot of secrets. And Andrew thought he'd been on the verge of divulging some of them to him. But he had never got the chance.

Had these same men been watching his father? And now perhaps they'd realized that he was trying to pick up where his father left off. Somehow it seemed unlikely, as he still had almost no idea what his father had been up to that might have attracted the attention of the wrong people. He passed his gaze across the crowd, returning it eventually to the spot where he'd seen the man.

The man in the tuxedo was walking toward him.

Now Andrew began to panic. This wasn't supposed to happen. None of these men had ever approached him. And he didn't want to know what the man was going to do when he reached him.

The lawn was getting crowded enough that it would be easy to disappear. He began to move away from his family, toward a large group of people walking toward the stage. He ducked behind them and walked with them for about ten feet, then moved quickly under a nearby tree. Looking around the tree, he couldn't see the man in the grey tuxedo anywhere. Had he lost him?

Then he noticed a familiar figure standing under another tree just a short distance away. May Li was staring into the distance, a look of serene calm about her as if she were somehow insulated from the noisy environment. She had her graduation gown slung over her arm and was wearing a long, slender dress of deep red, in stark contrast against her pale skin and long black hair that came down almost to her waist.

Andrew felt his heart begin to race as he watched her. He'd been immediately taken by her beauty and quick wit when they'd met in November his freshman year. By the second semester, she'd found herself a boyfriend. It didn't surprise

Andrew—a girl as beautiful as she was wouldn't remain single long. Still, it had disappointed him. Since then he'd kept a friendly distance. But he'd heard recently that she'd broken up with her boyfriend. This might be his last chance. He had no idea whether she was going to stay in Boston after graduation, or even in America.

He began walking toward her, trying to think of something clever to say, but as he walked, his mind seemed to go blank.

"Uh, hi May."

She looked over at him, and a smile broke across her face, "Hi Andrew."

"How's it going?"

"Oh, not bad, it's just so hot. I'm trying to keep cool while I wait for my parents."

"That's going to be difficult today." He looked around, but he still didn't see the man in the tuxedo. "I don't know why they're having the ceremony outdoors."

"I was thinking the same thing."

Andrew met her eyes. "Really?"

"Yeah. This heatwave is definitely not normal. But people should be getting used to a new normal by now I suppose. You'd think they would take better precautions."

It made sense to Andrew that she saw things the same way he did. He always knew they were similar. He lowered his voice, "Who do you think is causing it?"

May blinked and stared at him for a moment. "What do you mean, 'Who'? I think it's being caused by climate change."

"But you said it was 'not normal.' Don't you think the government might be doing something to change the weather?"

May seemed to consider this for a moment. "Well, the Chinese government does that sometimes. But I don't think the U.S. government is capable of it. They don't have that kind of control over this country."

"Tian gao, huangdi yuan," *Heaven is high, and the emperor is far away*. The words just slipped out of Andrew's mouth without him really thinking about them.

May's eyes widened and her mouth opened slightly. "Ni hui jiang zhongwen?" *You can speak Chinese?*

"Dui." Andrew couldn't help but smile at her reaction.

"Ni zenme meiyou gaosu wo ya?" *Why didn't you ever tell me?*

"I don't know, it just never occurred to me. Actually, I haven't spoken it for a long time."

"So why did you say that phrase?"

"My nanny used to say it all the time when my mom was away. What you said about the U.S. government just reminded me of it."

"Your nanny was Chinese? So that's how you learned to speak it?"

"Yeah, when I was really young. And then my dad put me in a Mandarin immersion school."

May gave him a puzzled look. "So strange. I wonder why?"

"I've always wondered why too. But my mom doesn't seem to know, or at least she doesn't want to tell me, and I'll never be able to ask my dad."

"Why is that?"

"Because he died twelve years ago."

"Oh, I didn't know that. I'm sorry."

This was not going in the direction Andrew had wanted it to. They weren't supposed to be talking about his dead father. But somehow his father kept coming up in all his conversations, like a ghost that wouldn't stop haunting him.

"So, what are you doing after graduation?" Andrew changed the subject.

"Well, my parents want to go eat seafood, since Boston is famous for it…"

"No, I meant, do you have a job? Are you going to stay in America?" He tried to disguise the hopeful tone in his voice.

"Oh, you mean that. No. My father found me this job back in China. It's based in Beijing, working for a big state-owned enterprise."

"Oh, that sounds cool." What was a state-owned

27

enterprise?

"It's not really what I wanted to do, but it's very prestigious. I guess it's OK for now. You know," she paused, "I really wanted to stay in America and try to become a journalist here, but my parents insisted that I come back to China."

"Parents always think they know what's best for us, don't they?"

"Well, I guess they do, sometimes."

"My mom always tries to control everything I do, it's really frustrating."

"But don't you think she's just doing it because she loves you?"

"Oh, I guess so. But she wants me to get a regular office job. And I want to do something more... unconventional. Something where I feel like I'm making a real difference, you know? I'm just not sure what yet."

"I'm sure you'll think of something," said May. Her eyes were the color of dark chocolate. Andrew couldn't help but stare into them. May returned his gaze for a few seconds, and then looked away. Andrew thought her face had turned a little red.

"Andrew, there you are. I've been trying to get this family together to take a picture."

Andrew looked around, alarmed. If his mother had been able to find him, surely the man in the tuxedo would too. But he was still nowhere in sight.

"Oh, hello, miss," Andrew's mother turned to May as if just noticing her.

"Mom, this is May, she's a friend of mine."

"Oh, I see. And where... are... you... from...?"

"Mom, you don't have to do that, she speaks perfect English," Andrew muttered.

"I was in some of your son's classes, Mrs. Oxley. I'm from China."

"Oh. Lovely," Andrew hoped May wouldn't detect the sarcasm in his mother's voice. "Would you come over and help take a picture of our family, dear?"

"I'd be happy to."

"Excellent," they walked back over to where the family was gathered. "Now everyone *please* come over here and let's get this done so we can go get some seats before they are all taken."

"Well, looks like I showed up just in time."

Andrew turned around. His Uncle Cooper was walking toward them. It was eerie how much he looked like Andrew's father, with his shaggy brown hair and slightly out of control beard. Of all his extended family members, Andrew had wanted to see his uncle the most at his graduation. Cooper was just a few hours drive up in Maine, and though he had been almost a constant presence in Andrew's life before his father died, now he rarely came to visit, and when he did it was almost always unplanned and brief.

"Nice of you to show up," said Andrew in as bright a tone as he could muster.

"Cooper, what a surprise to see you here," his mother didn't even try to conceal her disdain. "Here, you're just in time to help us take an O'Brien family picture, so we can let this young lady go find her family," she snatched the camera from May and thrust it into Cooper's arms.

May looked startled, then she looked over at Andrew, made a playful, funny face at him, and then walked away. Andrew watched her go. He would much rather have followed her than stayed for the picture. When would he ever see her again?

They found some seats among the thousands that were spread out across the lawn. Andrew continued to look around for the man in the tuxedo, but he was nowhere to be seen.

It was a little past noon, and Andrew could feel the sweat soaking into his graduation robe. He looked at the weather app on his phone. The temperature had climbed to 106 degrees. That was unheard of in Boston for that time of year.

"I really think we should go inside, Mom," Andrew urged. "I heard they were setting up TVs inside for people to watch who didn't want to sit outside."

"After we managed to find such good seats? You'll just have to put up with the heat a little longer Andrew."

"This isn't about me, Mom." Andrew knew what she was thinking: a little suffering builds character. His generation was too pampered, she thought. It was hard to get her to take him seriously.

"I don't want to hear another word about it," she whispered to him. Just then, the Tufts president began speaking into the microphone. The ceremony had begun.

Andrew felt an overwhelming feeling of helplessness begin to creep through him. It was the same feeling he'd had twelve years ago. He'd wanted to get to his father and pull him back on board, but he was only nine and was just regaining his feet after nearly washing overboard himself. After his father disappeared into the ocean, he and his Uncle Cooper had barely made it to shore. It was a scene he'd replayed countless times over the years. Even though he knew on some level there was nothing he could have done differently, it didn't stop the guilt.

He drifted into a heat-induced daze, partly conscious of the ceremony, and partly lost in memory. But as the keynote speaker was announced, he suddenly came back to reality and sat up. The speaker, William Rothschild, had graduated in the same class as his father. Andrew wondered if they had known each other. As the CEO of one of the largest privately-owned oil companies in America, Rothschild Industries, he was also very controversial. Andrew noticed that a small crowd of protesters had formed near the stage and were being held back by security personnel.

"Now I know this is a graduation ceremony, and you're all expecting a speech with the customary optimistic and encouraging commentary," Rothschild began. "But I'm here to give you a warning." He paused and looked around. There was a murmur from the crowd. "We live in a world of growing instability. There are many factors contributing to this, but I'm mainly talking about the climate. Yes, as much as it might surprise you and the concerned citizens who've gathered over here," he gestured toward the protesters, "I'm here to tell you that our climate is changing. The good news is, there are technologies emerging today that can help us solve this problem. And as you all go out into the professional world, there will be great career opportunities for you in these fields."

"The bad news is, our climate is changing more quickly than anyone thought. And because of that, there may not be time for anything but the most rapid and drastic response."

Andrew wondered if Rothschild really believed his own words. Surely he had just given in to political pressure and was trying to draw scorn away from his company by saying that the climate was changing. And what did he mean by a rapid and drastic response?

"The heat and drought we are experiencing right now are…" Rothschild appeared to falter. He reached up and wiped his brow with a handkerchief. "What I'm trying to say is…" He looked around and a frown crossed his face. "We are all in danger. We need to get inside."

A sound of collective shock rolled through the crowd. Andrew stood up out of his seat and immediately felt dizzy. And then he heard the cries and shouts from the crowd a few feet away. Someone was calling for a doctor. And then, through the daze of the heat, he realized that what he had thought was just loud chatter from the crowd for the last several minutes, was actually other people across the lawn shouting in distress. Andrew's head was spinning, and now he finally realized that one of the people shouting was his mother. He looked around and saw that Grandpa Joe had collapsed. His mother was knelt over him, pouring water on his brow and trying to wake him. Andrew bounded over to his grandfather. Joe hadn't passed out completely and was mumbling something incoherently.

"He's having heatstroke," Andrew said.

"He's going to be fine," his mother snapped, as she continued pouring water on Grandpa Joe's forehead.

"I'm calling an ambulance." As Andrew reached for his phone, sirens began wailing in the distance. Andrew looked around and realized that Joe wasn't the only one who'd collapsed. Others must have already called the hospital. Moments later, the President was back at the microphone, announcing that the ceremony would be temporarily adjourned until the evening when things had cooled down. He advised everyone to get out of the sun, especially elders and small children. Too little, too late, Andrew thought.

The lawn erupted into chaos as people scrambled to get inside. Andrew helped his brother lift Grandpa Joe and carry him off the lawn, into a nearby building to wait for the ambulance to arrive. After finding a couch to lay him on, Andrew realized they'd forgotten Grandpa Joe's cane, and he went back outside to search for it. He found it lying under the canopy where they had been sitting in the now almost deserted lawn. As he reached down, he heard a voice from behind him.

"You Andrew Oxley?" It was a man's voice, with a distinct southern drawl. Andrew turned around. The man in the grey tuxedo stood in front of him. He was tall and bulky, with slightly graying, curly hair sticking out from under a cowboy hat. Underneath the tuxedo he wore a white shirt. A grey bow tie and pocket square rounded out his outfit. Andrew thought it seemed strangely formal, even for graduation. He was also surprised to see how little the man was sweating. Something about his demeanor made Andrew relax a little.

"I'm Howard Harrison. I understand you're friends with my boy Michael."

Andrew's brain took a moment to process the information. Michael Harrison had been a friend of his since sophomore year. And now Andrew remembered Michael once jokingly making a drunken threat to their classmate about how his dad had worked for the NSA and could obtain files on them. Another chill passed over him.

"That's right. Nice to meet you Mr. Harrison."

"I've got somethin' important to discuss with you, son."

"Are you one of the people who have been watching me? Why?"

Mr. Harrison smiled. "Yes we have, for some time now. Good on you to notice. But we're not who you think. We've been trying to determine if you were a suitable candidate, and I'm quite convinced that you are. Your country needs you, son."

"What? You're joking. What do you mean?" This was the last thing Andrew had expected. His head was still swimming from the heat, and he wondered briefly if he was hallucinating.

"Do I look like I'm jokin' with you?" Mr. Harrison gave him a stern look, then reached in his pocket, pulled out a business card and handed it to Andrew. "I've arranged to have you flown to Washington D.C. two days from now for an interview at our headquarters. I'll explain everythin' then. You'll be able to make it, I assume?" Something about the tone in Mr. Harrison's voice told Andrew he didn't have much of an option.

"Uh, yes sir, I think so."

"Good. My secretary will be in touch to provide you with the flight details." He turned and strode off. Andrew looked down at the card in his hand. *Howard Harrison, Executive Director, Institute for American Exceptionalism* it read.

Andrew stared after him for a moment, then glanced down at the card again. What kind of job could Mr. Harrison have in mind for him?

CHAPTER 3:

THE INSTITUTE FOR AMERICAN EXCEPTIONALISM

Andrew watched through the open window as they drew closer to the large, plantation-style house. It seemed to him like a strange building for the headquarters of a think tank.

"This is some kind of government institute, isn't it?" asked the taxi driver as he pulled up and Andrew handed him two twenties.

"Honestly, I don't really know much about it."

"You know, every time I ask people about this place, they don't seem to want to talk about it." The driver raised an eyebrow at him.

"I'm just here for a job interview."

"Oh yeah? What kind of job?"

Andrew paused. "Well, I'm not really sure yet."

The driver chuckled. "Interviewing for a job you don't know anything about, with an organization you know even less about. Good luck."

"Uh, thanks. Keep the change."

The driver smiled, nodded, and then drove away.

Andrew faced the building, pausing for a moment to take it in. The house was framed with freshly painted white, Greek columns running all around the perimeter, and extending from the eve of the roof to the ground. Most of the front and side lawns were covered with thick hedges, which formed a sort of wall around the building. In the center of the front lawn was a shallow pond with two fountains spraying jets of water into the air, on either side of a stone walkway. Next to him was a small sign that read, *The Institute for American Exceptionalism.*

As Andrew approached the pond his heart began to beat faster. What was he doing there? He was beginning to feel that it had been foolish to fly all the way down from Boston on such short notice for an interview with an organization he'd never heard of. And maybe Mr. Harrison had an ulterior motive. Still, he'd said he wanted an unconventional job...

He reached the front entrance, took a deep breath, and knocked.

A tall, slim blonde woman answered. She looked to be in her early 30s and was wearing a semi-sheer white, lacey blouse, and a long white skirt that fit her body, emphasizing her curvy figure.

"You must be Andrew," she said with a cheerful smile. "You're right on time. I'm Shirley, Mr. Harrison's assistant."

"Nice to meet you," Andrew shook her hand.

"Come in please, Mr. Harrison is eager to see you." She turned to walk down the long entrance hall. Andrew hurried after her. It was still sweltering outside, and he was relieved to be inside an air-conditioned building again. As they walked Andrew stole some quick glances into the rooms that lined the hall. They had all been converted into offices, and most of them were crammed with desks and cabinets, overflowing with stacks of papers. Men and women were scurrying about, examining documents or shifting them neatly into new stacks.

At the end of the hall they came to a single door, which Shirley opened slowly, and then ushered Andrew in. The room appeared to have once been a den or a study, but now it was mostly void of furniture, except for a few armchairs, and at the far end, a large, mahogany desk with a tall chair behind it and a small armchair in front. Wooden bookshelves and paintings covered most of the brown, wood-paneled walls. The whole thing made Andrew feel as though he'd just stepped back in time several decades.

At the far end there was also a door, from which Howard Harrison was emerging. He closed the door carefully and, noticing their presence, he straightened up and smiled across the room at Andrew and Shirley.

"Welcome to the home of the Institute for American Exceptionalism. Well, what do yah think, son?"

"It's, umm, quite impressive, Mr. Harrison."

Looking satisfied with Andrew's answer, Mr. Harrison turned to Shirley "Shirley, will you get us some coffee and biscuits?"

"Certainly, Howard." She smiled at Mr. Harrison, who seemed to wince as she turned and left the room.

"Have a seat, son," Mr. Harrison motioned to the chair in front of the big desk. Andrew sat.

"That was quite a heatwave we had a few days ago, wasn't it? Is your grandfather recoverin' well?"

So Mr. Harrison had seen his grandfather collapse. "Yes, he's doing all right now, but the doctors wanted to keep him on for another week to monitor his condition."

"I understand he's currently still at Mass General?"

Andrew blinked. "How did you know that's where he was?"

"It's my business to know these things, son." Mr. Harrison winked at him. "Well, I'm glad to hear that he's doing well. Now, let's get down to business. The fact is, some of the things we're 'bout to discuss are very sensitive. Can't have you going 'round tellin' folks, you understand?"

Andrew nodded.

"That's good, son. I can tell you're a good Christian boy, very honest, yes, and I'm sure you won't tell anyone. Just the same, my lawyers insist that I have you sign this non-disclosure agreement before we move forward." Mr. Harrison produced a small stack of papers and slid it across the desk to Andrew, pointing at the bottom and handing him a pen. "Sign here, please."

Andrew glanced over the many pages, his thoughts

tripping over each other as he tried to take it all in. He looked up at Mr. Harrison, who seemed impatient to get started.

"With all due respect Mr. Harrison, I haven't even been told what this job is yet, and..."

"Oh, don't worry too much about it, son. This is just a standard NDA document."

Andrew looked down at the agreement again. He didn't want to take an hour to read through the mess of papers. He hesitated for a moment, then signed quickly and slid them back across the desk.

Mr. Harrison smiled and tucked the papers away in a drawer. Then he leaned back in his armchair. "Thank you, son. Now first, let me tell you a little bit about this project of mine," he looked around the room, his eyes sparkling with pride. "I founded the Institute for American Exceptionalism about five years ago after leaving a long career with the CIA and NSA," Mr. Harrison paused and stared at him. Andrew squirmed a bit.

Then Mr. Harrison continued. "For nearly a century, America has kept the peace and spread prosperity around the world. And it's because of the exceptional and unique nature of our society that we've been able to maintain this. But there are strong forces in motion that threaten to upend that world order," Mr. Harrison had been looking off into the distance, but now he turned his gaze on Andrew and stared at him intently.

"After a long career in government, I finally realized that our intelligence agencies have become too bloated and short-sighted to recognize the real threats to America. That's why I left and founded the Institute, as we call it for short. We mostly started out consulting for large U.S. technology firms trying to counter commercial espionage from other countries. But in the last few years, I've begun to uncover what I believe is the greatest foreign threat America has ever faced."

Mr. Harrison paused and looked expectantly at Andrew.

"What's that, Mr. Harrison?"

Mr. Harrison suddenly got to his feet and began pacing next to his desk. "We've been having a lot of strange weather these last few years, don't you think?"

So Mr. Harrison *did* know about his interest in the weather. "Yes, it seems like it."

"Droughts and heatwaves are getting longer and more severe in many parts of the country, while floodin' is becoming more common in other parts. Hurricane season is getting longer and the storms are more intense than before. In fact there's a new hurricane forming off the coast right now – far earlier in the season than usual. Let me ask you a question. D'ya think there's a reason for all this *unnatural* weather?

"Well, from what I've heard, it's being caused by climate change," replied Andrew.

Mr. Harrison grimaced. "That's the general consensus among the public, yes. But let's be honest with each other Andrew. I know what you've been up to. And I think you've realized more than most people that these extreme weather events are happenin' at a much faster rate than even the most pessimistic scientists predicted. In fact, most of this extreme weather is likely being caused by somethin' far more sinister."

As he said this, Mr. Harrison brought his face down close to Andrew's and stared at him for a moment. Then he turned abruptly and walked a few paces around his desk, where he retrieved a small stack of papers and held them up for Andrew to see.

"This is a report on what is potentially the most powerful weapon ever created by mankind. The High-frequency Active Auroral Research Program, or HAARP, is a massive radio frequency transmitter that was constructed by the U.S. Department of Defense up in Alaska in the 1990s. Its stated purpose was to analyze the ionosphere and investigate the potential for developin' *ionospheric enhancement* technology for radio communications and surveillance."

Andrew stared blankly at him. He hoped he wasn't supposed to understand what all of that meant. He vaguely remembered hearing about HAARP on a forum somewhere, but had never understood what it was.

Mr. Harrison paused, then continued in a slower, quieter voice.

"I've been working in the intelligence community long enough to know that their publicly stated purpose for a project often hides the true purpose. Several sources of mine within the DOD have confirmed that this was in fact an experimental machine for manipulatin' the weather. The machine was capable of sending high-energy pulses many miles up into the atmosphere. If those energy pulses could be directed and controlled, they could feasibly be used to spark the formation of tropical storms, or reroute the jet stream to cause major droughts or floods in certain parts of the world."

"But I thought... weather control..." Andrew hesitated for a moment. But it seemed Mr. Harrison already knew everything about him. It was no use hiding. "...was mostly done by planes spraying chemicals in the air."

"That is how it began. During the Vietnam War, the U.S. government realized that by sprayin' silver oxide into the sky over the Ho Chi Min trail, they could increase rainfall and slow down the Vietcong. That same kind of thing is in wide-scale use today, mainly by private entities trying to redistribute rainfall. That seems to be where this whole notion about chemtrails came from. But I'll tell you son, in my decades working for the U.S. intelligence community, I've never heard anything to suggest that the U.S. government is spraying chemicals in the sky with ordinary airplanes. If you ask me, they've become too bloated and ineffective to pull off such a deception of the public. Those trails you see left by planes in the sky are likely nothing more than condensation."

Andrew was surprised, and, if he was being honest with himself, a bit disappointed to hear this. He'd have expected Mr. Harrison to divulge secrets about chemtrails to him. But he was starting to get the impression that bigger things were at play here.

"Now admittedly, for decades weather control has been a very imperfect science. Most of the first cloud seedin' attempts were only mildly successful at best. Weather systems are chaotic. There are millions, perhaps even billions of tiny factors influencin' the development of different atmospheric conditions. For that reason alone, they are very difficult to predict, let alone control. However, technology has a way of advancin' faster than we ever expected. Recent advances in data science have allowed us to come closer and closer to understandin' these systems. I believe that someone now finally has the data gatherin' and computin' power to take into account all those minute factors and model how millions of variables impact the weather precisely. And as a result, control of the weather is within their grasp."

Andrew wondered why, if that were the case, the forecasters still couldn't get it right. But then he supposed that if someone was manipulating the weather and they didn't know about it, their models were sure to be wrong. "So you're saying the U.S. government has been using this HAARP thing to mess with the weather," Andrew ventured.

"Not quite, son. Unfortunately for America, there has been quite a bit of global backlash against projects to control the weather. Public scrutiny has made it very difficult for the U.S. military to continue with projects that are so visible. That's why HAARP was never officially classified as a military project. After the existence and true purpose of HAARP got leaked to the public, there was pressure on Congress to defund the program, and in 2014 it was shut down. The U.S. government bureaucrats had lost their appetite for experimental projects, making HAARP an easy target. But there are other countries where such public scrutiny does not exist. Countries that are trying to gain any tactical advantage on America that they can."

Mr. Harrison fell silent and stared at Andrew.

"Are you saying that other countries are working on a HAARP? Like what countries?"

At the sound of his question, Mr. Harrison spun around, leaned forward and down so his face was just inches from Andrew's.

"Haven't you guessed it by now, son? Why do you think I brought *you* here, of all people?"

The answer came to Andrew immediately. "China," he

said.

"That's right!" Mr. Harrison said, with a whisper so forceful that a tiny bit of spittle ejected from his mouth and landed on Andrew's cheek. But Mr. Harrison didn't seem to notice. He straightened up and looked out the window, while Andrew quickly wiped the spit away.

"Actually we should say, *The People's Republic of China.*" Mr. Harrison went on. "Let's not forget that they are still godless communists. We've entered the second Cold War, son. China is engaged in a global struggle to unseat the United States from hegemony, and they are meeting us on a broad array of fronts. They know that wagin' a conventional war is no longer an option, so they've been turning to other types of warfare. For decades they've been waggin' a cyber war, attackin' American companies, government institutions, and even the Pentagon itself..."

Shirley had reentered with a tray of coffee and biscuits. She had walked over and set them down on the desk, all the while staring at Mr. Harrison pacing the room.

"He's in it now," she whispered to Andrew, seeming slightly in awe. But Andrew was distracted by her proximity. A sweet scent of strawberry was wafting past his nostrils. He looked over and saw that her shoulder was now slightly exposed as she leaned sideways.

"...and this is the second rise of communism." Andrew jolted back to the present as Mr. Harrison walked past him, feeling guilty for thinking about Shirley in that way. "Now they are wagin' clandestine weather warfare on the United States. They are tryin' to further weaken our economy so that their economic growth will continue to outpace us, and as a result, they will soon have the wealth to support a level of military strength that will surpass ours."

"We are now grapplin' with the worst threat this country has ever faced. Even in the war on terrorism, it was relatively straightforward to recognize and detect the weapons our enemy was using. But when your enemy is manipulatin' the very climate of the earth, how do you tell the difference between which events are natural and which ones your enemy is creatin'? And how does the public tell? All this talk of climate change is the perfect disguise for them to hide behind."

"But how do you know that it's the Chinese who are doing this?" asked Andrew.

"Ah-ha, now you're getting to the heart of the matter, my boy. About fifteen years ago, one of the largest state-owned Chinese companies, the National Oil and Chemical Company of China, or NOCCOC—tried to buy the DOD contractor that owned the patents for the HAARP technology. It just so happens that this contractor is an energy company called ARCO. Why an energy company, you might wonder? Well, they originally developed the HAARP technology because they thought it might help them to explore for oil and gas deposits. So it seemed plausible that an oil and gas company like NOCCOC would be interested in it. The DOD recognized the danger of this technology fallin' into Chinese hands, and blocked the acquisition."

"Just months later, ARCO's systems were hacked, and most of their files stolen, including the blueprints for the HAARP technology. They were never able to trace the attack back to a source, but you can guess who the prime suspect was. Then, just three years later, a massive hurricane hits the east coast, causing unprecedented damage. It was almost as if it were being directed at all the major American Atlantic coastal cities. After hittin' New York hard, it seemed to be dyin' out over Boston, but then it hit an unusually warm patch of water off the coast, and picked up strength again, headin' north toward Maine."

"Where my father's sailboat got caught in the storm," Andrew said quietly.

"Yes, I know about that too, son." Mr. Harrison didn't say anything for a moment, and then continued. "We believe the Chinese picked up where the U.S. government left off with HAARP. They have developed it further so that they now can intentionally modify the weather on a global scale. Combinin' its power to create hurricanes with stealth, nuclear submarines that can generate enough heat to warm the surface waters just off the coast of Boston, they caused the storm to gain strength again. Now let me ask you this, son: since the hurricane had already passed most of the major U.S. coastal cities, why would the Chinese care about inflicting damage along the coast of Maine?"

"I really don't know, Mr. Harrison."

"Did you ever notice the dozens of large storage tanks right outside of Portland when you were a boy?"

Immediately Andrew knew what he was talking about. "Of course. I always saw them from the highway."

"Well did you know those tanks are full of oil? In fact, that storage facility is a major component of our nation's strategic petroleum reserve. And what did that hurricane do? It destroyed those tanks."

Now Andrew remembered the news stories he'd heard on TV after the hurricane about the oil spill. It had devastated the Maine coastline. He'd seen disturbing videos of seals and herons covered in gooey, black oil. But he'd been so preoccupied with his father's death that it had seemed unimportant at the time.

Mr. Harrison watched Andrew's face. "I can see that you remember. But one piece of news you may not remember is who bought those tanks at a bargain price after the disaster."

Andrew looked up. "NOCCOC?"

"It seems like you're startin' to put the pieces together like I did, son. In fact, for the last 12 years, every time there's been a major disaster that destroyed critical infrastructure in the U.S., NOCCOC and other Chinese state-owned companies have come in to bid on their purchase and reconstruction. Kinda funny, ain't it? You know these state-owned companies are supposed to seem like private entities, but they're really just arms of the Chinese government."

"But Mr. Harrison, if the HAARP facility is in China, how do they change the weather in the U.S.?"

"Ah. You're forgettin' that weather is interconnected across the globe, son. We suspect that the Chinese HAARP is located somewhere in northeastern China, perhaps close to Peking. Well, the jet stream actually passes over Peking. It then heads out across the Pacific and then crosses the North American continent, startin' up north near Alaska and travelin' down across the United States. By heatin' up that wind current over Peking, the Chinese HAARP can change the course and pressure levels of the entire jet stream."

"The increased pressure differentials cause wide fluctuations in temperature across North America, which leads to unexpected heat waves, cold snaps, and increases in hurricane strength. You remember the so-called Polar Vortex, right? We believe the Chinese use GPS satellites to collect real-time data on the Jet stream as it moves, and use that data to compute exactly what adjustments they need to make to their HAARP energy output in order to direct the path of newly formin' hurricanes, and perhaps even create new ones at will."

Andrew was trying hard to process all this information. Finally, someone was confirming almost everything he'd suspected for years. And yet it was also not quite what he'd thought. Perhaps it was China and not the U.S. government. It actually made more sense, when he considered it.

And now one question remained in his head above all else. "So what do you want me for, then?"

Mr. Harrison stopped pacing and looked at him. "Ain't it clear, son? We need your help to fight this war. Most people would think what I'm proposing is far-fetched. But I know you've been paying closer attention to what's going on than most people, and I knew you would understand what we're trying to do. You also speak Chinese and are skilled in hand-to-hand combat."

"Isn't the government doing something about this?"

Mr. Harrison gave a deep sigh. "As I told you before son, the U.S. government has gotten too complacent to recognize this kind of threat. When I brought it to their attention, they didn't take it seriously, despite the fact that I've been right before when no one believed me."

"So it's up to us. You know, you're a rare breed, Andrew.

It's very rare to find a white person who can understand Chinese as well as you. And looking like a foreigner will actually give you a distinct advantage when you're tryin' to collect secret information in China. Anyone who looks Chinese will be expected to understand the language. But as long as you keep your Mandarin fluency a secret from everyone you meet – and I mean *everyone* Andrew, you never know who might be workin' for the government – no one will know that you can understand them when they speak Chinese. If you do your job right, why, they should feel comfortable enough to have secretive conversations right in front of you."

"So what you're saying is, you want me to be a spy?"

"If you like that term."

Andrew's adrenaline started pumping a little, as a feeling of excitement coursed through him. What teenage boy who'd watched James Bond hadn't imagined one day being recruited to be a spy? And now it was actually happening to him. Andrew pictured himself wearing a double-o-seven-esque suit and carrying a small pistol.

"We've named this Operation Hurricane Eye, and your mission is this: We want you to find concrete evidence that China has developed technology to manipulate the weather for hostile purposes. Once you provide us with this, we plan to expose that evidence to the world. When the world knows what despicable work China is up to and the U.S. has the unquestionin' support of the world community, America can put pressure on China to bring a quick end to the use of weather warfare once and for all."

"And you're sure you want me? There's no one else?"

"For reasons I've already told you, you are the ideal candidate. Right now, there is no one else."

Andrew's mind was racing. So Mr. Harrison really had been keeping a close eye on him. Andrew had never imagined this would happen to him. It seemed unreal. And then, suddenly, his heart leaped as another thought crossed his mind.

"Mr. Harrison, where in China would you be sending me exactly?"

"Why to Peking, of course. All the state-owned enterprises are based in the capital. You'll be targetin' NOCCOC for information first."

May would be in Beijing. He would have another chance with her if he went. His momentary elation was cut short however by the thought of leaving all his friends and family behind. What would they think? His mother would never let him go do something so dangerous.

"Now of course you'll need an alibi," continued Mr. Harrison, as if reading his thoughts. "Otherwise folks will start wonderin' what the heck you're doin' in China anyway. Well, we've got just the thing. You're goin' to be an English teacher at NOCCOC. It will be the perfect way for you to gather information, unsuspected."

"You want me to pretend to be a teacher? But I've never taught anyone in my life."

"Don't worry about it, son. We'll train you for that. It shouldn't be too hard."

Andrew's mind was spinning. A teacher. A spy. These were labels he'd never thought he'd be given. It almost seemed like Mr. Harrison thought he was someone else. And yet, it was very enticing…

"Well my boy, that just about wraps things up. I'd like to give you some time to go home and think about all this, but we do need your answer within the next twenty-four hours…"

"Twenty-four hours?"

"Why yes, my boy. We need to get you ready so we can get you off to Peking within the month. We've got no time to waste."

"I need at least three days, Mr. Harrison. I've got to talk this over with my family. I mean, even going to China just to teach English is going to be a lot for my mom to swallow…"

Mr. Harrison's eye twitched. "Fine, but no more. Think about how many lives you could save, son."

That night Andrew stayed in a hotel room that the Institute had booked for him. As he brushed his teeth, he looked at himself in the mirror, trying to picture himself walking into a fancy bar in China wearing a black tuxedo. Could China really be controlling the weather like this? But everything Mr. Harrison had said that day seemed plausible.

He knew it would be difficult to convince his mother. He certainly would not be able to tell her the truth. But he hated the idea of lying to her, and he wasn't very good at it. It would have to be a very prestigious English school that wanted him to teach if there were going to be any chance of his mom agreeing.

And then he thought of his father again. Would he approve of this path? His father had spent many years in China, and he'd always seemed to have a strong appreciation for the country and its people. But Andrew knew that the people and their government were two separate things. Maybe his father had been at odds with the government. And now, he realized that maybe it was the Chinese government's fault that his father was no longer alive.

CHAPTER 4:

THE CASTAWAY

"I don't care how prestigious this job is, I'm not going to let them send you to China."

His mother was reacting a lot worse than Andrew had expected. He'd returned from D.C. that morning; his plane was one of the last ones to take off, as the hurricane Mr. Harrison had mentioned barreled into the coast of Maryland. But since his family was throwing a graduation party for him that afternoon, his mother had been preoccupied all day with preparing the house for guests. Now, as the party was winding down, and only extended family remained gathered in the living room, she had finally asked him what the job was and how the interview had gone.

"Relax Mom, I haven't even accepted the job yet. I'm just saying, I think I would enjoy this more than being cooped up in an office in Boston. Besides, you're a teacher, and…"

"And it barely pays the bills. I don't want my son who has a *science* degree becoming an English teacher. I'm surprised they even think a boy your age can handle the kind of responsibility that comes with being a teacher."

"I'm not a *boy* anymore, Mom."

"But you are still *my* boy, and I won't have you shipping off to that wretched country like your father was always doing."

"Wretched country?" Andrew had never heard his mother talk about China before. It was a subject she'd always avoided. "Is that why you were so rude to May?"

His mother's eyes narrowed. "So that's what this is about. You have a crush on that girl, don't you? Well, get the idea out of your head. There's no future for you with a girl like her."

"Why not?"

"Because you're never going to date a Chinese girl."

Andrew stared at her. How could he even respond to something like that? "So you think you're going to just keep controlling my life forever?"

"That's enough from you, young man. If your father were here…"

"He would have wanted me to go," Now Matthias and Uncle Cooper who had been talking nearby stopped and turned to look at Andrew and his mother. Andrew knew he was walking on thin ice. His mother always got her way in the end.

"Why else do you think he had me go to Chinese school?" Andrew continued. "He wanted me to learn Chinese so that I could go to China someday."

"Don't you dare use your father against me, young man. You have no idea what he would have wanted."

"But you don't know either. Or at least you don't want to tell me. Why did he want me to learn Chinese, then?"

"Andrew James Oxley, I don't want to hear another word from you about this. You are to call Mr. Harrison tonight and tell him that you decline his offer." His mother turned to walk away. This was always how it ended. He never wanted to fight with her, so he would usually just give in and never get what he wanted. But not this time.

"What if I don't?" Andrew was surprised at how clear and firm his voice sounded.

Slowly, as if a wave were rippling out from where Andrew and his mother stood, the room fell quiet. Andrew's mother turned back to face him. She was giving him a look that meant death. But for the first time, Andrew didn't care. All he wanted right then was to disobey her.

"You will not leave this house again until you call him and reject the offer. Do I make myself clear?"

So she was grounding him. She hadn't done that since he'd left for college.

"Very clear," he said, and then turned and headed for the door.

"Where are you going?" His mother yelled after him. But Andrew ignored her. He reached the front door, opened it, and without another word to the room full of people who were silently watching him, he walked through the door and closed it behind him.

He made it to the street before his feeling of triumph melted away and fear began to sink in. He had just defied his mother in front of the whole family. And now he realized it was something he'd wanted to do for a while. He had no idea what she would do, but he figured he probably wouldn't be able to come back to his house.

Just as he began considering which of his friends he could ask to stay with, he heard the front door open. He turned, expecting to his mother, but instead Uncle Cooper walked out. He crossed the front lawn in just a few strides, heading right for Andrew, then brushed past him and opened the passenger door of his truck. Turning to Andrew, he said. "Get in."

He was speaking in a commanding tone of voice that Andrew had never heard him use before.

"Where are we going?"

"To my house."

"But that's all the way up in Maine."

"It's not really that far. Where else are you going to stay? Surely you don't want to spend the next few days with your mother after that. Anyway, I wouldn't be surprised if she tried to lock you in a closet to prevent you from going to China."

Andrew had never heard his uncle talk like this. Seeing no better options at the moment, he climbed into the truck. Cooper got on the other side and they took off.

"I have to admit, I've never seen anyone talk to Abigail that way. You were like a bull in a china shop back there."

50

"A what?"

"It's a saying. You've never heard that before? Can you imagine what would happen to a shop full of china if you introduced a bull?"

"It would probably break everything."

"That's the idea. The dynamic in your family revolves around Abigail's authority. Shatter that, and everything falls apart."

"You know my mother is going to hate you for taking me in."

Cooper looked thoughtful for a moment. "She's a very strong woman, your mother, and she usually hates anyone who helps her when she thinks she doesn't need help. Since it's only thanks to me that she's been able to raise you three children single-handedly, I'm pretty sure she already hates me quite a bit."

"What do you mean?" Andrew was confused. He'd barely seen Cooper since he was twelve. How could he claim to have been helping his mother take care of them?

"Andrew, you must know that school teachers like her make next-to-nothing. Where do you think she's been getting the money to raise you all these years? Your father never had any life insurance. So when he died, what else was I going to do? I started sending your mother money every few months. And I've been doing that for the last twelve years. Your mother has a lot of pride, but she wouldn't let pride get in the way of making sure you kids were taken care of. And God knows the rest of her family couldn't have helped, they barely get by as it is."

Now Andrew understood why his mother always seemed annoyed when Cooper showed up. Was that the reason why Cooper rarely came around, because his mother was annoyed with him? Andrew's anger toward this mother resurfaced. "So I guess she kept your visits short because of that."

Cooper didn't say anything for a while. When he finally spoke his voice was much softer. "It would be easy to blame your mother for my absence. But the truth is, if I had really wanted to see you, Abigail Oxley would not have been able to stop me." Cooper paused again. His words shocked Andrew. So Cooper hadn't wanted to see him. "The truth is, I'm a coward," Cooper continued. "Every time I see you Andrew, it reminds me of that day. Thinking of what I could have done differently. Thinking of how I could have saved him. It was just too painful for me to deal with. That's why I stayed away, and tried to forget."

Andrew's thoughts drifted back to that fateful day, 12 years earlier.

***

He had been on the sailboat with his father and Uncle Cooper, looking at the water, and the growing swells. The size of the waves was making him a little nervous.

"I'm not afraid of a little wind," he said to his father, trying to hide his growing uneasiness.

Ray Oxley smiled. "That's my boy."

Then Andrew thought back to something his father said earlier. "How come you said this hurricane was unnatural?"

A dark look crossed his father's face. "Because my instinct tells me this hurricane is man-made. Humans have far more influence now over the natural world than most people think. We now have the power to change global weather patterns."

Andrew was about to ask his father if someone created the hurricane on purpose, or just by accident, when Cooper cut in. "Ray, we'd better jibe now. We need to start heading away from this thing," Cooper urged.

Suddenly Andrew felt drops on his head. He looked around and realized that the storm was approaching more quickly than he'd first thought, and the boat was beginning to rock from side to side as the waves grew to four and five-foot swells. Suddenly a wave broke over the side of the boat, splashing water across the deck.

"If we're going to use the spinnaker, we need to be in a position where we can head in the direction of the wind," Ray said, looking toward the coast.

"The wind is going to be too strong soon for us to even hoist the spinnaker," Cooper shouted.

Ray turned to Cooper. "You're right. Let's pull it out and start getting it ready."

Five minutes later they were drenched in pouring rain. The wind was howling and the waves were lashing at the sides of the boat, sending it up and down as the swells climbed higher.

"OK, it's now or never. Ready to jibe?" His father's voice was muffled by a gust of wind and the pouring rain.

"Ready!"

"Andrew, you've got the helm, you'll need to turn us 90 degrees to the right when I give the command. OK, now!"

Andrew turned the wheel hard, but his fingers were slipping on the soaking wet wheel. Bracing his legs against the railing in order to give himself more leverage, he pushed with all his might. The boat whirled around and caught a giant swell as it did so, which crashed over the deck and sent it spinning off in the wrong direction. Andrew tried to steer it back on course, but another wave suddenly crashed over the stern, covering him in salty seawater and causing him to lose his grip on the steering wheel entirely. He fell on the deck and slid toward the edge as the sailboat rocked to the side. For a second he thought he was going to roll off the boat into the churning sea below, but the railing stopped his progress just in time.

"Andrew! Hold on!" Ray dashed up to where Andrew lay trying to regain his feet, and pulled Andrew up with one hand, while grabbing the wheel with the other. He began cranking the wheel, his face set dead on the Portland Headlight shining off in the distance. Andrew could see the look of determination on his father's face, and felt his strength as his entire being focused on turning the boat while holding tightly to Andrew's hand. For a moment, his father seemed invincible.

When they were finally facing inland, Andrew saw Cooper begin raising the spinnaker. The giant sail climbed up the mast rapidly and then spread its vast wings to catch the wind, billowing forward as if it too was reaching for the lighthouse and firm ground. The boat began to pick up speed. They were now racing along, but the swells rising under the boat threatened constantly to pull them off course.

"Cooper, come up here and grab the helm. I'm going to tie Andrew in. I'm afraid he might get washed overboard if a big wave comes."

Ray carried Andrew down to the main mast, grabbed a rope off the deck and began tying a makeshift harness around Andrew's waist.

It was so dark that Andrew didn't notice it at first, but slowly, looking over his father's shoulder, he realized that he could not find the horizon anymore. A great wall of darkness had blotted out the sky and was growing, coming closer and closer, and as it did so the boat began to tip to the side.

"Look out!" Andrew cried.

Cooper noticed it in time, grabbed hold of the nearest rope and wrapped it around his wrist, but Ray, concentrating intently on finishing the knot for Andrew's harness, ignored his warning for just a few seconds too long. And in those seconds, the wave crashed over the boat.

For a moment Andrew was suspended underwater and couldn't tell which direction was up. He flailed around wildly, trying to right himself. He needed to breathe badly. Just as he began to worry that he might drown, he suddenly found himself lying on the deck again as the water washed over the side. He looked around wildly for his father.

And then he saw him.

The door in the railing on the side of the boat had come unlatched and was swinging out over the ocean, and his father was just barely hanging on with one hand.

"Dad!" Andrew cried. He scrambled to regain his feet. Cooper apparently had seen Ray too, because Andrew heard him shouting his name from behind, but Andrew knew Cooper was too far away to get there in time. I've got to get to him, Andrew thought. He grabbed the mast and pulled himself up, but just as he was about to run to his father, another wave arose from the ocean, and like a watery tentacle it snatched Ray from the edge and hurdled him out of sight, into the dark sea below.

The sound of Andrew's scream had been lost in the howling wind and rain.

***

Andrew didn't say anything for several moments. Somehow, he'd never imagined that his uncle felt as guilty as he did for his father's death. "You were keeping the boat on course. There's nothing you could have done differently. I'm the one who was closest to him. I should have gotten to him quicker."

"You were too young to be able to help him. I should have found a way to lock the steering wheel. I could have jumped down and pulled him back up in seconds."

Andrew didn't say anything. He didn't want to keep thinking about that day. After a few moments Cooper seemed to realize this, and changed the subject.

"So, the Institute for American Exceptionalism wants to send you on a good-will mission to teach English in China?"

"Uh, yeah."

"And you're planning to accept the offer, despite your mother's wishes?"

Andrew stared out the window. "I don't know. I just finally got tired of her telling me what I could and couldn't do."

"I can see that. But I also heard you say that you thought you would enjoy this more than, what did you say, being cooped up in an office?"

So Cooper had been listening to his conversation. "Yeah, I think teaching would be more interesting."

"What about living in China?"

"Well, you know I've always been curious about it..." Andrew trailed off. He didn't want Cooper asking him all these questions.

"Uh huh," Cooper continued to drive on in silence. They turned onto highway 95, heading north toward Maine. "You know I actually saw Howard Harrison give an interview on CNN this morning. It was about this crazy theory he apparently has, about the Chinese controlling the weather."

Andrew's eyes widened, but he tried not to react. He hadn't realized Mr. Harrison had gone public with his theory already. Cooper stole a glance at him as he continued to drive. "His basic argument was that the weather disasters of recent years are far too intense to be caused by climate change, and that in fact the Chinese are using climate change as a veil to hide behind, while they secretly wreak havoc on our economy. Naturally all the climate scientists are up in arms about it. It's a very controversial position, which I suppose is why the media is giving him plenty of air time."

"Uh, yeah I guess so."

"He never mentioned anything to you about it?"

Andrew gritted his teeth and then retorted, "I was there for an interview, why would he talk about that?"

"Because I don't think you were interviewing for a teaching position."

Andrew tried not to look at his uncle and act casual. "What makes you think that?"

"Andrew I know I haven't been around very much, but I knew your father well enough to be able to tell when he was hiding something, and you have the same giveaways. Also, sending people to teach English in China just doesn't sound like something Howard Harrison would do. He seems too paranoid to organize something like that. And besides, no one in China would trust a teacher sent by his organization if they heard what he was accusing them of."

Andrew didn't say anything. He was annoyed at his uncle for prying. And Cooper didn't think he was good at keeping a secret. Well, he wasn't going to tell Cooper anything.

"Andrew, you don't have to tell me what the interview was really about. I'm sure Howard Harrison made you promise to keep it a secret. But my guess is that being a teacher is just a cover for something else... something like investigating how the Chinese are controlling the weather. And if that's the case, I think you should go."

This time Andrew didn't try to hide his surprise, but he

wasn't sure what to say next. Should he ask Cooper why? Or would that make it look like he was admitting Cooper was right?

"Not to bring up something we both don't want to talk about again, but do you remember what Ray said that day when he saw the storm approaching?"

His uncle could have no idea how many times he'd thought about what his father had said. "He called it unnatural. He said he thought it was man-made."

"That's right. I think the work Ray was doing in China all those years had something to do with weather control," Cooper glanced over at Andrew again.

"I thought you just said that Howard Harrison is paranoid. You're saying you think he's right?"

"I don't know if he's right or not, but I think he's onto something. Maybe someone is controlling the weather, even the climate itself. Technology has advanced far enough now that so many things are possible, things we couldn't even imagine when I was a kid."

"Ray kept many secrets, Andrew. He kept them from both me and your mother. But I'm going to tell you as much as I know. Ray started going to China many years ago with Doctors Without Borders. China's economy has advanced rapidly in the last few decades, but some of the rural areas still had high rates of death among babies and younger people. What he discovered was that in the towns and villages that he visited, most people were dying from air, water and soil pollution. So he shifted his focus toward environmental action. It shouldn't surprise you that he butted heads with Will Rothschild a few times, given that Rothschild Industries is one of the biggest polluters on the planet."

"Anyway, something about his experience in China began to change him. It seemed as if he had a greater purpose on his mind, and everyday life began to interest him less and less. Over the years, he became more and more involved in his work in China. I'm sure you remember his frequent trips there. As he got more and more secretive about it, I got the impression that he was involved in something dangerous. Like there were powerful forces working against whatever he was doing, and he needed to cover his tracks. He insisted that I not ask him about it, saying that he didn't want me getting involved. 'You're my insurance policy, Cooper,' he used to say to me, and I could never tell if he was joking. Well, that turned out to be true quite literally."

"And it never occurred to you before that I might want to know these things? That I might want to know if there was a path my father had in mind for me?" Now Andrew was angry with his uncle. He was angry with him for his cowardice, for not being there when what he'd really needed all those years was a father, not his silent financial support.

Cooper didn't reply, and after a few minutes he turned the radio on. They spent the rest of the drive up to Maine not saying much. When they finally arrived in Portland and turned off the highway, Andrew soon realized that they were driving to the house where his family had lived before they moved down to Boston. He remembered his mom telling him that Uncle Cooper had bought it from her; the first of his financial assistance no doubt. As they pulled into the driveway next to Back Cove, a sense of nostalgia flooded through Andrew. He hadn't been back since he was a boy. He remembered having sword fights with his brother in the front yard and his dad sitting in his favorite chair on the porch, sipping tea and reading the newspaper.

"You can sleep in your old room again," said Cooper as they walked up the front steps. "I haven't changed it much. Don't really have use for all these extra rooms, so I rent them out to travelers now and then."

Andrew tried to imagine Cooper staying in this house all alone, and felt a little sorry for him. "How come you never married or had kids, Uncle Cooper?"

"Oh," he paused. "Too much of a hassle. I like my peace and quiet." Cooper looked around, then picked up a remote and turned on the TV. Then he walked out of sight into another room. Andrew looked around, memories flooding back to him like presents appearing under a Christmas tree. The evening news was playing, and as Andrew listened he heard the anchor mention the hurricane, so he turned the volume up.

"It's certainly early in the year for a hurricane, but this tropical storm appears to be gaining strength, possibly fueled by the intense heatwave that has stretched across the Northeast in the last few days. It made landfall in Maryland early this morning, and, heading north quickly, it's already hitting New York City. We may be looking at unprecedented damage for a storm so early in the season. The good news is, it should begin to die out as it makes its way further north."

Andrew had a bad feeling as he heard the anchor say this. That's what everyone had thought twelve years ago, too. But before he could dwell on it much more, Cooper returned carrying a small, heavily decorated wooden box, which he set down on the dining room table, then motioned for Andrew to come over. "Open it," he said.

"What is it?"

"A present. From your father."

The box was beautifully painted with blue designs on a white background, which Andrew knew was a traditional Chinese pattern. Carefully, Andrew unhooked the clasp that held the lid and opened it. Inside, nestled in casing lined with silk, was a small porcelain teacup. The cup was also painted with blue and white and depicted a natural scene with two figures in the foreground. Andrew looked closely and saw that they appeared to be a monk and a cowboy. That seemed unusual; a cowboy on Chinese porcelain?

"This was given to Ray by a close colleague of his in China. He said it was custom made and one of a kind. He left it to you when he died, but knowing the way anything related to China upset your mother, I decided to hold on to it for you until you moved out of her house." Cooper paused. Andrew picked up the teacup and turned it over in his hands. It was very light, and he realized it was probably quite delicate. Then he noticed a small insignia stamped on the bottom of the cup. It was the shape of a bull's head, also painted in blue.

"I think if you can find out who made this," Cooper continued, "You might be able to find the people he was working with. Then, just maybe, you can uncover the great mystery of what Ray Oxley was doing in China all those years," he paused, "And maybe even find out what he had in mind for your future."

CHAPTER 5:

HURRICANE ANDREW

Andrew woke to the sound of something smacking repeatedly against his window. At first, he thought someone was trying to get into his bedroom, but as he became more alert, he realized the sound wasn't consistent enough for that. As he sat up in bed, he began to hear other sounds: the creaking of the house, and the whistling of the wind through a crack somewhere above him. As he approached the window, there was another loud smack that made Andrew jump, but now he realized that it was a branch from the large maple tree that stood near the house. He looked out the window and saw the great tree writhing around like a mad man.

The hurricane had come to Maine.

Andrew knew he wouldn't be able to fall back asleep, so he went downstairs and turned on the news.

"…After leaving an unexpected and unprecedented path of devastation along the mid-Atlantic coast, Hurricane Andrew has continued on to New England, where it slammed into Boston several hours ago with more strength than any hurricane in recorded history. Significant areas of Boston have been flooded and several hundred homes and businesses destroyed…"

It was eerie that someone had named the storm after him. Not really after him, he reminded himself. It just happened to have the same name. He wondered why no one had predicted this. Hadn't the same thing happened twelve years ago? Then he took in a sharp breath as the camera panned over his neighborhood in South Boston. Most of the houses were sitting feet deep in seawater, and many were in ruin. The house his family lived in was nearly 100 years old. Could it have survived such a storm? And as the camera continued, Andrew was almost unable to believe his eyes as he saw the spot where his house had stood.

The house had partially collapsed.

Anxiety began clawing its way through his entire body. Immediately he tried to call his mother, but it went straight to voicemail. His brother's and sister's did the same. All his anger at his mother for their argument the day before had now washed away. All he could think about was that his family might be in trouble and that they needed him.

Then he got another call from an unknown number. He fumbled with the phone, his hands trembling, and finally managed to answer it. "Andrew, it's Rose. Thank God you're awake. I'm at the hospital with Grandpa."

Andrew breathed a short sign of relief. "What about Mom and Matthias?"

Rose didn't say anything for a moment, and then continued in a softer voice. "You need to come back. They were supposed to come here last night after stopping by the house to pick up some things, but they never came. And no one's cell phones are working." Her voice trailed off.

Andrew's anxiety returned even stronger than before. He had a very sick feeling in his stomach.

"Did you call the police? Is someone searching the wreckage?"

"Why would I call... what wreckage?"

Andrew swallowed hard. "I just saw our neighborhood on TV. The house is partially collapsed."

"Collapsed?" her voice squeaked, "Oh my God, oh my

62

God..."

"Hold on Rose, I'm coming now. We're going to find them."

"Yes, please come back Andrew. Please, please, please."

"I love you, Rose. I'll see you soon."

"What's going on?" Andrew turned to see Uncle Cooper standing behind him.

"I need you to drive me back to Boston right now."

His uncle stared at him, "Have you looked outside? We're not going anywhere for several hours. Besides," he paused, "I thought we were going to spend some time together."

"Our house collapsed."

"What? How do you know?"

"I just saw it on TV."

"Are you sure it was...?"

"It was our house. And no one can get in touch with my mom and brother." Cooper was silent. "I have to go find them. If they were in the house...I have to get them out."

"I'm sure they had enough sense to get out of the house."

"My sister just said that they were supposed to stop by the house, and that was the last time she heard from them."

Cooper was silent for a minute. "I know it sounds bad, but there's really nothing you can do right now..."

"Just like there was nothing we could do for my father? I'm not going to sit back and wait for another member of my family to die!" Andrew could feel his neck getting hot.

"That was different. We were right there. Boston is a hundred miles away right now."

"I don't see any difference. There are probably dozens of houses that collapsed. Who knows if the search and rescue have even made it to our house yet."

"Andrew, it's just not possible right now to drive in this storm."

"And how are you going to feel if they're found dead in a couple days and we just sat here and did nothing?"

Cooper looked shocked and hurt. "Don't talk like that, Andrew."

But Andrew didn't care if he was making his uncle feel uncomfortable. "If you're too scared to drive in this storm, then give me the keys, and I'll drive back myself."

Cooper stared at Andrew, and Andrew glared back at him, his eyes unblinking. "If we get washed off the road, neither of us is going to do them any good."

"But we have to try."

Finally, Cooper signed. "Get your jacket."

**

The drive down to Boston was tough, and a few times the wind nearly blew them off the road. But Cooper's truck was heavy, and its four-wheel-drive gave them extra traction in the pouring rain.

As they came into Boston on Interstate 93 and ascended the bridge that would take them over the Charles River, Andrew could see that most of Boston and the surrounding towns had undergone severe flooding. To his right, he saw that the neighborhoods surrounding Bunker Hill were nearly all flooded, as if the hill was once again under siege by a foreign invader. To his left, he saw Cambridge and MIT, which were also largely immersed in seawater. Somehow the Charles River Dam had survived the storm. The dome atop the Boston Museum of Science stood triumphantly above the chaos. They continued across the bridge unimpeded, while the line of cars and trucks in the opposite lane practically stood still. It seemed that everyone except them was trying to get out of Boston.

Before they reached the tunnel that took the highway under the city, Andrew could see that it was blocked off and that cars were being diverted into downtown. The storm must have flooded the tunnel. As they got nearer he could see that a lake of ocean water had settled in the tunnel, and it looked like part of the tunnel had even collapsed. That great engineering marvel that had taken the city over a decade to construct had succumbed to the power of the sea. As he listened to the sirens in the distance, he knew that his city was in deep trouble. This was an attack far more brutal than the Boston Marathon bombing. It would take the city decades to fully recover.

When they finally reached a road that led to the shores of South Boston, Cooper slowed. The road was covered in water. He turned onto the road and Andrew felt the inertia of the water hit their tires. Seeing the water this close made his pulse quicken, and his head begin to spin. He tried not to look at the water, and instead focused on the houses passing by on the side of the road.

After what seemed like forever, they finally reached their house. As Andrew opened the door and saw the water at his feet, he began to feel nauseous. His mind flashed back again to twelve years ago, when he'd been temporarily submerged in seawater on the deck of the sailboat. He looked around at the scene outside. There were a dozen other partially or fully collapsed houses in the neighborhood. Firefighters and National Guard were dispersed between them searching for survivors, but no one was searching his house. He had no choice. He began taking deep breaths, and, trying not to look at the water, he slowly lowered his feet into it.

The nausea got worse as he waded through the seawater up to the wreckage of his home. He could feel the water creating a vortex around each of his feet as he moved them. He could hear the splashes and smell the salt. By the time he'd reached the house, he was ready to vomit. But as he climbed out of the water onto the stairs, the nausea began to subside.

"Matthias, Mom, are you here?" He began frantically tearing through the sodden, disintegrating pieces of sheetrock and shingles, listening for a sound; anything that would indicate life. It was still raining hard, and soon Andrew was soaked, but he was so focused that he barely noticed.

"Careful Andrew," his uncle called from the truck. "The house doesn't look safe. Something could shift and the rest might collapse." But Andrew ignored his uncle's warning and continued pulling apart pieces of debris. And then finally, he heard something. It was the slightest sound, but he could hear a distinct and consistent tapping sound somewhere above him, under a collapsed portion of the roof. And then he heard the very faint and muffled sound of a voice.

"Hey, there's someone alive over here," he shouted at the nearest fireman, waving his arms around. "Come help me dig them out. Hurry."

A few firemen rushed over and cautiously entered the house. They began climbing the stairs slowly, testing them as they went. Andrew tried to follow them but one of the firefighters held him back. "Leave this to the professionals. The house is very unstable."

After several tense minutes and some chopping sounds above them, the firefighters returned. Matthias was walking with no visible injuries, but he looked quite shaken. Their mother was being carried and was barely moving. Blood was splattered across her clothes.

"We were trying to get to the roof, and got stuck in the attic when the house began to collapse," Matthias said, his voice trembling. Then he motioned to their mother. "She's badly hurt. I tried to stop the bleeding, but she's lost a lot of blood. She's been slipping in and out of consciousness."

One of the firemen called in an ambulance, and several minutes later it arrived. "We're coming with her," Andrew insisted defiantly when the paramedic tried to stop him and Matthias from climbing in.

"We've got to stop and pick up some other patients on the way. No space for relatives to come along."

"Are you taking her to Mass General?"

"Yup."

"Then we'll follow."

Andrew alerted Rose that they had been found, and she was waiting for them at the door to the hospital when they arrived. When she saw Matthias climb out of the car she ran over and wrapped her arms around him. "Thank God you're alright," she sobbed. Then she saw their mom getting wheeled out of the ambulance on a stretcher. "What happened to Mom? Is she going to be OK?"

"We've got to get her to the emergency room right away," was all the paramedic said.

A few hours later, Andrew, Rose, Matthias and Cooper all waited for news on Abigail's condition. Finally, a doctor came out of the operating room, a grave look on his face. Immediately Andrew felt a sinking feeling in his chest. He knew what that look meant. Then the doctor addressed them, "We've done what we can, but several of her vital organs have been irreparably damaged and the internal bleeding is too great."

For a moment there was silence as the news sunk in. Then Matthias' voice pierced the quiet, "So she's going to die, is what you're saying." He had that blank look that Andrew knew meant he was trying to pretend he wasn't in pain.

The doctor looked down at Rose and then looked away. "I'm afraid she doesn't have much time left."

"No!" Cried Rose, and she ran past the doctor into the operating room.

Stiffly, as if his legs had turned to lead, Andrew followed Matthias and Cooper into the room. They found Rose clutching their mother, sobbing into her shoulder. Abigail looked like she could barely keep her eyes open. They gathered around, Andrew trying to hold back tears as he looked at her, once such a strong woman, and now so feeble.

"Andrew," she said quietly, "Come closer." Andrew obeyed, walking up next to Rose, and taking his mother's outstretched hand.

"The doctor told me... my condition." She was having trouble getting words out. "Promise me you'll stay here and... take care of Rose and Matthias. Don't go running off to China... like your father."

Andrew bit his tongue.

"Promise me, Andrew."

"I promise I'll make sure they're safe."

There was a pause. "Andrew... I know I've been hard on you sometimes, but it was only because I love you."

"I know mom."

"I'm proud of you..." her voice trailed off, and then her head fell and she was silent.

Rose's sobs grew louder. Matthias swore softly and covered his face in his hands. Cooper looked on gravely, his hand on Matthias' shoulder.

Andrew looked around at them all, still trying to hold back his tears. He had to be strong for Rose. But the tears came anyway, silently rolling down his cheek. He'd now lost both of his parents to a hurricane. And his grandfather had nearly been struck down by a heatwave.

He looked over at Cooper, who looked back at Andrew. Cooper seemed to understand what he was thinking, because he nodded slightly. Andrew knew his uncle would take care of his brother and sister.

And he would go to China.

CHAPTER 6:

THE WOODS

Andrew dodged to the side as another soldier popped up from behind a broken wall, pointing a handgun at him. Swiftly he circled around to the side and delivered a Kung Fu chop to the soldier's gun, knocking it to the ground. Without hesitation, he then kicked at the soldier's legs, and the soldier collapsed. Pausing for a moment, Andrew felt somehow unsatisfied as he looked at the cardboard figure lying broken on the ground. It was the sixth cardboard soldier he'd disarmed in the last three minutes, and it was starting to bother him. Why wasn't he training against real people?

"Keep moving, son," the voice of Mr. Harrison bellowed through a speaker hidden somewhere overhead. "You've still got to get into that room at the end of the hall before time runs out."

Andrew continued down the hallway, glancing around as he went. About a week ago Mr. Harrison had driven him deep into the woods in Virginia, down a long dirt road and through a barbed-wire fence, until they pulled up in front of a large, decrepit looking house. There they had met a martial arts teacher who had helped Andrew brush up on his skills and a seemingly schizophrenic handyman who had taught Andrew a variety of miscellaneous skills, including how to pick a lock, and how to plant a small video camera or bug. Now they were running him through an obstacle course that took him through a maze of severely damaged rooms and hallways in the old house.

He approached the door at the end of the hallway, which was inscribed with a large red X, and began to pick the lock on the door. He was getting pretty good at this, and he had it open within fifteen seconds. Inside the room was mostly empty, except for a large desk sitting at one end. He moved toward it, looking around for cameras or other security systems. Seeing none, he circled around behind the desk, planted a bug underneath, and then began to open one of the drawers to search inside. But as he did so, an alarm began to sound, making Andrew jump. Within moments, however, the alarm stopped and Mr. Harrison's voice blared over another speaker, "Did you notice the small wire sticking out from under that drawer, son? It was rigged with an alarm. Pay closer attention to detail next time."

"Why would someone place an alarm on a drawer and not the whole room?" Andrew shouted at the loudspeaker.

"Why not?" retorted Mr. Harrison's voice. "You never know what kinds of unexpected things you're going to find in China, son. You've got to be prepared."

Andrew sighed and walked downstairs, to the room where Mr. Harrison had been watching him on video.

"You've certainly made progress, son. And it's going to have to be enough because today we move onto your English teacher training." Mr. Harrison led him into a room that was set up to look like a classroom. A fat, balding Caucasian man sat at a desk at the far end. He glanced up as Andrew and Mr. Harrison entered, then looked back down at the papers in front of him without changing his expression.

"This is your teaching instructor, Mr. Humphrey. He was an English teacher in China for almost two decades, and he's going to teach you everything you need to know about VIP tutoring in China."

"VIP?"

"Oh, of course, I forgot to fill ya in. We've been in contact with a private tutorin' company in Peking that agreed to hire you. And lucky for us, not only do they have an exclusive corporate trainin' contract with NOCCOC, but one of the classes they needed taught is a one-on-one, VIP class for none other than NOCCOC's CEO, Mr. Cheng.

"I'm going to be teaching English to the CEO? Mr. Harrison, I don't know if I can handle…"

"Like I said, son, Mr. Humphrey is going to give you a thorough trainin'. By the time he's through with you, Mr. Cheng won't know what hit 'em, ain't that right Gene?"

Mr. Humphrey gave a loud grunt and didn't look up from his papers.

"It just so happens that Mr. Cheng used to be in the Chinese military, and still has close ties to top officials there. I've even heard there's a rumor that he's vyin' for a top government position. Now, mah instincts are telling me that him bein' ex-military, as well as CEO of the company that's benefitin' most from China's weather control, is more than just a coincidence. What luck we had to get you a class teachin' him. You'll have a prime opportunity to gather information."

The idea of teaching such a powerful man unnerved Andrew a bit, but he was also relieved that he wouldn't be teaching a full class. He'd never been good at public speaking, and the idea of getting up in front of a classroom had made him more nervous than anything else.

As Mr. Harrison left the room, Andrew stared at Mr. Humphrey, waiting for him to look up or his expression to change. After a long moment, Mr. Humphrey finally looked up at him. "Well sit down, won't you? We've got a lot to do."

As Andrew sat down, Mr. Humphrey heaved himself out of the chair and over to the chalkboard. Then he wrote two words on the board in big, block letters:

FACE

HIERARCHY

"These are the two most important concepts you'll need to understand as a teacher in China." Mr. Humphrey spoke as if he'd recited the line a hundred times, to the point where it no longer really interested him. "The fear of losing face, or making others lose face, is the primary factor that drives people's decision making in China. This means that your students are unlikely to challenge you in class and your colleagues are unlikely to give you honest feedback, for fear that they might cause you to lose face. It also means they will not respond well to criticism."

"The second most important thing, hierarchy, ties into this as well. Chinese people immediately place everyone they interact with into either a higher, lower, or equal position to them. It's less acceptable to make your superior lose face than your subordinate. It also means that subordinates usually will not question the decisions of their superiors, because they fear making them lose face. As a teacher and a white foreigner, you will generally be considered higher up in this hierarchy than most people that you interact with, the important exception being your student, the CEO. While he will respect your position as a teacher, he will always see himself as your superior. It is therefore extremely important that you do not cause him to lose face. These are both deeply rooted concepts in Chinese culture that date back to the influence of the philosopher Confucius on early Chinese society."

As Andrew tried to absorb this information, he recalled some of his early childhood memories of interacting with his Chinese nanny. It didn't seem like she had tried to save him face at all. In fact, she'd always been very strict and highly critical. His thoughts began to wander back to his family, and the pang of loss shot back up through him. He needed to stay focused, now more than ever, so that his brother and sister would someday be safe.

CHAPTER 7:

THE LAND OF CONFUSION

As Andrew dragged his two suitcases out of the baggage claim area into the lobby of the Beijing airport, he was met by a crowd of people holding signs and jostling for the best position to be seen by the people getting off his plane. As he walked through the crowd, dazed from his long nap on the 20-something-hour flight from New York, he caught sight of a sign that read "Oxly Anderu." Holding it was a Chinese girl wearing thick, wide-rim glasses, high heels and a very smart looking pants-suit that showed off her figure. Apparently, she hadn't recognized him, even though he'd sent several pictures of himself to the English tutoring company at their request. As Andrew walked up to her, she finally noticed him. She turned to stare at him, blinking several times.

"...Osley? Osley An-de-ru?"

"Yes, that's me."

"Hallo, my name is I-phone. Nice to meet you," she reached out and shook Andrew's hand so many times that Andrew began to feel that she would never let go.

"I-phone?" repeated Andrew.

"Yes, it is my English name. Because it sound like my Chinese name, Ai Fong. You like it?" She grinned at him.

"It's...ah...very original."

"You just like picture, Teacha Osley... so handsome."

Andrew blushed a little. He couldn't remember the last time a girl as pretty as this had called him handsome. He also wondered why, if he looked just like the picture, she hadn't recognized him.

"Come, come, it is late. We get you some food, then you sleep. Big day tomorrow." She grabbed one of his suitcases and began dragging it toward the door, stumbling slightly in her high heels. Andrew wondered why she was dressed so nicely for such a menial task as picking him up from the airport. As the doors to the outside opened, an unfamiliar smell filled Andrew's nostrils. He coughed slightly, and looked out at the vast dome of the airport that curved around them, then to the sky, where the setting sun reflected in bright orange and red against a dense fog. Throngs of taxis crowded in to scoop up passengers headed into the city. I-phone waved down one of them, and helped the driver stuff Andrew's suitcases into the trunk. The driver grinned at Andrew, showing his stained and cracked teeth, and blurted out, "Hallo!"

"Hello," said Andrew, then he paused for a second. It couldn't hurt to show them that he knew a little Chinese. "Ni hao," he said, trying to make it sound as if he didn't know how to pronounce the word properly.

"O, vera good Chinese," chimed the cab driver. Apparently he was easily impressed.

As they climbed into the cab, I-phone said, "We eat at restaurant near your apartment. Then tomorrow I take you sightseeing."

Overwhelmed by all the new sights and sounds, Andrew didn't say much as they drove down the highway, while I-phone chattered away with the cab driver about the traffic and weather. The driver had a thick accent and added the "er" sound at the end of so many words that Andrew had a hard time eavesdropping on their conversation. At one point the driver asked I-phone why she was picking up a "laowai," which Andrew guessed was slang for foreigner, to which she replied that he was a new teacher.

"Laowai hui shuo zhongwen?" asked the driver. Andrew

found it amusing that the driver was just now asking her if he could speak Chinese.

"Bu, bu, ta gen biede laowai yiyang," responded I-phone. Andrew felt a little wave of resentment. It seemed that Mr. Harrison had been right; I-phone just assumed that since he was a white foreigner, he couldn't understand Chinese. Well, maybe this spying thing won't be so hard after all.

They continued down a part of the highway lined with trees for about 20 minutes before Andrew saw any signs that they were in a city, but soon large concrete apartment buildings began to appear here and there. As they drove up onto a bridge, Andrew looked below and saw several more multi-lane highways crisscrossing each other, every one packed with cars that had slowed to a crawl. The taxi they were riding in also began to slow, and soon they were caught in dense traffic five lanes wide on each side, inching through the city.

"Beijing traffic jam very serious," remarked I-phone, shaking her head up and down. "All Chinese people wanna own car, but not enough space. China have too many people."

Andrew watched as the concrete apartments along the highway were slowly replaced with glass skyscrapers, as they inched deeper into the city. Giant neon signs glowed through the fog. Besides the fact that they were all made up of Chinese characters, Andrew wouldn't have been able to tell that he was in China. Everything looked so modern and sterile. Where were the pagodas? Where were the bamboo forests, the rice fields, and farmers wearing straw hats that his father had always described in his stories? Well, after all, his father had mostly been working in rural areas. As they drove on they passed several buildings under construction. Andrew stared up at their massive steel frames, rising dozens of stories until they disappeared into the fog. Andrew could barely make out the shape of cranes high above, their long necks stretching over the buildings.

And why was it so foggy? Normally Andrew would have expected the air to feel moist in the fog, but instead his throat and eyes felt dry. And it made everything look a little more grayish-brown than he would have expected. Then he remembered reading about the pollution in Chinese cities. And to his horror, he realized this wasn't fog... it was air pollution. He'd never expected it to be this bad.

"We here," declared I-phone. They had pulled up outside a very modern-looking gated apartment complex. Behind the gates were two rows of what appeared to be thirty-story, concrete apartment buildings, separated by a park in the middle. As they drove through the gate, the guard in the gatehouse stared at Andrew through the window, his head moving to follow him as they passed. Andrew watched him too, and as they drove away, Andrew saw him reach for his phone. Suddenly Andrew felt uneasy.

The apartment turned out to be quite modern and spacious. He had a large bedroom with a queen-sized bed, and even his own living room and kitchen. There was a lone magnet on the refrigerator that said *Welcome to China* in English, with a red Chinese dragon below the words. As Andrew turned away, he noticed a faint glint in the black eye of the dragon. Turning back, he stared at it. Something wasn't right about it. He leaned in closer.

The eye looked like a lens.

Andrew's heartbeat quickened. I-phone was still in the other room, talking to the agent who had shown them into the apartment. Andrew looked around and found a kitchen knife. With it, he carefully cut into the plastic surface of the magnet. He pried at what was inside, and finally it popped out and landed on the floor. Andrew bent down and looked at it. Sure enough, it was a tiny camera.

Andrew stamped on it and ground his foot until he heard a faint cracking noise.

Were there others? Andrew would have to thoroughly search the apartment when he was alone. But more importantly, he wondered who had put it there. Did someone already suspect why he had come to China?

"OK, now we go eat," called I-phone. "I take you to good restaurant nearby, I think you like very much."

As they walked back out to the busy street, Andrew looked into the gatehouse. The guard was there, but this time he seemed to be ignoring Andrew. What was going on? Andrew was so distracted that he wasn't really paying attention to where they were walking, until I-phone stopped abruptly and pointed. Andrew looked around, expecting to see a Chinese restaurant, but instead he saw something vaguely familiar.

"Is this a fast-food restaurant?" Andrew asked, confused. The name over the door read 'Ken De Ji.'

"Yes, this is your... how do you call it? Kentucky Chicken?" I-phone grinned at him. Then her face twisted into a pensive frown, "You like eat here, yes Teacha Osley?"

"Oh, sure I-phone." Andrew had been looking forward to eating authentic Chinese food, but at that point he didn't really care. All he could think about was that someone had been anticipating his arrival in China and that they clearly wanted to keep a close eye on him.

***

It was the evening of the day before Andrew was to start teaching classes, and he realized he hadn't yet discussed his lesson plan with I-phone. I-phone had packed his first few days in China full of sightseeing, including trips to the Forbidden City and Tiananmen Square, the Great Wall, the Temple of Heaven; all the famous tourist spots around Beijing. Andrew had welcomed all the activity. At least when he was outside, moving around through crowds of people, it was less likely that someone was watching him. He hadn't found any more cameras or bugs in his apartment... but that didn't mean they weren't there.

As he began describing the lesson plans he had prepared with the help of Mr. Humphrey to I-phone over dinner, a puzzled look began to form on her face. Then, as if she had just realized what he was talking about, she let out a little exclamation of surprise.

"No, no, Teacha Osley... you no teach President Cheng. He is too demanding anyway. You be much happier teaching class to engineers."

"What? No I-phone, I was told I would teach President Cheng. That's what this lesson plan is for."

"Ah, but plans change. You will teach engineers first."

"And when were you going to tell me this, I-phone?" Andrew asked, raising his voice slightly now. This was not supposed to happen.

I-phone gave Andrew a look of confused innocence. "No need to be angry Teacha Osley, I thought you already know. We tell your boss."

"Well if you did, my boss didn't tell me. This was not part of the plan. I didn't prepare to teach a full class. I was hired to teach the CEO."

I-phone stared at Andrew and then her eyes suddenly seemed to become larger and she stuck out her lower lip into the biggest pout Andrew had ever seen, "Come on Teacha Osley, don't make my job harder. You just teach class, OK? Pleeeease??"

"I don't care if it makes your job harder, I-phone. I signed up to teach a one-on-one class. If you don't correct this, I'm... I'm going to talk to your boss about this," Andrew hoped that the idea of losing face to her boss would compel I-phone to change her mind. But it was a bluff; he had no idea who her boss was, or how to contact him. The thought that something like this would happen hadn't even occurred to him.

I-phone started at him for a moment, then when she spoke, her voice was still sweet, but there was a hint of iciness. "You just deal with me, Teacha Osley. No need talk to my boss. See, he have no choice anyway. NOCCOC have demands, and we listen, undastand? They say Mr. Cheng need old teacha with more experience teaching him. He is very demanding."

"Fine. Let me call *my* boss, I'm sure he can straighten this out," Andrew didn't know what else to do. Why hadn't Mr. Harrison given him more guidance on what to do in this situation? If he were forced to get up in front of a class, they would surely realize he wasn't a real teacher very quickly. Then his cover would be blown.

He got up and walked out of the restaurant. A few people stared at him as he went. Once outside, he took out the cell phone that Mr. Harrison had given him exclusively for them to communicate and dialed Mr. Harrison's secure number in Washington. It would be early morning there and Mr. Harrison would just be getting ready to head to the office. After several rings, Andrew heard Mr. Harrison's voice on the other end, "Hello mah boy, what did you have for dinner tonight?"

"Brunswick stew and banana pudding," said Andrew, answering their secret question the way Mr. Harrison had instructed.

"That's good Andrew, but make sure you say 'nana putin.' That's the way we say it in North Carolina. That way I know for sure it's you."

"Yes sir, I'll try that next time."

"Good, now what have you got for me, son? How's it goin' so far?

"This teaching assistant, I-phone, reassigned me to teach a group class instead of teaching the CEO, and I have no idea how to teach a group. They're going to realize I'm not really a teacher and..."

"Now hold on a second there, son. Why did she reassign you?"

"She says NOCCOC is demanding a more experienced teacher for Mr. Cheng."

"Well now, I suppose that is a reasonable demand."

"Can't you do something about it?"

"Like what?"

"Use your contacts, with Mr. Humphrey or whomever, to talk with her boss and get this straightened out."

"I'm afraid that won't be possible, son. We got you a job, but we have no control over how they assign the classes. You've got to figure this one out on your own. These kinds of things happen all the time. You can't expect things to always go as planned. You've just got to improvise."

There was a long pause. Andrew was beginning to panic. Mr. Harrison didn't seem to realize how much he was afraid of public speaking. "Mr. Harrison, I don't really know if I'm cut out for this job after all…"

"What do ya mean, son?"

"Maybe you should find someone else…"

"Now listen here, son. You can't turn back now. You're committed. Things have already been set in motion and… there's no time to find someone else. Now I don't want to hear you talkin' like that again, you understand?"

"Yes, sir."

"Just sit tight, and I'll see what we can do. But no promises." There was a click and then a tone.

Trying to calm himself down, Andrew took a deep breath and walked back into the restaurant. He sat back down across from I-phone, who looked at him curiously. It seemed he had no other choice right now. He'd have to figure out how to teach the class.

"OK I-phone, I'm going to teach the class for now. But you can't expect me to come up with a new lesson plan in just a few days. Can we postpone the class?"

"Oh, you don't worry Teacha Osley," I-phone continued on in her perky manner, as if nothing had happened, "NOCCOC students English level not very high, so you teach beginna to intamediate level. Should be very easy."

"So we can't postpone it?"

To his surprise, I-phone laughed. "Don't worry Teacha Osley, you be fine." She appeared to think for a moment, then continued, "Most important thing is, just make it interesting."

Great, thought Andrew, how the hell am I going to be 'interesting?' But I-phone's nonchalant attitude toward the whole thing had relieved some of his panic, at least for the time being. Still, he couldn't help but wonder how this had happened. Maybe it was just bad luck. Or maybe whoever had put that camera in his apartment was doing more than just watching him.

CHAPTER 8:

THE BOSS

"The boy's havin' cold feet already."

"I find that surprising, considering his motivations."

"I'm worried he might have realized what's really goin' on. I mean, why we really sent him there."

"What makes you say that?"

"Just a feelin'. He asked me to bring him home. Said he wasn't fit for the job. Frankly I'm not surprised."

"Do you think my suggestion to use the Oxley boy was unwise?"

"No, it's not that. I still think he's the right choice. He's skilled enough to be believable, but still naïve enough that he will eventually be discovered. But we only gave him a few weeks of trainin'. He must have realized that's not nearly enough time to train a real spy."

"You know as well as I do that we were running out of time. Waiting for him to graduate was already delay enough. If we don't get some traction before the UN Climate Summit, we could see the U.S. committing itself to sending billions of dollars in aid to China. Now I know you don't want that, Harrison…"

"A' course not. But even if they pass a new treaty, the Senate still has to ratify it. Can't you bide us some time on that end?"

"That would be tough. I have much greater influence in the House. But the Senate is a different story."

"Well, I'm just afraid he's going to realize what's going on, and bail on his own."

"Even if he does, I wouldn't be too worried. Having a decoy is not a vital part of the operation."

"I respectfully disagree. We need him to draw attention away from our primary operative. He's been having a lot of difficulty. Foreigners in China are being watched more and more closely. And with all the media attention that The Institute is getting these days... well, I just worry the Chinese might start lookin' more closely at what we're up to."

"So what do you propose?"

"I think we need to start training a backup decoy."

"And who would that be?"

"I don't know, but I'll start lookin' for someone."

"That would be a waste of your time, Harrison. You've got enough on your plate already. Besides, I don't think we've really seen what this boy is made of yet, especially given his father's history. He might surprise you."

"God, I hope so."

"So make it work then. Do whatever you need to do to build up his confidence. I've got to go."

Howard heard a click and hung up the phone. Sitting down in the armchair behind his desk, he stared across the room at the portrait of him and Henry Kissinger that hung on the opposite wall. It had been taken when he'd met Kissinger at a gathering of the intelligence community back in the late 2000s, where Kissinger had given a speech. Kissinger had been his hero since childhood, so it had been the thrill of a lifetime to meet the man in person. Whenever he was having difficulties at work, he would think back to that night and ask, what would Kissinger have done?

He hadn't gotten much sleep the night before, and from the look of his schedule, he had a long day ahead. There was a meeting with the intellectual property theft department at ten o'clock to see what progress they'd made on tracking seed theft. Then there was the board meeting at one o'clock, where they'd be scrutinizing his budget plan for the next year. And finally, the Washington Post was coming to do a follow-up interview with him at five o'clock about the weather warfare hypothesis, which he knew would be tough, because the Washington Post clearly thought his ideas were hogwash.

He needed a smoke. Continuing to stare at the portrait, his hand reached deftly into his top left drawer and retrieved his pipe. Packing in the tobacco and lighting the pipe, Howard sat back in the armchair and crossed his arms, continuing to hold the pipe between his teeth and take long, slow puffs. He began to relax. Now he could think.

Howard had supervised dozens of spies over the three decades he'd been working for the United States intelligence community. But only once before in his career had he deployed a decoy. It was not a decision he had made lightly. He knew that at best, the decoy would end up in Chinese prison. And even though he fully intended to use his influence in the U.S. government to convince them to bargain for the boy's eventual release, there were no guarantees. This time, it had been especially difficult for Howard to bury his feelings of guilt. When he looked at Andrew, he saw something of his son, Michael. It seemed especially cruel to cut short such a young life.

But how would he function if he continued doubting his own judgment like this? That was perhaps the most worrying thing. He had always trusted his gut, despite all the naysayers who thought he was crazy, who thought he was doing the wrong thing. And in the end, he'd proven them all wrong time and time again. That's how he'd courted so many wealthy donors onto the Institute's board of directors. He had a reputation for keen insight.

Using Andrew as a decoy had been one of his more brilliant ideas, really. Well, it hadn't been completely his idea; the board chairman had suggested it, but he had developed it into a formal operation. To take a fresh, naive college graduate with fluent Chinese, and pass him off as an English teacher who didn't speak a word of Chinese – there was no way he'd be able to keep that façade up for long. From there his disguise would slowly unravel, and soon Mr. Cheng would be focusing his resources on watching Andrew, leaving an opening for his primary operative to complete his mission.

Howard sighed and decided he was worrying too much.

The chime of his grandfather clock startled him. It was ten o'clock already; time for his meeting. Howard placed the pipe carefully back in its drawer and headed for the door.

He managed to make it through the day, but the five o'clock interview was nearly a disaster. The reporter asked several hard-hitting questions that he just didn't have the answers to and had to dodge. As he was packing up his briefcase and preparing to head home, the door to his office swung open, startling him. In pranced Shirley, throwing her hair back over her shoulder and smiling as she approached his desk.

"Ms. Hawthorn, I thought I told ya, I want ya'll to knock before enterin' my office."

"Oh, but that doesn't apply to me, does it, Howie?"

"Well, I suppose, if it's urgent…"

"Very urgent…"

Instead of stopping in front of his desk, Shirley continued around to Howard's side. She was carrying a stack of papers, which she placed gingerly on his desk. In doing so, she stuck her hip out to the side and leaned forward, exposing some of her cleavage. "Here's the revised budget proposal from the meeting this morning, all ready ahead of schedule. I'm sure the board will be impressed with how quickly you're able to get back to them."

"Thank you, Shirley, good work." Howard glanced at her chest, and then looked quickly away, "And stop callin' me Howie. It sounds unprofessional."

"As you like, *Howard*." She continued to lean against his desk, watching him intently.

"Is that all Ms. Hawthorn?" Howard fumbled with his briefcase.

"If that's really all you need, Howard. I know it's been a long week for you. How about a little massage to help you relax?" Without waiting for a response, Shirley moved behind Howard's chair and, reaching down in front of the high, leather backrest, began to massage the back of his neck. Instead of feeling more relaxed though, Howard began to feel tense. Shirley's massage was making him feel very uncomfortable. This could easily be misinterpreted. And these days, someone was always watching...

Shirley stopped the massage and slid around the chair until she was half sitting on Howards lap, her face very close to his. She leaned closer and closer, so that Howard got a nose full of her sweet strawberry perfume. It was intoxicating... but he knew what she was trying to do, and knew he couldn't.

He pushed Shirley away abruptly and got up from his chair. "What in the hell do ya think you're doing Ms. Hawthorn? I've got a wife of 32 years, ya know. This is not how you behave around your boss."

Shirley had opened her mouth slightly and was momentarily frozen, but she regained her composure quickly and smiled disarmingly. "I don't think there's anything wrong with me helping you relax. Besides, Mrs. Harrison doesn't have to know anything. It's just you and me in here," she giggled, "and no one else would dare disobey your order to knock first." She moved slowly toward Howard again, swinging her hips back and forth, but Howard turned away.

"It ain't right, Ms. Hawthorn. I made vows before the Lord, and I don't mean to break those vows." He paused and looked at her sternly. "Now you'd best be gettin' on home."

For a minute Shirley just continued to smile sweetly at him, searching his eyes for a sign of weakness. But after several moments passed, her expression hardened and she stopped smiling.

"You're a real piece of work, Howard. How do you get off?"

Howard was taken aback. "I hired you to be my secretary, Ms. Hawthorn, nothin' more."

"I see what's happening to you. You're getting more and more tense every day. I've overheard some of your conversations with Mrs. Harrison. A powerful man like you needs a woman who treats you right." She put her hand on his shoulder and began to slide it down, but he brushed it away.

"I can't believe you. No one ever rejects me. Where do you get the nerve?"

"The vow of marriage is one of the most important vows a man can make. It's a vow that should not be broken."

"Wake up, Howard. People are breaking it all over the place."

Howard stood up. "Ms. Hawthorn, if you still wanna have a job here, I suggest you get out of my office."

"Oh, I will have a job here for quite some time, Howard. Otherwise, the whole world is going to know about Operation Hurricane Eye and what a phony organization you're running here."

"Are you blackmailing me, Ms. Hawthorn?"

"Oh Howard, I'm just trying to get you to stop suppressing your desires. That's not really blackmail."

Shirley turned and walked out of Howard's office.

Howard sat back down heavily in his chair. His secretary had just threatened to blackmail him—his own secretary. Now he was truly under siege from all sides.

As much as he hated to admit it, he knew it wouldn't be hard for her to discredit him. He was still operating largely from his gut feeling, without much evidence. Not that real evidence mattered to the media these days. But with all the fake news circulating around online, how could he really hope to make his story more credible than hers? Whoever could generate the most drama—that's who people would listen to.

It was the dramatic nature of his claims that had bought him so much airtime in the first place. And of course, the stagecraft they had employed to make the announcement. They had made it look like an unintentional leak, in order to get the media's attention. Then when they had finally allowed the media to "corner" him, Howard had admitted that yes, they had intelligence to suggest that the Chinese government was carrying out very covert attacks on the U.S. by manipulating the weather.

They'd found some scientists to testify that yes, it was indeed very possible for a country to manipulate the weather and that in fact it had been done for decades. It didn't take long before experts were being interviewed all across the major news networks to question whether these strange weather events were really being caused by climate change, or by China. Climate change was the perfect disguise for China to hide behind, everyone agreed. But like all media fads, this one was in danger of deflating, and he had yet to get the real decision-makers to take him seriously. But once his primary operative had recovered concrete evidence, everything would change.

***

When he arrived home late that evening, Howard discovered that his wife, Anna Harrison, had already prepared dinner. Plates of fried fish, potatoes, pickled vegetables and biscuits waited steaming on the table. He had always marveled at Mrs. Harrison's unique skill in mixing Russian and Southern cuisine. And tonight's dinner was especially fancy.

"This is quite a spread here, my dear. What's the occasion?"

"Michael tells me he has ze announcement to give us." Anna's tone was stiff and unbending.

It was about time Michael had an announcement for them. He couldn't keep living at home forever. He needed to be a responsible adult and join the workforce. Part of Howard had hoped he would come work for the Institute. But it seemed Michael had some other plans. What those plans were, he didn't have a guess— Michael had been very reluctant to share them with him.

Michael came out into the dining room and sat down at the table without looking at Howard. Anna joined them, said grace, and they began to eat in silence. After several minutes,

Howard finally spoke.

"Michael, your mother tells me you have somethin' to tell us."

Michael, who had been staring at his plate as he shoveled food into his mouth, finally looked up. He finished chewing very deliberately, as if he had decided to savor every bite, and then sat up straight in his chair.

"Out with it now boy. You're moving slower than molasses."

Michael took a deep breath. "I got a job with the New York Times. So I'm moving to New York with my boyfriend and we're going to find an apartment together."

Anna stopped chewing and glanced quickly at Howard, then went back to eating without a word.

"Well, it's a very prestigious newspaper, even if it is rather slanted," Howard forced a chuckle. "I suppose you'll be starting out as a delivery boy?"

"Actually, as an editorial assistant. No one has delivery boys anymore, Dad. News is mostly online."

"Nonsense. How else would they hire inexperienced young people like you, boy? I hope you didn't fake your resume to get that position."

"No sir."

"Good. Now tell me, are you dating anyone these days?"

"I told you dad, I'm moving to New York with my *boyfriend*."

"I mean dating anyone in a romantic sense. Any girls from school you have your eye on?"

Michael stood up abruptly and leaned forward, "I don't date *girls* dad. I have a BOYFRIEND. How many ways do I have to say it before you'll get it through your thick head?"

Howard was on his feet, "Don't you talk to me that way, boy. Now stop lying and tell me what this is all about. You don't have to be ashamed if she's not pretty. Your old man never dated pretty girls, at least not until I met your mother."

"Ashamed? Clearly I'm not the one who is ashamed, dad. Why is it so hard for you to accept the truth?" Michael threw back his chair and stormed out of the room.

"The boy is clearly a pathological liar," Howard stared at the empty seat where Michael had just been, breathing heavily. "Where did he ever get these silly ideas from?"

Mrs. Harrison stopped eating, put down her fork and turned to face Howard. "Ze boy is right, you know. You can't accept anything zees days unless it fits with your view of ze world."

"And what's wrong with my view of the world, Anna? Are you telling me I should just allow him to spread lies and pretend to be a homosexual like this?"

"You just need to start accepting zat not everyone is going to agree with you all the time, Howard. Michael is his own man now, and he can make his own decisions."

"I'm disappointed in you, Anna. Of all things, I would have expected you to side with me on this."

Anna stood up. "I've put up with your bigotry all zees years Howard, but I'm not going to let you do ze same thing to our son." She threw down her napkin and left the room.

Howard watched her go, and then put his face in his hands. "God, help me," he said quietly. "Help me to make them see your light again."

CHAPTER 9:

INTO THE DRAGONS DEN

As Andrew got out of the taxi and saw the NOCCOC building for the first time, he felt as if he had just walked out of a dollhouse into the much larger scale of the real world. The building was a massive steel and glass box, stretching eight stories tall, and running what appeared to be nearly the length of a football field. Carefully pruned gardens and fountains lined the cement walkway leading from the street to the main entrance. Dozens of men and women dressed smartly in suits walked in and out of the building, chatting amiably. The building was located on Chang'an Street, a major boulevard running through the heart of Beijing, where most of China's largest state-owned enterprises had their offices, and just blocks from Tiananmen Square. The sky was clearer that day, and as he looked around, he saw similar buildings lining the street, all the way down to where he could see the walls of the Forbidden City.

Through consulting with Mr. Humphrey over the phone, Andrew had cobbled together what he hoped was a workable lesson plan for a class of 20 students. He had written everything down so that he knew exactly what to say, in case he got nervous and lost track of where he was. He had been starting to feel that maybe this wouldn't be so bad, but seeing the majesty of the building, his fears had resurfaced.

As they entered the main lobby, a man wearing a suit and badge greeted them.

"Please, follow me," he said in English, as if each word were carefully calculated. As they walked through the cavernous lobby, Andrew could almost see his reflection in the smoothly polished marble floors.

"NOCCCOC is the largest oil and chemical company in China, and also one of the largest companies in the world," began their escort, directing his attention at Andrew. "The company has nearly 500,000 employees worldwide, and we recently expanded our business into Southeast Asia, Africa, and the Americas. We have over 100 offices around the world. This building was built about 15 years ago to serve as our headquarters."

They stepped into an elevator, and as their escort pushed the button for level five, Andrew noticed that the button skipped the fourth floor.

"I-phone, how come there is no fourth floor?"

"Oh, four in Chinese is unlucky. Chinese word for 'four' sounds like word for 'death.' So most buildings in China just skip fourth floor."

Just then a young woman stepped into the elevator, and Andrew's heart leaped into his throat.

"May?"

She turned, and gave a soft cry, putting her hand to her mouth.

"Andrew? How…what are you doing here?"

Andrew realized that with all the excitement, he'd forgotten to tell her he would be going to Beijing.

"I, um, I came to work here… as an English teacher. I kind of didn't get a chance to tell you. But, here I am." He grinned, trying to stop all the blood in his body from rushing to his face. "But I didn't expect to see you here, at NOCCOC, I mean."

"Well, I work here now, this is the job I was telling you about, the one that my dad insisted I take." She raised her eyebrows and sighed, then turned to face Andrew, a little half-smile on her face. "It's so nice that you're here. Ni zhu zai nali?"

She was asking him where he was staying in Chinese. He had forgotten that she knew he could speak Chinese. The words Mr. Harrison had said to him in their initial interview and had repeated many times throughout his training, floated back into his mind. *Above all son, don't let* anyone *know that you can understand Chinese.*

She was going to blow his cover wide open. He looked tentatively over at I-phone, who had been watching them curiously.

"Ah, what was that?" said Andrew, trying to feign a look of genuine confusion.

May wrinkled her forehead and frowned, "NI – ZHU – ZAI – NALI?"

"Sorry, I'm not sure what you're saying. I don't speak Chinese," Andrew couldn't look at her. He felt horrible lying to her face like this.

"Ni zenme ke neng ting bu dong wo shuo de hua ne?" Now May was starting to sound upset.

Thankfully, they had just arrived at the fifth floor. "Well, see you later..." said Andrew, and hurried off the elevator, followed by a confused looking escort and I-phone.

"So rude, that girl," remarked I-phone as they walked. "How you know her? And why she think you undastand Chinese?" She gave him a scrutinizing look.

"I think she confused me with someone else," said Andrew, turning away. He had just now realized the impossibility of ever having a romantic relationship with May here. In fact, he should probably stay away from her altogether as she could seriously compromise his mission. All his hopes of having a second chance with May were unraveling very quickly. The thought was so devastating that he barely noticed as I-phone led him further down the hall, into a crowded classroom, and up to the front of the room. It wasn't until he heard I-phone say, "Here is Teacha Osley," and the room suddenly fell silent, that he snapped back to reality.

"Uh, hi." He said, caught off guard by the sudden silence.

Now he became aware of how big the class was. There must have been at least 50 people present. He had never stood up in front of so many people in his life. He began to sweat a little. Why had they given him such a big class on his first day?

"Today…" he stammered, "…today we will be studying…" But his mind was drawing a blank. You rehearsed this several times on the way here, he told himself. Think…he looked down at the lesson plan he'd prepared.

"…studying different types of English greetings in a letter." Numbly, he walked to the chalkboard and began writing, *To Whom It May Concern…*

"Does anyone know another way to start a letter to someone you don't know?" he said, turning back to face the class.

Silence.

He looked around at the student—a strange feeling, since he'd very recently been in their shoes. They were all dressed in very similar business attire and were sitting very stiffly, most of them avoiding his gaze. They were each crammed behind little desks that seemed too small for adults. I'm probably half the age of most of the people here, Andrew thought. But their shyness somehow helped to slightly settle his nerves. So he wasn't the only one who was nervous about their first class.

"Anyone?" He gazed around the room, watching several of them turn their heads down as he did, and a few others turned to each other and whispered quietly in Chinese. It was too far away for Andrew to hear them. Well, better call on someone.

"How about you in the red blouse?" Andrew pointed to a woman sitting near the back. She looked around, and then, realizing he was talking to her, stood up. *What is she doing?* Andrew thought. But then she spoke.

"We can say, *Dear Sir or Madam,*" She said, and then sat down almost as quickly as she had stood up."

"That's right," said Andrew, scribbling this onto the chalkboard. "Now what about ways to end a letter?"

This time there was a little murmur among the students, as some of them turned and whispered to each other in Chinese again. Andrew was about to call on someone when one woman sitting in the front row stood up. She was wearing a white lacy shirt and perfectly round glasses.

"Excuse me, Mr. Oxley, but most of us studied this in fourth grade. Do you have anything new to teach us?"

Andrew stared. This woman had just spoken to him in nearly perfect English. Clearly these students were a lot more advanced than I-phone had said. What in the world was he going to teach them?

He felt a void growing deep in his chest as if his insides were being sucked out by a hose. What was he doing here? How had he thought he would ever make it in China posing as an English teacher, let alone trying to be a spy? He felt a deep longing to return to his family, to America, and live out a normal life. He had never been so far from home, in such a strange place…

"…Teacha Osley?" Andrew realized he had been silent for several seconds and I-phone was giving him a concerned look.

"Oh, sorry, I'm, uh, just not feeling well today. Well, um, I guess since you guys already know this, let's jump ahead to writing the body of a formal letter.…"

***

An hour later, Andrew watched as the NOCCOC employees filed neatly out of the classroom. He had made it through the class. He had a feeling, though, that I-phone was not happy with his performance. As the last of the employees left the room, she walked stiffly up to him.

"I have otha class to go attend now Teacha Osley. You go have lunch in cafeteria on first floor. I come get you later." And without another word, she turned and left.

Andrew felt only slightly vindicated. Hadn't he told her this wouldn't work? But he was more concerned now with how long he could keep this up. He found his way back to the elevator and pressed the button for the bottom floor, going over the class in his head as he did. A minute later, he emerged into a busy hallway with a long line of chattering workers waiting to be served. As he waited in line, he noticed several people staring at him. Did he really stand out that much?

After retrieving his food, Andrew squeezed into a seat at one of the many long tables. Feeling as if he were back in high school, he began eating by himself, when to his surprise a tall white man sat down across from him. Andrew couldn't help but stare at his outfit. He was wearing a tight, black v-neck shirt and jeans. His hair was gelled into a Mohawk, and he wore two thick, black, leather bracelets. The whole outfit was such a stark contrast to the neat suits everyone else was wearing, he couldn't help but stare.

"How are you doing, dude? And here I dought I was da only foreigner who worked at NOCCOC. What are you doing here?"

Andrew couldn't tell where his accent was from, although it sounded slightly British. "Well, I'm the new English teacher for the employees here," Andrew replied.

"Dat's totally awesome, dude. You're American I take it? I grew up in Germany, but my mum is British. Dat's why my English is so good," he grinned. "M'name's Fritz Nimitz. Or as some of my American homies like to call me, 'Frizzle, my Nizzle.'"

Andrew just stared for a moment, wondering how Fritz had made these friends. "Hi Fritz, I'm Andrew. So what do you do here...?"

"I'm a geologist. You know, the cool science," Fritz winked at him.

"Oh, right. I was a biology major in school, and I..."

"Hey, check it out," Fritz pointed across the room behind Andrew. He turned and immediately noticed a slim and stunningly beautiful woman wearing a short skirt and low-cut shirt walking delicately toward the front of the food line, cutting about 20 people. Andrew watched her casually pick up a tray of food, and walk across the room to a solitary table, turning heads as she did so.

"Who is she?" asked Andrew.

"Dat's Yang Fei. More commonly called 'Gui Fei' around here," Fritz snickered again. When Andrew just stared at him blankly, he continued, "Don't you know da Chinese legend of Yang Gui Fei? She was da emperor's favorite concubine. Well, Yang Fei over der provides da same service for our own emperor, da President of NOCCOC, Lao Cheng." Fritz stared off into space for a moment. "Ah, Yang Fei. You know, I went on a date with her once." Andrew looked at him skeptically. This guy had been on a date with what appeared to be the most attractive girl at NOCCOC? He found it hard to believe.

"Dey must be having a fight or something because she usually eats with the boss," Fritz continued.

"Why do you call Mr. Cheng 'Lao' Cheng?"

"Oh, yea, dat's what dey call him behind his back. 'Lao' means old, so it's kind of an insult in Chinese to call someone dat. Do you speak Chinese by da way?"

"Uh, just a little."

"Ok, well don't go telling anyone I told you dese names. If dey were to find out, you'd probably have your droat cut in your sleep. Dat's what happens when you make a Chinese person lose face. It can get nasty…"

Fritz had trailed off and was staring at something behind Andrew.

"Hi, Andrew."

He turned and saw May standing behind him. His heart jumped into his throat.

"I just wanted to say, I'm happy to see you here, and if you need any help with your new life in China, just, um… let me know."

Andrew just stared at her. His mouth had gone dry. He started to open his mouth to say something, but nothing came out. After a few seconds of silence, May looked at the ground, then turned quickly and walked off. Andrew felt an impulse to run after her, but instead, he just watched her, helplessly, as she disappeared into the crowd.

"What was dat about Drew?" Fritz was staring after May. "Damn, you already got a hottie dat's totally into you. How long did you say you've been here?" Fritz was looking at Andrew with renewed interest.

"This is my first day, actually."

"Wow. Well you clearly have a way with women my friend."

Was that true? Was May really interested in him? It didn't matter anyway. Now his chances with her were as slim as his chances of making his classes 'interesting.'

CHAPTER 10:

THE MAGICIAN AND THE APPRENTICE

Andrew collapsed onto the couch in his apartment. He'd taught two more classes that week, and at the end of his last class, I-phone had issued what he was pretty sure was a not-so-veiled threat. "Students dropping like fall leaves on windy day. I think maybe they want new teacher," she had said. "You teach one more class, then if students want, we transfer you," she had said in a matter-of-fact tone. But when Andrew had asked her what class he'd be transferred to, she had dodged the question.

As Andrew contemplated his options, his phone began buzzing. He looked and saw that it was Fritz calling. He hesitated a moment before accepting the call.

"Drewster. You got plans tonight? Come out to a bar with your pal Fritz. There's someone I want you to meet."

"Thanks, Fritz, but I have a lot of work to do this weekend if I want to keep my job."

"Keep your job? What's da matter?"

"My classes are not going well. I'm just… not a very good teacher."

"Hey, that's great." Great? It seemed like Fritz hadn't understood.

"What do you mean? What's great about losing my job?"

"Da guy I want you to meet tonight. He can help you

become a better teacher… among other things," Fritz chuckled nasally. "C'mon, it will be fun."

The idea of going out to a bar with Fritz didn't thrill him, but Fritz had stirred his curiosity. "Alright, sure."

Following Fritz's instructions, he took a cab to an area called Sanlitun, where there appeared to be quite a few bars and restaurants. The smog had been hanging heavily over the city for the last few days, and as he got out of the car, it started to drizzle.

He entered the bar and soon spotted Fritz off to the side, leaning against a wall and talking to a very tall, attractive Chinese girl. Andrew inched toward them until he was standing right next to Fritz, who seemed to be trying very hard to remain engaged in the conversation, and was sweating profusely. After a few seconds, he noticed Andrew. "Ah, Drew buddy, how you doing?" Fritz appeared to force a grin and then gave Andrew an awkward half-hug. "Drew, I'd like you to meet…" Fritz hesitated for a moment, smiling weakly at the girl, who folded her arms across her chest, "…Shao Lin?"

"Xiao Li," the girl groaned.

"Ah, right, Xiao Li…"

At that moment, one of the girl's friends came over and took her arm, whispering something in her ear.

"Sorry, I go now," she said in broken English and disappeared into the crowd.

"Damn, dat girl was so hot." Fritz said, in a tone that sounded like he was mourning the death of a family member.

"How do you know her?"

"Know her? I don't. I just started talking to her."

"Really? But how did you get a girl like that to talk to you when… I mean, no offense, you're a good-looking guy… not that *I'm* attracted to you, but…" Andrew trailed off.

Fritz smirked. "How else, but with practice, and guidance from my mentor. Speaking of which," he looked over at the bar entrance, "here he comes now."

Andrew turned toward the entrance and saw a six-foot-tall, solid Caucasian man step into the bar. He wore slightly baggy jeans, a well-fitting t-shirt that revealed his muscular upper body, and had a bandana tied around his head. Something about his movements and the look on his face projected an air of utter confidence. He was shadowed by a shorter, skinny Chinese guy who was similarly dressed, wearing a tight designer t-shirt, except that his head wasn't covered by a bandana, but by a large tuft of spiky, thick, black hair. Spotting Fritz, the two newcomers headed in their direction, parting the crowd like the Red Sea as they moved through it.

"How're you doing mate?" the man reached out and clasped hands with Fritz. His voice was deep and controlled, and despite his imposing figure, his presence was quite calming. Then he turned to Andrew. "I'm Mazken, nice to meet you, Andrew," he gave a casual smile. The fact that Mazken already knew his name sent a little chill down his back, but for the first time in a while, Andrew felt like he was talking to someone who was genuinely pleased to meet him.

"I'm Charlie Wu," said the Chinese guy in only slightly accented English. He was now leaning against the wall lighting a cigarette, and he leaned forward to shake Andrew's hand, grinning with the cigarette between his teeth. Unlike Mazken, Charlie seemed to be overflowing with restless energy.

"Nice to meet you," Andrew said to both of them, and then fell silent, not sure where to go from there.

Mazken grinned at him, "You're pretty talkative, huh? Slow down, you don't need to tell us your life's story all at once," He laughed a deep laugh, and Fritz joined in, mimicking him. Charlie just grinned again and dragged on his cigarette. Then Mazken stopped and looked searchingly at Andrew, scratching his chin. "You're American, yeah? And I suppose you're here teaching English?"

Now Mazken's gaze was unnerving him. "Yeah, how did you know? I teach classes at NOCCOC."

"At where? At no cock?" Mazken chuckled, and Fritz joined in again.

"It stands for National Oil and Chemical Company of China."

"Uh-huh. But is that really why you're in China, Andrew?"

Andrew felt his face begin to heat up. "What do you mean?"

"I suppose you just graduated from college and didn't know what you really wanted to do with your life. You grew up as an outcast and always wanted to find adventure somewhere else, so you came to China to try and find yourself. But so far you aren't having much luck."

It felt like Mazken was staring into his soul, and seeing more than he wanted anyone to see. How did he know all these things? And if he could see all this, did he know that he wasn't really there to teach English at all?

As if continuing to read his mind, Mazken smiled disarmingly, "I'm making you uncomfortable, aren't I? Don't worry mate, I won't expose all your secrets here," Mazken winked at him.

"I don't understand how you knew all that. We've never even met before."

"There's a lot you can learn about a person by being a keen observer of human behavior."

"And dis guy is about as keen as dey come. He's amazing," Fritz chimed in. Mazken just continued looking warmly at Andrew, ignoring Fritz's comment."

"So you don't claim to be a psychic then?"

"There are some people who've called me psychic. But it's really just hard work and careful study."

As Andrew marveled at Mazken's words, he realized that the man standing in front of him had all the traits he wished he had. If he could read people like that, surely that would make him a better spy. And if he could be that confident, he'd probably be a much better teacher.

"I want to learn how to do that."

Now Charlie chimed in, "Everyone say that. But few people actually have the talent and the patience to learn." Mazken gave Charlie a look. "But you seem like you would be good at it," he added hastily to Andrew, as he dropped his cigarette butt into a nearby glass of beer while its owner was looking the other direction. Seeing the look of horror on Andrew's face, Charlie grinned and added under his breath, "Don't worry. I know that guy, and he is a rich a-hole. He have it coming."

Andrew turned back to Mazken. "I'm definitely willing to work."

Mazken gave Andrew another deep, soul-searching gaze, "Why do you want to learn?"

"Because," how to answer without giving himself away? "To be honest, I don't really know what I'm doing as a teacher. If I could read my students better... maybe I could come up with more interesting lessons for them. And I'm still really not confident standing in front of a room full of people."

Mazken didn't break his gaze. "I think I can help with that. But like Charlie said, it's not easy. Even my best students needed a lot of patience, hard work, and practice. And even if you turn out to be good, you need to be open to feedback if you want to keep improving," his eyes landed on Charlie.

"Why do you look at me? I listen to your feedback... sometimes," Charlie grinned.

"That's not a problem," said Andrew. "When can we start?"

Mazken smiled. "We can start right now."

"But we're in a bar."

"Yep. This is the perfect place to learn how to pick up beautiful girls."

"What? But I thought you were going to teach me to be confident and read people?"

"Did you ever see the movie The Karate Kid?"

"Yeah."

"Remember how Mr. Miyagi has him wash all his cars, but what he doesn't realize is that by doing so, he's already practicing karate?

"Right."

"Well, have a little trust in your new mentor, mate. Now watch this." Mazken turned and walked directly toward the girl

Fritz had just been talking with. Without any hint of hesitation or nervousness, he tapped her on the shoulder and gave a little wave and a smile. The girl smiled back. Then Andrew heard Mazken begin talking to her in Chinese, though he couldn't make out most of what he was saying over the noise of the bar. But the girl seemed to be engaged. She was easily the most attractive girl in the bar. How was he doing it?

"See her body language, how she turns toward him and strokes her hair?" said Charlie. Then Andrew saw Mazken wave his arm in their direction. "See ya later," said Charlie, who stuffed a piece of gum in his mouth, and then, seemingly as an afterthought, thrust his nearly empty pack of cigarettes into Andrew's hand.

"But I don't smoke," Andrew protested.

"No problem, just keep it in a case a girl asks you for one." And Charlie walked over to join Mazken and the girl. Andrew watched as Charlie began to engage the girl's friend, with similar results to what Mazken had achieved. Soon he saw the two girls laughing and moving closer to the two men. Mazken was so loud and energetic that some people at nearby tables began to look over at them.

"Look at dem work der magic," Andrew had almost forgotten Fritz was still with him.

"That's the girl you were talking to, though, Fritz. Doesn't that annoy you?"

"Nah, she wasn't da right girl for me, dude. I'll find another one."

Pretty soon Mazken was heading for the door with the girl in tow, and Charlie and the other girl followed them. "Give me a call tomorrow and we'll arrange lesson two," said Mazken as he passed, handing Andrew a card.

"Where are you going?"

"Taking these girls to another bar. Motion creates emotion, mate." Mazken winked at him again, and they were gone. Suddenly Andrew felt a little shove on the shoulder. He looked over and saw a well-dressed, muscular Chinese man glaring down at him.

"You drop cigarette butt in my drink?" the guy demanded in English.

"Me? No, I don't even smoke…" protested Andrew, and then he looked down at the cigarette pack in his hand, and realized why Charlie had given him the cigarettes.

"Andrew, I think we're late to meet our friends at dat other bar, huh?" Fritz said, grabbing Andrew and steering him quickly out of the bar, as the Chinese man glared after them.

CHAPTER 11:

THE JUNGLE

The next day, Andrew found himself sitting in a dingy, hole-in-the-wall noodle restaurant near the Workers Stadium, having dinner with Mazken and Charlie. He watched Charlie dramatically recounting what had happened the night before.

"...and then she asks you, 'where are we going?' And you say 'back to my flat,' and she say, 'What are we doing there?' And you... what do you say?"

"I said, 'We're going to bake a cake, of course. Didn't you know, today is Australian Cake Day?'"

Mazken and Charlie burst out laughing.

"What's Australian Cake Day?" asked Andrew.

"It's a holiday that I made up off the top of my head. It doesn't really exist. I just needed some reason besides, 'we're going back to my place to bang.'"

"Plausible deniability," Charlie said.

"When you're trying to get a person to do something that makes them feel a little uncomfortable, but which you know they really want to do, it helps to have some kind of excuse," explained Mazken. "Basically, it's a surface reason for doing something that isn't the real reason. People often prefer to deceive themselves rather than admit the truth."

"But you lied to her... don't you think that will somehow come back to you later? How is she ever going to trust you?"

"Not really," continued Mazken. "We actually did bake a cake. And it was delicious," he grinned. "The thing is, I knew she already *wanted* to come back to my place. I was just helping her to do it in a way that would save her face—so she wouldn't have to admit to herself that she was going to have sex with a guy she'd just met. Think about this for a minute, Andrew. Do you remember any situations in your life where someone you knew preferred to deceive themselves rather than admit the truth?"

Andrew thought back to after his father had died. His sister was so young at the time that his mother had told her their father had gone on a long vacation. For years after that, Rose had asked, "When is Daddy coming home?" to which his mother had answered, "Not for a while yet." Even though he knew after a while that Rose had figured out what had happened, she continued to pretend their dad would still be coming home someday. Andrew nodded his head.

"Truth is relative. It's the person with the stronger frame—the person who sticks to his version of the truth with the most confidence—that will ultimately control reality. So the first thing you have to learn to influence human behavior is to have unshakeable confidence in your vision of reality."

Andrew noticed that Charlie had gotten up and gone over to another table, where a group of Chinese men were playing cards, and appeared to be trying to join their game.

"But how do I learn to be confident?"

"That's the tricky part. I could just tell you to be more confident all day, but you won't achieve this without first conquering your greatest fears. You know, I was a lot like you once, Andrew. I spent much of my teenage years feeling isolated, getting into fights, and finding as many ways as I could to escape from reality. But I knew I wanted to... that I could be something more, so one day I decided to stop being angry at the world, and began observing the world around me. I became a student of human behavior and started conducting my own social experiments. I would say and do things just to see how the people around me would react. After that I started to notice some things all human beings have in common. Above all are dreams. Wishes. Hopes. For a few people, they're even concrete enough to be called goals. But how many people are even anywhere close to reaching those dreams? Almost none, because most of them are too afraid to take action. Fear can paralyze us."

"Well Andrew, just like me, you took action by coming to China to look for a new life. And tonight you've taken action again by coming to meet us. That makes you special, and it means you might have what it takes. But we still need to find out what's holding you back. So let me ask you: What is your greatest fear?"

Immediately Andrew felt a dull pain in his chest. "Losing another family member. My father died when I was nine. And my mother just died... recently."

"Fear of the loss of a loved one. Yes, that's a very natural fear. And it's also one that you can conquer. But are you sure that's your greatest fear?"

"Well, I think so."

"Think back to times in your life when you were the most fearful. What caused that fear?"

Once again, Andrew thought back to when his father had died. The years after that were full of fear. He'd felt more alone than ever. And he'd felt a responsibility to try and take his father's place to some degree. He'd helped to take care of his sister and brother. And he'd also felt like his mother and other relatives had always expected him to grow up to become as successful as his father.

"I guess my greatest fear is really that I'll fail to do what I was meant to do. Does that make any sense? Like I have a destiny, and I have a vague idea of what it is, but I'm afraid I won't find it, or even if I do, that I'll fail to live up to it."

"So fear of failure."

Andrew paused, "Yeah, I guess that's what you could call it."

"Would it surprise you to learn that this is a very common fear, especially among men?"

"Well, I guess not. I mean it makes sense. But why do you say 'among men'?

"Because the fear of failure is closely related to the fear of rejection. And most men have a very strong fear of rejection. It's an evolutionary trait rooted deep in our DNA." Mazken looked around the restaurant. "Say, how would you feel if I asked you to walk over to that girl right now and start talking to her?"

Andrew looked where Mazken was pointing and saw a stunningly beautiful girl wearing a slim dress and high heels, sitting around a table with a few other similarly dressed girls. His heart began beating faster.

"Well, are you going to go talk to her?"

"You actually want me to do it?" The thought of it made Andrew begin to feel shaky, and even a little feverish. Surely that girl would reject him in front of everyone in the restaurant.

"Just the thought makes you want to crap your pants, doesn't it?" Mazken grinned.

"What are girls like that doing in a restaurant like this anyway?"

"Just one of the strange things you see every day in China. These girls were probably farmers not long ago and just came to the city. They must be getting ready to head over to Mix. That's the club where all the models and actresses go. In fact, that's where we're going tonight."

"What? You mean you really want me to go talk to these girls tonight? I thought you were just going to teach me today…"

"That *is* the lesson. The only way to get over your fear is to take action. And the longer you delay, the harder it will be."

Just then they heard a commotion coming from the card table. Andrew could see that Charlie was grinning and there was a little gleam in his eyes, as he collected money from the other players.

"Alright Charlie, you've hustled enough money out of these blokes for now, let's get over to the club before you take a beating," Mazken began to walk out, and Andrew quickly

108

followed, with Charlie reluctantly joining them.

***

Ten minutes later, as they walked into the main room of the club, a shock wave of electronic music smashed into Andrew. As the wave swept over him, a new sensation overwhelmed him: flashing disco lights, the smell of perfume mixed with sweat and alcohol, and crowds of people shouting, laughing, and moving in amorphous clumps around the club.

"Welcome to the modern-day jungle," said Mazken, as he navigated them between crowds of people surrounding tables toward the other side of the room. "This is where you will witness human nature at its rawest. It's that primitive feeling of being on the hunt, and being hunted, which draws the rich, the bored and the desperate to clubs like this. If you watch carefully, you'll observe a primal mating game is taking place here. The dominant men flaunt their resources and influence by buying bottle service and bringing as many friends as they can, so they can try to convince the most beautiful women to mate with them. Some women are taken in by this display, but most women are not as attracted to money as they are to things like social status, confidence, and an interesting personality. Ultimately, practically everyone here is looking for someone to mate with, whether they admit it or not. And many of them will go to amazing lengths to get what they want."

"The greatest way to understand human nature is to learn to seduce. Many of the most influential people in history: kings, entrepreneurs, explorers, spies…" Mazken looked directly at Andrew, and for a moment Andrew thought he'd been discovered, but then Mazken looked away and continued, "….have also been great seducers. Treat this club like an interactive classroom, Andrew. You will learn more from just talking to girls and observing what goes on here than you ever will from reading a book or listening to me lecture."

"But it's so loud, and there are so many people around, how am I supposed to even get anyone's attention, let alone get these girls to talk to me? I can barely even hear what you're saying."

"The first step is just to be more interesting than anything or anyone else. If you look around, you'll start to notice how bored some of these girls are, despite all the stimulation to their senses. Try this: go up to that girl over there and just wave at her and smile, then if she smiles back, give her a high-five."

"What? That's so lame..."

"Just do it. Charlie will be your wingman if you need one. Don't think about it, just go now."

Andrew reluctantly shuffled over to the girl who was standing a few feet away, leaning against a wall. He smiled weakly at her and gave a little wave. The girl just frowned and turned away from him. Feeling defeated, Andrew turned and walked back over to Mazken and Charlie.

"Good job," said Mazken.

"But she totally rejected me."

"And that's your first lesson. You're going to get rejected a lot. Get used to it. Every rejection will make you stronger."

"So you told me to smile and wave just so I would get rejected?"

"No. That actually has about a fifteen percent chance of working, which is a much higher percentage than most other approaches. Believe me, I've tried just about everything.... Hey, there's another one." Mazken grabbed Andrew, turned him around, and shoved him so hard in the direction of another girl that he practically ran into her. She looked up, surprised, and without really thinking this time, Andrew smiled and waved at her. To his amazement, she smiled back.

"Show some enthusiasm. Give her a high-five," Mazken bellowed at him over the music. For a second Andrew was embarrassed at Mazken's blatant instruction, but then he realized that this girl probably didn't understand English. So he kept smiling and moved his hand up in a high-five motion. The girl hesitated for a moment, then slapped his hand and giggled. Andrew couldn't believe this was working. But now the girl was looking at him expectantly, and he didn't know what to do next.

"Ni hao, wo shi Andrew," he said, trying to make his Chinese sound elementary.

The girl giggled again. "Ni de zhongwen hen hao." She was complimenting his Chinese, just like the taxi driver. Before Andrew could think of something else to say though, a Chinese guy came over and put his arms around the girl, giving Andrew a menacing look. The girl seemed annoyed and tried to pull his hands off her, but he just kept looking at Andrew. It looked like his time was up. Andrew smiled weakly and then walked away.

"Why did you leave?" Mazken demanded.

"Didn't you see that guy come up and put his arms around her? I'm not going to hit on someone's girlfriend."

"She probably wasn't his girlfriend. In fact, there's a good chance she didn't even know him."

"What? But why would he do that?"

"To stop a foreigner from hitting on her. Deception comes in many forms."

Even though all of this was a little overwhelming, Andrew felt elated, like he had just climbed a difficult mountain and made it to the top. He had actually started an interaction with a beautiful girl that he had never met... even if it had only lasted a couple of seconds.

"OK, now it's time for you to wing Charlie. He's going to start talking to a set of two girls, and when he's ready, he'll wave you over to join him. When you get there, he's going to point to one girl and say, 'She's the bad girl.' That's code for, 'This is the girl I'm interested in.' Then it's your job to talk to the other girl."

Andrew looked around for Charlie and saw that he had already approached two girls who were standing near one of the big tables. Charlie was leaning against the wall as he talked to them, and soon Andrew saw the girls start laughing. Then Charlie turned toward Andrew and waved at him. Here goes nothing, thought Andrew.

"Zhe shi wo laowai de pengyou, An-de-ru," Charlie introduced him. "So she's the bad girl," Charlie said, pointing to the girl closest to him. Andrew began talking to the girl's friend. She was quite pretty and was being somewhat friendly. Andrew couldn't believe how well things were going. But a few minutes later, he heard raised voices and looked over to see a tall Chinese guy confronting Charlie. Looking around, Andrew noticed that everyone at the large table was looking at Charlie and this guy. He must be the leader of their group. But apparently Charlie wasn't backing down. He hadn't budged an inch and was also talking in a raised voice. Then Andrew saw a glass fly across the room, bounce off Charlie's shoulder, and land on the floor, shattering instantly.

And then the room erupted into chaos.

Andrew saw the tall guy take a swing at Charlie, who ducked smoothly, turned, and kicked the guy in the stomach. It appeared Charlie had also studied martial arts. But more of the guy's friends had already converged on Charlie and were coming at him from all sides. Andrew knew Charlie wouldn't last long if he didn't help. As one of the Chinese guys lunged for him, Andrew smacked the guy squarely across the head and sent him tumbling sideways. A jolt of adrenaline rushed through him. He spun around and kicked another guy who had Charlie in a headlock, causing him to let go of Charlie and double over in pain.

"Thanks," shouted Charlie, and spun-kicked two more guys who were lunging at him.

"You two better get out of there quick, security is on its way," Andrew heard Mazken's voice, though he couldn't see where he was. The voice just seemed to be echoing around him.

"But why are they after us? It was that guy who started it."

"Doesn't matter," said Charlie, "That guy is rich and comes here all the time. Security is only here to protect people like him. Let's get out of here."

They raced toward the door, shoving people out of the way and knocking over a small table as they went. But when the front door came into view, they saw it blocked by two big security guards. They were trapped.

CHAPTER 12:

LESSONS

Andrew stared at the security guards in front of them, not sure what to do next. He looked at Charlie.

"No choice, we must take these guys out," shouted Charlie. "Jump kick after I count to three."

"But we'll be arrested for sure," Andrew began to protest.

"No, we are arrested for sure if we stay here." Charlie grabbed Andrew by the arm and began running full tilt toward the two guards.

"One, two... three."

He and Charlie jumped at the same time, kicking the two guards to the side, and landing in the entryway. They both stumbled and then ran out into the parking lot.

"Over here," Mazken was already waiting in a taxi with the door open. Andrew wondered how he'd made it out faster than them. He and Charlie ran up and jumped in. "Qu, qu, qu, kuai, kuai, kuai!" *Go, go, go, quick, quick, quick,* Mazken shouted at the driver.

The driver didn't move but just turned to look at Mazken. "Qu narr?" *Where?*

"It doesn't bloody matter where we're going, kai che!" *Just drive!*

The driver stared at him blankly and began to light a cigarette.

113

"This is a getaway, you idiot. Charlie, how do you say 'getaway' in Chinese?"

"Uh, we don't have a word for this," said Charlie.

The driver began muttering under his breath, and Andrew heard him say the word "laowai." Mazken whipped out a hundred bill and shoved it in the taxi driver's face. "You see that security personnel running toward us? They are going to arrest us *and* you if you don't go *now*." The driver looked at the men, then at the hundred, and it finally seemed to click. He floored the gas, just as one of the guards reached for the door handle, and the taxi sped away.

"Charlie, what the devil did you think you were doing?" Mazken said. Until now Mazken had always seemed so calm, but now he looked completely irate.

"That guy is a rich asshole. He thinks he's better than everyone else just because his dad is in Politburo."

"You just picked a fight with a guy whose dad is one of the most *powerful men in China?*"

"He needs someone to teach him a lesson…"

"Real nice going Kong Kong."

"And I told you, stop calling me that."

"What's Kong Kong mean?"

"His first name in Chinese is Kong. But kong also means empty. So saying it twice implies that his head is empty," Mazken glared at Charlie. Charlie just glared back. "I swear I'm not getting you out of another one like that, mate. Picking fights with these guys is not going to bring justice to China. You're not bloody Robin Hood or something."

"How did you get out of the club so quickly?" Andrew asked Mazken.

Mazken grinned. "I was already outside calling a cab when you heard my voice. I was broadcasting over the Mix intercom. Charlie hacked it a few months ago so that we could access it remotely at any time. Security would have got to you a lot sooner if I hadn't prevented them from using their radios to call for backup."

"So actually, it's thanks to me that we get out," interjected

Charlie.

"Qu narr?" droned the taxi driver.

"Yes, as usual, most of the credit goes to you, Charlie," Mazken said as he rolled his eyes. Then he turned to the driver, "Qu Xiu Ba."

"We're going to another bar? After that?"

"Why not? You've still got a lot of learning to do, mate."

By the end of the night, Andrew was feeling a little bit like a bull charging at an elusive red cloth. He'd been rejected dozens of times, but every once in a while he managed to have an extended conversation with a beautiful girl and even managed to get a few phone numbers, a feat he'd never previously thought possible. At one point, for just a moment, he'd even been the center of attention of a large group, who were all laughing at his jokes. That had never happened to him before. And his confidence was growing.

"So, tell me five things you learned tonight," said Mazken as they sat down to a late-night snack at a 24-hour McDonalds.

"Well, umm, it's not as hard as I thought to talk to beautiful girls?"

"There's one."

"And, umm, it seems like really all you have to do to get their attention is to be more interesting than whatever else they were doing. It seemed like there were a lot of people at those clubs who didn't really even know how to carry on a normal conversation."

"That's because most of them don't, at least not in that setting. They were just as uncomfortable there as you."

"Most of those girls just seemed so bored. It actually wasn't that difficult to be more interesting than their friends."

"Exactly. Add confidence, and you have a winning combination. Most people are sheep. And sheep will follow a cunning wolf anywhere."

Andrew felt a surge of confidence that he'd never felt before. It was intoxicating. And that was a little scary.

"Embrace it, mate," Mazken was looking at him intently. "Much of what we can achieve in life is ultimately determined by our dominant thoughts. Don't let the seeds of doubt root themselves in your mind. Rip them out like weeds in a garden, and replace them with the flowers of positive thinking. You will become unstoppable. Now how are you going to use your new skills to improve your life, starting tomorrow?"

"Well, my next class is on Monday. I think I'll feel a little more confident in front of the classroom, at least."

"Just a *little* more confident? How about this: pretend your students are a bunch of beautiful girls. How will you hold their attention?"

***

Andrew stood in front of his class, as he had for the last week, and looked out at an almost barren classroom. Since he'd begun teaching, his class had shrunk to less than a quarter of its original size. The ones who were there were distracted, some of them texting or chatting on their phones, and others typing away on their computers. I-phone sat off to the side, visibly agitated. He looked around the classroom. There were five guys and five girls. Perfect.

Andrew cupped his hands around his mouth and bellowed, "Attention students. Please take your seats. Class will start in thirty seconds." The strength of his voice seemed to surprise the students, and some of them looked around at each other as if to say, *is he serious*? "That's right, you heard me. Twenty-five seconds." Andrew was surprising himself at how commanding he could make his voice sound. But he was still quite nervous. What if they didn't listen and just ignored him? But finally, they seemed to have gotten the message, because they all began to take their seats and put their phones away.

"Today's class is going to be a little different," Andrew began. "Today, we're going to play *The Dating Game*." He wrote this on the blackboard in big letters. There was a murmur from the students.

"You will be split up into pairs. Each will take turns asking questions of the other person about things such as their career, family, hobbies, likes, and dislikes, etc. You will have 20 minutes to prepare, and then perform in front of the class." He paused and looked around. There were mixed reactions from the NOCCOC employees. A few of the girls looked excited, while the guys all looked a little nervous. "BUT, there's a catch. During the dialogue, you must correctly use at least five of the following words and phrases," He began writing on the board:

> *Microbiologist*
> *Over the hill*
> *Personal assistant*
> *Long-range missile*
> *The weather outside is frightful...*

Andrew tried to think of the most random words and phrases he could. It would be better to make this a challenge. After he'd written ten phrases, he turned back to the class, whose murmur had now grown louder. "Whichever pair uses the most phrases correctly will win a special prize."

The employees began chattering to each other in Chinese again. Clearly they were competitive, and it seemed Andrew had managed to grab their attention.

"Any questions? No? Good. Now, choose your partner and get started." As Andrew watched the NOCCOC employees obediently and enthusiastically working on their dialogues, he felt a sense of power and control over his life. For once, his class was actually going really well. Twenty minutes later he had them begin their presentations. They were still shy, of course, but he could tell they were finally having fun as they attempted to use the random words and phrases he'd come up with.

"You're breaking up with me already? I will shoot a long-range missile at you," one of the female employees threatened, and then began giggling uncontrollably.

"Ok, I agree to date you, but only if you will be my personal assistant," another one of the students declared.

As the class finished and the employees began to file out,

talking excitedly amongst themselves, Andrew knew that he had succeeded. His feeling was confirmed when he saw I-phone grinning at him from across the room, as she talked with one of the managers. But then he noticed out of the corner of his eye that someone was moving toward him. He looked over and realized it was May.

"That seemed like a really good class, Andrew," May said as she walked up to him. "I came in at the end, but everyone was saying good things about it."

Andrew pretended to be very busy sorting papers and didn't look up. Once again Mr. Harrison's warning shot into his head. She knew his secret. Associating with her might jeopardize everything. But then Andrew felt a little pinch of rebellious anger. Mr. Harrison had refused to help him. And who was he to tell Andrew whom he could associate with? After all, part of the reason why he'd come here was to have another chance with May. And now he'd learned some skills that would help. He could handle this; he'd just have to be cautious.

Andrew finally looked up. May was frowning at him slightly.

Andrew smiled, "Yeah, I think it went pretty well. What's important is that everyone had fun." He paused. "What do you think about my teaching style?"

"Oh, I like it very much. Maybe they will let me join your class sometime so I can experience it first hand," she smiled coyly at him.

"Well, you know my class is very selective. Only the best students get to join," he tried not to smile, but it crept onto his face anyway. "Are you a good enough student?"

"Don't you know that I am? After all, we were classmates. How could you forget?" She sounded a bit indignant, but Andrew was pretty sure she was teasing him back. This was going well.

"Well, how about we discuss it over dinner this Saturday?"

"Oh, well, I was supposed to have dinner with some

friends...." *Oh, no.* He'd been too direct, and now she was rejecting him.

"...but I suppose I could tell them I'll meet them another time." She smiled at him. He felt a little lightheaded and tried to stop himself from grinning like an idiot.

"You two so cute," Andrew looked around and saw I-phone. She was looking back and forth between the two of them with a delighted look.

CHAPTER 13:

THE DATE

"How come you don't want anyone to know that you understand Chinese?"

"What? Where did you get that idea?"

At Mazken's suggestion, Andrew had asked May to join him in the park before going for dinner. 'Dinner is such a normal, boring guy date,' Mazken had said. 'Show her that you're not like every other guy. Take her somewhere interesting.'

May smiled, "Don't play dumb with me. Why else would you pretend you didn't understand me when we met in the elevator?"

This was the moment Andrew had feared. What was he going to tell her? He didn't want to lie to her, and he wasn't very good at it either. But obviously he could never tell her the truth…

"Oh, that," he gave a nervous laugh. "Well, you know…"

"I think I do know. If your students knew you speak Chinese, they'd use it as a crutch to communicate with you. You want them to have an immersion experience. And also, I bet you don't want people like your teaching assistant to know that you understand what they are saying about you."

Andrew stared at her. She'd just given him an out without him having to come up with a lie. He realized he'd been holding his breath, and slowly began to let it out.

"Yeah, that's exactly what it is," he said quickly, smiling. "How did you know?"

May gave a little laugh, "I'm smart, you know. How else do you think I got into college in America?"

"That's true."

May smiled and looked away, over toward the lake that they were now approaching. The Beijing smog had been slowly building up over the last few days until earlier that morning, when Andrew hadn't been able to see more than 200 feet in front of him. But then, as if someone had switched on a fan, a steady wind began blowing through the city.

As they approached the edge of the lake, May paused and looked down.

"The water is much lower than it should be. I remember coming to Beijing when I was a kid. My parents took me to see the Forbidden City and Beihai Park. Back then the lakes were very full. It's the same way all throughout northern China."

"Why do you think that is?"

"It's because there's a drought. It's quite severe. The Chinese government is concerned enough that they built a giant canal all the way from southern China to the north in order to divert some of the water. But even that didn't solve the problem."

"Why doesn't the government just whip up some more rainstorms then?"

May gave him a funny look. "I don't think it's that simple. The government's ability to control the weather is limited. This is a long-term problem caused by climate change."

"You told me you didn't think the U.S. government could do that. But why not the Chinese government?"

"Don't be ridiculous. Sure, they can shoot chemicals into the air that cause moisture to condense into clouds, but if there's very little moisture in the air already, it doesn't have much of an effect. The environmental problems have gotten to be so severe, that they are starting to threaten the government's legitimacy. You'd think that if they did have that kind of power, they would use it to clean up pollution and end the drought, right?"

It seemed like a good point, but Andrew was suspicious. May had seen what was going on in America, and it seemed much worse than here. Why was she defending the Chinese government? But it would be risky to pursue this line of conversation much further.

"You know, you remind me a bit of an American boy I knew in school when I was younger."

"I do? How so?" He was glad she had changed the subject

"Well, to start you look a little bit like him. Not so tall, light-colored hair... and very handsome."

"I'm glad you added that last part."

May giggled. "You are also very playful and mischievous."

"I'm mischievous?"

"Come on, Andrew," she giggled again, "The whole pretending not to speak Chinese act? Did you forget already?"

"Oh, that. But my Chinese really isn't that good you know," he grinned at her. This seemed to be going well. Don't mess this up, he told himself. Turn the conversation back to her. Keep things moving. Motion creates emotion.

He took her hand and led her away from the lake, further down the path. "So if you wanted to go to America so badly, why are you back here in China now?"

"I told you before, my parents insisted that I come back to China to work for at least a little while after school. Well, they say a little while, but I think they are trying to keep me here. They probably think they're going to set me up with a Chinese guy so that I'll get married and settle down here for good. Like I said, they are very nationalistic. You know, they are so crazy that if they met you here, they'd probably suspect that you were a spy or something." She laughed.

Andrew did the best he could to force a laugh. He suddenly wasn't very eager to meet May's parents anytime soon.

"But why did you come to China anyway, Andrew? How come you never told me that you wanted to come to China?"

Andrew swallowed. At least he'd been anticipating this, and he'd prepared an answer that was as close to the truth as it could be. "Well, it was a surprise to me as well, I mean, I didn't know I would be coming here until a few days after graduation. But I was offered this opportunity to teach English here and, well, it seemed like it would be a good experience."

"But you know, so many foreigners come here to teach English, and most of them just play around and don't take it seriously. You could be putting your Chinese skills to better use."

Andrew felt like she'd just taken a hot iron and branded him in the ribs. If only he could tell her that he *was* putting his Chinese skills to good use. But why did he have to justify himself to her?

"You don't think I take teaching seriously, after seeing my class?" He retorted.

"I don't mean that. But there are so many English teachers here, and I thought you said you want to make a difference."

Andrew didn't say anything. He'd never be able to tell her how he was making a difference, or why he'd really come here. And he hated that.

They had paused on a bridge over a small river. May was standing very close to him, holding his hand, and looking out over the park. Andrew looked at her, and their eyes met. He began moving his head closer to hers, staring at her small, tender lips, opening his mouth slightly.

And then she turned and looked away. Andrew stopped abruptly and moved his head back. Why had he done that? It was far too soon.

May gave a little shudder, and Andrew realized that she didn't look well. He had been so focused on the attempted kiss, but now he saw that she was paler than usual, and little beads of sweat were forming on her brow.

"Are you OK, May?"

"I'm fine, I'm just a little… tired. And hungry. Let's go eat, shall we?"

***

They went to dinner at a nice Italian restaurant near the west gate of Chaoyang Park. The area had a little village filled with restaurants and nightclubs. Andrew thought it seemed very romantic on a warm summer night like this. The area was busy, but not with the usual claustrophobia-inducing crowds that were common to other parts of Beijing.

They said very little throughout dinner. Andrew was still feeling awkward from her rejection of his kiss, and despite what she'd said about being tired and hungry, May was barely eating anything. Andrew paid for dinner, and they walked out of the restaurant away from the west gate and toward the road. Andrew figured the night was over. She'd likely want to go home and rest now. "I was going to show you the view from my apartment, but I suppose you probably just want to go home. I'll put you in a cab."

"No that's O, we can go see your apartment," she said, and she seemed to be trying to muster what energy she had. "I'm sure it's a lovely view."

Now Andrew's confidence returned. It would have been much easier for her just to go home. For some reason, she wanted to spend more time with him.

Andrew took her on a brief tour around his apartment. They went out onto the balcony, but right after he opened the door, he and May both started coughing. Andrew looked out across the city, and saw that the sky had turned hazy again, but now the color looked browner, and the wind was stronger than ever.

"Sandstorm," said May, between coughs. "Let's go back inside."

"Why are there sandstorms here?"

"Beijing is near a desert, and the desert is expanding toward the city every year. The drought makes the sand really dry, and most of the forest that used to act as a shield from the desert was cut down, so the sand spreads easily."

They went to his bedroom, where May noticed his father's porcelain teacup sitting on his bedside table. "This is very beautiful. And the design is very strange…"

"Yeah, my father left that for me when he died. It was given to him as a gift from someone in China, but I don't know who."

"See the design on here? This reminds me of a very ancient and famous painting from the Song Dynasty, called Hu Xi San Xiao. Except there's something funny about it. See the two men in the middle of the stream? There are supposed to be three of them, and they should all be monks. But here there are only two, and one of them is dressed very strangely... it looks like he's wearing a cowboy hat."

"But why would the painter change an historic painting like that?"

"I don't know. But look, there's a blue cow on the bottom of the cup. Maybe that has something to do with it."

"That's a bull, I think. See how it has horns?"

"It could be an ox, too, like Oxley. Maybe that blue bull was meant to symbolize your family name?"

Andrew hadn't considered that. But if that were the case, it didn't bring him any closer to figuring out who had made it.

"Hey Andrew, ni shu shenme?"

"What?" For some reason, Andrew didn't understand.

"What's your Chinese zodiac? What year were you born?"

"Oh, well believe it or not, it's actually the year of the bull."

"That's even more perfect. Hey, I'm going to call you Xiao Niu."

"That's not really very flattering in English you know, to call someone *small bull*."

"Xiao doesn't really mean small in this case, it's just a common way to give someone a nickname in Chinese," she giggled.

"Ni shu shenme?"

"Wo shu hu. Tiger."

"I'm surprised. You're so gentle. Tigers are supposed to be fierce."

"I can be fierce too. You just haven't seen it yet." She grabbed his arm surprisingly hard with her fingertips, imitating a clawing cat. Then she looked up at him. Andrew felt a strange boldness come over him, like he had never felt before. He was going to try again. He turned to face her, his body nearly shuddering with anticipation as he looked her in the eyes, and then began to lean in, slowly. His face was within a foot of hers, then just a few inches. He began to close his eyes. But at the last second, he felt a slight breeze and his lips landed on May's cheek, as she turned her head to avoid his kiss.

"Sorry Andrew, but I'm not... I can't do that."

Andrew was embarrassed again and more than a little bit disappointed. Did that mean she didn't really like him after all? Then what was she doing here? Were they really just friends? He let go of her and turned away.

"Andrew, don't misunderstand me. I like you a lot. I always have. But like I told you, my situation is... complicated."

"You mean with your parents?"

"Yes. I know you Americans think it is best to be independent and choose your own path, but we Chinese have a stronger obligation to our family. I'm not sure that I could really go against my parent's wishes."

"Isn't that why you went to America though, so you could make more of your own choices?"

"But that doesn't change where I come from. What if we wanted to get married someday? Would you stay in China?"

Andrew was startled by this comment. "It seems like that's thinking pretty far ahead. Let's just take this one step at a time."

"You don't understand the kind of pressure my family puts on me. They expect me to get married soon," May's voice was becoming softer, despondent.

"That seems unfair."

"But it's the way it is, and I can't change it," She looked at the ground. "I'm really not feeling well, and I don't want to ruin your night. I think I should go home now."

Andrew didn't know what else to say, so he walked her downstairs and waited for her to call a car. May gave him a little hug and a sad look and turned to climb into the back of the taxi. "I'll see you at work," she said.

"Let's have lunch sometime."

May gave him a small smile, and then closed the door. Andrew watched her drive away. The whole night had been so confusing. Andrew thought back to what he had thought was a joke about her parents thinking he was a spy. Was she just playing with him?

CHAPTER 14:

THE MASTER BECOMES THE STUDENT

"Why did you let her leave?" Mazken was interrogating him.

"She said she wasn't feeling well."

"That was probably just an excuse. There was something else that was making her feel uncomfortable."

"Well, yes, she said she wasn't sure if we could be together because her parents wouldn't like it."

"Of course, typical Chinese. Always have to get their family's approval. Well anyway mate, overall I'd say you've put your new skills to excellent work so far. In fact, I think you've achieved results quicker than almost any other student I've had."

"Really?"

"Yep. You're part of our brotherhood now, Drew. And your training is just beginning. I'm going to teach you how to seduce the most beautiful girls in China. Forget about this girl; there are so many more out there. Then someday, when you've mastered these skills, you can teach this stuff like me and Charlie."

As he finished up lunch, said goodbye to Mazken and Charlie, and returned to the NOCOCC building, I-phone ran up to him, nearly tripping over her high heels, with a very excited look on her face. "We have important new assignment for you, Teacha Osley."

Oh no, thought Andrew. Just as things we're going well, they were going to take him out of NOCCOC and bring him somewhere else, and he'd have to start the mission from square one. "That's OK I-phone, I'm fine teaching at NOCCOC, I don't want to go anywhere else."

"No no, new assignment for you here. You finally get your wish. President Cheng want to take class with you."

Andrew stared at her. A small shiver ran up his spine. This was almost too good to be true. He thought back to the camera he'd found in his apartment. Was this a trap?

"Why does he want me now, I-phone?"

"I think word travels that your classes are so good, teacha Osley. But actually he have not decide on you yet. We provide him three teacher to choose from, and he will see demo class from all of them."

"So I'll teach a demo class for him, and if he likes me, then he'll take class with me?"

"Yes, yes." I-phone nodded her head up and down several times.

I-phone's story was starting to sound more plausible. "So what does this demo class involve? What should I teach?"

"Oh, that up to you Teacha Osley. He already have good basic English, like me," she gave Andrew a wide grin, "Intermediate level, you know?" You vera good teacha now, I know you figure it out. Just most important, make sure it interesting. Now I must go to meeting." I-phone grinned at him and began to walk away.

"Wait, when is the demo class?"

"Tomorrow afternoon, three o'clock." she said over her shoulder.

Of course, leave it to I-phone to spring something this important on him at the last minute. As one of the most powerful businessmen in China, Lao Cheng would no doubt have very high standards. And Andrew would have one chance to make a good impression. But wasn't this what he'd been preparing for?

***

The next day, I-phone escorted him up to Lao Cheng's office. When they reached the door, Lao Cheng's secretary Yu Mama was sitting at her desk in the entryway. Andrew was surprised to realize that she was quite old. Her hair was grey, her forehead wrinkled, and her mouth twisted into what looked like a permanent scowl. Andrew wondered why Lao Cheng didn't hire someone younger to be his secretary.

Yu Mama greeted them and then without saying anything further, walked over to the door and opened it slightly, sticking her head through. Andrew heard her ask in a quiet but firm voice whether Lao Cheng was ready for them. Then she poked her head back out, and without a word, pushed the door further open and beckoned for them to enter. Andrew turned to I-phone, expecting her to take the lead, but found that she was heading in the opposite direction.

"You OK now Teacha Osley, I go," I-phone said, and then scurried away.

Andrew had never seen I-phone so eager to get away, as if just being this close to the CEO frightened her. Feeling even more apprehensive than before, he turned and entered the office.

He was immediately taken aback by its size. It appeared as though his whole apartment could fit into this room. The walls were decorated with immaculate artwork, mostly traditional Chinese paintings. Unlike the hallway outside, the floor was carpeted, and on top of that in one part of the room was a beautifully woven rug. On the side of the room closest to him was a leather sofa and armchair with a coffee table, facing a mantle, where a few beautiful Chinese porcelain vases rested, giving this part of the office the feel of a large living room. To Andrew's right, the entire wall was a large glass window, looking out over Chang'an Street. Not too far in the distance, Andrew could see the Forbidden City and Tiananmen Square. On the opposite end of the room were two large wooden doors.

In front of them was a desk, where Lao Cheng sat, watching him.

Even sitting behind the desk, Andrew could see that he was a big man; not obese, but he looked like he ate very well. He appeared to be in his late forties or early fifties, and was partially bald, with just a little hair growing in the center of his bald patch. He wore thin, rectangular glasses that would have made him appear grandfatherly, if not for the cold eyes behind them.

Andrew breathed in slowly to try and calm his nerves, and got a strong whiff of cigarette smoke mixed with some sweet, flowery fragrance. He hesitated inside the door, taking this all in. Then he felt a slight breeze and heard the door behind him click shut.

He was alone with Lao Cheng.

"Please, come in," the acoustics of the room somehow amplified Lao Cheng's voice, and it seemed to echo off every wall. Andrew walked slowly toward the desk. A small chair had been placed at the desk opposite Lao Cheng, which Andrew assumed was for him, and he sat down.

Lao Cheng looked up and stared at him for a moment, then he smiled and said, "Welcome you to my office." His voice was low and gravely, and he spoke slow and methodically. Andrew returned his smile and said, "Thank you, President Cheng. I look forward to being your teacher."

Lao Cheng's smile began to fade, then he nodded his head once and gave a little grunt, which Andrew interpreted to mean that he'd understood. Then Lao Cheng turned to the door and bellowed, "Ma Ma. Lai liang bei cha."

A minute later Yu Ma hurried in with a tray carrying a teapot and two teacups. She carefully placed the cups and pot on the desk in front of them, poured tea for the two of them, and then left just as quickly.

"Chinese tea, vera good." Lao Cheng said, pointing at the cups and smiling like a proud father. He lifted his cup slowly and drank, and Andrew mimicked him. Then he set the cup down to the side and looked at Andrew, "OK, now we start class."

Andrew smiled weakly. Lao Cheng emanated a supreme confidence that was intimidating, and Andrew would have only fifteen minutes for the demo.

"Well, let's start with some simple introductions. I'm going to tell you my name, my favorite pastime, and where I'm from. Ok, here we go. I'm Andrew, my favorite hobby is playing video games, and I come from Boston, in the USA. Do you know Boston?"

Lao Cheng stared at him intently as he spoke, but when Andrew finished, he leaned back, a disappointed look on his face. "Yes, yes, I know Boston," he said impatiently.

Uh oh, was he boring him already? "Ok, how about you?" Andrew prompted cautiously.

Lao Cheng paused and reached into his desk drawer, from which he withdrew a pack of cigarettes. Andrew watched as he lit one and began puffing on it. As Lao Cheng let out a long puff, he seemed to relax a little. Then he frowned for a few moments before speaking. "I'm President Cheng, my favorite hobby is-a going to... how do you call it? Oh, karaoke! Ha ha ha." His laugh was deep and hearty, sounding something like an evil Santa Claus. "Oh, and I come from-a Chongqing. Do you know-a Chongqing?" he asked.

"Sorry, I don't know it. What's it like?"

"Chongqing is-a big city in western China," he paused, "If you-a never go to Chongqing, you don't know-a China." He laughed again. Andrew had the feeling Lao Cheng was laughing at some inside joke that only he and his cavernous office were in on. Andrew smiled and forced a little laugh, trying to pretend like he understood the joke.

"I guess I'll have to visit it."

"Yes, yes, I take-a you there sometimes," Lao Cheng said off-handedly as if it were a given.

"OK. Now I thought for our main lesson today, I can teach you some vocabulary and phrases related to oil extraction and trade since that's what you do here at NOCCOC," he paused, waiting to see Lao Cheng's reaction.

"Yes, yes, that's-a good," Lao Cheng sounded impatient again.

Andrew took a deep breath. He'd done some research on this and was prepared. "Ok, so oil under the ground is called *reserves*. I understand NOCCOC has the largest oil *reserves* of any company in China?"

"Yes, yes," Lao Cheng nodded his head impatiently. Andrew decided he needed to speed things up.

"Ok, now after the oil field is drilled, the *crude* oil gets *extracted* and sent to a *refinery*, where it gets refined into many different products, including *gasoline*."

Lao Cheng was looking more interested now. His eyes darted up as if trying to access a certain part of his brain and confirm what Andrew had just said. "Oh, yes, yes," he finally replied.

"So our key vocabulary here are crude, extracted, refinery and gasoline," Andrew said, writing these in a notebook that he'd prepared for Lao Cheng. "The final step is for the finished products to be shipped around the world in *tankers* and sold on *world markets*."

"What about-a new gas?" Lao Cheng asked.

At first, Andrew didn't know what he meant, then he realized Lao Cheng must be referring to shale gas, which he'd also read about.

"Yes, *shale gas* gets extracted through a process that we call *hydraulic fracturing*…"

"Hydra… fracking…" Lao Cheng tried to repeat.

"Actually you can just say *fracking* for short. So through fracking, shale gas can now be *extracted* at a competitive price. Shale gas is the same as *natural gas*, which can be used for heating, power plants, and transportation fuel…"

"Natural gas-a cleaner than coal," Lao Cheng interrupted.

"Yes, I suppose it is…"

"Shale gas make-a China get cleaner, help reduce-a… climate change."

Andrew was taken aback. Didn't oil executives usually deny that climate change was happening? Lao Cheng was only the second one, after Rothschild, that he'd heard admit that climate change was happening. But then as Andrew thought about it, it began to make sense. If Lao Cheng were indeed helping China to manipulate global weather, of course, he would want people to believe that it was being caused by climate change. Andrew was about to reply, but then he saw Lao Cheng's mouth opening and realized he wasn't done yet.

"China make-a big progress to reduce-a climate change…. but China still developing country… America need-a do more." Lao Cheng sat back, seemingly satisfied with what he'd said. And then, he made a hacking sound deep in his throat, and to Andrew's horror, spit on the rug beside his desk.

Andrew flinched but tried not to make his disgust visible. Just like Mr. Harrison had thought, it seemed like Lao Cheng was using climate change as a disguise, and effectively pointing the finger at the U.S. for causing it. With weather control technology, he could make it appear that the effects of climate change were accelerating, putting even more pressure on the U.S. to do something about it. It was, Andrew realized, a very clever strategy.

Despite his better judgment, Andrew couldn't restrain himself from arguing. "But China is actually very developed now. It just became the world's largest economy."

Lao Cheng brought his fist down hard on the desk and leaned forward, "China have-a more people. America people still richer than Chinese people."

This Andrew couldn't argue with, and he decided it was better not to do so; it was certainly not going to help him get the class if he was causing Lao Cheng's temper to flare.

Just as he was about to move on, the door to Lao Cheng's office opened and Yu Mama hobbled in. "Xia ke le," she declared. Great, thought Andrew, the class was already over. He didn't want to end the class on a negative note like this. He'd been a fool to argue with Lao Cheng, and now he'd put the whole mission at risk. But Yu Mama was beckoning forcefully for him to leave. He stood up, thanked Lao Cheng, and walked out.

Andrew continued to curse himself as he waited nervously for the results. A day passed, then two, without a word from I-phone. Andrew figured this was not a good sign. What had he done? He'd screwed the whole thing up. Then, three days after the demo class, I-phone appeared at the end of his regular group class and approached him, looking concerned.

"I hear you argued with President Cheng? You vera brave, Teacha Osley, vera brave. No one argue with President Cheng."

"I didn't get the class, did I, I-phone?" But to his surprise, I-phone smiled.

"I do not undastand why, but he want you be his teacha."

"What? Wow, that's great news," With all these people tip-toeing around him, maybe Lao Cheng liked someone who challenged him. I-phone was looking at Andrew like she wanted to kiss him, making him feel slightly uncomfortable. "So when do I start?"

"Tomorrow aftanoon." I-phone replied, then looked at him cautiously, "I hope that OK?" Once again, she'd left him almost no time to prepare, but Andrew wasn't even surprised now. This was his big opportunity. As Lao Cheng's teacher, he'd finally have a real chance to collect some meaningful intelligence. Things were finally in motion.

CHAPTER 15:

A FRAGILE STATE OF AFFAIRS

By his second class, it seemed to Andrew that Lao Cheng had forgotten about his desire to study English, and was content to spend most of their time lecturing Andrew about various aspects of Chinese history and society. In fact, for some reason he now seemed determined to convince Andrew of the superiority of Chinese civilization. Halfway through the class, he decided to give Andrew a tour of his office, explaining the different Chinese artwork and its significance.

"This is Chinese porcelain," Lao Cheng stated, pausing in front of the mantle. "You know China invent-a porcelain? China have 5,000-year history, so invent-a many thing. And west countries, they steal-a many invention from China."

Andrew thought this seemed ironic, considering how much technology China was stealing from the West these days, but he held his tongue.

"Chinese porcelain very high quality. Everything hand-painted. Take a look," Lao Cheng lifted one of the porcelain vases off the mantle and handed it to Andrew. Then, Lao Cheng looked toward the back of his office. "Excuse-a me, I use-a toilet," and he strolled to one of the doors in the back of his office, leaving Andrew alone for the first time.

This was the opportunity he'd been waiting for, though he hadn't thought it would come so soon. He reached in his pocket and took out a tiny video camera. The camera had a wireless video feed that would allow him to remotely monitor activity in Lao Cheng's office.

He carefully placed the vase back on the mantle and looked around. It seemed that the mantle was, in fact, the best place to put the camera, since it faced Lao Cheng's desk directly and was painted black, the same color as the camera, so it would blend in well. He reached between the vases and pushed the camera all the way to the back wall. And just as he was doing so, he heard the door open behind him.

Andrew hadn't expected Lao Cheng to come back from the bathroom so quickly, and the sound made him jump. In doing so, his arm jerked sideways, bumping into the vase that sat on the edge of the mantle.

He watched helplessly as it fell and smashed on the floor beside him.

Andrew quickly snatched the camera off the mantle and turned to face Lao Cheng. "I'm so sorry President Cheng, it was an accident, you startled…" but he stopped, noticing that Lao Cheng's eyes were wide and his lips pressed together in an angry grimace. Better not make it sound like he was accusing Lao Cheng and make things worse. He was definitely in danger of losing his job now. Why had he been so careless?

"Let me clean it up," he offered and stooped down to pick up the pieces. As he did so, he noticed he was very close to the potted plant that sat next to the mantle. If he was being fired, this might be his last chance to place the camera. With his back to Lao Cheng, he pretended to search the dirt at the base of the plant for pieces, and quickly placed the camera in the dirt, tilted up so it would face Lao Cheng's desk.

At the same time, the main door to Lao Cheng's office opened, and Andrew looked to see Yu Mama standing in the doorway. She must have heard the crash. But had she seen what he just did? With her face blank and emotionless as usual, she just stared at Andrew and the remains of the broken vase. There was no way for him to know.

"Mama, qing bang ta shoushi yixia."

"No, no, that's OK, I can clean it up myself; it was my fault," Andrew didn't want Yu Mama getting anywhere near the plant. She looked at Lao Cheng, and to Andrew's relief, Lao Cheng nodded and gave a small grunt. Yu Mama turned and walked swiftly out the door.

As Andrew picked up what remained of the bottom of the vase, he noticed a familiar symbol painted on one of the pieces. It was a small, blue bull's head. Andrew stared at it, wondering how common this insignia was. Did every piece of Chinese porcelain have this symbol, or was it the mark of a specific brand? That gave him an idea. He turned to Lao Cheng, who was still watching him.

"President Cheng, once again I'm very sorry. Please let me replace this vase for you. Where did you get it?"

Lao Cheng's anger seemed to be cooling, "No, no, it is no problem," he said, waving his hand. Yu Mama had returned with a trash can and thrust it at Andrew, where he deposited the broken pieces.

"No really, I feel bad and I want to replace it for you," Andrew insisted. "Where can I find a shop that sells this brand of porcelain?"

"Oh, it doesn't matter. It is no problem," Lao Cheng repeated dismissively and began walking back to his desk.

Andrew didn't want to push Lao Cheng any further, but this was the first real lead he'd come across as to the origin of his father's cup.

"President Cheng, I insist. Where can I buy a replacement for you?"

To Andrew's surprise, Lao Cheng spun around and slammed his fist on his desk, "No more question. Class is over." He walked around to the back of his desk and began dialing a phone number. Andrew looked at his watch. They still had a half-hour of class left. That wasn't a good sign. Yu Mama had appeared again and was waving her arm at him, directing him toward the door. As he left, she shut the door rather hard behind him.

Andrew stared at the door for a minute, his mind racing.

Was Lao Cheng calling I-phone right now to tell her he was canceling the class? He looked around to make sure no one was watching, then pulled out his cell phone and pulled up the feed from the video camera he had just planted. He could see Lao Cheng was still on the phone. The camera was just barely picking up the sound of his voice, so Andrew listened closely.

"I want the new systems ready for tests before the end of the month. No, you don't need to be fully operational, just ready for small scale atmospheric tests," Andrew heard Lao Cheng saying in Mandarin.

Lao Cheng was talking on a cell phone. Even from a distance, Andrew could tell that it was a much older model, which seemed strange. Then Lao Cheng glanced in the direction of the door. Andrew froze. Did he know he was still there? Lao Cheng paused and Andrew held his breath, then Lao Cheng continued, *"I want a report on my desk on your progress at the apple orchard before the end of the week."* Then he hung up. He and Yu Mama began talking about his schedule. Andrew closed the video feed, turning to go, and nearly bumped into Yang Fei.

He didn't know how long she'd been standing there staring at him with a little half-smile, half-smirk on her face. She was leaning to the side with one arm on her hip, while the other hand twirled her hair. Andrew remembered what Fritz had said about people comparing her to a legendary concubine, and he could see why.

"Are... are you waiting for Lao... President Cheng?" He realized the question was stupid after it left his mouth, but he was feeling very self-conscious. Had she seen what he was doing?

Yang Fei put a hand over her mouth and giggled nervously, but didn't say anything. Then Andrew realized she probably didn't understand English. Now was his chance to say something more interesting. Remembering a line Mazken had taught him, he feigned looking at Yang Fei as if considering her for the first time. "Ni de toufa shi zhende haishi jiade?" *Is your hair real or fake?* he said, pointing at her hair and smiling, while trying to make sure his Chinese sounded elementary.

Yang Fei looked surprised and then giggled again. "Dangran shi zhende." *Of course it's real.*

"Wo bu xiangxin," *I don't believe you*, he teased further.

"Zhende," she whined, giving Andrew a pouty face.

Andrew was about to continue, when he realized this was straying into dangerous territory. He was flirting with Lao Cheng's mistress and using his Chinese a little too openly.

"Uh, I have to go... bye-bye," he said, waving at her as he walked quickly out into the hallway.

"Bye-bye," she replied. Out of the corner of his eye, Andrew noticed she was staring after him as he walked away.

Andrew had a feeling he'd just overheard something important. But what did Lao Cheng mean by "apple orchard?" It sounded to Andrew like a code name. Maybe it was the name for the weather modification facility. And now he knew what to do: he needed to get his hands on the report Lao Cheng had requested.

CHAPTER 16:

PEOPLE WATCHING

"The boy is doing better than I thought he would. He managed to work his way into teachin' Mr. Cheng after all."

"I told you Harrison, the boy is resourceful."

"Yes, I'm starting to admire his determination. Almost makes me think we might be wasting talent by using him as a decoy."

"Don't start second-guessing yourself again."

"Of course not. Now that he's closer to Mr. Cheng, it shouldn't be long before he's discovered."

"How is your other operative doing?"

"Still having difficulty. Honestly, I think he's gotten paranoid and is being too cautious. But now that our decoy is really in play, that should change soon."

"We need to speed things up. We've only got about two months until the climate conference."

"You think I ain't aware of that? I'm pushing him as hard as I can."

"I hope so. We wouldn't want this to be all for nothing."

The chairman hung up the phone. Did he really doubt Howard's commitment to the operation? Of course, he was doing all he could to get results quickly. He'd been losing sleep over the matter for weeks.

It was almost six o'clock. He needed to leave; otherwise,

he risked being late for an important dinner that he and Anna were hosting with the director of the CIA and his wife. It would be another opportunity for him to try and convince the director of the legitimacy of their operation. He grabbed his jacket and briefcase and headed for the door, trying not to return Shirley's gaze as he walked past her desk. He'd been trying to minimize contact with her ever since she'd come onto him in his office, which was of course quite difficult. He'd begun leaving his office door open so that she wouldn't be able to try to start anything again. It was annoying, but for now he'd just have to tolerate it until he came up with a better solution.

He walked out into the parking lot and got into his SUV. As Harrison started up the car, he looked across the parking lot. People-watching had always been a hobby of his. He liked trying to guess what kind of mood people were in as they left work at the end of the day. As he watched he noticed an Asian man walking to his car. There was something about him that seemed odd, Mr. Harrison thought. He walked very stiffly, and his clothes seemed a little big on him, as if they were meant for someone who weighed about 30 pounds more.

Then the man glanced in Mr. Harrison's direction. It was only for a split second as if confirming something he saw, but not wanting anyone to know that he was doing so. Had the man been looking at *him*? Mr. Harrison put the SUV into gear and pulled out of the parking lot. It occurred to him that with all the publicity he'd been getting recently, perhaps the Chinese government had sent a spy of their own to keep an eye on him.

CHAPTER 17:

HACKING THE MASTER

"You crazy, man. Hacking the club comm system is one thing, but NOCCOC is huge."

"I only need you to disable the cameras in and around Lao Cheng's office."

"But to do that, I still need to hack the whole system. You can bet Lao Cheng's office is the most heavily protected."

"But you can do it?"

"Why you want to get into his office man?"

Andrew knew Charlie would ask, but he hadn't been able to come up with a good excuse. So he had decided to try another tactic on Charlie.

"Hey, you know what, never mind. It's OK if you can't do it."

"I don't say I can't do it, I just want to know why."

"Now that I think about it, it does sound too difficult, even for an experienced hacker. I'm sure NOCCOC has tons of security."

"Hey, you don't know me, man. I'm a master."

"But I'm sure NOCCOC has plenty of really smart people building their systems. They'll be able to keep you out."

He could tell Charlie was starting to get worked up. He was fidgeting around, shifting his weight back and forth.

"Keep me out? Keep me out? Not a chance."

"Then you'll do it?"

"Only if you tell me why."

"Tell you what, Charlie. You do the hack first, then if I'm successful, I'll tell you why."

Charlie squirmed. He knew Charlie's pride and curiosity were getting the better of him.

"Fine, fine. You just wait and see. NOCCOC won't know what hit them."

Andrew figured the best strategy for breaking into Lao Cheng's office would be to wait until late in the evening when everyone had gone home. The problem was that some people stayed at NOCCOC really late, including Yu Mama.

A few days later, Charlie sent him a text. *Done*, it said.

He waited until eight o'clock – surely Yu Mama would be gone by then – and headed for Lao Cheng's office. But as he stepped off the elevator on the eighth floor, he nearly ran straight into May.

"Andrew," May exclaimed. Andrew silently cursed his luck. This was horrible timing. "What are you doing here this late?" he asked her, and then realized she'd just said the same thing.

"I, er, was just doing some lesson prep for tomorrow."

"You're so dedicated."

"Thanks." There was another long pause.

"I was working late too," she was avoiding his gaze, "We've got a new marketing campaign coming out soon, and I'm in charge of… international marketing."

"Oh, that's great. Good for you."

"Yeah." May raised her head to look him in the eye. Her eyes were so big. And she looked so beautiful in the dim glow of the poorly lit hallway.

"Andrew I… I'm sorry I've been a little distant." She moved closer to him. "I know this is a difficult situation for both of us." She put her hand on his shoulder. Andrew's insides began to churn. "I just don't know what to do."

Andrew was surprised that she was apologizing. But now all he could think about was her hand on his shoulder and the curve of her body. And there was something about the look in her eye. Suddenly he pulled her in close to him and kissed her. She responded by kissing him passionately. They swayed there in the hallway for half a minute, then May pulled him through a door that was slightly ajar and into an empty office.

There was a couch inside the office, where May pulled him down and began kissing him even more passionately than before. Andrew couldn't believe what was happening. He began to pull away, but May pulled him back to her, moving his hands onto her hips, and prompting him to remove her shirt. Andrew began kissing her shoulders, then her chest, and down to her breasts. Then he began to remove her pants. Soon they were both naked, and, trembling with anticipation, Andrew began to make love to her.

Afterward they lay on the couch in silence. Andrew couldn't believe what had just happened. His inhibitions, which he'd tossed to the wind in the heat of the moment, now returned full force. He worried that someone might find them there.

"We should get going," he murmured to her.

"Just lie here with me for a few minutes. Don't worry, everyone else has gone home already."

They lay in silence for a few minutes, Andrew holding her and stroking her hair.

"Andrew, can we start over?"

"Umm, sure."

May didn't say anything else for a few moments.

"You never really told me why you came to China."

"Didn't I?"

"Well… you said you came here because you got offered a teaching job. But back at school, you told me you wanted to do something meaningful."

Andrew wasn't sure what she was getting at. He didn't say anything.

"…And, sorry if I'm offending you, but teaching English to a bunch of SOE employees doesn't seem that meaningful."

Andrew could feel himself tensing up. Why was she being so persistent with this question? And now he began to wonder what she had been doing on the eighth floor, at this time. This wasn't where her office was. And if everyone had already gone home, she had no reason to be up here.

"So I'm just wondering, why did you really come to China?" When he didn't say anything, she gave him a slightly mischievous look. "Come on Xiao Niu, you can tell me."

Andrew sat up, brushing May's arms away. "Why is it so important to you to know?"

May frowned. "Is it really that hard for you to tell me?"

Suddenly Andrew began to laugh. It was so obvious, wasn't it? She was working for Lao Cheng. Why hadn't he seen it before? Why else would she have suddenly taken an interest in him again?

"What's funny?"

"It's so obvious what you're up to. Did you really think I would fall for it?"

"Fall for what?" She was giving him a confused look.

"Oh don't play dumb now. I know what's going on here. This is all just an act."

"An act? What are you talking about?"

Andrew didn't reply, but began getting dressed. He couldn't be around her anymore. It was too upsetting.

May followed suit, putting on her clothes as well, but as she did, Andrew heard her begin quietly sobbing. His anger at her began to melt away as quickly as it had come. "Hey, come on now…"

"What's wrong with you Andrew?" May snapped. "Guys can be so cruel. One minute you want to be with me, and the next you push me away?"

"You know, I was starting to feel the same way about you."

May glared at him, then got to her feet. "I wish I'd never met you," she hissed, then turned and ran for the door, slamming it behind her as she left. Andrew just sat there, staring after her. They had grown up in completely different worlds. Chinese people seemed to have a different sense of what was right and wrong. Everyone seemed to think it was OK to be constantly deceiving themselves and others. How could he ever trust someone from a world like that?

Andrew heard the sound of the elevator arriving and listened closely for the sound of May getting on. When she had gone, he ventured out into the hallway again and looked around. No one else was in sight. Was it safe now for him to continue on to Lao Cheng's office? No, she might have alerted someone to his presence there. He'd have to wait.

The next day he returned to the eighth floor even later, hoping that no one would be around this time. As he got off the elevator, he took out his phone and opened the app that Charlie had created for him to control the cameras. He made sure he'd switched all the cameras in and around Lao Cheng's office over to stock footage of empty hallways and rooms, before proceeding. As he passed the office where he and May had made love the day before, he felt a sharp pain in his chest. Trying to shake the feeling off, he rounded the corner to Lao Cheng's office. Yu Mama's desk was empty, and as usual, the door was locked. Andrew looked around again, making sure no one was in the hallways, and then began to work away at the lock. Within 15 seconds, he had the door open. He quickly slipped in and closed the door behind him.

He'd been surprised and relieved when Lao Cheng had continued having class with him, despite his fumble. And so far, it seemed like no one had noticed the spy camera. Maybe he really was outsmarting them. Now that he was alone in Lao Cheng's office for the first time, he felt an odd sense of power. He could do whatever he wanted here. But he needed to focus. The logical place to start seemed to be Lao Cheng's desk. But just as he began to cross the office toward the desk, his heart nearly stopped as he heard Lao Cheng's voice.

"What you doing in my office, An-de-ru?"

Andrew looked around wildly, but he didn't see Lao Cheng anywhere. Where was the voice coming from?

"You in big trouble now," the voice continued. And now Andrew realized it was coming from a speaker in the ceiling. "Your friend Charlie very clever, An-de-ru. You better tell him what you up to. Ha ha ha…"

Andrew exhaled and put his palm to his forehead. Charlie must have taken recordings of Lao Cheng's voice and mashed them together. He should have known that bastard would play a joke on him like this. Still feeling a little unnerved, he continued across the room. Walking around to the back of the desk, Andrew realized that there were nearly a dozen different drawers. He reached for the first one, but paused, remembering the training session with Mr. Harrison where the drawer had set off an alarm. He examined the drawers closely. There were no signs of an alarm system. Slowly, he began inching the first drawer open. Once it was all the way open, he breathed a sigh of relief.

He began searching through the drawers methodically, looking over every multi-page file to see if it referenced an apple orchard or anything related to weather modification. It had been many years since he'd read Chinese characters, so he had to read carefully to make sure he wasn't missing anything important.

After searching through several of the top drawers, he opened the largest one at the very bottom of the desk. Rather than being organized into a filing system, all the papers inside were simply stacked on top of each other, and immediately the top document caught his eye. The title was "Ping Guo Yuan Tian Qi Shi Yan Shi" *Apple Orchard Weather Experimentation Facility*. This was it. As he flipped through the pages, he realized that it seemed to contain everything he needed: references to a HAARP-like facility that could control everything from wind currents to precipitation to hurricanes. But something about it didn't feel right. For one thing, it was much shorter than he'd expected – only about five pages. And it all seemed a little too easy. He looked around again, but there was still no one else there. No, he was just getting paranoid. He needed to have confidence, like Mazken had taught him. He really was just a better spy than he'd first thought.

CHAPTER 18:

THE CHINESE HAARP

"This is quite… something, son." Andrew had taken photos of the document, translated it, and faxed it to Mr. Harrison over a secure line. "And you found this document in his desk, you said?"

"Yes, I overheard him talking about a facility called the Apple Orchard on the phone. He was saying something about running tests… which is a little strange, since they've clearly already been using it for years, but maybe they've just made some upgrades."

"Yes, well, this is an exciting development. Good work, son. But your work isn't done yet. What we really need is a visual confirmation that this facility exists, and any other information you can collect on-site about the details of how it's operated. A video of the facility in action would be best. By God… this really could be it."

Mr. Harrison seemed just as surprised as Andrew at how quickly he'd managed to uncover this information. But Andrew knew Mr. Harrison was right—he needed to go check it out in person to be sure.

Andrew had assumed that the apple orchard was a code name, but as he said the name to himself over and over in his head, he knew that it sounded familiar – like the name of a place he'd been to, or heard of. So he put the question to

Charlie.

"Ping Guo Yuan? Of course, I know it. It is the last subway stop on line one."

Of course. He'd read the name on the subway map. "Is that a famous apple orchard or something?"

"Actually I don't think there is an apple orchard there anymore," Charlie pondered. "That area is very industrial now. Why do you want to go out there?"

Andrew hesitated. He knew he had promised to tell Charlie what he was up to. And he realized that it would be better to have someone like Charlie with him, in case he was able to gain access to the computers controlling the facility. He knew Charlie didn't like the Chinese government, but would he still help him if he knew the truth of what he was doing?

"Charlie, what if I told you that I know where there's a government database that could make us a lot of money?

Charlie looked at him curiously, "What kind of database is it?"

"It contains information on when and how the Chinese government is going to modify the weather."

Charlie stared at him. Then his eyes widened, "So if we know that, we can bet on prices of agriculture products. We can make a killing." Charlie was practically jumping with excitement.

"Uh... yeah, exactly." Andrew wondered why Charlie had so easily accepted his assumption that the Chinese government was modifying the weather.

"Hey," said Charlie, his elation momentarily suspended and a look of suspicion on his face, "How you know about this?"

"I found a report about it in Lao Cheng's office."

"But, how you know to search there in the first place?"

"Well... I'm a hustler, just like you Charlie."

"Hustler? What is it?"

"It means someone who's always looking for a new way to make some quick money. You know, kinda like a businessman."

"Oh, yeah, I know it. Yeah, yeah, I'm a hustler. Hey, I have this idea to do import-export business too. You wanna help me?"

"Uh, let's just take this one step at a time, alright? Meet me tomorrow and we'll go find that database."

"Where is it?"

"At the apple orchard, of course."

***

The ride on the subway out to the end of line one from the center of the city took almost an hour. When they emerged, Andrew felt like they were no longer in Beijing. Unlike the clean, glitzy buildings and streets in the center of the city, everything out here seemed old and grimy. The nearby apartment buildings and storefronts were older and more decrepit than most of those in the center of Beijing. The soot that hung in the air seemed thicker too, making Andrew double over in fits of coughing. As they walked, they were shadowed on one side by a long concrete wall. At one point they came to a gap where the wall had crumbled, and Andrew looked past it to see that the wall was an enclosure, and inside was a grove of small trees. They were all dead and leafless, like a Garden of Eden that had been hit with a poisonous gas.

Andrew looked around and saw that Charlie had gone to talk to one of the locals. When he returned, he said, "We take the 538 bus to the foot of the mountains, then transfer to the 108 bus …"

"How do you know that?"

"The man just told me."

Andrew looked at him disbelievingly. "How do you imagine *he* knows where to find a secret government facility?"

Charlie shrugged, "It is not a secret to people who live nearby. When the government built something, everyone in the area knows about it. He said there is a giant network of metal built by the government that hums all day and night. It is near a village on the other side of the mountain."

As they walked to the bus stop, they passed the gate to

what looked like a large factory. But when Andrew looked inside, he saw a grisly mess of collapsed buildings, and melted steel towers. On a wall just inside, Andrew saw that someone had spray-painted in red the letters E-J-F. Underneath them were five Chinese characters:

覆巢无完卵

The translation, as Andrew understood it, was something like, *when the nest is overturned, no egg is left unbroken.*

"Charlie, do you know what EJF means?"

Charlie looked back at him and narrowed his eyes. "It means Economic Justice Front. Where did you see that?"

"Inside that factory."

Charlie came back and stared for a moment. Andrew thought he looked melancholy.

"What do you think they meant by writing that?"

Charlie shrugged. "Maybe a threat to the Communist Party? They are a secret group that claims to stand for the common people, since the Communist Party now favors the rich. Actually I think they are an international group, which is why their initials are in English. They go after and destroy assets of corrupt government officials. This factory must be owned by one."

They continued to the bus stop. After two short bus rides, they came to the base of the mountain and started to climb. As they descended the other side of the mountain, Andrew became aware of a humming sound permeating the stillness. Then as they came around a corner, and the trail opened up into a clearing, suddenly it was right below them. They stood on a rise, looking out over a vast array of metal poles and wires, covering what looked like at least a half square mile.

"This is it. We found it, Charlie."

Charlie seemed temporarily stunned by what they were seeing. His giddiness had all gone away.

"Come on, we need to get closer," Andrew took some pictures with his phone, and then began to climb down toward the installation, and eventually Charlie followed him, now very quiet. Not surprisingly, a barbed-wire fence surrounded the facility, so Andrew began circling the perimeter, searching for a way in. Soon they came to a road leading to a gate, and a large building that stood about 50 yards away from the fence. Andrew quickly ducked behind a tree and pulled Charlie with him when he saw that there were about a dozen uniformed men walking around near the entrance.

"See those soldiers? I bet the computer systems are inside," said Andrew, as he watched them. "One of us needs to create a distraction to draw them away from the door so the other one can get inside. I think you should create a distraction." Andrew looked back at Charlie and saw that he was lighting up a cigarette. "Charlie, someone is going to smell that. This is not a good time."

"Of course it is a good time. This whole thing stresses me out, man."

"But I need you to create a distraction."

"You create distraction, man. You're the white ghost who doesn't speak Chinese; you're a walking distraction. I know computers."

"But if they see me in a place like this they will be more suspicious. How many white people do you see out here?"

"Exactly, that is why it is distracting."

Andrew reached up, grabbed the cigarette out of Charlie's mouth, and threw it on the ground. "Stop joking around and be serious for once, will you?"

"Hey, why you do that?" Charlie looked around for the cigarette, but it had disappeared in the leaves. "No one going to smell a cigarette from here."

"It's distracting you from focusing on what we need to do. This is a high-security government facility that we're about to break into."

"That is what worries me man. I don't know if we should mess around with something like this."

"This is not the time to be having second thoughts, Charlie." Andrew paused and then changed his tone. "Think about how much money we could make from information like this."

"And you know what happens if we are caught? Probably they execute me, and deport you."

"That's a risk we just have to take."

"Oh, easy for you to say. You are not the one who is executed."

Andrew was about to respond when a familiar smell passed his nose. It was the smell of something burning. He looked around and saw that a small pile of leaves near their feet had caught on fire. Charlie saw it too and yelped. Andrew tried to stamp the fire out, but it was catching too quickly in the dry underbrush of the woods. Pretty soon the flames were leaping up as high as their knees.

Charlie began jumping around and cursing. "Let's get out of here."

They began running through the woods around the clearing. As they did so, they heard shouts from the soldiers, and Andrew turned to see that several of them were running over toward the fire.

"Hey, that is our distraction," said Charlie in a loud, excited whisper.

They continued to run through the woods until they were as close as they could get to the building. There was no one near the entrance, and the one guard who hadn't run over to put out the fire was watching the others do so, turned in the other direction.

"Let's go," whispered Andrew. They ran across the clearing to the door. Andrew was preparing to pick the lock, but to his surprise, he found the door was unlocked. He opened it as quietly as possible, and they slipped inside.

They were in a giant room with a tall ceiling, filled with large, very old looking mainframe computers. It appeared the soldiers had been camping out in the building because there were clothes, mattresses, and other items lying around. Charlie went over to the nearest computer and examined it. "I think this is not working anymore," he said. "No lights on; no power source. Even if it does work, this thing is so ancient, I don't know how to download from it."

"Well let's look around. There's got to be more modern computers here somewhere." But after walking once around the room, Andrew could tell there was nothing else there.

"This place looks like it was not used since 1990s."

"But you see that giant machine outside. This is definitely where the Chinese government is controlling the weather."

"Man, how you know for sure?"

Andrew ignored Charlie. But he was starting to doubt it himself. If this facility was so important, why wasn't it more heavily protected?

"They must be controlling it remotely now. The database must be somewhere else."

"Seriously man, how you know about this place?"

"It doesn't matter. The database isn't here. We better leave before the soldiers come back."

"I can't believe you convince me to come here and risk my head for nothing," Andrew had already returned to the front door, and continuing to ignore Charlie, he opened the door a crack and peeked outside. The soldiers had already put out the fire and returned. Some of them were near the door.

"Looks like we're going to have to fight our way out of here."

"Man, this is not a day I want to get shot."

"They don't have guns. We should be able to take out the first few and then make a run for it."

Just as he said this, the door opened. For a second he was face to face with a stunned looking guard. Andrew reacted quickly, striking him on the head with the intent of knocking him out, but as he did the man shouted, "Laowai!"

Andrew kicked the door open and began to make a run for it. "Come on," he shouted at Charlie. One of the soldiers tried to block his path, but Andrew kicked him hard in the stomach and the man fell to the ground. Behind him he heard another shout and then someone else fall to the ground. Charlie must have taken out the other guard. He continued to run, but when he heard more shouts and realized no one was following him, he looked back. Charlie had been pinned to the ground by the guard, who was now holding a knife in his face, shouting at him in Chinese.

Andrew looked around and saw that the other soldiers were now halfway across the clearing. He sprinted back toward Charlie as quickly as he could. The guard who had him pinned heard Andrew coming and turned to face him, but Andrew delivered a swift chop that knocked the knife from his hand, and then kicked him in the stomach. The guard collapsed. He grabbed Charlie's arm, pulled him to his feet, and they began running, just as the other soldiers were about to reach them. The soldiers were now between them and the path on which they had come, so Andrew headed down the dirt road. He was a good runner and was outpacing the soldiers easily, but Charlie had begun wheezing, and was falling behind. The soldiers would catch him soon, and then there would be too many for the two of them to fight off. Andrew looked around and saw a van parked in a side lot up ahead. He didn't see any other options, so he headed for the van.

He reached the van and yanked on one of the doors, which came open. He climbed into the front seat. "Get in, get in," he shouted at Charlie. Charlie quickened his pace and reached the van, diving into the front seat. Andrew shut the door just as the soldiers reached them.

"See if you can find the keys," he shouted at Charlie, who began searching around frantically. Andrew was about to begin trying to hotwire the car, when Charlie shouted, "here it is," and handed the keys to Andrew. As he did so, the window closest to Charlie shattered, spraying glass everywhere. One of the soldiers reached in, trying to unlock the door, but Charlie smacked his arm against the shattered glass, and the guard pulled it away, howling in pain. Andrew started the car and stepped on the gas. The van lurched forward, and the soldiers jumped out of the way, shouting frantically. Andrew gunned it and the van sped off down the road. Charlie was still breathing heavily, but when Andrew looked over at him, he smiled and began to laugh. "We escape, haha!"

Andrew just smiled. He was already worrying about the consequences of them being discovered. Surely the news would make it back to Lao Cheng that a foreigner had broken into the facility. But would he suspect Andrew? There was something strange about this whole situation. Why weren't there people monitoring the facility at the site? Why were there a bunch of ancient computers, no longer in use, housed in that building? And why did the government build this apparatus somewhere that was so easy for the locals to find? Although this facility seemed like the proof Harrison was looking for, Andrew realized he would need to dig deeper. He would need to find a way to get more guarded information from Lao Cheng.

CHAPTER 19:

A DANGEROUS GAME

The idea came to him the next day at lunch.

Andrew knew that his English classes had made him quite popular at NOCCOC. Recently he'd noticed that some of the women in his class were staying longer after class to ask him questions that seemed trivial. At lunch, they would sit a small distance away, at the same table as him, glancing in his direction and giggling every now and then. He couldn't help but enjoy all the attention. But now there was just one woman whose attention he wanted to capture.

"The mistress of one of the most powerful men in China? I like your ambition, mate." Mazken said when Andrew told him that he wanted to seduce Yang Fei. "You'll have to make yourself very intriguing to her. Beautiful women like her are used to stealing all the attention from guys around them. Best thing you can do is to set her up to see you giving more attention to another chick, or better yet, a group of other chicks. It's social proof. If other chicks like you, then she should too."

But now that he had the idea, Andrew wondered if he could really do it. Despite the fact that they weren't really dating, he felt that he'd be betraying May. And Yang Fei was practically the favorite mistress of an emperor. Could he really seduce someone like that? But he couldn't see another way forward.

As soon as Andrew noticed Yang Fei walking into the cafeteria the next day, he looked away, making sure he didn't make eye contact with her, or give any signal that he'd noticed her presence, and quickly sat down with a group of women who were in his class. As Yang Fei was getting her food, he began telling a joke to the women that he knew would get them talking loudly and hopefully laughing, especially if he told it in Chinese. He had stopped worrying about people knowing that he could speak Mandarin. As long as he kept it rather elementary, no one would know how fluent he really was.

"Ni ting shuo guo waixing ren lai Zhongguo de gushi ma?" *Have you heard the story of what happened when aliens came to China?*

There were mixed replies, combined with small outbursts of pleasant surprise that Teacher Oxley knew so much about Chinese culture.

"*Well, if they went to Beijing, the nationalistic people in Beijing would put them in a museum to offer evidence of the greatness of China,*"

There were some head nods and giggles. Out of the corner of his eye, Andrew saw Yang Fei paying for her food.

"*If they went to Shanghai, the crafty people of Shanghai would create an exhibition to showcase them, and charge people lots of money to see them.*"

There were a few more laughs. Now Yang Fei was looking around for a place to sit. But had she spotted him?

"*And if the aliens went to Guangzhou... do you know what the people there would do with them?*"

"Ba tamen chidiao le," *They would eat them,* said several of the women in unison, and then they all burst into laughter. Several people nearby turned to look at their group.

"*Are you making fun of people from Guangzhou? That's my favorite game.*"

Yang Fei was now standing across from Andrew. She'd taken the bait. Mazken had guessed correctly that she wouldn't be able to resist stealing center stage.

"*Actually we were just about to start making fun of girls*

from Shanghai," said one of the other women. Andrew noticed that most of them looked disappointed that Yang Fei had arrived, and even a little intimidated.

"*Because we all know how people from Shanghai have fake hair,*" he said, winking at her.

Yang Fei apparently remembered the joke he'd made when they first met, because she smiled, while rolling her eyes and flipping her hair back, letting out a little high pitched 'eh' sound. He had her attention, but now he needed a hook.

"*Of course, not everyone fits the stereotypes. I know of a personality test that will tell me whether you're a typical Shanghai girl or not.*"

Yang Fei raised one eyebrow and put a hand on her hip, looking at him expectantly.

"*It just involves asking you four questions. Why don't you sit down,*" Andrew motioned for her to sit across from him, and two of the other women moved to the side to make room for her. Slowly and deliberately, Yang Fei sat down across from him.

"*OK, first question. What is your favorite color, and what feeling does it give you? Describe it.*"

The other women were watching and listening intently now.

Yang Fei answered immediately "*Pink. It makes me feel happy and energetic.*"

Andrew thought he could have guessed that one, but pretended to be mildly surprised. "Hen you yisi," *Very interesting*, he mused.

"*What does it mean?*" she asked.

"*Hold on, I need to ask all four questions first.*" Some of the other women giggled. Yang Fei gave him a look of annoyance and folded her arms across her chest, but Andrew knew this was just part of the game.

"*What is your favorite animal?*"

Yang Fei appeared to think for a moment, and then said, "Yuyan."

Andrew didn't know what that meant. "*Can you describe*

it?"

"It's a small bird that rarely lands, but is almost always flying."

The other women were talking amongst themselves. Andrew still didn't know what bird she was talking about and looked around for help. Finally, one of the other women looked at him and said in English, "It means the bird called swift."

This one was genuinely surprising to Andrew. *"And how does it make you feel?"*

Yang Fei paused, looking around as if she were pondering the question, and then her eyes landed back on Andrew. *"Alive, spontaneous... free."*

Her look was a little unsettling, but Andrew continued to hold her gaze.

"Now imagine yourself in a doorless, white room. Everything is white – the ceiling, walls, floor. How do you feel?"

Yang Fei broke his gaze and looked down before answering, *"Relieved, calm, safe."*

"And finally, imagine you are next to a large body of water and are about to jump in, how do you feel?"

Yang Fei didn't break his gaze this time, but stared into his eyes, *"Excited... and a little helpless."*

Now the other women were quietly watching Andrew and Yang Fei. As she continued to look at him, Andrew felt like he had gotten a glimpse into her soul. And behind the lively, confident woman he saw on a daily basis, he thought there was a hint of fear and sadness. Finally, she broke his gaze. *"So what does it mean?"* She insisted.

"Ok, so your favorite color is how other people see you... happy and energetic."

There were some snickers. Yang Fei smiled a knowing smile, "Dangran." *Of course.*

"Your favorite animal is how you see yourself... or rather, your ideal self. You would like to always be alive, spontaneous, and free."

Yang Fei didn't say anything to this one. *"And the next*

one?"

"*The room is how you view death. You said you feel relieved, calm, and safe. I guess death doesn't scare you.*"

Yang Fei nodded her head slightly.

"*And the last one, where you are about to jump into the water, that shows us how you view romance... and sex. So you feel excited, but also a little helpless.*"

There were some laughs again, and the women began talking excitedly amongst themselves. "*So what do you think, was that accurate?*"

"*I think so,*" said Yang Fei. Her usual flippant bubbliness was momentarily gone.

The lunch hour was over, and the cafeteria was emptying out quickly. The women who had been sitting with them began to get up and head back to work. Yang Fei stood up as if to leave as well. Andrew could barely hold his composure, he was so nervous at this point, but he knew he couldn't pass up this opportunity.

"*You know, you're not quite what I expected,*" he began.

Yang Fei looked at him and shrugged her shoulders, "*Is anybody?*"

"*You seem more adventurous than I thought. And I like adventurous girls. We should go on an adventure together sometime.*"

"*Sure, I guess.*" She was trying to pass it off as no big deal, but Andrew could tell she was interested. He got her phone number and made sure she programmed his number into her phone. As he did so, he noticed her looking around anxiously.

"*I take it you like music?*" He asked.

"*Of course.*"

"*There's a jazz concert at a bar in the Central Business District this Friday. Why don't we go to that, and then go explore the city after?*"

"*Text me,*" was all she said. Then she walked off.

Andrew realized that he had been taking a big risk by visibly getting her number in the middle of a public place like the cafeteria. No doubt that's what Yang Fei had been anxious about. Would she actually meet him?

CHAPTER 20:

A NEW ASSET

Andrew waited nervously for Yang Fei outside the bar. He had called her earlier that day and she had responded that they were still on. When a taxi pulled up and Yang Fei got out, Andrew could barely contain himself. She was wearing a very tight, sparkly dress. The shoulder straps were flesh-colored, making her body from the breasts up appear naked, except for a feathery scarf that was draped over her shoulders.

"Hi," Andrew croaked. His mouth had gone dry. He was glad he'd decided to take her to a fancy place. She would have been far too overdressed for anywhere else.

Yang Fei smiled her usual seductive smile and held out her hand for him to take. He led her into the bar, and they sat down at a table near the stage. Andrew ordered two cocktails for them, and then the concert began. During the concert, they said very little. It was hard to talk over the music anyway, but Andrew was beginning to feel awkward. What was he supposed to say to this beauty queen? She was too much for him.

After the concert finished they left and took a taxi to Houhai, a small lake in the middle of Beijing surrounded by bars and restaurants. Now that they were out in the open air, Andrew noticed that the wind had picked up and was quickly blowing away the usual smog that clouded the city. Even after sundown, the summer heat was still stifling, so Andrew welcomed the cooling breeze.

"*Did you grow up in Shanghai?*"

"*I was born in a small town outside Shanghai, but I moved to the city when I was fourteen.*"

"*Why?*"

"*To work in a factory.*"

Andrew stopped and stared at her. "*You worked in a factory?*"

She nodded. "*My parents sent me to work there because they weren't making enough money to support me and my two younger sisters.*"

"*You have two sisters? But what about the one-child policy?*"

"*My parents really wanted to have a son, so they kept trying after I was born, and after my second sister was born. But after three daughters they stopped trying. They kept both my sisters a secret and never registered them, so the government doesn't know they exist.*"

"*That must be hard. What was it like working in a factory?*"

"*It was very unpleasant. Older men were always looking at me, and some of them tried to touch me. When I tried to stop them, some would get angry and hit me. At first, I was passive and didn't fight back much, but after a year or so, I learned that I didn't have to just let them do what they wanted. I became friends with the manager and he protected me from the other men.*"

Her sudden outpouring stunned Andrew. This was not at all what he'd expected. He wondered what she had to do to become 'friends' with the manager, but decided not to ask.

She seemed to be warming up to him and continued. "*When I turned eighteen, I went to work for a KTV bar as a hostess. Girls like me can make a lot of money doing that, you know? I did that for a few years and was able to send a lot of money back to my parents, so they were eventually able to pay the fine for having my sisters and get them officially registered.*"

They asked me to come home after that, but I didn't want to go back to village life. I wanted to try and make it here on my own."

"After a while, I was tired of servicing men at the KTV every night. That's when I met Lao Cheng, and he offered to hire me to work at NOCCOC. I thought it was a way out, but of course, I should have known what he really wanted." She stopped talking and looked off across the lake.

"I had no idea. I always thought..." Andrew trailed off.

"Ni yi wei wo mei chi guo ku," *You thought I'd never eaten bitter before,"* she whispered.

Andrew was confused for a moment and then realized this must be a Chinese expression for experiencing some sort of hardship.

"That's right," he replied. He put his arm around her without even really thinking about it. She didn't reject it. He looked out behind her at the crowds of people walking along the lake, going in and out of the bars and restaurants, and as he did so, he saw a familiar face. He blinked; trying to make sure he was seeing right, but soon he had no doubt. May was walking toward him, with a young Chinese man at her side, his arm around her shoulders.

A surge of panic pumped through him. She couldn't see them together. Not if she was working for Lao Cheng.

"Let's go sit in that bar over there," he quickly steered Yang Fei off the path and into the bar. There were some tables with big, cushy looking couches, and Andrew pulled Yang Fei down onto one of them. She was giving him a confused look. Andrew glanced out the window and saw May walking past. She didn't seem to have spotted them.

Relieved, he turned back to Yang Fei. He thought about putting his arm around her and then decided against it at the last second. Then he quickly decided to order some drinks. As they drank, Yang Fei began to giggle excessively, laughing at almost anything Andrew said. He noticed that she seemed even more at ease with him now than before. Maybe she had just needed someone to hear her story. It seemed to bode well for him—they both relaxed, and she seemed to be having a good time. It was time to keep moving, as Mazken had told him.

He called a taxi and they both got in. Pretty soon they arrived at his apartment and Andrew began to get out, taking her hand to pull her with him, but she hesitated. *"Where are we?"*

"Oh, this is my apartment..."

Yang Fei narrowed her eyes at him. *"Why are we going to your apartment?"*

Plausible deniability, Andrew thought to himself. *"Well, I have a nice bottle of wine there and I thought we could have one more drink before I send you home."* Andrew paused, and then added, *"And I have a great view from my balcony, I want you to see it."*

Yang Fei just continued to stare at him, not moving.

"Come on, it will be fun, then I'll send you home," Andrew insisted. He pulled on her arm again, and this time, she let him lead her out of the cab and into the building.

When they entered his apartment, he took her on a tour, first to the balcony, then to his kitchen where they retrieved the wine and some glasses, then finally to his bedroom, where they sat on the bed. Andrew poured them each a glass, and they both sipped on them. Soon Yang Fei saw the framed picture of his family and grabbed it from his bedside table.

"Wow, you have a sister and a brother. Are you the oldest too?"

"Yeah."

Yang Fei examined the picture. *"Do you miss them?"*

"Yes." He replied.

"I miss my family too," she said, and Andrew turned to look at her. He saw the pain in her eyes, and for a second he hesitated. Was he going to cause her even more pain with what he was about to do? But as he looked at her, he felt a primal passion stirring inside him. She was so beautiful and looked so vulnerable right now. He wanted to protect her, to wrap his arms around her and shield her from the world. He leaned forward and began kissing her neck.

She flinched and pulled away slightly, but when Andrew persisted she let him continue. Slowly, he worked his way down her shoulder blade and then under her neck, and soon was unzipping the back of her dress. When the dress had come off he slipped his hand between her legs, and she began moaning. And then his clothes were coming off too and he was on top of her. As they moved together, passion overtaking them, she pushed him off and rolled over so that she was on top of him, and as she did so, Andrew accidentally bumped his bedside table.

His father's teacup, which had been perched near the edge, slid off and fell to the floor, shattering into several pieces.

"Congratulations, mate, sounds like you pulled off a masterful seduction," Mazken told him over lunch on Monday. "No doubt old Cheng wasn't keeping her entertained. Now she's got her sugar daddy and her youthful lover."

"You mean you sleep with Lao Cheng's mistress?" Charlie blurted out.

"Yes Kong Kong, have you been paying attention to anything we've been saying?"

Charlie looked wide-eyed at Andrew. "Man, you have no idea what you get into."

"What do you mean?"

"I thought you know man, you the one who work for him." Charlie lit up a cigarette and then continued. "Lao Cheng have a legendary temper."

"Yeah, I've noticed that."

"Not just that. He is ruthless. They say that every time someone stands in his way to getting power, he will first make friends with them, then invite them to his personal karaoke bar," Charlie continued. "You know that is the kind of place where government officials go to have a good time, right? You know they don't really go there to sing karaoke, right? Most of them are really just brothels in disguise. Well these enemies of his, they are suddenly caught with a prostitute and charged with corruption. He is very cunning, and also very unforgiving. You know that his first wife died of cancer? That's the official story at least. But there's a rumor that he poisoned her slowly as revenge for cheating on him."

Andrew had grown stiff listening to Charlie. Somehow the news wasn't that surprising, but it was still unnerving.

"So what are you saying I should do?"

"If I were you, I drop the whole thing now and get out of China. If he ever find out, you dead man."

Andrew realized now that he needed to be more careful about keeping their relationship a secret from everyone at NOCCOC. No more public dates. He'd already had a close call with May.

And now he faced the next dilemma. He needed Yang Fei's help to uncover Lao Cheng's secrets. But that would almost certainly mean telling her why he was really there, or at least, some version of why he was there.

He knew that she had fallen for him. But could he trust her?

Late one night, Andrew was drifting off to sleep, when he heard a knock on his door. Then his phone began vibrating, and he saw that Yang Fei was calling him.

"*I'm outside, let me in.*"

Andrew went to the door and opened it. She was standing there, makeup smudged all around her eyes and tears running down her cheeks.

"*What happened?*"

She didn't say anything, but just walked into Andrew's apartment, headed straight for his bathroom and shut the door. When she had emerged, she had washed her makeup off and applied new eyeliner. She went to Andrew's bedroom and lay down on his bed.

Andrew walked over and sat down next to her, running his hand over her hair. "*What happened?*" he repeated.

"*I told him I was done, that I didn't want to see him anymore. I expected that I would lose my job. That's OK because I could get another job working at a KTV again, or at a nightclub. I almost just told him that I quit, but I wanted to let him fire me so that he could have some satisfaction. But instead, he said I would keep my job and that everything would stay the same. At first, I didn't understand, but then he asked me how my parents and sisters are doing.*" She began sobbing again. "*When I told him they were fine, he said, 'Your dad works in construction, doesn't he? That's a very dangerous job. It would be unfortunate if he had an accident.'*"

Andrew's hand stopped for a moment. He knew what the implication was.

"*You should have seen the look on his face. He loves it when he knows he has power over someone.*"

Andrew bent down and put his arm around Yang Fei. "*What if there was a way you could turn the tables on him. What if you could take away his power?*"

"*There's no way. He is one of the most powerful men in China. And I'm just a foolish girl.*"

"*What if I knew a way?*"

Yang Fei turned to look at him, frowning. But when she looked into his face, the frown softened. "*How?*"

Andrew took a deep breath. "*I know he is leading a secret government program to manipulate global weather patterns. That's why I'm really working for him, so I could spy on him. If this was exposed to the international community, the Chinese government would likely use him as the scapegoat, and he would lose his power, probably even get put in prison. But I've been trying for weeks, and I can't find the information myself.*"

Andrew had expected her first reaction to be one of disbelief, or even anger as she realized this was the reason he'd been interested in her from the beginning. She would likely demand to know how he knew this, and what his motivations were. And he had prepared his defense.

She stared at him, searching his face, and taking in what he had said. And then to his surprise, she replied, "*Tell me what you want me to do.*"

CHAPTER 21:

THE OTHER FOREIGNER

Andrew was headed for Lao Cheng's office. For three days straight, his class with Lao Cheng had been canceled, and it was beginning to make him nervous. I-phone hadn't given him any reason why. Finally, he decided to find Yu Mama and ask her, but when he arrived on the eighth floor, she wasn't at her desk. In all his time at NOCCOC, Yu Mama had never been absent when Lao Cheng was in his office. He walked up to the door and gave it a tentative push. To his surprise, it began to inch open. Inside Lao Cheng was nowhere to be seen. Instead, Yang Fei was standing near his desk, staring out the window. She looked tired.

She heard him enter and turned quickly, then seemed to grow tense when she saw it was him.

"Do you know why Yu Mama isn't here?" he asked.

"She has been out sick for a few days. I've been taking her place."

Andrew walked toward her, but before he could get very close, she put a hand up and shook her head.

"Lao Cheng is in the bathroom. You should go. I don't want him to see us together."

"Wait. Have you made any progress while Yu Ma was out?"

"We shouldn't be talking here, there are cameras," she

171

said, but at the same time nodded her head. "*Meet me after work. I have something important to give you.*" They heard the toilet flush. "*Now go, quickly.*" Andrew walked quickly toward the door, and out into the hallway. There had been an urgent tone in Yang Fei's voice that made him feel uncomfortable.

Andrew headed for the cafeteria for lunch. As he devoured a bowl of noodles, out of the corner of his eye he saw a strange sight that sent a chill through his body. Four of the building's security guards had entered the cafeteria and seemed to be looking around for someone. Surely it wasn't him. He continued eating his noodles, trying to ignore them. But as he did so, they began walking in his direction. As they approached, he overheard them arguing in Chinese, "*Is that him?*" "*It's got to be, do you see any other foreigners around?*" "*I heard there is another foreigner who works here too.*"

The men finally stopped in front of him. "Excuse-a mee. You Osley?" One of them said in very broken English.

"Who's Osley?" Andrew replied, trying to feign the best look of confusion that he could."

The men looked at each other, "Teacha Osley," the leader replied.

Andrew continued to give them a confused look, then pretended to realize what they were talking about. "Oh, Teacher Oxley? No, no, I'm the *other* foreigner. I don't think the teacher is here today."

The men looked at each other confused, but one of them had a triumphant look on his face. "*See? I told you there were two of them.*"

"No Teacha Osley?" the leader repeated, looking confused.

"You know, he may have gone out to lunch. If he's supposed to be here, I'm sure he'll be back. Want me to let him know you're looking for him?" Andrew realized the guard probably hadn't understood most of what he said, but hoped he would get the gist.

The lead guard still looked confused, but after conferring with the others, they seemed to decide that they had the wrong

172

guy, and left the cafeteria.

Andrew got up, trying not to move more quickly than normal. He had no idea why the guards would be looking for him, but he knew it couldn't be good. They were almost certainly doing Lao Cheng's bidding, and if Lao Cheng was sending guards to fetch him, then something had happened. Whatever was going on, he needed to get out of NOCCOC as quickly as possible without making a scene.

But what about Yang Fei? If Lao Cheng knew about him, she might be in danger as well. He called her.

"Feifei, there are security people looking for me. I think they know about us. We both need to get out of NOCCOC quickly. Where are you?"

There was a pause and he heard her breathing quicken. *"I'm on the 8th floor, at Yu Mama's desk."*

"Come meet me in the lobby immediately."

"OK, I'm coming." She hung up.

Andrew walked out of the cafeteria and ascended the escalator to the ground floor, trying not to look like he was in a rush. Then he walked casually across the marble floors of the great entrance hall, through the normal lunchtime crowds that were strolling around, toward the main exit. As he did so, he noticed that there were two security guards standing in front of the main door. They were still allowing people in and out, but this was not a normal security procedure. They were positioned in a way that they could easily stop anyone from leaving. Andrew was approaching them from an angle, so they hadn't seen him yet.

He stopped behind the front desk and stood there waiting, trying to stay out of sight of the security guards. Two minutes passed. Where was Yang Fei? He looked at the security guards, trying to figure out how they were going to get past them. Maybe they could sneak up and then run between them at the last minute? But just then, he heard a voice blare through one of the guard's radios. Andrew couldn't hear what it had said, but suddenly the guard turned in his direction and spotted him. There was no doubt in Andrew's mind now. They were there to keep him from leaving. Then he saw rapid movement on the other side of the lobby. There were three more security guards running toward him. He couldn't wait for Yang Fei any longer.

He began running toward the door and the security guards, who were now bracing themselves, blocking his path. As he reached them, he jumped and delivered a kick to the chest of one of them. Clearly they hadn't been expecting his assault, because the guard crumpled to the ground, and Andrew continued past him, now at a full sprint out into the plaza in front of NOCCOC. Even though it was the middle of the day, the sky outside had grown dark. Big drops of rain were falling from the sky, and in less than a minute, Andrew was soaked.

He heard shouts behind him, and realized that about half a dozen other security guards were running after him now. In front of him was the busy, eight-lane boulevard of Chang'an. He jumped over the fence into the bike lane and to his surprise, landed in a small pool of water. It had been raining so hard that the streets had begun to flood. The nausea immediately began to take hold. But he needed to move. Scooters and motorcycles beeped at him as he began to dodge through them, while the security guards continued to pursue him. There was no way he could cross the street in this rain and with the heavy mid-afternoon traffic on Beijing's largest boulevard, so he continued forward into Tiananmen Square.

And then he saw the lightning.

It struck the gate of the Forbidden City, lighting up the giant portrait of Chairman Mao with an eerie glow. The throngs of people in the square who had been scrambling to find shelter from the rain uttered a collective sound of fear and surprise, as the thunderclap rolled across the square. Andrew was amazed by how close it had struck. But he didn't have time to think about it, because the security guards were closing on him. He began dodging through the crowds, trying to shake his pursuers. As he neared the center of the square, the crowds became thicker. He could hear the sounds of the security guards behind him shoving people out of the way. They were almost upon him.

He was not more than 20 feet away from Chairman Mao's mausoleum in the middle of the square when lightning struck again at the top of the obelisk. The shock wave caused Andrew to stumble, and he felt a small surge of electricity run through his body. As he recovered from the shock and continued to run, a new fear swept through him. What were the chances that two bolts of lightning would strike in such close proximity to him within just a few minutes? A thought crossed his mind that he knew seemed crazy, but that he couldn't dismiss. Was Lao Cheng somehow controlling this storm?

He continued running toward the other end of the square. He could feel the water rising around his legs, slowing him down, and making him want to vomit. He needed to get higher. He was approaching Qianmen, the back gate to Tiananmen Square, which had a staircase leading up to the ramparts of the old gate tower. He began to climb the stairs. The security guards followed. Maybe he could find somewhere to hide.

At the top of the stairs was an open plaza. He ran to the other side, looking for a door in the wall of the tower, but there was none. He looked down at the street on the other side. It was becoming a raging torrent of water. Even the cars couldn't seem to fight it, their drivers abandoning them in the middle of the road. And then he felt a hand on his shoulder. One of the guards had reached him. He turned quickly, grabbed the guard's arm and twisted. The man howled in pain, as Andrew sent him spinning into another one of the guards. But the others managed to dodge them and continue toward Andrew. He couldn't hold them all off. He looked back at the racing water, and was taken back to his childhood again and the feeling of nearly drowning in the churning water that had swept over his father's boat. But he had no other path. Before another guard reached him, he jumped from the ramparts and into the water.

He couldn't believe how fast it had risen. Fighting to keep his head above water and not let the panic consume him, he was carried down the road and out of the square. Finally, he managed to grab onto a nearby car and pull himself out, where he promptly vomited. Pausing for a moment to recover, he noticed a short wall next to the car. He climbed up to the top and looked around at the flooded streets. It would be very difficult for them to come after him in this flood. If this storm had indeed been Lao Cheng's doing, he clearly hadn't anticipated the flooding.

But what about Yang Fei? His thoughts returned to her as he realized she was likely in more danger now than he was. But he couldn't go back to NOCCOC to warn her. He took out his phone, but it was soaked in water and wouldn't turn on. Then a thought occurred to him and he stared at his phone. What if Lao Cheng was tracking his phone? He almost certainly was, and he probably had been monitoring his conversations as well. For that matter, he probably knew where Andrew lived and would have men heading there now. Surely he also knew who Andrew's friends were; who he'd been spending the most time with in the last few weeks. He needed to warn Mazken and Charlie. He needed to get a new phone. He needed to find a new place to live. He needed to disappear.

CHAPTER 22:

THE FALL OF CONSORT YANG

Cheng filled one of the glasses on the bar in the back of his office with baiju – 'white alcohol,' as it was translated in English. The Russians would probably call it vodka. Not that his English or Russian were very good, he knew, but that didn't really matter. He raised the glass and downed it in one gulp, then glanced at the door to his office.

Why had he ever agreed to pretend to be taking English lessons? He knew the little American, Andrew, who was supposed to be teaching him, had really been sent there as a spy by another American, a man that he despised: Howard Harrison of the Institute for American Exceptionalism. But he was supposed to play along and pretend like he didn't know, because it was all part of the plan.

He was getting tired of it.

It was bad enough that his employees were beginning to talk about it behind his back. 'The boss needs English lessons, did you hear? He's so behind the times.' In fact, it was giving even more momentum to the nickname they called him behind his back, Lao Cheng. But even worse, this little ass of an American thought he was actually doing a good job at passing for a teacher; thought he was pulling the wool over the eyes of Cheng. And then he had the nerve to try and plant a spy camera in his office and in the process break one of his vases.

But Andrew had no idea what he, Cheng, was capable of. As a former member of China's military intelligence community, he was still tapped into all the sources of intelligence employed by China's state security apparatus, right down to what was happening inside his own building. There was very little that could get past him.

It was his American collaborator, Will Rothschild, that had suggested he plant false documents for Andrew to find. It could serve as a useful distraction for them, he'd said. Lao Cheng had agreed reluctantly to play dumb and let the little American teach him English while thinking he was gathering valuable information to share with the media. But for some reason, even after Lao Cheng had planted documents that would lead him to the old HAARP replica near Ping Guo Yuan, Andrew and Harrison hadn't yet revealed what he'd found. Ever since then, Lao Cheng had been trying to figure out what the little laowai was up to.

So it had come as a very unpleasant surprise when he was informed that Andrew had been sleeping with his mistress. Cheng could feel his face growing hot with rage. Screw the plan, he was done pretending now. He couldn't wait to smash the little American's face in. But no, that would be too quick. He would enjoy it much more if the pain were drawn out.

The door to his office opened, and two of his security personnel came in, dragging Yang Fei. Cheng waited, expecting them to drag Andrew in next.

"Xiao Meiguo ren zai nar?" *Where is the little American?* Cheng demanded. The security people looked at each other, and then looked at the ground. If neither of them wanted to answer, it could not be good news. "*Where is he?*" Cheng demanded more forcefully.

Finally one of the men muttered, "*He ran out of the main entrance.*"

"*And is someone going after him?*" Cheng asked, trying to suppress his impulse to strangle one of them.

"*Of course, sir. Five colleagues are pursuing him.*"

"*Well, why are you still standing here? Go after him*

yourselves. I want him NOW."

The two men hurriedly left his office.

Yang Fei stood in front of him, clearly trying to look indignant, but he could tell she was afraid. Good. She should be.

Cheng just stared at her for several seconds, letting her fear build. Then he spoke. *"One of your colleagues has informed me that she saw you out with my personal tutor recently. Is this true?"*

He could see her processing this and deciding what to say. Yes, let me catch you in a lie, Xiao Fei.

Finally, he could see her decide. *"Yes, I was out with him. Can't I have friends here? Or is that not allowed?"* Her defiant tone didn't surprise him. It was the same one she'd used a few days ago when she tried to leave him.

"But your colleague said she saw him putting his arm around you. Now I don't think that's something friends do."

"Fine, he's my lover. I told you I was done. I don't want this to go on anymore. I want to live a full life."

"Have you forgotten how I got you out of that KTV rat hole? If it weren't for me, you'd still be giving blowjobs to strange men every night."

"I could have gotten myself out of there with time. This life I have now, this is just a nicer cage."

"There's no such thing as a free life, Xiao Fei. Everywhere you go, someone is going to be your boss."

"Maybe that's true, maybe it isn't. But I don't want it to be you anymore."

Cheng stared at her. He was not used to people talking back to him like this. Even for independent-minded Yang Fei, this was something new. There was something else going on here.

"You've really fallen in love with him, haven't you?" Suddenly she blushed and looked at the ground. It wasn't just that. As the realization dawned on him, a new wave of rage crashed into him. She'd helped the little American somehow. She'd helped him get some real information.

Cheng walked right up to her, his voice quivering. *"What information did you give him?"*

Now she looked up at him, wide-eyed. Their eyes met for a moment, and then she tried to run. But Cheng was ready. He grabbed her arm. She tried to pry his arm away with her other hand, but she was tiny compared to him. She didn't stand a chance.

"You betrayed me," he growled, grasping her arm tighter.

"No, I didn't give him anything."

"Liar."

"Really I didn't."

"But you were going to give him something."

She didn't reply. He put his other hand around her throat and began to squeeze. *"What was it?*

"It was... nothing... just some coordinates..."

"Where?"

"Some place out in Inner Mongolia."

That was it. He let go of her throat and grabbed her other arm, turning it behind her back. She cried out in pain. Taking both her wrists in one of his hands, he began dragging her toward the mantle. She began to kick and scream, but he knew no one would do anything about it. This was his domain. There was a stone near the edge of the mantle that had been coming lose, and now Cheng ripped it out of its place. He raised it above his head. Yang Fei saw what he was doing and cringed, waiting for him to strike. But instead, Cheng turned and hurled the stone at his window.

The panel of glass shattered, leaving a large hole, as the stone fell to the plaza, eight stories down. A warning shot for anyone below, Cheng thought vaguely.

Yang Fei looked at him in surprise. Then, as he began dragging her again, the horror of realization seemed to hit her. She cried out and thrashed around, but she was no match for him. He continued to drag her toward the broken window.

CHAPTER 23:
THE BLUE FEDORA

After about an hour, the water had begun to subside. Andrew found an abandoned motorbike and began riding along the sidewalk toward his apartment, stopping at a China Mobile store to buy a new phone and sim card. When he finally arrived in his neighborhood, he began to proceed cautiously toward his apartment. Everything seemed to be normal. He doubted Lao Cheng's security had managed to get here first with all the streets flooded. Cautiously, he got off the bike and went up to his unit. It didn't appear that anyone had broken in. He opened the door as quietly as he could, and went in. He needed to be quick, taking only the essentials. As he stuffed some clothes into a backpack, he noticed the pieces of his father's broken cup on his bedside table. He stared at them. He couldn't just throw them away, so he swept them into his backpack.

As he left his apartment, he felt a prickly sensation on the back of his neck, and he looked around. Out of the corner of his eye, he noticed a man walking a distance behind him to his left. Had Lao Cheng's men caught up to him?

There was a bus stop up ahead, and a bus had just pulled up and was letting on passengers. Andrew marveled at how the busses were still running, even just after a flash flood. He quickened his pace slightly, but didn't break into a run, and remained on the sidewalk far away from the curb, for fear the man would realize what was going on and catch up to him too quickly. If only he could time it just right...

He reached the bus stop just as the last person was getting on. At the last second, he sprinted sideways and hopped through the doors just as they were being shut. As the bus pulled away, he looked out the window. The man stared at him as the bus drove away. There was something strange about him. He was wearing a blue fedora. Why would one of Lao Cheng's thugs wear such a ridiculous thing?

An hour later, he arrived at Mazken and Charlie's apartment.

Charlie answered the door only half-dressed and looking like he'd just woken up.

"Drew, what are you doing here?"

"I need to talk to you and Mazken right away."

Charlie rubbed his eyes. "It is that urgent?"

"Yes," Andrew pushed his way past Charlie into the apartment.

"Is that Drew?" came Mazken's voice. He emerged from his room, wearing nothing but a bathrobe and slippers. He walked past Andrew to the refrigerator, poured himself a glass of milk, and chugged the whole thing. "This can't wait until after breakfast?"

"Breakfast? It's after one o'clock..."

"Charlie and I taught a class last night," Mazken said. "So for us, it's breakfast time."

"I just barely escaped from NOCCOC with my life. Security came looking for me, and they clearly were trying to take me to Lao Cheng. And now both of you are in danger too. I think you're gonna have to move to another apartment at least, maybe even change your phone numbers..."

"Lao Cheng catch you sleeping with his mistress, right? I tell you be careful, but you don't listen to me."

"So why are we in danger, Andrew?" Mazken asked. He was now doing pushups in the middle of the floor.

"Just trust me, Lao Cheng is angry enough now that he'll do anything to find me."

"Like capture and torture us for your whereabouts? I doubt

182

he's *that* angry."

"Charlie was right all along. He discovered my relationship with Yang Fei, and now he wants revenge. And his search for me will lead him to you. You have to get out of here. We don't have much time." Andrew was beginning to panic. They weren't taking him seriously enough.

Mazken got up and faced Andrew. "I've lived in this apartment for five years and it suits me quite well. This is where Charlie and I do our business. This is our home. And it has good Feng Shui," he swept his hand around the room, as if this were obvious, "So you're gonna need to give us a much better reason to move than telling us that you're paranoid."

Charlie stared at him; his eyes narrowed, then said, "I think there is something you do not tell us."

"Good job Charlie," Mazken's tone sounded slightly sarcastic, "you're getting better at reading people. You're right, there is something he hasn't told us."

Andrew looked at them. Could he trust them? Or more importantly, could he trust Charlie? He was Chinese after all. But Charlie hated the Chinese government. He would appreciate what Andrew was trying to do, wouldn't he?

"Ok, I don't think Lao Cheng is after me because of my affair with Yang Fei..." Andrew began. "I think he's after me because he's discovered that I'm a spy."

Mazken just smiled slightly. But Charlie practically jumped in the air with excitement. "I knew it. That's how you know where is weather control facility." Then he frowned. "You spy for U.S. government?"

"Well not exactly. It's an, er... non-governmental organization actually."

"So they sent you here on a mission to sabotage the Chinese government's weather control technology," stated Mazken. He'd gone back to his pushups.

Andrew looked at him. "You've known all along what I was doing here, haven't you? How did you know?"

"The same way I knew everything else about you when we first met. I started with a little deduction, and your reactions to certain things I said told the rest of the story. You wear your emotions on your sleeve, mate. It's a wonder Lao Cheng didn't discover you sooner. But I have to give you some credit; ever since you started studying with me, you've gotten a little better at hiding them," he stood back up and grinned.

"How come you care if Chinese government control its weather?" Charlie pressed him.

"See, the Chinese government isn't just changing the weather in China; they are secretly manipulating the weather in America in a way that's weakening its economy. And I'm here to find proof."

Charlie crossed his arms and continued frowning at him.

"I thought you hated the Chinese government, Charlie. Their power needs to be checked," he looked at Charlie deploringly. Charlie's expression didn't change. "OK, well whatever you think, I'm pretty sure Lao Cheng has known about me for at least a few weeks and has probably been tracking all my movements. That means you two are in danger. His men could be on their way here right now for all I know."

"Let's start packing, Charlie."

Andrew turned to look at Mazken with relief. "So you are going to move then?"

"I believe everything you've told us, mate. And if that's the case, then the most prudent action is for us to get the hell out of here. We don't have much to pack between us. We can all stay in a hotel tonight, then go searching for a new flat tomorrow.

"I cannot share a flat with someone who spies on China."

"Come on Kong Kong, don't be dense. You're probably already on the blacklist for associating with him. And I'm sure Lao Cheng knows about your little trip out to Ping Guo Yuan. You haven't got anything to lose."

"It is the principle. If I start to help him now, I betray my country."

Mazken scoffed, "Since when do you care about principles? Stop talking nonsense and get packing."

Charlie didn't move, but leaned against the wall and

pulled out a cigarette.

"What are you going to do Charlie? Are you going to turn me in?"

Charlie shook his head vigorously. "No, we are brothers now, I cannot do that."

"That's right mate, and brothers help each other out."

"Not only that," now Andrew moved toward Charlie until he was pressed against the wall, "But if you really aren't going to turn me in, then I wonder what you're going to say to Lao Cheng's thugs when they show up here in a few minutes. I'm sure they will be really sympathetic."

Charlie remained silent, but Andrew had a feeling he'd gotten the point. Finally, he put the cigarette out, turned and went into his room. Andrew could hear him moving things around and then saw through the crack that he had pulled a suitcase out. He breathed a sigh of relief.

"He'll come around eventually, mate," Mazken said cheerfully. Then they heard a commotion outside in the hallway. "Sounds like our friends might be here already," Mazken raised his voice, "Charlie, no time to pack, we need to go now mate."

They were on the fifteenth story of an apartment building, so there was only one way out. As Andrew opened the door, he braced himself for a fight, but there was no one immediately outside. Instead, the commotion was coming from just down the hall. Confused, Andrew poked his head out, and saw a group of men surrounding the apartment next door.

"Good thing these door numbers slide on and off so easily," said Mazken, grinning at him.

It took Andrew a moment to understand what he meant. "You mean you switched the door numbers? But how did you know...?"

"I didn't. But I had a dream last night that you came to us and said we were in danger and that I'd better switch the numbers. And my dreams seem to have a strange habit of predicting the future."

Andrew just stared at him in disbelief. Then Charlie

appeared. "What is happening?"

"Lao Cheng's thugs are bothering our neighbors, and I have a feeling we're next. Let's go." They closed the door and strolled toward the elevator, pretending nothing was wrong. As they waited for the elevator to arrive, one of the thugs looked over at them, and seemed to make the connection.

"Tamen zai zher!" *There they are*, he shouted. At that moment, the elevator door began to open, and the three of them hurried inside. Andrew slammed his finger on the button to close the door, and managed to close it just before the man reached them.

When they'd descended to the lobby, Charlie opened up the elevator control panel and pulled a few wires. "Other elevator is already out of service. Now this one is too," he grinned.

"They're probably already taking the stairs, Kong Kong. Let's get out of here."

CHAPTER 24:

THE TAIL

"What's happened, Harrison?"

"How'd ya know I'm callin' with bad news?"

"Every time you call me after 2 AM, it's bad news."

"It's a double whammy this time. You want the really bad news, or the bad news first?"

"The really bad news."

"Our primary operative has been captured."

There was a long pause. "And the bad news?"

"The Oxley boy was discovered as well, and just barely managed to escape capture."

"And that's bad news?"

"The boy is our only hope now. He managed to uncover something more important than our main operative ever did. He found a report in Mr. Cheng's desk detailin' the capabilities of a weather modification apparatus on the far west side of Beijing. I think he was on to something. But now he's goin' to have a harder time continuing that investigation, with Lao Cheng after him."

"What else is there to investigate? If he found this report, that should be good enough to put some weight behind your thesis. Pull him out now, before things go too far."

"There was somethin' off about that facility he found. He found a control room that was abandoned. Doesn't think the machine is in use. Thinks they must have built a new one somewhere else."

"Does it really matter if we find their newest one or not?"

"We need to make sure we find the real one if we're going to force them to shut it down."

"This is unnecessary, Harrison. If he's captured, there are a hundred ways they could use him against us."

"He's goin' to continue the mission. He was makin' progress, and I dare say he'll find a way to get back in there. Besides, Cheng's sure to have put an exit control on him now, so gettin' him out of China will be difficult."

"So now you think he's capable of being a real operative?"

"Cheng discovered him, and yet he managed to escape from the buildin' without gettin' captured. That's quite somethin'. Gives me more confidence that maybe there's more to him than we thought."

"Still, he was amateur enough to get discovered in the first place. What exactly did he do to get himself caught?"

"You won't believe this, but he managed to seduce Cheng's mistress and was usin' her to get information. Now that's creative. Just give him a week to get back on his feet and see what he does. I have a feeling he can turn this whole thing around."

"I wish for once that you'd run this organization based on more than just a feeling. It's hard to justify the money I'm putting into this otherwise," the chairman suddenly seemed unusually agitated.

"Just one week. I'll give him a kick in the butt."

"OK. But you'd better show me some results." The phone hung up.

Howard left his study and headed back to his bedroom, where his wife was still sleeping soundly. After all these years, she'd learned to sleep through his middle-of-the-night emergency phone calls. But she had never quite gotten used to his lifestyle. Maybe all those years were starting to add up. He watched her sleep, as he had so many times before. It calmed him. All this was worth it as long as she was by his side.

***

The next day, as Howard was leaving the office and heading to his car, he noticed the same Chinese man that had been watching him a few weeks prior also getting into his car. As Howard pulled out of the parking lot, the Chinese man pulled out right behind him. A few turns and several miles later, the Chinese man was still right behind him. Why had the man chosen today to follow him? Did this have something to do with the discovery of their man in Beijing? Well, he wasn't going to lead the man right to his house. Howard made a sharp turn off the main road onto a small side road, and the Chinese man continued right behind him. He was definitely being followed.

Howard picked up his cell phone and called the Director of Homeland Security. It rang several times until finally the Director answered.

"Harrison. What can I do for you?"

"There's a Chinese man following me in my car. I'm pretty sure he's been spyin' on me for the last several weeks. I'm drivin' down Pine Street near Oak Grove in Fairfax. Ya'll got a unit in the area? I might need backup."

There was a pause. "Are you sure he's a Chinese spy? This could really backfire if we're wrong again, Harrison. One of our officers just came under heavy fire for racial profiling…"

"I'm sure they did, but this is the real deal. You got someone?"

There was another pause. "I'm sending Officer Turner in your direction right now. She should be there in a few minutes."

"Dandy. I'll send you my exact coordinates shortly."

Howard continued driving for another few minutes, and then pulled over to the side of the road in an upscale suburban neighborhood. There were people out walking their dogs and children playing in the front yards. If this guy was going to start anything, he wanted there to be plenty of witnesses. He saw the Chinese man pull up behind him, turn off his car, get out and start walking toward him.

Before the Chinese man could reach him, Howard jumped out of his car, brandishing a pistol that he kept in the glove compartment. The Chinese man looked up, his eyes widened and he jumped back, putting his hands out in front of him. "Don't shoot, I'll give you my wallet or my phone, whatever you want."

"Why have you been followin' me?"

The man gave him a confused look. "I haven't been following you."

"Don't lie to me. You've been followin' me all the way from my office."

"No, I wasn't following you. This is my home."

"You expect me to believe that I happened to park right in front of your house?"

Just then a black SUV pulled up and flashing lights appeared in the front window. A woman dressed in civilian clothes got out, but Howard saw that she carried a concealed firearm and a badge. "Officer Turner with Homeland Security," she said, turning to the Chinese man. "Please come with me sir, we need to take you in for some questioning."

"Why me? What did I do?"

"Sir, I'm an officer for the federal government. Now don't force me to arrest you. If you'll just come with us, it will make things much easier."

"I want to talk to my lawyer first before I go anywhere."

"I'm afraid that's not how this works." She reached out and grabbed the man, spinning him around and pinning him to Howard's car.

"Hey, what are you doing?" the man protested.

"Sir, I'm placing you under arrest. You have the right to remain silent..."

As Officer Turner read him his rights and then loaded the man into her car, Howard got back into his car as well. He was relieved that she had shown up. He was too old for this kind of thing. He started his car again. As he was pulling away from the sidewalk to follow Turner, he looked in his rearview mirror at the house in front of which they had stopped and saw a small Asian girl walking out of the front door onto the lawn, staring after them.

CHAPTER 26:

THE OTHER SPY

There was a knock on Cheng's office door. This had better be his head of security. And he'd better have good news for him.

"Jin lai," *Come in,* he shouted.

The door opened and his head of security shuffled in. He was not behaving like a man who had good news.

"*Speak,*" Cheng demanded.

"*Sir, we nearly caught him as he was escaping through Tiananmen Square.*"

"*Nearly?*"

"*Well, you see he ran up on top of Qianmen tower, and then jumped into the flooded street where the water was already above our necks and rushing very quickly, and I'm sure you understand, no one was going to follow him at that point.*"

"*Who, exactly, was sure that I would understand?*"

The man was looking very uncomfortable. "*Well sir, uh, there were several men pursuing him, I'm not sure who exactly...*"

"*Well, find out who, exactly, and then inform all of them that they no longer have a job here.*"

"*Uh, yes, sir.*"

"*And I assume your men are still searching?*"

"*Oh yes, absolutely sir.*"

Cheng stood up. *"Good. Now don't return to my office until you have some good news."* The head of security nodded vigorously, and then made a hasty exit.

Cheng stood there for a moment, then brought his fist down hard on his desk. With all the cameras and men at his disposal, why hadn't they caught him yet? Could it really be that hard to catch a stupid little American and his two friends? Cheng tried to clear his head and think. He needed to take a new approach.

"Ma ma," he called. A few seconds later, the door to his office opened and Yu Ma walked in. Of all the people in the world, he trusted her most. She had always been there for him, and she could get things done.

"I need you to draw on your personal connections. Make sure every hotel owner and taxi driver in this city knows that there will be a large reward for whoever turns in the little American."

"It will be done." She turned to go.

"One more thing. Before you do that, please send the employee May Li to my office."

She turned and nodded, then left the office.

About ten minutes later, May entered his office, a timid look on her face.

"Qing zuo xia Li Mei" *Please, come sit down May Li,"* Cheng gestured for her to sit in the chair in front of his desk. Slowly, she came over and sat down, looking cautiously at him.

"I didn't properly thank you for telling me about my tutor and Yang Fei," he began.

"Oh, it was nothing. I just thought you might want to know," now she looked uneasy.

"I need you to help explain something to me," Cheng continued. *"You went to college with Andrew Oxley, correct?"* She nodded. *"And you were friends with him, yes?"* She nodded again. *"Well, that's the puzzle. I can't figure out why you would tell me that he was seeing Yang Fei, when you must have known it would put him at risk."*

May squirmed a bit. *"Well, the truth is,"* She paused.

"You see, him and I started dating recently," She stopped and took a deep breath. *"We began dating after he came here. So he was cheating on me with her."*

"I see. So we were both in the same boat."

May gave him a fake smile and nodded. She was beautiful. Not as beautiful as Yang Fei, but still well above average. Perhaps he could persuade her to become his new mistress. But that would have to come later.

"There's something you need to understand about me, May, if you don't already. Loyalty is very important to me. I reward those who are loyal, and punish those who are not. I'm sure you heard about what happened to Yang Fei. When I confronted her, she confessed to me, and then decided to take her life, rather than live with the shame of her betrayal." He looked intently at May, who squirmed in her seat again. *"I just wish she had done it in a way that didn't require breaking my office window,"* He laughed. May forced a short laugh too.

"Tell me May, are you still angry at Andrew?"

May stared into space for a moment, then her eyes narrowed. *"Yes. He treated me very poorly. I want him to suffer the way he's made me suffer."*

"I agree. Not only did he treat both of us poorly, but it turns out, he's also an American spy."

She looked up at him, seeming surprised. *"A spy?"*

"That's right. He was sent here to steal military secrets from me. Can you believe those Americans? As soon as they start to lose their edge, they turn to stealing from other countries. It's outrageous."

May nodded her head in agreement. *"I experienced their arrogance first hand when I was in America."*

"I need you to help me put an end to it, May. I need you to help me find him."

She looked surprised again. *"But you must have so many resources available to hunt for him. How could I possibly help?"*

"He trusted you, May. I'm sure you can get him to trust you again. I'm sure a woman like you knows how to get her

way with men," He smiled at her.

May gave him what looked like a fake smile again. He had a feeling she was going to play hard to get. But they all came around to him, eventually.

"Convince him that it's safe to meet you somewhere. And then when he comes, my men will be waiting."

CHAPTER 25:

REINFORCED GLASS

Andrew was walking by himself down the Sanlitun bar street. Around him, the crowds of people were drinking, laughing, and having a good time. But he felt removed from all of them. He wanted to join them, but he was worried about drawing too much attention to himself.

"Come with me, my boy. We have some important matters to discuss." Andrew turned to see Mr. Harrison walking toward him. "Let's go drink some tea together. Alcohol ain't no good for the body or the soul."

Andrew wasn't surprised to see Mr. Harrison there – he knew Mr. Harrison was coming to check on him. He followed him away from the bar street, through the maze of shops and department stores that made up the outdoor mall, toward the other side of Sanlitun, where they found a traditional Chinese teahouse. Andrew wondered since when Mr. Harrison had been a tea drinker. But then he realized it was part of southern tradition, too. As they walked through the entrance, Andrew noticed there was a blue bull's head engraved over the door. Suddenly he felt excited. Maybe this was where his father's teacup had come from.

They headed toward a table where a group of Chinese men already sat. As they approached the table, one of the men, who had been facing away from Andrew, turned around.

"To An-da-rew Osley," the man raised his teacup in a toast, and to his horror, Andrew realized that the man was Lao Cheng, "May he rest in peace."

Now the other men at the table got up and began closing in on Andrew. Andrew turned and ran out of the teahouse. Soon Lao Cheng's men had surrounded him. As they closed in, Andrew heard a girl calling to him frantically off in the distance. "Andrew, Andrew! They're trying to take our baby." It was May's voice. Frantically Andrew began punching and kicking at the men around him, fighting his way through them. There seemed to be hundreds of them now, but they backed away as he kicked ferociously, until he saw May crouching on the street up ahead, clutching a little bundle wrapped in a blanket.

He approached her, and she smiled at him, a smile mixed with relief and sadness. He leaned down and pulled back the blanket to get a look at their baby. But what he saw didn't look like a baby at all, but a little monster made of black tar. It snarled at him and lashed out, biting into his outstretched hand. Andrew cried out in pain and woke up abruptly.

He had been taking a nap on the pull-out couch in a hotel room. They hadn't gotten much sleep the night before as they had tried to give Lao Cheng's men the slip. Looking around, he saw Charlie, his head tilted sideways and his eyes half-open, trying to read the newspaper. On the other side of the room, Mazken was sitting cross-legged and silent, facing a corner where he'd made a temporary shrine.

Lying back, he thought about the strangeness of the dream he'd just had. Did it mean something? More than likely he was just anxious that Lao Cheng was going to find him. Out of habit, Andrew pulled out his phone and began checking his email. He was surprised to see at the top of his inbox that he had a message from May. The subject read: *We need to talk.* He opened it and read the body.

Your phone is off. We really need to talk.
Come meet me in Sanlitun tomorrow evening?
Love,

May

No mention of the fact that he'd disappeared from NOCCOC. Maybe she didn't know, but it seemed like the commotion would have been hard to miss, and rumors would have spread. Feigning ignorance seemed like further proof that she was working for Lao Cheng.

"Hey, Drew, I think you need to read this," said Charlie, handing the newspaper to Andrew with a solemn look on his face, pointing to an article on the second page. The title read in Chinese *"NOCCOC Employee Commits Suicide."* Andrew's throat went dry. He had a feeling he knew what it meant, but he didn't want to believe it. He continued reading:

"An employee at NOCCOC named Yang Fei reportedly committed suicide Tuesday afternoon by smashing through a window on the 8th story of the NOCCOC building and jumping to her death. After investigating the matter further, officials concluded that she was experiencing too much pressure from her direct manager, who was known to work his employees very hard. "That manager has since been fired," said Zhao Fengshui, Director of HR for NOCCOC. "We will not tolerate that sort of thing here. We want NOCCOC to be a harmonious and happy place for our employees." Zhao also noted that they were taking further steps to make sure this kind of thing would not happen again. "First thing tomorrow we're having all the large glass windows in the building that are at least three stories up reinforced," he said..."

Andrew read the first part of the article over again, and then again. Maybe there was a mistake. Maybe they had gotten the wrong name. Despite how trapped she felt, he knew she never would have committed suicide.

Yang Fei couldn't be dead.

But how could they confuse her with anyone else? Andrew found that he was short of breath. He was feeling dizzy. He put his hand on the table to steady himself.

"Hey, are you alright, man?"

The eighth story was where Lao Cheng's office was. And there was no way Yang Fei was strong enough to break through a window like that on her own.

This was murder.

And they were all covering it up. The paper had just called it a suicide, plain and simple. There was no question of foul play. And of course, Lao Cheng had just found a scapegoat, in the form of Yang Fei's direct supervisor, to take the fall.

"Mazken, get in here. Something wrong with Andrew."

Andrew tried to take a breath, but he was starved of air. He doubled over, gasping.

"Andrew, look at me." He looked up to see Mazken standing over him. "Concentrate on the sound of my voice. Everything is OK. You are taking deep breaths. Everything is OK. Feel the oxygen filling your lungs. Breath in. Breath out. Everything is OK."

Andrew felt a sense of calm returning. After several long moments, he was finally able to breathe again.

"What happened?" asked Mazken, his voice very slow and deliberate.

Andrew didn't say anything, but handed him the newspaper.

"Yang Fei suicide," said Charlie.

"No, that article is bullshit. She was murdered."

"Is that all? Big surprise there, mates."

"What the hell does that mean? Don't tell me you could have predicted her being murdered. You just know everything, don't you?"

"Lao Cheng is a powerful man with a really bad temper and a big case of megalomania. He discovered that someone close to him has betrayed him and is collaborating with someone who is spying on him—which not to mention is a HUGE loss of face—so he killed her and covered it up. Big surprise."

"So that's all you're going to do is analyze this. You don't even care that someone died."

"Why should I care?"

"Oh, I don't know, because anyone who's not a psychopath would care."

"Let me ask you Andrew, why do *you* care so much?"

"Why do I care? Because she was part of my life."

"Did you love her?"

"That doesn't matter. She's a human being for Christ's sake."

"And you, mate, are a spy. It's your job to use people and then lose them. You shouldn't become so emotionally attached."

"I should have tried harder to get her out of NOCCOC that day, rather than just trying to save myself."

"Then you likely would be dead now too. You can't blame yourself for that."

"The hell I can't," Andrew was shouting now. "She was helping me spy on him. I was sleeping with her. If she hadn't gotten involved with me, she would still be alive." Now he was sobbing.

"If you mess around in a china shop, you break some things," said Charlie quietly.

Andrew turned on him, "What are you going on about?"

"It's an American idiom. Bull in a china shop, right? When you do reckless thing like sleep with powerful man's mistress, something gets broken. Someone gets hurt."

"You're not helping Charlie, just stay out of this."

"Charlie is right," said Mazken. "If you're going to be in the business of spying, you need to be able to live with the decisions you make. But she made decisions too. It was ultimately her decision to sleep with you. It was her decision to help you. She was just as reckless."

"But I used her. You just admitted it. I followed you and your training and your tactics, and she fell in love with me. That's why she agreed to help me spy on him."

Mazken's voice remained calm and steady. "She clearly wanted to be rid of him. And she took a major risk to do that. You gave her an opportunity to liberate herself. I think she would have thanked you for that."

"Now you're just trying to spin it in a way that gets rid of your own guilt."

"There's nothing for me to feel guilty about."

"Well, you know, I really wish I could be as heartless as you. I'd feel a lot better right now."

"Life is going to throw you around a lot, Andrew. You're just getting a taste of it."

"I've tasted plenty of it. Both my parents died in accidents where I couldn't save them."

"And when I was a kid, my father used to beat me. Eventually, I decided that instead of continuing to be a victim, I would accept it for what it was, and move on.

Andrew stared out the window, at the vast cityscape below. Millions of people were going about their business, living, laughing, crying, and dying. Then he remembered something. "She said the white room made her feel relieved, calm and safe."

"Ah, you used the four-question psychology test on her," Mazken nodded.

"She didn't have an easy life. I hope that means she's at peace now. Do Chinese people believe in heaven, Charlie?"

Charlie looked pensive for a moment. "Yes, but it is different from Western heaven."

"Do people go there when they die?"

"Some people believe that is true."

"But you don't?"

Charlie shrugged. "I like to focus on life, not on death."

Andrew didn't see how he could do that right now. The feeling of guilt was too strong. He knew he should move on, but that wasn't going to be possible for the time being. He stared for a minute at the picture of Yang Fei that had been printed in the article. Then he carefully tore it out and put it in his wallet.

"Hey, cheer up Drew, at least you still alive." Andrew didn't say anything for several moments. Charlie seemed to be uncomfortable with the silence because he continued. "You know, now that you have time on your hands, you should help me start my import-export business."

"Oh get off it mate, you've been going on about that for ages."

"But I didn't have anyone to help me sell abroad. Drew can help me sell in America."

"In case you forgot Charlie, I'm here on a mission."

"Forget about that silly mission, man. Who cares if Chinese government controls the weather? Governments do sketchy stuff like that all the time, huh? Who knows, all we can do is try to make some money and have a good time."

"So you don't think that when you see an injustice in the world, you should try to do something to change it?"

"Man, I seen lots of injustice, and sometimes I try to do something about them, but I learn," he grinned at Mazken "Nothing good ever come from kicking the hornet's nest."

"I don't know if beating up the son of a Politburo member qualifies as 'doing something,'" Mazken commented.

"You know my parents run a business in Wenzhou. One time when government official demand a bribe from them to keep our factory going, my dad refuses to pay, and tries to appeal to the provincial court. And you know what happens? He loses, and local government thugs come to beat him up. He is nearly killed." Charlie paused. "I don't like Chinese government either, but they are too powerful."

"But I've got to find a way," and then a dreadful thought came to Andrew's mind. "Is Lao Cheng powerful enough to prevent me from leaving China? Like to get border security to stop me from leaving?"

"You better believe it. Oh man, I don't think about that."

Somehow Andrew didn't feel any worse knowing this. It seemed he'd already hit his low.

"So much for you helping me," Charlie went on. "I have a great idea too."

"What was your idea?"

"Chinese porcelain," Charlie declared. "It becomes more popular in American recently."

All of a sudden Andrew was much more interested in

Charlie's business idea. He reached in his backpack and dug out the pieces of his father's cup.

"Like this?" He showed the pieces to Charlie. Mazken leaned over to look as well. "Have you ever heard of a brand of porcelain with a blue bull as its symbol?"

Charlie shook his head. "Why you carrying those pieces?"

"These are from a cup my father left for me. My uncle said it was a gift from someone in China. Someone who was close to him."

The phone rang.

Mazken and Andrew looked at Charlie.

"Why you look at me?"

"This is your room on paper, mate. Answer it."

Slowly, Charlie picked up the phone. Andrew heard a voice on the other end say, "Hello?"

Whoever it was, they were speaking English.

Immediately Charlie hung up the phone and looked at them.

"You didn't tell them you had two laowai friends with you when you checked in, did you?" asked Mazken.

"Of course not."

Mazken looked at Andrew. "We'd better go now." Andrew nodded.

"Why?"

"Clearly someone figured out that Andrew and I are here. Remember how I said your name was probably already on the blacklist Charlie? Damnit, we never should have come to a hotel."

"But where else can we go?" There was silence for a minute.

"I know," said Charlie finally. "I have a friend—a businessman who lives north of Third Ring Road. He hates government. He will never tell about us."

"You better be right."

There was a pounding on the door.

"That's our cue to exit, mates," Mazken ran to the door and turned the deadbolt. The pounding started again, this time much harder.

Andrew looked around wildly. The only other way out was the window. He ran over and looked down. They were only on the second floor, but the pavement appeared to be a long way down. Not too far from the side of the building, there was a single parked car. At least, Andrew hoped it wasn't too far.

"Come on," he waved to the others and then opened the window.

"That's a long way," said Charlie, looking down.

"We've got no other choice."

There was a loud crashing sound as something smashed against the door.

"Time to jump," said Mazken.

Andrew held his breath and then jumped.

CHAPTER 27:

THE BLUE BULL PORCELAIN COMPANY

"Hello?" May's voice sounded just as sweet as ever.

"May, it's me, Andrew." He needed to keep this call short. He, Charlie and Mazken had made it to Charlie's friends house, and now he was outside using a public phone to call her. He looked around, nervously.

"Andrew, I'm so glad to hear your voice. I heard rumors… that you had been fired from your job at NOCCOC. Is that true?"

Andrew wondered if those were really the rumors she'd heard.

"Oh, yeah, I was. It was probably for the best though. I think I might start an import-export business with my friend instead."

"Oh, that's great," said May, her voice pitched a little higher than usual.

"How about you? How is NOCCOC treating you?"

"It's alright. My boss is on vacation this week, so things are a little more relaxed. I really hope I can get out of there soon though. I really admire that you've decided to start your own business, Xiao Niu."

"Don't call me that name anymore."

"Why not? I like it."

"I just don't want to be called that anymore, OK?" He was starting to regret making this call. "Why did you need to talk to me anyway?"

"Can't you come meet me in Sanlitun tonight? I'd rather tell you in person."

"I'm busy."

May didn't say anything for several moments, and then he heard her take a deep breath. "Andrew, I'm pregnant."

Andrew nearly dropped the phone. These were just about the last words he would have expected to hear come out of her mouth. His mind flashed back to the dream he'd had the night before.

"Are, are you sure?"

"Andrew, I wouldn't be telling you this if I wasn't sure."

"And you think it's mine?"

"I know it's yours. I haven't been with anyone else."

"But how is that possible? We used protection."

"I don't know... I guess it didn't work."

"You guess? May, you realize this is the most horrible timing."

"Is it? Were you about to go back to America and leave me here?"

"Of course not, where would you get that idea?"

"Just from the way you've been acting recently. It makes me think I might not want to have anything to do with you anymore."

"Well, like it or not you'll have something to do with me now."

"I could get an abortion, you know."

"You can give it up for adoption, too."

"What if I don't want to give my baby away?"

"May, you're being ridiculous. What are you going to do, keep it and raise it?

"Why not? I don't want to stay here forever, you know. I thought maybe we could make a life together back in America."

Andrew hesitated for a moment. It was a nice thought, but he knew it wasn't practical, at least not now. "That's not going to work."

"Oh? Why not?"

"I, I… don't ask me why."

"You know, I thought you would be more responsible."

"Responsible? You think this is my fault?"

"It's on both of us."

"I don't know why we're even having this conversation. And by the way, don't you have a boyfriend now? How does he feel about this?"

May was silent for a moment. "How do you know about that?"

"I saw you walking with him on the street."

"He's not really my boyfriend. He's just someone my parents set me up with."

"So you were just going to use him to make me jealous, huh?"

"Oh, I'm sure it won't bother you. You American playboys are all the same. You'll just go and find some other Chinese slut now and play with her emotions, then leave her high and dry too."

She had gone too far. He slammed the phone down on the receiver.

She had no right to say those things. She had no idea what he was doing, what he was going through. Or did she? She was probably just trying to get him emotional so that he'd admit something or tell her where he was. Well, he wasn't going to talk to her again. She could continue to play around with whomever. He didn't care. He wasn't going to let her lead him right into Cheng's grasp.

But of course, he did care. He couldn't stop the thought creeping back into his mind: she was pregnant with his baby. He'd loved her for years now. Did she really work for Cheng? Was this really happening?

He was walking back toward Charlie's friend's apartment complex, when he noticed something familiar out of the corner of his eye. It was a man wearing a blue fedora. Surely it was the same man as before. It seemed the man had tracked them down. What would he do now?

As Andrew approached the front gate, the man began walking faster, as though he was trying to intercept Andrew before he reached the gate. Andrew began walking faster too. The man quickened his pace to match, and soon they were both running toward the gate. Andrew reached the gate first, yanked it open and then closed it just as quickly before the man had reached him.

"Wait, Mista Osley, Mista Osley," the man called out.

This didn't seem like something a man who was there to kill him would say, but maybe he was trying to get Andrew to let his guard down.

"What do you want?" asked Andrew from inside the gate.

The man was bent over, trying to catch his breath. "I been looking for you long time. Ever since you disappear onto bus. Why you run away from me?"

"You were following me and I don't know you. Why wouldn't I? There are people out there who want me dead, you know."

The man's eyes widened, "Oh, no, Mista Osley, I no want you dead. I just want you come visit my uncle's factory. You want to start import-export business. So I come to find you, see if you interested to export my uncle's product."

Now Andrew was confused. How would this man have known about Charlie's business idea, and that he was somehow involved in it? "You tracked me down just to come visit a factory? What do they make there?"

"My uncle make world's finest porcelain," the man said, smiling. "It's called Hebei Blue Bull Porcelain Co. Very famous."

Blue Bull. It couldn't just be a coincidence. This had to be the company that made his father's teacup. Andrew's head began to spin with excitement. But then he checked himself. What if this was a trap? Could Lao Cheng possibly know that he would be tempted, more than anything else, to go visit a factory with that name? It was possible, but not likely. And Andrew knew he couldn't pass up an opportunity like this.

"Fine, can you take me there tomorrow?"

"Oh yes Mista Osley, we go first thing tomorrow. I pick you up here at 9 AM. See you tomorrow... Oh, my name is Chu," the man said, and he walked off.

When he opened the door to the apartment, Andrew got a strong whiff of marijuana. He found Mazken and Charlie sitting at the kitchen table surrounded in smoke, playing a rowdy game of cards and drinking baijiu with two beautiful girls that Andrew hadn't seen before.

"Drew, Say hello to Bo Xi and Zhang San."

Andrew gave a quick smile in their direction, then turned to Charlie and Mazken. "Are you guys crazy? What if these girls are working for Lao Cheng? And I thought they executed people for having pot here?"

"Ah, don't worry about it, mate, these chicks are clean. The government doesn't really check up on foreigners for this stuff. And Charlie here is practically a laowai now, aren't you Charlie?"

Charlie grunted and continued concentrating hard on his cards, while stealing glances at one of the girls' low-cut shirt.

"Come join us, Mate. Boobsee here was just teaching me how to play Chinese poker.

"Not Boobsee, BO XI. Ah, taoyan," *annoying,* said the girl. Mazken grinned drunkenly and threw his arm around her.

"Charlie, did you tell anyone about your import-export business idea?"

"Of course man, I already toured some factories. You change your mind?"

"Did you mention my name to any of them?"

"Why would I do that?"

"Well, a man just approached me about visiting his porcelain factory tomorrow and somehow he knew about your import-export business idea."

Charlie finally looked up from his cards. "How does he know?"

"I have no idea. But what's especially strange is, I think it's the factory that made my father's teacup. I have to go check it out. You want to go with me?"

"Nah, I am busy tomorrow."

"It's Sunday, and we are on the run from people trying to kill us. What could you possibly have to do tomorrow, besides sleep in until noon?"

"Ha, gotcha," Mazken threw down his cards. "Drink, you crack heads."

Charlie and the two girls downed their glasses of baijiu.

"You say this man came to you? His product is probably no good then."

"How do you know that?"

"Think about it this way. When has a pretty girl ever approached you in a bar? Only the ugly ones and prostitutes do that. But you don't want to sleep with them."

Andrew rolled his eyes at the crass comparison. "I have a feeling that's not going to be the case with this one."

"Don't worry about it, man. If you're interested in the business now, there are plenty of factories out there," Charlie reached in his pocket and pulled out a cigarette.

Andrew reached up and knocked it out of his mouth, then slammed his fist down on the table. "I NEED to visit this one tomorrow, OK? Are you coming with me or not?"

"Hey, calm down man. Fine, fine, what's gotten into you?"

Andrew straightened up and took a deep breath. He didn't know why he'd lashed out at Charlie like that. "Sorry, I guess I'm just too stressed. I just found out May is pregnant."

Mazken and Charlie both stared at him. "Well mate, an abortion seems like the only option. Take her to the clinic tomorrow. You don't want that kind of trouble right now."

"But I'm worried that she's working for Lao Cheng. That's why I didn't go to meet her in person. It could be a trap."

"Well then, are you sure she's really pregnant, mate?"

Andrew was caught off guard by the suggestion. It hadn't even occurred to him that May could be lying about something like that.

Mazken smiled and continued. "Chicks do manipulative

stuff like that all the time. What better way to get you to come to see her?"

Andrew didn't believe that May was capable of doing something like that. But if she was working for Lao Cheng… maybe he had misjudged her.

"You need to unwind a bit, mate. Sit down and have a drink and a smoke with us. Boobsee here will keep you company."

"Not Boobsee!"

Mazken grinned. "See, she's so much fun."

CHAPTER 28:

AN OLD FRIEND

Chu pulled up in a beat-up Honda Civic that looked like it might fall apart before they made it to the factory. As they began to drive, Chu turned on the radio and began blasting Chinese pop music, singing along with it enthusiastically. They drove northwest for an hour and a half, passing through the mountains that surrounded Beijing until they reached a small town that looked like it had only been built a decade ago. The factory stood apart from the town, at the end of a long road, next to a small river.

Andrew noticed that this building looked much different than other factories he'd seen in passing: it was new and permanent looking with cement walls and big glass windows. Instead of a run-down dorm for the workers to stay in, Andrew noticed that a few small clusters of single-family homes surrounded the factory. Further out, in a nearby field, Andrew saw a large array of solar panels. It seemed awfully modern and high tech for a porcelain factory.

Chu led them through the main entrance and into a large lobby. "Please, wait here a moment," he said, and walked through a set of double doors.

"This place look very expensive. They must get government money for some special project," Charlie commented.

"Why do you say that?"

"No place this nice is not getting government support. Otherwise, they look just like all those other factory. Question is, what they funding, and do they make any profit?"

A few minutes later, Chu returned, followed by a man that Andrew guessed was the factory owner. He wore plain clothes and a pair of glasses with perfectly round lenses, with a very strong prescription so that his eyes looked bigger than normal. He was quite short, with slightly graying hair, but walked with authority and composure.

He stopped in front of Andrew and looked him up and down. "So you are Andrew Oxley." It was a statement rather than a question, and Andrew noticed how this was the first Chinese person he'd met who could pronounce his name correctly. His English also had a slight British accent.

"Yes, I am."

"You must be related to Ray Oxley, yes?"

Andrew let out a small gasp. "He was my father."

The man smiled. "Ah, jolly good. You look very much like him," he reached out to shake Andrew's hand, "I'm Jonah Wong. It's a pleasure to meet the son of Ray Oxley." Then he turned to Charlie, who was staring at them with his mouth slightly open, and frowned at him over his glasses, "And who are you?"

"Charlie Wu," said Charlie, who, like a schoolboy caught delivering profanity, promptly closed his mouth and grinned from ear to ear.

"He's my friend and... business partner."

"Uh-huh," said Jonah, looking Charlie up and down. "And what exactly is the business you're running?"

"Import-export. Maybe we sell your porcelain to America, if you are lucky," Charlie jabbed.

"That's a kind offer, but I already have some very generous American clients and I'm not really looking for more right now."

"Then why did Chu here ask us to come tour your factory?" Charlie demanded.

"That's an excellent question," said Jonah, turning to stare at Chu, "Why did he invite *both* of you to come?" Chu gave him a sheepish look.

Andrew didn't have time for all this back and forth. This man knew his father! This was almost definitely where the cup came from. But why did he track Andrew down? "Sorry Mr. Wong, but…"

"Please, call me Jonah."

"OK, Jonah. How exactly did you know my father?"

Now Jonah stared at him over his glasses. "He didn't tell you?"

"Well, I don't know if you know this, but he died about twelve years ago."

Jonah was silent for a moment, then said quietly, "I did know."

"You do? Did you know each other well?"

Jonah paused. "Very well. He was a good friend."

"I was only nine years old back then, so he didn't really tell me much… and he didn't tell me anything about what he was doing in China. I was hoping you could tell me."

Jonah stared at him for a long moment, as if considering him. Then he quickly changed the subject. "Well boys, to be honest, I don't usually show the inside of my factory to anyone, but since you came all this way I'll make an exception today. Now, a few rules before we get started. One, don't talk to any of the workers without my permission. Two, don't go off anywhere by yourself. Understand? OK, let's go." He walked briskly back through the double doors into a long hallway. Andrew and Charlie hurried after him, with Chu bringing up the rear.

"He just plays hard to get," whispered Charlie to Andrew, "What he says about too many clients is just a ruse. He really wants us to look all along, but this way he gets us more eager to buy." Andrew's family drama, and how it was connected to the potential sale, didn't seem to concern him…

The building was full of activity, as people bustled in and out of dozens of offices along the main corridor. Soon they passed through another set of double doors and came into a huge room, which appeared to be the main floor of the factory. Immediately Andrew noticed the large windows that dominated most of the walls on three sides. Daylight was flooding in, and a warm breeze also seemed to permeate the factory walls.

"It's so light in here," Andrew exclaimed.

"We had the architect design this room with large windows facing south, to capture as much daylight as possible. It saves on energy costs, and the natural lighting has positive health benefits for our craftsmen."

Looking down from a balcony, Andrew saw scores of workers going about their business. But instead of the usual assembly-line style factory floors he'd expected, there appeared to be much less order to this factory. Each worker was working on his or her own piece, doing most of the work by hand. There were people working on shaping clay, there were several kilns where the pieces were being fired, there were people sanding and buffing the final pieces, and there were people painting them.

"As you can see, we don't believe in assembly-line work here," said Jonah. "All of our workers are very skilled in their craft, and each works on one piece at a time. We have very little specialization: a craftsman typically works on one piece until it's finished, with the exception of painting. Ok, let's head down to the floor so you can get a closer look."

As they walked across the factory floor, Andrew could see how much care was being put into each individual piece. "These workers must be quite expensive, huh?" said Charlie, who was looking skeptical.

"Each *craftsman* is paid a fair wage. We don't believe in skimping here. By paying them more than they would make elsewhere, we are not only able to retain skilled workers year after year, but they are also much more satisfied and fulfilled with their work. We also provide them with housing, which you may have noticed around the factory grounds. Each family has its own house so that they are comfortable and have their privacy, and of course, they only have a five-minute commute by foot."

"That is very convenient," said Charlie, with a little too much sincerity. Then he looked around. "Mr. Wong, may I use your bathroom?"

"Certainly. Chu will show you the way." Chu led Charlie back across the factory floor.

Andrew reached into his pocket and produced the pieces of his father's broken teacup. The blue bull's head had survived intact. "Are these from one of your pieces?" he asked, showing them to Jonah.

Jonah's eyes widened, then he took the pieces of the broken teacup as Andrew handed them to him. Examining them, he finally said, "This is the teacup I gave to your father many years ago. It was one of the first pieces produced here. I painted it myself." He looked up at Andrew, with agony on his face. "How did it break?"

Andrew looked at the ground, "I was careless and knocked it off a table."

"We may be able to repair it," said Jonah, studying the pieces. "It broke quite cleanly. Come with me." They walked across the factory floor until they reached a man sitting on a bench surrounded by dozens of broken pieces of porcelain.

"Shao Xiansheng, neng bu neng jiejue zhe pian ciqi?"

Mr. Shao took the pieces from Jonah, examined them, and then nodded.

"What does that picture you painted on it mean? Someone told me it's a famous Chinese painting, except you changed it a little."

"Yes, it was a variation on the Three Monks Laughing at Tiger Brook. It's a 900 year-old painting from the Song Dynasty. The painting symbolizes the desired harmony between the three main philosophies in China: Buddhism, Confucianism and Daoism. When I painted it, I wanted to update it a little for modern times, so I painted a monk and a cowboy together to symbolize the desired harmony between the Middle Kingdom and America. This was my gift to your father to symbolize our cooperation."

"What kind of cooperation?"

Just then, Charlie and Chu returned. Jonah narrowed his eyes at Charlie. "Quite a long trip to the bathroom, wasn't that?"

"You want details?" retorted Charlie, "We get up early this morning, so I have no time to take a..."

Just then Andrew's cell phone rang. He looked and saw that it was Mazken, and figuring he could call him back later, ignored it.

"So Jonah, you were saying about you and my father...?" His phone started ringing again, and Andrew looked and saw that it was Mazken again. "Sorry, this must be urgent, excuse me," he picked up the phone.

"You've got to get back here immediately, mate. I just ran into Fritz, and he's insisting that he needs to see you right away."

"Can't it wait? We're actually making some great progress at this factory visit."

"He says he has an important message for you from Yang Fei."

"What? How is that possible?"

"He says she gave him something just before she was killed, and told him to give it to you."

Andrew thought about the last time he'd seen her and how she said she had information for him. Could she have passed this information to Fritz at the last minute? He had to find out right away.

"...Ok, we're on our way."

Andrew hung up and turned back to Jonah. "I'm really sorry Jonah, but we have to go, I have an urgent personal matter that's just come up. But I'd like to come back sometime and finish this conversation."

Jonah gave him a shallow bow. "You are always welcome back here, Andrew Oxley. And don't forget, you'll need to retrieve your teacup once it's repaired. I hope this can serve as a sign of our families' friendship continuing down through generations."

"I still have so many questions for you…"

"And I will have answers when the time is right. Chu, will you drive them back to Beijing?" Chu nodded curtly.

Andrew gave a little bow back, and feeling slightly awkward, headed for the exit. The whole way back, Chu played Chinese pop and sang along just as obnoxiously as the first time.

"There is definitely something fishy about that factory," said Charlie quietly, so Chu wouldn't hear. "After I go to bathroom, Chu is not watching the door, so I sneak out and go find accounting office and look at their books. You know how much they charge for that porcelain? About five times more than I ever see porcelain sell for. I know foreigners will pay higher price than Chinese, but this is outrageous."

"But maybe it's just really high quality?"

"No, no, you misunderstand. This price is five times more than even *highest quality* porcelain. Like I say, there is something fishy."

CHAPTER 29:

IN THE NAME OF JUSTICE

"It's no use, Harrison, we haven't been able to find any dirt on him."

The Director of the CIA was leading Howard through a hallway lined with cells where they usually held suspected spies. This was where they had been holding the Chinese man for the last three weeks while they investigated his background.

"He's been completely clean since he arrived in the U.S. ten years ago. And we of course looked into his story that he lives at 1257 Pine Street, right where you pulled over when you thought he was following you. Well, he does indeed live there. Quite a coincidence, there's no denying that. But he's got a wife and a young daughter. We thought you might be onto something for a little while when we discovered he works on computer modeling, but we've done a thorough trace of his online activities over the last year, and found nothing suspicious. We've got nothing to charge him on, except perhaps tax evasion. But even that would be stretching it."

They reached the cell, and the Director motioned to one of the guards to open the cell. "Howard, at this point, if you can't get something out of him, we've got to let him go."

"Thank ya, Pete. I'll take it from here." Howard tried not to sound too short with the man, but he couldn't help it. Of course they weren't going to find any dirt on this man. A

Chinese spy would be very good at covering his tracks. He would have to use some unconventional interrogation tactics.

Howard walked into the cell and saw the Chinese man lying on the bed, his back facing the door.

"So your name is Jeffrey Chen, is it?

The man rolled over to look at Mr. Harrison, and a look of recognition mixed with anger crossed his face.

"You're the guy who called the police on me. Have you finally figured out that I've done nothing?"

"These ain't the normal police. You're bein' held by the CIA, sir. Do ya know why?"

"You think I'm a spy? Who are you?"

Howard realized now that the man had nearly perfect English. That was rare for a Chinese immigrant. It almost made him start to doubt that he'd really caught a spy. The Chinese government had certainly sent their best.

He walked up to the man and bent down so their faces were level. The man didn't cringe or move away. "You know what I think, *Jeff*? Can I call you that? I think you know exactly who I am. I think you were sent by the Chinese government to keep an eye on my operation, ain't that right?"

"I don't know what you're talking about. I'm driving home one day and notice your car in front of me, you drive to my house, then accuse me of following you," He paused. "Ok, I see, how much do you want?"

" 'Scuse me?"

"How much do you want? I know now, you just kidnapped me 'cause you know I'm rich. I can pay. Just let me go home."

"Say, that's not a bad idea. Why don't you just pay me $300 billion dollars? Got that Jeff? I know you're good with numbers, but just in case, that's a three with eleven zeros after it. In fact, you can just make that check out to the U.S. taxpayer, 'cause that's how much your government's weather tamperin' has cost this nation in economic damages over the last several years."

Jeff stared at him blankly. "Come on, how could you possibly think I've got that much money? You're crazy."

That was enough. Howard pulled out a pair of handcuffs, rolled Jeff over on his back, and cuffed his hands to the bed.

"Hey, what're you doing?"

"Quit playin' dumb with me. Now you're goin' to cooperate and tell me what your government has been up to because you ain't leaving here until you do."

"But you're already holding me here illegally. You still haven't given me my phone call. When I finally talk to a lawyer, I'm going to sue your ass."

"Let me make it more clear. You are bein' held here as a prisoner of war. There's no phone call. Now, tell me why the Chinese government sent you here."

"I have no idea why the Chinese government would do anything. I'm not in the communist party, and I haven't been back to China for ten years, so you're asking the wrong guy."

"Stop *lying* to me." Howard reached over and grabbed a towel and pitcher of water off the bedside table, then he held the towel over Jeff's nose and mouth, and poured the pitcher of water over him.

Jeff thrashed around and made a noise that sounded like it would have been a scream if he hadn't been choking. Howard continued pouring water over him, then bent down and whispered in his ear, his voice quivering as he did so.

"Now, you're goin' to name the exact location of the facility your government has been using to manipulate the weather in America. I need to know now. Tell me or I swear, you might just have a little accident. Then, who would take care of that nice daughter and wife of yours?"

He finally pulled the cloth off of Jeff's mouth, and then undid the handcuff on one side. Jeff sputtered and spit water out as he turned on his side, gasping for air. When he'd finally caught his breath, he looked up at Howard, with tears in his eyes.

"I wish I knew what you were talking about. All I want is to get back to my wife and daughter. They probably have no idea what happened to me. They're probably thinking I've already disappeared forever, just like my parents."

"Your sob story ain't gonna work either." Howard moved toward him, ready to put the towel back over his mouth.

"Wait, I'll tell you what I know. But first, you answer my question. How do you think the Chinese government is able to control the weather in America?"

"We know you've developed a powerful ionosphereic heater. More powerful than the one developed by the U.S. military," Howard said.

"And this iono…whatever heater, it can change weather patterns in America?"

"That's correct."

"So, how do you expect it can change the weather in the U.S., without affecting the weather in China?"

"What kind of a ridiculous question is that?"

"It's not ridiculous at all," said Jeff, who was now sitting up and concentrating very intently on Howard. "I do computer simulations for my work. One of my clients is an insurance company, and they had me do some climate modeling not long ago. And what I realized in doing it is that changes in weather and climate are all interconnected. If you create a storm over here, maybe you'll have a drought over there."

"But if ya'll can model the outcome, then you can predict what will happen in China, and adjust your device to prevent bad weather in China."

"That would be impossible. There are too many variables. Even with all the computing power of humanity combined, I don't think anyone could figure out how to do that."

"Well, your government clearly has."

"You really think China could advance that far past the U.S. in technology? China may have the largest economy now, but they can only hope to keep up with the U.S. in technology because in China you still can't think freely. That's why I came to the U.S. I'm just an ordinary citizen who wanted to be free."

"You really expect me to believe that story? How come you were watchin' me then?"

Jeff looked at the ground. "I admit, I have watched you a few times. I saw you one day across the parking lot, and you looked so much like my immigration officer, I couldn't help but stare at you."

"Ha," Howard couldn't believe this guy. He had a story to explain everything. Howard would need to work a little harder to poke holes in it. Perhaps if he could catch this guy in a lie, he would start to crack. "What's the name of your immigration officer, then?"

"Frank Harrison."

"You've gotta be kiddin' me. You expect me tah believe your immigration officer is my brother? My younger brother *is* an immigration officer, that's true… but you coulda pulled that intel from my file."

"It *is* true. Go ask your brother then. I got a green card to study here 15 years ago, then I was finally able to apply for U.S. citizenship this year. When you locked me up, I was waiting for a response on my application. You think a Chinese spy would go through all that work to become U.S. citizen and give up Chinese citizenship?"

"There couldn't be a more convincing alibi. That's devotion to the mother country right there."

"You know, I always thought your brother was very nice. I never guessed his brother could be so cruel."

"Watch your mouth, or I might just shut you up with this cloth again."

"When I finally went to submit my application for citizenship, I did hesitate for a minute. You know why? Because recently I've started to think that maybe the U.S. isn't the land of the free anymore after all. And now you've confirmed my worst fears. What am I being charged with? Where is my fair trial?"

"You're a damn godless, communist spy. We've got pinko commies running half this country now. If we give you a trial, you'll wiggle your way out of punishment and we'll never get the intel we need. We're at war, here."

"Really? I never heard that war had been a declaration between China and the U.S."

"That's just it. The world don't tolerate open war

anymore, so countries like China have got to wage war secretly. And the only way to respond to secrecy is with secrecy."

"So now you're just going to make random arrests? Make people disappear without a trial? That's what happened to my parents when they defied the Chinese Communist Party. Sounds to me like you're no better than the godless communists now."

"This ain't a random arrest. It was authorized under the U.S. Patriot Act. In America, we have laws that say what the government can and can't do."

Jeff closed his eyes, "There is no crueler tyranny than that which is perpetuated under the shield of law and in the name of justice."

Howard was startled to hear the man say this. It sounded very familiar, and as he racked his brain, he realized he'd heard it from one of his professors many decades ago while in college. Somehow it had stuck with him all these years. This man was getting to him. He couldn't let this spy weaken his resolve. But there was also a little voice in the back of his head that said: *He's right. You've got nothing to charge him with. You should let him go.*

"And what if it turns out you are a spy and we let you go? Then we might have missed a key opportunity to uncover the Chinese government's plot."

"I think that if you keep a close eye on me, you'll realize I'm not a spy. I just work hard and provide for my family, like an ordinary person. You'll see I've even started going to church. Besides, your NSA seems to have no problem with surveillance."

Howard still wasn't convinced. But torturing this guy wasn't getting him anywhere. And although he didn't like to admit it, Howard was starting to feel a pang of guilt for keeping this guy away from his family for so long. If this Jeff Chen turned out to be a spy after all, he would kick himself many times and never doubt his gut again, but for now, he realized there wasn't much else he could do.

"We'll let you make your phone call," Howard said. "And

if further investigation doesn't come up with any black marks on your record, we might let you go."

Jeff closed his eyes and nodded. "That's a start."

CHAPTER 30:

THE FILES

"Whaz up Drew-dog? Long time no see. How you been doing?"

Mazken had told Andrew to come to meet him and Fritz in Sanlitun rather than their house, which Andrew thought was a wise decision on Mazken's part. He hadn't seen any sign of Fritz since he'd run away from NOCCOC, and he was worried that one of Lao Cheng's men could be trailing him.

Andrew wasn't in the mood for small talk, especially with Fritz, "How come you didn't tell me about this message sooner, Fritz?"

"Dude, I've been trying ever since you escaped from Lao Cheng, but it seems you all must have changed your phone numbers, huh? Smart move, but you should have told your pal Frizzle about it."

"We were taking precautions, mate," said Mazken. "Drew didn't want us to be in contact with anyone from NOCCOC after that."

"Are you sure no one followed you here?" asked Andrew, looking around nervously.

"Nah, don't worry about it Drewster, the Frizzle is much smarter den dat. I've noticed dis guy trailing me for weeks, so I gave him the slip after I ran into Mazken. Dude, I feel like I'm in a spy movie or something. What's going on anyway?

How come Lao Cheng is after you?"

"Drew have genius idea to sleep with…" Andrew stepped on Charlie's foot hard and Charlie cried out in pain.

"Because I *am* a spy," Andrew blurted out before Fritz could ask what Charlie had been about to say.

"What? Don't mess with me dude, I know when someone's messing with me."

"It's true. That English teaching thing was my cover. I was sent here because my boss suspects that the Chinese government is using weather control to wage a secret war on America, and Lao Cheng is behind it. I've been trying to find proof."

"No way," said Fritz, his eyes wide with excitement. "You know, I always suspected something like dat was happening. I say, if the Chinese government can control da weather here, why not in other parts of da world too, right? And dey could totally use dat as a weapon."

"That's right. And Yang Fei was helping me spy on him," Andrew hoped Fritz wouldn't make the connection between what Charlie had just started to say, and the fact that Yang Fei had been helping him. He didn't want Fritz to know that he'd slept with her.

Fritz looked away, "I would have done anything for her. So when she asked me to deliver this message to you, I didn't hesitate for a second."

"So what's the message?"

Fritz was silent for a moment, and then to his surprise Andrew saw a tear run down Fritz's face.

"The last time I saw her was in the lobby of NOCCOC the day you escaped. It was crazy dude, I wish you could have seen it from my perspective. Der were dozen's of Lao Cheng's goons rushing toward the door when you fought your way out. I was like, damn, that boy Drew must have really pissed Lao Cheng off. Then suddenly, Yang Fei was there, tugging on my sleeve, and looking at me desperately. 'You have to help me,' she said. 'Der's no way out, and dey'll be coming after me soon too,' den she handed me this envelope," Fritz reached in his bag and pulled out a thick envelope, and handed it to Andrew. "'Find Drew and give dis to him,' she said. 'It's vitally important. Can I count on you, Fritz, darling?'"

"Yeah, I am sure those are exact words she use," Charlie snickered.

Fritz ignored him. "Dat bastard needs to pay for dis, Drew. I hope whatever is in here helps you bring him down. Someone like dat who can cover up a very obvious murder has far too much power."

"So you think she was murdered, too? Charlie and I read that story about her suicide in the newspaper, and I couldn't believe it."

"I know she was murdered. She would never have committed suicide."

"Thank you for your help, Fritz."

"Der's one more thing you should know, Drew."

"What's that?"

"I overheard a conversation between dat girl who came up to you at NOCCOC when we first met and her colleague."

Andrew tensed up. "You mean May?"

"Yeah, I think dat's her name. So I just happened to walk past her cubicle and heard her talking in a hushed voice with another girl. I wasn't going to listen, until I heard her mention your name. I was hoping she might know something about where you'd gone, you know? So I ducked down behind da cubical. I heard her saying how she didn't know where you were and dat she was worried about you. Her friend asked, 'What did you say when you talked to him on the phone?' 'Well,' and May lowered her voice even further so I had to listen very carefully. 'I told him I was pregnant,' she said. Her friend gasped and then asked, 'Are you really,' 'No, no, not really,' she replied.

"I bloody knew it," said Mazken.

"Wait, der's more. Den she started sobbing. 'I wish I hadn't told him dat, but I was feeling desperate and I didn't want to lose him. I had a feeling he might leave China, and dis was da only way to get him to stay,' or something like dat. I

227

may have not quite heard it right. It's hard to understand Chinese when people are whispering.

It took a moment for this news to sink in. It seemed like she wasn't working for Lao Cheng after all. Why else would she confess this to her friend? And now it was really starting to sink in. He'd made a big mistake.

"Drew, are you OK?" It seems that Fritz had noticed the look on his face.

"Not exactly. All this time I thought she was working against me. But it sounds like she just wanted the same thing that I did."

"Ah yes, women can be confusing like dat."

"You'd make a better spy than I would have guessed." Fritz just grinned. Then Andrew put his hand on Fritz's shoulder. "I will find a way to make Lao Cheng pay," he said, "I promise you that."

Fritz looked at him and smiled. "If you need any more help, I'm at your service."

They left Fritz and returned to Charlie's friend's apartment. Once there, Andrew opened the envelope. It contained a series of email printouts. As Andrew scanned through them, he noticed several mentions of something called the *Chinese Center for...* followed by a word that Andrew wasn't familiar with. When he used his dictionary, the translation came up as *Geoengineering*.

"What is geoengineering?" asked Charlie, looking over his shoulder.

"Sounds like engineering the earth, or the globe... or maybe global weather."

"Wow, so you think this is what you look for?"

Andrew read on. The emails described a number of chemicals that the center had been experimenting with, which would be spread around the upper atmosphere.

"What's the matter, mate?" Mazken had apparently noticed the confused look on his face.

"Well, this is not quite what I was expecting. My boss, the head of the organization I'm working for back in America, thought that the Chinese government would be using a large metal apparatus shooting ionic-pulses... like the one Charlie and I found out at Ping Guo Yuan. But this report is talking about using airplanes to spread chemicals in the upper atmosphere."

"A machine shooting out ionic-pulses? That sounds like something from Star Trek, mate. Planes spreading chemicals sounds a lot more... realistic."

Had the chemtrail theory been right all along? But this didn't quite match. Most of the chemtrail theories supposed that the government was using these chemicals to create artificial global warming. But these documents were talking about using chemicals to *cool* the Earth's climate. Andrew read on. The emails mentioned that a visit was scheduled in two days from an executive of Russia Oil & Gas. So the Russians were in on this as well. That would be news for Mr. Harrison. Andrew found it curious that both governments put this project in the hands of their state-owned oil companies, but it seemed fairly insignificant. Perhaps it was just a good way to cover the project up.

In the text of the last email was what looked like a set of GPS coordinates. Andrew put the coordinates into his phone, and the pin came up in the middle of an empty field. He zoomed the map out.

"I've got to go to Inner Mongolia."

"Why would you want to go there, mate? The girls are not as hot as you might have heard."

"That's where the weather control operation seems to be based. I've got to go and collect more evidence. I need proof that they are using this to influence weather in the U.S.," he looked at Charlie and Mazken. A plan was beginning to come together in his head. "And I'm going to need your help."

"No way, man. I not go on your investigation again. You know what almost happen last time."

"Someone from the Russian state oil company is supposed to visit this center the day after tomorrow. I'm going to show up a day early and impersonate him. But I can't do it alone."

"Interesting idea," mused Mazken. "But none of us speak any Russian."

"Actually I took some Russian in college, I can speak a little bit. But I doubt we'll run into any Russian speakers there. All that matters is that I speak English with a Russian accent. All white people look the same to Chinese, right Charlie?"

"You go without me."

"Come on, Charlie. I need a Chinese assistant and interpreter that's chaperoning me while I'm in China."

"And what's my role?" asked Mazken.

"Bodyguard, of course." Mazken grinned. Charlie folded his arms.

"Fine Kong Kong, stay here, we'll find some other Chinese rando to act as interpreter. They're a dime a dozen around here. Just don't tell Lao Cheng's thugs where we've gone when they show up, alright?"

"Ha, that's not going to work on me again."

"Just wait and see, mate. You know Fritz isn't smart enough to really avoid being followed. I'm sure one of Lao Cheng's men saw us meet with him and then followed us back to this apartment, and is probably calling for backup as we speak."

Charlie's face went pale. "You just try to manipulate me again, like you do everyone else."

Andrew wasn't really sure now if Mazken was actually making this up, or if he was serious. The possibility seemed pretty real, now that he considered it.

"Like I said Charlie, go ahead and stay here and find out. But if I were you, I'd come with us. I've heard Chinese prison really sucks."

Charlie bit his lip and seemed to be holding his breath.

"Let's go, Drew. No more time to waste here if Lao Cheng's men are on their way."

As they began walking out, Charlie finally burst. "Fine, I go. I hate you Mazken. You no-good scoundrel."

"Scoundrel? Where'd you pick that word up? Your English is improving, mate," Mazken chuckled.

"Just how you gonna get to middle of Inner Mongolia anyway?"

"There must be a train or a bus that goes there, right?"

Charlie let out a forced laugh, "Ha, no train or bus where you wanna go. That is middle of no man's land. The grassland stretches for hundreds of kilometers. Maybe there are not even paved roads."

"So what do you suggest?"

"There is only one way to get that far into Inner Mongolia."

"…Don't tell me we have to ride horses?"

Charlie shook his head, "Russian jeep."

"And where are we gonna find one of those?"

Charlie grinned, and Andrew had a feeling whatever he had in mind wasn't going to be entirely legal.

CHAPTER 31:

TRANSPORTATION

"Ok, very simple plan. I go talk with them, create distraction, you two pick lock on jeep, start it up, and away we go." Charlie had led them to a very industrial part of southern Beijing.

"How'd you know about this Charlie?"

"Short time ago I help them sell Mongolian vodka, but the business never take off."

They were crouching at the corner of the warehouse. Around the corner, a half dozen Mongolian men stood around smoking and talking. In the parking lot, about a hundred feet away, were parked six heavy-duty green jeeps.

"You sure this is a good idea? You might have the Mongolian mafia coming after you when we get back to Beijing."

"Nah, these guys is small time. They a bunch of cheats too; they never pay me for several cases of vodka I sell for them. No one wants to do business with people like this."

"They have six jeeps—what's to keep them from chasing after us once we steal one?"

Charlie wrinkled his face, "Good point, hmmm…"

"They are going to see us walking up to the jeeps too, even if you are talking to them, mate. There's about 30 meters of open parking lot and nowhere to hide. You've got to lure them inside, then lock them in," said Mazken.

"OK, OK, I know. I tell them I find new market for their vodka and want to talk about a new deal."

"When you hear the jeep start up, get out of there quickly and bolt the door behind you, ok? If you get into trouble mate, you just holler and we'll smash the door down with that jeep, yeah?"

"OK, I go now," Charlie walked back out to the main road and then strolled into the parking lot from the road. They watched him greet the Mongolian's, who didn't look happy to see him, but didn't look angry either.

"So far so good. At least that crack-head didn't piss them off too badly," Mazken commented. They watched him continue talking with the men, and then, as if on cue, they headed toward the door of the warehouse. However, two of the six men remained outside. Charlie glanced at them as he went through the door, but Andrew knew he couldn't do anything to make them all come. He and Mazken would have to deal with the remaining two.

"OK, follow my lead," said Mazken, and he strolled out around the corner into the parking lot. Andrew quickly followed him, wondering what Mazken was doing.

"G'day, mates!" Mazken said to the two men, who jumped and looked at him.

"Where does one find a good food joint around here? Me and my mate here were looking for some dinner."

The two men looked at each other, then one of them replied in a heavy accent, "No Engrish."

They were now about three feet away from the men. "No what? See, I was tryin' to find somewhere to eat on this map here, let me show you," Mazken walked up to one of the men while holding his phone as if to show something to the man. Realizing what Mazken was doing, Andrew got closer too. When they were both right next to them, Mazken delivered a sharp and quick chopping motion to the back of the man's head, while Andrew struck the man next to him across the forehead. Both men crumpled to the ground without a sound.

"Nicely done," said Mazken, slapping his hands together. "Now for the jeep."

As they sat in the front two seats, trying to hotwire it, Andrew turned to Mazken. "Why are you doing this? It's pretty dangerous, what we're about to do, you know. You didn't have to help me."

"The way I see it, mate, life is just a big experiment. If you don't take a few risks now and then, you don't learn anything. In my life I've been beaten, I've had bullets flying at me, I've climbed some of the highest mountains in the world, I've slept with lots of girls, I've even drunk tea with her Majesty the Queen of England. Yeah, I'll tell you about that one sometime. But I've never broken into a top-secret government facility. I figured that's something that should be on my bucket list, you know?"

"Well, I guess when you put it that way... but why did you convince Charlie to come?"

"Sometimes that kid needs a kick in the butt to make him do the right thing. Just like you. You know he loves his country, but he hates the Chinese government. He comes from a family of merchants that refused to join the Communist Party, and suffered as a result. He's wanted to do something to disrupt the system all his life, but he's become resigned and cynical. Maybe helping you will give him the jumpstart that he needs."

Just then the car engine began to turn over and then started up. "Here we go," said Mazken, and they both turned to look at the warehouse door. Moments later the door burst open and Charlie ran out. He came a few paces toward the jeep, then stopped, seeming to remember what he was supposed to do, and turned back to the door.

"Damnit, Kong Kong forgot to lock them in."

Charlie ran toward the door and slammed it shut just as one man was about to cross the threshold, hitting him square in the face. Charlie quickly bolted the door, then ran toward the jeep, now panting and huffing.

"Screw those bastards, they think they so sly, they try to make me pay in advance for vodka cases again. Well, they no mess with Charlie no more."

Mazken floored the gas and they took off toward the fourth ring road and the highway leading toward Inner Mongolia.

CHAPTER 32:

A SURPRISE ARRIVAL

"Wei?"

"Mr. Cheng, Dr. Stone wanted me to inform you that your Russian guest has arrived for his scheduled visit to the Geoengineering Center."

Cheng sat up in his chair and raised his eyebrows. *"Who?"*

"Sir... it's Mr. Ivanovich from Russia Oil and Gas. Don't you remember?"

"Of course I do. But he was scheduled to visit tomorrow."

"Well sir, he's here now. There was a little confusion at the gate. Just like you sir, we thought he wasn't coming until tomorrow. But apparently Mr. Stone got it straightened out. I watched him go into the Center with Dr. Stone."

"Jeep? He was supposed to come by plane."

"Apparently his plane was too big to land on our runway. They must have landed in Beijing and drove here."

Cheng stared at the phone. Something about this wasn't right.

"Who else is with him?"

"I saw one bodyguard and a Chinese interpreter."

"Can you describe Mr. Ivanovich? What did he look like?"

"Well, he was wearing a suit, skinny build, dark hair, about 170 centimeters tall I'd say..."

That was it. Cheng had met Mr. Ivanovich years ago, but

he knew the man was much more than 170 centimeters tall. This was clearly an imposter. And judging by the fact that there were three of them, this could only mean one thing: the little American had somehow found his way there.

"Thank you, soldier. Please send a message to Dr. Stone that Mr. Ivanovich must not be allowed to leave the Center."

"Uh, yes sir. Is something wrong?"

"That's not Mr. Ivanovich. It's an EJF terrorist who's come to destroy the facility."

Cheng hung up the phone. It was better that the soldiers thought they were with that pesky terrorist group. It was just more straightforward. If anyone suspected that another government had even the slightest idea of what was going on here, there might be those who wanted to postpone the launch. He'd waited long enough for this moment, and he wasn't going to risk another setback.

The fact that Andrew had shown up here, now, was an amazing development, in so many ways. He still couldn't understand how they had avoided capture so far, when they had clearly stayed in Beijing the whole time, right under his nose. Was he losing his edge? Or had someone else betrayed him and kept them out of his sight? The primary suspect of course would be May. She hadn't yet proven her loyalty to him. And hadn't all of her supposed attempts to find them so far failed?

But May could not have known about the Geoengineering Center. The only way the little American could have found out about that was through Yang Fei. Hadn't she been planning to give Andrew the coordinates, but had failed to do so before he caught her? He'd become quite good at knowing when people were lying to him, and Yang Fei's eyes had not betrayed a lie. Was it possible that she had deceived him?

If so, it had taken Andrew an unusually long time to find his way to the Center. But that could be explained in any number of ways. Maybe they had waited until the day before Mr. Ivanovich's scheduled visit so that it would look more like a scheduling mistake. Or maybe they had decided to just lie low until the heat of Cheng's search of them had faded. Or maybe, there had been a delay in them receiving the information because Yang Fei had hidden it somewhere for them to find. One thing was certain: they clearly had help that he wasn't aware of. Who would dare betray him, betray their country, to help this little American? It was hard for Cheng to imagine.

He would not underestimate Andrew again. This time, they would not escape. He would see to it personally.

CHAPTER 33:

GEOENGINEERING

Andrew was searching his brain wildly for a way out, but there was nothing. He'd just about resigned himself to being taken prisoner when he suddenly heard Mazken begin laughing. Had he finally cracked? Andrew looked over at him. Mazken just continued to laugh. Now the soldiers had paused, looking at him too, seeming momentarily confused.

"What's so funny?" Demanded Dr. Stone.

"I just realized what's going on here, comrade," said Mazken, in what Andrew could tell was his fake Russian voice. "You were expecting Ivan Ivanovich. But he is not what you expected. And that's because this is Ivan Ivanovich *junior*."

Andrew looked at Dr. Stone. He seemed suddenly confused. Well, that was progress.

"You see, Mr. Ivanovich has started training his son to take over for him, as Mr. Ivanovich senior is nearing retirement. He wanted Junior here to start going on important business trips by himself."

Mr. Stone turned his gaze abruptly to Andrew. All Andrew could do was stare at him and nod.

"And if this is the case, why didn't you land your jet on our runway? How did you get here?"

Of course a Russian oligarch would have flown directly here instead of coming in a jeep. How was Mazken going to explain this?

"There wasn't enough space on your runway for the size of his jet."

Mazken's tone held a touch of disdain. Andrew knew what he was implying. *Our jet is too big and important for your tiny runway.*

Dr. Stone still looked suspicious, *"Let me check with Mr. Cheng to make sure this is alright."* He pulled out a cell phone.

"Sure, go ahead and lose face to Mr. Cheng for getting our appointment wrong," now Charlie was stepping back in. *"Since you've already embarrassed Mr. Ivanovich, I'm sure Mr. Chen will be very forgiving. In fact, I'll make the call myself and Mr. Cheng can talk directly with Mr. Ivanovich."*

Charlie had clearly recovered too and was back to his clever self. He knew the man would not want to risk losing face with Lao Cheng. There were many people who were afraid of him.

Dr. Stone hesitated and looked at Mazken again, who suddenly looked grave and made a fist with one hand, while clasping it with the other. Even the two soldiers flanking Dr. Stone seemed to cringe a little in Mazken's presence. Finally Dr. Stone put the phone away. *"No, no, I guess it doesn't matter."* Then he switched to English and addressed Andrew.

"I apologize for the misunderstanding, but we just learned that a terrorist group may be trying to target this facility, so we're taking extra security precautions. I hope you can forgive me." He turned and barked a command at the soldiers, who immediately let go of them, and lowered their guns.

"It was an understandable mistake... comrade," Andrew said in what he hoped was a convincing Russian accent.

"Ha, yes, comrade," Dr. Stone laughed nervously. "Well, welcome to the Chinese Geoengineering Center. Please park your vehicle inside the gate, and then I will meet you at the main entrance." He turned and headed back toward the building. Andrew looked at Charlie, who gave a wide-eyed look and a tiny shrug. Mazken grinned and winked briefly at them, then resumed his scowl as they climbed back into the jeep.

A few minutes later, Andrew, Mazken and Charlie followed Dr. Stone down a long hallway, past rooms filled with hundreds of men and women sitting at computers in cubicles. Some stared at them as they passed. A group of soldiers passed them as they walked down the hallway. The whole facility felt like it was on high alert. Andrew was feeling more nervous with every step.

Soon they emerged into a large room filled with many scientists sitting at computers, and some scrambling back and forth between their computers and a giant holographic simulation of the earth in the center of the room.

"This is our main simulation laboratory," said Dr. Stone. "As you know, there are so many factors to take into account that our scientists are working around the clock trying to think of every possible scenario and its impact on the global climate." Dr. Stone paused and looked at Andrew. He seemed to be sizing Andrew up; judging whether he was really the tough Russian executive he was supposed to be. Andrew tried to look somewhat disinterested and gave a sharp nod.

Dr. Stone looked away quickly and continued. "We have been using the latest in holographic technology to visualize the effects of various levels of geoengineering using sulfur dioxide aerosol. Does the Russian laboratory use technology like this?" He looked eagerly at Andrew.

For a moment Andrew froze. Was this a trap? Perhaps the doctor already knew the answer and was testing Andrew.

"Why don't you show me what it's capable of before I judge," Andrew replied in his gruffest voice.

Dr. Stone turned to one of the technicians standing near the hologram and nodded. The technician pressed a few buttons, and the hologram began to change, showing several small dots moving across the globe and leaving lines behind them that began to spread out in a random pattern.

"We have been running simulations around the clock for the last few months, and it seems we've come up with something close to the ideal levels to create the global temperature drop that we're looking for: about 1 degree Centigrade, for now. We've been simulating the effect this will have on global weather patterns with our holographic earth image here. So far it seems that if we spray about a million tons of sulfur dioxide aerosol into the atmosphere annually with our small fleet of planes, that should stabilize the global temperature back to pre-industrial levels. Of course, if we were to use sulfur aerosols, those would have to be replenished regularly, as the particles fall out of the sky every two years or so. And the total amount would have to increase over time as global warming continues to increase. We suspect it would require doubling the original concentration within three decades.

The holographic image began to change, showing the clouds getting gradually denser. "With these amounts we should see an immediate reduction in the extreme weather events that have been increasing in intensity over the last several years, as well as a slow in the melting of the Arctic and Antarctic glaciers that are leading to sea level rise."

This wasn't right. Where was the hurricane creation simulation? Where was the weapon that would cause droughts, floods and heat waves in the U.S.? Instead, this man was talking about reversing global warming.

"Is this similar to what your researchers came up with?"

Andrew looked around and realized Dr. Stone was addressing him again.

"Uh, yes, it's about the same."

Dr. Stone raised an eyebrow and then nodded. "But here's the exciting thing," he turned to the technician again. "*Show them particle X.*" The image immediately returned to its original state. Then the dots, which Andrew now assumed represented planes, began moving across the globe again. This time, instead of white, their contrails were a light yellow color.

"We just had a breakthrough in creating an artificial nano-particle with similar properties to the sulfur aerosol particles. But this particle was made with electrostatic materials that can use photophoretic forces to remain suspended in the stratosphere longer," he paused. "We estimate that they will be able to stay in the atmosphere for nearly 50 years without needing to be replenished," he looked at them with an expectant smile. Andrew just stared. He hadn't understood half of what Dr. Stone had just said, but it seemed, based on the way the man was looking at him, that they had made a significant breakthrough.

Dr. Stone's smile faded, and he continued. "Of course this means we need to be extra certain that we've got the concentration right the first time, but once we put them up there, the world would cool permanently for five decades and save us a lot of money on replenishing."

So they wanted to cool the temperature of the entire earth in order to slow global warming. And once they began spreading this particle into the atmosphere, it would be irreversible for fifty years. Andrew wasn't quite sure what to make of it. But something about it made him feel uneasy.

"Now let's move on to the main event. I know you really came to see the planes," Dr. Stone led them out the other side of the simulation room, and soon they found themselves in a giant hanger, where one of the planes they had seen outside appeared to be under construction.

"We've developed and built specialty planes for high altitude flights that can also carry a heavy payload. We started with a B-2 stealth aircraft design, since these planes will need to avoid detection, then we had to lengthen the wingspan to something similar to the U-2 spy planes, and added a more powerful engine so the plane can get 13 tons of the particle up to 60,000 feet – well into the stratosphere where it can be released for the greatest effect. As you can see, we're just putting the finishing touches on the last plane now. But they are basically ready for take-off. We made sure they were ready a week sooner in order to accommodate the new timeline," he added, glancing sideways at Andrew.

"Each plane ended up costing about a billion dollars to build, but we only need about half a dozen of them for the operation. And since the costs will be spread out between

NOCCOC, Russia Oil & Gas, Canadian Oil, Arabia Co, and Rothschild Industries, they should be quite affordable. Oh, excuse me for a moment." An aid had run up to Dr. Stone with a message.

Canadian Oil? *Rothschild Industries*? For a moment Andrew thought he'd heard him wrong. He had named the company of Will Rothschild, who had spoken at his graduation. There were Americans working with them on this project. Andrew's head was spinning. And clearly it was not governments, but the oil industry that was behind this geoengineering project, whatever their purpose was. Andrew had a million questions he wanted to ask, but he was afraid if he didn't choose his questions carefully, he might blow their cover.

"What they do here, it doesn't look like they create weather disasters like you say," Charlie hissed to Andrew while Dr. Stone was giving instructions to the aid. "You think they have any other research?"

"Other research? What other research would we be working on?" Dr. Stone had clearly overheard them.

"Like how to create and control localized weather events," Andrew said.

"Ha, we gave up that research years ago." Dr. Stone began walking out of the hanger back into the lab and indicated for them to follow him. "Have the Russians still been messing around with the HAARP technology?" Dr. Stone seemed to be having a hard time hiding the fact that he took pleasure in thinking that the Russian's were clearly behind the times.

"Ah, yes, we think it has great potential... especially for military applications," Andrew stated, trying to sound confident.

"I would be quite surprised if you managed to find a use for it," said Dr. Stone. "We found it impossible to predictably create or control localized weather events. There were just too many factors involved, and too much feedback. Changing the weather in one region of the earth had unexpected consequences in other regions. Some of our ionosphere heating experiments ended in disaster. You must have heard about those freak ice storms in Hong Kong several years ago? And anyway, everyone is far more concerned now with the impacts of climate change than with controlling local weather."

So, Mr. Harrison had been wrong all along. Lao Cheng wasn't working on a conspiracy to control the weather in the U.S. But why were he and these other oil companies concerned about climate change? It was the oil industry that for the longest time had denied that climate change was even happening. But Andrew realized he didn't have time to make sense of all this now. He was still on a mission. He needed to get proof of what was going on here. Whatever the reason, these were still secrets that needed to be revealed.

They had arrived back in the computer lab. Andrew signaled to Charlie, the one signal that they had planned beforehand. "Thank you for the tour, Dr. Stone. Mr. Ivanovich would like me to download your most recent findings and data so that we can compare it with what we've discovered." Rather than waiting for permission, Charlie turned toward the nearest computer and signaled for the person sitting there to move aside. But as he did so, Dr. Stone grabbed his arm.

"Why do you need to download the data now? We can send it to your colleagues later," Dr. Stone had switched back to Chinese.

"Oh, of course..." Charlie glanced at Andrew and Mazken, then turned back to Dr. Stone. "But Mr. Ivanovich would at least like your latest report so he can read it on the flight back. He's very busy you know, and won't have time later."

Dr. Stone stared at him for a moment, "Fine, I'll have my assistant print you a copy. I'm sure that will be much more... convenient for his reading. Now if you'll excuse me for a moment, I have something to attend to."

Dr. Stone instructed the man at the computer to print the document and then walked off, leaving Charlie, Andrew and Mazken alone with the assistant.

"Do you think it is enough?" Charlie whispered.

Andrew just shrugged. He didn't want to risk their conversation being overheard. He looked at Mazken, who seemed to be enjoying his bodyguard role. He was still staring sullenly forward, but Andrew caught him winking at a pair of woman scientists who were staring at him from down the row of cubicles.

As the report was finishing its print, Dr. Stone returned, accompanied again by two soldiers with automatic rifles. Andrew could tell there was something wrong. Then the two soldiers parted and a man stepped into the room that Andrew knew all too well, and that sent shivers down his spine.

"Hello An-de-ru," said Lao Cheng.

CHAPTER 34:

DIVISION

He knew they didn't have time to think. Andrew looked at Charlie, and then both of them lunged toward the gunmen.

The men seemed unprepared for this assault, and Andrew and Charlie managed to knock the guns out of their hands. As they did so, one of the guns went off, shooting a hole in the ceiling. There were screams from all over the room, as several scientists ducked for cover under their desks.

The soldiers were clearly trained in martial arts themselves, but he and Charlie had the element of surprise. Soon the two soldiers were lying on the ground, unconscious. Dr. Stone looked like he was about to run, while Lao Cheng reached for his phone, but suddenly Mazken's voice bellowed, "Bie dong." *Don't move.*

Andrew turned and saw that Mazken had picked up one of the guns and was pointing it straight at Lao Cheng. He was holding it very comfortably as if he'd been trained to use one. Andrew looked around and quickly grabbed the other gun off the floor.

"I knew you weren't Russian the whole time," blurted Dr. Stone. "You're with the Economic Justice Front, aren't you? Well, you're not going to destroy this facility."

The Economic Justice Front? Is that what Lao Cheng wanted them to think?

"Shut up," Mazken commanded in English, and Dr. Stone went silent. "Andrew, do you have what you need?"

Andrew quickly scanned the report that had been printed and realized that it was a computer diagnostic report. Useless. He quickly pushed the man at the computer out of the way.

"Charlie, help me look through these files, they printed a useless document."

Lao Cheng began to chuckle, "You not find-a anything,"

"This is the guy who hacked into your NOCCOC security camera system. He can hack anything, *Lao Cheng*," Andrew added. If he could piss him off enough, maybe he could make a mistake that would allow them to escape.

Lao Cheng's eyes flared with anger.

"Forget the damn files man, we gotta get outa here."

Lao Cheng's anger faded and a smile broke across his face. "Even if you get-a files, you never escape. My soldiers at-a every exit, and more coming now."

"Cao," Charlie swore in Chinese.

"I don't think we can hold off a whole company of soldiers with just two guns, mates."

Andrew had an idea. He grabbed Charlie and began steering him toward the computer, as he whispered, "They must have some sort of evacuation alarm. Get on the computer and find a way to set it off." Charlie nodded and sat down at the computer. "But search for the files we need first," Andrew hissed. "Otherwise they might get suspicious. And do you really want to leave here empty-handed after we came all this way?"

"We might not leave here at all, man." But he began typing away furiously, staring at the computer screen with his head tilted to one side and his mouth slightly open. Andrew had seen this look before. It was a rare moment when Charlie was concentrating hard.

"Look for information on particle X, designs of the planes, and anything you can find about the companies involved," Andrew said using a normal voice again.

"My soldiers come-a soon. Then we take you somewhere

to die-a slowly."

Andrew pointed his gun at Lao Cheng's crotch. "Keep talking and I'll make sure you die slowly. You're going to pay one way or another for killing Yang Fei."

Lao Cheng grimaced. "It is-a you who kill Yang Fei. When I find out she-a spy for you, I have-a no choice."

"Got it," Charlie exclaimed.

New pages began coming out of the printer.

Then the alarm started going off. Andrew looked around. Sure enough, all the scientists in the room had been hiding under their desks, taking Mazken's 'don't move' command as applying to them too. But at the sound of the alarm, they began to rise cautiously, looking around.

"Mei yi ge ren wang chukou zou qu," *Everyone head toward the exits*, Charlie shouted at them. "*You will not be harmed.*"

They didn't need a second prompting. All the scientists began to hurry toward the doors on either side of the room.

"Bie ting tamen jiang the hua," *Don't listen to them*, Lao Cheng shouted. "*It's a false alarm. These traitors set it off. Stop them!*" But his words seemed to be lost amongst the scrambling workers.

Andrew picked up the documents coming out of the printer and scanned through them. It was a collection of schematics showing how particle X worked, the designs for the planes, and there was also a budget detailing the contributions required from each of the involved companies. It would be enough to grab headlines.

Andrew glanced at the printer. There were still pages coming out.

"We've got to go now Drew," Mazken growled.

"Hold on," Andrew practically yanked the last page from the feed.

"We're all set."

"Then let's get the hell out of here. Grab these two so we can use them as human shields and they don't alert the soldiers."

Andrew grabbed Dr. Stone around the neck, putting his hand over his mouth, and pointing the gun at the man's head. Mazken did the same with Lao Cheng. With Charlie in the lead, they dragged them into the crowd of people heading for the exits. With everyone jostling to get out as quickly as possible, the hallway was very crowded, and they were forced to walk at a normal pace.

When they had nearly reached the doors leading out to the parking lot, Andrew saw that there were two soldiers on either side of the doorway. Andrew tried his best to hide behind Dr. Stone, but he knew that soon they would be noticed. However, Charlie got to them first. Pausing in between them, Charlie delivered nearly simultaneous chops to both their heads and the men crumpled to the ground. There were a few shouts from the crowd, but Charlie smiled disarmingly. "Zou, zou, mei wenti," *Keep going, there's nothing wrong.*

"Pick up one of those guns Charlie,"

"But I don't know how to use it!" cried Charlie.

"It's not that hard to use. Just point it at the bad guys."

Outside now, Andrew scanned around quickly and saw that a group of soldiers had congregated by a flag pole about 50 feet away from the door, probably the designated evacuation meeting point. Soldiers always followed protocol. Behind them was a line of jeeps and trucks. Luckily, their jeep was parked separately in the guest parking area, and they had a clear path to it.

"Charlie, Mazken and I are going to walk with Dr. Stone and Lao Cheng between us and the soldiers. You walk behind us, with your gun pointing at them."

"But what if they start firing at us?"

"They won't, not as long as Lao Cheng is exposed." Dr. Stone began to struggle a little. Andrew gripped him tighter, "You better stop moving if you don't want a bullet in your head." Andrew looked at Lao Cheng, and could see the fire in his eyes. But Mazken was holding him tightly with his powerful arms.

As they began to walk, one of the soldiers spotted them.

He shouted, and the soldiers got into a formation, facing them.

"*We've got Cheng here. Don't shoot or he's dead,*" shouted Charlie.

"I think they can see that, mate."

Charlie shrugged "I just make sure."

They were about halfway to the jeep when Andrew saw one of the soldiers lift a radio to his mouth and say something that he didn't understand. He looked at Charlie.

Charlie had gone pale. "They have a sniper on the roof. Run."

Mazken smashed his gun across Lao Cheng's head, and the man crumpled to the ground. Andrew did the same to Dr. Stone, and they began to sprint for the jeep. The soldiers began to open fire. Charlie reached the jeep first, jumped into the driver's seat and started it up, as bullets grazed the windshield. "Luckily this is military-grade," he shouted, "bulletproof glass." Andrew felt something hit his foot. He braced for pain, but it didn't come. Must have been a dud. He had just literally dodged a bullet. He jumped into the back seat behind Charlie. Mazken stumbled, then heaved himself into the other seat alongside Andrew.

Charlie put the jeep into drive, then stepped on the accelerator. But instead of turning for the exit, he put his foot to the floor and headed straight for the soldiers.

"What are you doing Charlie? Are you crazy?"

"We've got to make sure they can't follow us." The soldiers saw them coming and scattered to both sides as the jeep plowed through them. "Mazken, you've got to shoot the tires of the other vehicles," Charlie shouted. Andrew looked at Mazken. He was leaning over, clutching his side.

"I think he's been shot," said Andrew.

"Someone needs to shoot those tires."

Andrew lifted his gun and began firing at the wheels of the other vehicles as Charlie drove past them. Once they had reached the end of the line, Charlie turned sharply and began heading for the gate.

"Did you get them?" Charlie yelled.

Andrew looked back and saw, to his surprise and delight that he'd managed to get at least one tire on each vehicle. "Yes, let's go."

"Cao," Charlie swore again. "They are closing the gate. That gate looks pretty heavy duty. I'm not sure this vehicle could knock it down." He floored the gas again. Andrew saw the gate rolling slowly closed. It looked like they had about three car widths. Then two.

They sped through the gap, knocking one of the mirrors off as they went.

"Woohooo, we made it!"

Now Andrew turned his attention to Mazken.

"Mazken, are you OK? What happened?"

"Oh, it's only a flesh wound," Mazken gave a weak grin.

"Mazken?" Charlie looked back at him.

"Keep your eyes on the road, crackhead. We can't afford to end up in a ditch."

Andrew pulled up Mazken's shirt. There was blood trickling out of a hole in his side. "We've got to get you to a hospital.

"The nearest hospital is back in Beijing."

Andrew's heart sank. Could Mazken make it that long? "Charlie, do we have extra cloth of any kind? We need to make a tourniquet to stop the bleeding."

Charlie looked around. "I don't see anything."

Andrew ripped off part of the shirt he was wearing and tied it around Mazken's waist, pulling it tight over the bullet hole.

"Ok, we're going to get you back to Beijing in no time, Mazken. Just hang on." They floored it on the long drive back, going as fast as the roads would allow. Charlie and Andrew took turns driving, and Charlie tried to pass the time by talking to Mazken, retelling all the stories of their adventures in Beijing over the last few years. The morning turned into afternoon, with the sun beating down, and Mazken began to slip in and out of consciousness. At one point he seemed to have passed out. They were approaching the edge of Beijing.

Then Mazken awoke and called out to Andrew and Charlie.

"I can't come there Mazken, I'm driving," said Andrew. "We're taking you to Peking University Hospital. I can see the edge of the campus up ahead. We'll be there in ten minutes."

"Pull over and come back here you crackhead, I'm not going to make it that long."

"What are you talking about? You're going to be fine."

"Andrew, you've got to do me one last favor," Mazken's voice sounded really faint now. "Contact my mum... Mabel Wilson in Rockhampton, Australia. I haven't talked... to her since I went into the military. She probably... already thinks I'm dead. Tell her how...I died. Tell her...that I love..."

Mazken's voice trailed off. "Hold on Mazken, we're almost there." Andrew flew onto another road and began dodging around cars.

"I think he gone, Drew."

"God damnit Charlie, shut up, will you? I don't need your pessimism right now. He's probably just passed out. We need to get him to a hospital now."

"Hey, don't get mad at me, it is not me who drag us into this."

"This is no time to start pointing fingers, Kong Kong."

"*Stop* calling me that," Charlie shoved Andrew. The jeep went swerving to the side. Andrew managed to regain control and just missed hitting a car. "Will you cut it out, Charlie? You're going to get us all killed."

"I knew this is bad idea. Why Mazken listens to you? We should just stay in Beijing and keep on with our normal life, not go with you off on some stupid mission."

"We don't have time to argue about this now. Mazken is about to die, and I need you to direct me. Where's the turn off for Peking University Hospital?"

Charlie looked around, "Right here," he pointed. Andrew slammed on the break and swerved right onto the road. Now he could see the hospital building up ahead.

"Contact my mum..." Mazken seemed to have woken up again momentarily, but then went silent again.

Minutes later they pulled up to the front door of the hospital with a screech as Andrew slammed on the breaks. He and Charlie jumped out and dragged Mazken, supporting him on either side, toward the front door. Mazken was not moving at all.

"*Get us a stretcher, will you?*" Charlie barked at the nearest hospital staff, who jumped and then scurried away. Moments later she had returned with a small group of nurses wheeling a stretcher.

"*What's his condition?*" Asked a doctor who had walked over.

"*He's been shot in the side.*"

The doctor blinked and stared. Andrew remembered that guns were not at all common in China. The only people who had them were the police... and the mafia.

It seems Charlie had noticed the doctor's surprise, because he reached in his pocket, pulled out a wad of 100s, and handed it to the doctor. Andrew also noticed that Charlie had turned sideways so that the gun he'd acquired from the center and clipped onto his belt was clearly visible to the doctor.

"*You'd better make sure he survives, understand?*"

The doctor stared at the bills, then glanced at the gun, and nodded. He followed the stretcher down the hall and out of sight. Charlie and Andrew watched as Mazken was wheeled off.

"Let's go back to your friend's apartment, Charlie. I need to call my boss and tell him what's happened. Hopefully, he'll have an idea of how we can stop these guys from starting this geoengineering."

"Not safe to go back to my friend's house, remember? Lao Cheng probably knows where we live."

"So where do you propose we go now?"

"Now *I* go home to Wenzhou and stay with my parents."

"What? But I need your help, Charlie. Didn't you hear what they're about to do? The climate of the entire world is about to get permanently altered by a bunch of corporate thugs. Don't you want to bring down Lao Cheng? And what about getting rich?"

"We didn't get any data, just your damn documents. And you hear Dr. Stone, there is no way to know exactly what will happen with local weather. It is too unpredictable. If it's not predictable, we don't make any money."

"What about taking a stand for something once in your goddamn life?"

"Don't tell me what to do. I listen to you too much already, and all you do is get me into trouble. And maybe you get Mazken killed. Soon, I am next. I am done with this." Charlie turned and walked back to the jeep.

"What are you going to do with that?"

"Sell it. Don't wanna be seen driving it around." Charlie started the engine.

"This is bigger than both of us, Charlie," Andrew yelled over the noise. "You can't hide from Lao Cheng forever. Sooner or later, he'll come after you and your parents."

"Chinese government comes after us many times. We are fine so far without your help."

Charlie put the jeep into gear and drove away.

For a few moments, Andrew just watched him drive away. A feeling of deep emptiness was welling up inside him. He needed to stay focused. He began fishing in his pocket for the phone he used to call Mr. Harrison.

"Hello? What did you have for dinner son?"

"Oh for the love of God, Mr. Harrison, I don't have time for this."

"Do not use the Lord's name in vain, son."

"I've made a breakthrough, Mr. Harrison. I uncovered the real plot that Mr. Cheng has been working on. But it's not what we thought."

"Not what we thought? What do you mean?"

"I just barely escaped from a research station far out in Inner Mongolia where they are preparing to dump billions of tons of this experimental particle into the upper atmosphere in order to slow down the warming of the entire planet from climate change. And guess what? They are working with a group of oil companies from Russia, Saudi Arabia, Canada and America."

"What are you talking about son? This must be another Chinese deception. They've been spreading lies about climate change for years…"

"No, no, I learned about it from Lao Cheng's emails. I asked the leader of the facility if they had ever experimented with local weather control, and he said they had, but were never able to perfect it. That explains why the Chinese HAARP station I found several weeks ago was practically abandoned. And this place was way out in the middle of the grasslands and heavily guarded. Clearly they don't want people to find it."

"Now, now son, you've clearly been misled somehow. Perhaps the director of that facility was feeding you false information."

"One of my friends was shot as we were escaping and may not survive, and we were lucky to escape at all. They clearly didn't want to be discovered."

"You had friends with you on the mission? I told you this mission is strictly classified."

"I needed help. How could you expect me to carry out this mission on my own in the first place?" Now that the thought occurred to Andrew, it seemed ridiculous how little help he'd been given. And Mr. Harrison didn't seem to be taking anything he said seriously. "I'm going to send you the report we printed at the facility. It explains everything."

"That won't be necessary, son."

"What do you mean?"

"If this is all you could come up with, then your mission has failed."

"But I thought you wanted me to uncover what Lao Cheng was up to? I did that. This is the truth. And it doesn't seem like something that should be kept a secret. You should use the Institute to expose what's going on."

"We will do no such thing. I asked you to find proof that the Chinese government was conducting weather warfare, and you failed to do that. We don't have any time left."

"But there isn't any weather warfare program, that's what I'm telling you. How am I supposed to complete a mission that's based on a false assumption?"

"I'm sorry son, we're done here."

Andrew said nothing for a moment. He couldn't believe what he was hearing.

"Fine, then I need to come home. You've got to get me out of China. Lao Cheng will almost certainly have issued an order to prevent me from leaving."

He waited for Mr. Harrison's response, but nothing came.

"Do you understand what I'm saying? I need your help, otherwise, I'll be stuck here," Andrew insisted.

Finally, Mr. Harrison spoke. "You disobeyed my instructions, son. So if you want to come home now, that's something you're gonna have to sort out on your own. We're not bringing you home until you can find me what I asked for." And Mr. Harrison hung up.

Andrew looked at the phone and then threw it as hard as he could at a nearby rock, where it burst into several pieces. Some of the hospital staff looked over with alarm.

Mr. Harrison was clearly delusional. Andrew couldn't believe he had ever trusted him. It seemed that Mr. Harrison had some agenda and had never been interested in the truth. Why had he ever come here? As he thought about it, he realized he'd been caught up in his mother's death. It was an irrational decision. How had he ever expected that he could become a real spy? How could he hope to stop something that was so much bigger than him?

Now he was utterly on his own, with no way out of China, and no one to turn to.

Except for Jonah Wong. He had been a good friend of Andrew's father, and he was the only person Andrew could trust now.

He pulled out his smartphone and was about to dial Chu, when he noticed an email message highlighted on his screen. It was from May. He hesitated, and then opened it.

I guess you must have blocked me on your phone because it never rings when I try to call you. I know you're mad at me... but I'm sick now and I'm in the hospital. Actually I never told you, but I've been sick for a long time. I wish you'd come and see me. I'm at the Peking University Hospital, room 804.

Love,
May

What did she mean? She hadn't seemed sick to Andrew. The words left a sinking feeling inside of him. What if she was fatally ill?

And now, by some glitch of the universe, she was at the same hospital as him. He couldn't leave without seeing her first. And maybe, if she really wasn't working for Lao Cheng, he could salvage their relationship.

CHAPTER 35:

NEXT MOVES

Howard Harrison sat at his desk, puffing on his pipe. Andrew had really disappointed him. Someone in China had clearly found a way to manipulate him into believing this rubbish about geoengineering, and now he was compromised. There was no way to recover the mission. In a week, the UNFCCC would likely come up with a new treaty committing the U.S. to spend hundreds of billions of dollars to fight climate change, while China continued to get a free ride. And weather disasters would continue plaguing America.

But the little voice of doubt in the back of his mind that Jeff Chen had created was now growing stronger. What if he and Andrew were right? What if there really was no weather war, but instead a different, international plot to cool the climate in response to global warming? But that was preposterous. Global warming had always been a hoax, created by the Chinese, and then advanced by those who wanted to increase the power of government. Even if it really was happening, it wasn't nearly as bad as they wanted the public to believe.

And why would oil companies get together to cool the climate in such an aggressive way? That would mean they had accepted man-made climate change as a real thing, which was absurd. China was the real threat here. Why was no one else paying attention?

Howard didn't like the fact that he was beginning to doubt his own convictions. He was getting too soft in his old age. Certainly he had been wrong before, but more times than not, when it was him against the establishment, everyone eventually came around to his way of thinking. And it was often in the face of utter defeat that he came up with a brilliant solution.

He needed to find inspiration now. But he also needed a plan. Surely the board chairman would be able to help him sort through this new turn of events.

He reached for his phone and began to dial.

CHAPTER 36:

THE PEKING UNIVERSITY HOSPITAL

When Andrew arrived on the eighth floor, he was stopped from entering the ward by a locked door. A man standing at a desk near the entrance motioned for him to come over.

"*Who are you here to see?*"

"*Li Mei.*"

The man typed something into the computer and stared at the screen.

"*She just finished intensive treatment and needs to rest. No visitors now.*"

Intensive treatment? "*Is she alright?*"

"*Her condition is stable, but only time will tell if she's fully cured. Heavy fatigue is a common occurrence among malaria patients.*"

Andrew was shocked. "*She has malaria? How is that possible?*"

"*She probably contracted it just like most people—from a mosquito bite.*" The man was looking more and more annoyed with him. "*Now what is your relationship to her?*"

"*I'm her... boyfriend.*"

The man raised his eyebrows at him.

"*I need to see her now.*"

"*I'm sorry but that's not possible. Like I said, she needs to rest."*

Andrew ignored the man and walked back over to the door, where he pulled out a paperclip and began picking the lock. It took the man a few moments to realize what he was doing.

"Hey, what are you doing? I said don't disturb her," The man came around the desk toward him. Just as he was about to reach Andrew, the door clicked open. Andrew was through it in a moment and began running down the hall, calling out for May.

"I'm here!" He heard her voice from behind one of the doors and burst into the room, where he found her lying on a bed. He walked up to her and took her hand between his, caressing it as he looked at her tired face. She looked back at him and smiled weakly.

"Is it true you have malaria?"

May looked away, then nodded her head.

Just then the man burst into the room. *"You must leave her alone to rest, young man."* He tried to grab Andrew's arm and drag him away.

"What are you doing!" May snarled at the man, and for a brief moment, she seemed energized again. *"I want him here."*

Startled, the man backed away. *"As you like, but he can't stay more than ten minutes."* Then he bustled out.

"Why didn't you ever tell me?"

She looked up at him again. "I didn't know it had relapsed until after you left NOCCOC, and then after that, well, we weren't on very good terms, and I thought you would... treat me differently."

"You mean I wouldn't want to be with someone who was sick?"

She nodded. "When it began to come back, I thought it could be treated permanently, but these doctors have been giving me medications for days, and they only seem to be somewhat effective. I need to get treatment abroad somewhere, like the U.S. They have more advanced procedures for treating it there."

"How did you get it in the first place? It seems like it was months ago, but then you would have been in the U.S..."

"Yes, I did get it in the U.S. I was on a spring break trip to Florida. We were touring the Everglades and I must have been bitten by a mosquito that was carrying it."

"But I've never heard of people in Florida contracting malaria..."

"Well, apparently I was one of several hundred cases that were reported for the first time in Florida this year. They said the warming climate is likely causing it to spread further north."

The warming climate. For the last few minutes he'd only been thinking about May, but now the events of the last twelve hours came to the front of his mind again. He was no longer working for Mr. Harrison, which meant he wasn't obligated to keep his mission a secret. And he was tired of keeping secrets from May. He didn't want there to be any more barriers between them.

"May, I have something important to tell you," he began. She looked at him expectantly. He opened his mouth, and then closed it again. "I don't know where to begin. I, I haven't been completely honest with you about why I came to China." It was time to just let it all out. "I was sent here to expose a secret weapon that the Chinese government was using against the U.S... except it turned out not to be true. I was investigating Lao Cheng because he was supposed to be the leader of the whole thing. And he is, but it's not what we expected—I mean the organization that hired me isn't—and I just found this secret facility in the middle of Inner Mongolia where they have some plan to start dumping billions of tons of particles into the upper atmosphere, and that's supposed to slow down climate change. But they are keeping the whole thing a big secret...."

He suddenly stopped, because May seemed to be stifling a laugh. "What's so funny?" He demanded.

"Nothing, you just sound like a schoolboy who's trying to come up with a million excuses for why he didn't do his homework."

Andrew opened his mouth to retort, and then closed it again. May began to giggle. "It's not funny." He insisted. "I'm trying to tell you that everything I told you about what I was doing in China was pretty much a lie."

May stopped laughing. "I know," she said quietly.

Andrew looked at her. She had a slightly guilty look on her face. "What do you mean?"

"I mean, I've known you were a spy for a while now."

"What? But if you weren't working for... Was I that obvious?"

"No, not at all. At least, you certainly had me fooled. But when you started seeing Yang Fei..." she trailed off.

"How did you know about that?"

"I saw you together at Houhai."

So she had seen him after all. "So you knew I was using her to get closer to Lao Cheng."

"Were you? You seemed more interested in her than that."

Now it was Andrew's turn to look guilty. "You're right, I was. I did fall for her a little bit." He stared off into space for a moment. "But that still doesn't explain how you knew I was a spy."

May began to puff out her lower lip and her eyes widened. "Don't hate me for this, Xiao Niu. I was so jealous of you and her and I, I went too far," she trailed off and looked at the floor.

And then it hit Andrew like an iron ball had smashed into his stomach. "You *told Lao Cheng* about us? But you must have known what would happen."

"I didn't think he would react the way he did."

"You didn't think he would react that way? I thought you were smarter than that, May." Andrew turned and began heading for the door. It had been a mistake coming to see her.

"Andrew, wait, just let me explain."

"You realize you almost got me killed. And look what happened to her. There's no explaining to do."

"Andrew wait, *please*." She was sobbing now. Andrew paused at the door. As angry as he was, he couldn't leave her like this. Not again. "There's more to it than that. I was trying to gain his trust, because I'm, well, you might say I'm a spy too."

Andrew let out a snort. "Seriously? For who?"

"They, I mean we are called the Economic Justice Front. I've been working with them since I came back."

"Wait, the men at the geoengineering center thought we were working for them too."

"That makes sense. They know we are onto them. We are fighting against the corruption of big companies like NOCCOC and the governments that enable them, in China and around the world, often by targeting and destroying their key assets."

"Great, good for you." It seemed that May had gotten his sarcasm this time because she gave him another guilty look.

"Andrew, I'm so sorry. I thought he would just fire you, and maybe Yang Fei too. But as soon as I told him I knew it was a mistake because his face went red and I could practically see his veins popping out. He immediately began making phone calls to security, demanding that both of you be brought to his office and to use any force necessary, and then I knew it was worse than I'd planned. I guess he was really in love with Yang Fei too. She seemed to have that effect on many men." There was still a hint of jealousy in May's voice.

"Well you don't have to worry about her anymore, do you? I bet you're happy about what happened to her."

"No, not at all." Her voice had turned pleading. "I never dreamed that would happen to her. I felt so horrible for many days. I still do. And the worst part is, Lao Cheng must have realized why I told him because he called me back to his office. And he *thanked* me for tipping him off," She had a disgusted look on her face. "Then he told me that you were an American spy and that you had escaped, and he needed my help to find you."

"So I was right from the beginning. You were working with him."

"Actually, I never tried to help him. None of this started until a while after we... hooked up in that office." Now May gave a slight smile. "I did what any good double agent would do. I *pretended* to cooperate. He said that I should try to find out where you were staying. At first, I told him you'd fled to Shanghai, but a few days later he called me back in and told me his men had almost caught you in a hotel in Beijing, and that you'd likely lied to me, probably because you suspected me. He insisted that I try to rebuild your trust and meet you if I could. Well, that's when I…" She stopped and looked down.

"That's when you decided to tell me you were pregnant?"

May looked up, "So you know it's not true?"

"A friend of mine overheard you talking to your friend at work."

May looked slightly relieved. "I was hoping Fritz would tell you about that conversation."

"You knew he was listening?"

"Come on, Andrew. You know Fritz is about as subtle as a freight train."

Andrew almost laughed. "I suppose you're right."

"Anyway, I was trying to get you to come meet me so I could…"

"So you could turn me over to Lao Cheng?"

"Of course not. Can't you see that I'm on your side? I assumed he was using my phone to track me, and I had already spotted the man he had tailing me, so I could have easily given him the slip and gone to meet you without anyone knowing. I wanted to tell you what was going on, but I couldn't tell you over the phone, in case he was listening. I knew that if I told you I was pregnant that would at least get your attention. You'd either want to come see me, and then I could tell you what was happening, or you'd be scared away. Either way, you'd be safe."

Andrew didn't say anything. He didn't want to tell her how impressed he was by how much she'd thought this through. It seemed that she had made a much better spy than him.

May watched him. "You mentioned earlier how you found a facility where they are planning to dump particles into the atmosphere and slow down global warming. You know that's exactly the place the EJF has been looking for. They're trying to stop them too. So it looks like the people we're both working for have the same objective."

"Not really. I'm not working for anyone anymore. My former boss thought the Chinese government was creating weather disasters in the U.S. to weaken its economy. When I discovered that wasn't true and told him, he didn't want to believe it and basically gave me the boot."

May sat up. "Then you should come work with us. You have vital information that they've been trying to find for months." She looked at Andrew and seemed to sense his hesitation. "What's the matter?"

"I don't know anything about this EJF. And the last guy I worked for turned out to be nuts. How do I know these people won't be the same?"

"Trust me, just come meet them and see for yourself. They are good people."

"Trust you? After what you did?"

"Well, who else are you going to trust now? Don't you want to expose these guys and see Lao Cheng get locked away? If so, you're going to need help."

Andrew knew she was right. And he wanted to believe her. He looked at her face, then at her arm, which she was using to prop herself up, and traced it down to her hand. And then he noticed her phone sitting on the bedside table. And suddenly he felt uneasy.

"Are you sure Lao Cheng isn't tracking you still?"

May looked where he was looking and seemed to understand. "No, I'm sure. This is a new phone."

"And no one is following you?"

"Like I said, Lao Cheng was having me followed for a while. So a few days ago I told him that I'd lost contact with you, and I put in my resignation at NOCCOC, telling him that I was moving back to Sichuan. Then I sold my old phone with the tracking device to someone who I knew was *really* going to Sichuan. Since then, no one has followed me."

"How do you know?"

"Well, it was pretty obvious when there *was* someone following. I could spot the guy from a mile away. You'd think they would be more clever about it."

"But what if Lao Cheng *wanted* you to know you were being followed, as a kind of subtle threat. Now that you aren't working for him anymore, if he is having you followed, they would be more secretive about it."

Now May looked alarmed. And immediately Andrew knew that there was no "if" involved. They were in grave danger.

"We've got to get out of here."

"Are you sure?"

"One hundred percent. If Lao Cheng already suspected that you weren't cooperating with him, he probably was even more suspicious of your sudden resignation. And if someone followed you here, Lao Cheng was probably alerted as soon as I arrived. I made quite a commotion downstairs just a little while ago. His thugs could be here any minute."

And just then, he heard the screeching sound of tires on pavement, as what sounded like several vehicles barreled into the hospital parking lot. Well, they weren't trying to keep their arrival a secret.

Andrew looked at May anxiously, "Do you have enough energy to walk...maybe run?"

"Of course," replied May confidently, but as soon as she sat up and swung her legs over the side of the bed, she swayed back and forth a bit and looked like she might faint.

"Easy there, here, let me help you," Andrew put his arm around her shoulders and began to support her, but she pushed him away, "I can get up myself."

"May, we don't have time."

"We don't have time for you to carry me out of here. I'm going to have to support myself. Just give me a few seconds." She eased onto her feet and threw her coat on over her hospital gown.

"OK, quickly, before the doctor comes looking for us." Andrew peered out from behind the door to May's room and spotted a fire exit at the end of the hallway. "Let's go."

They ran toward the exit and down the staircase until they reached the ground floor. But when they opened the staircase door, they saw that several uniformed men with guns had blocked the main entrance. Half a dozen more were just boarding the elevator, presumably heading up to the eighth floor. It would only be a matter of a minute or so before they discovered that Andrew and May were gone, and began searching the whole building.

"What are we going to do?"

May looked at the flight of stairs descending one more level into the basement. "I've got an idea. I got acquainted with a really nice lady who works in the morgue in the basement. I think she might help us."

When they arrived, the morgue seemed to be deserted. "Lu Yan? Lu Yan? Ni zai ma?" May called.

"Wo zai a," a short, plump woman wearing round glasses appeared from behind a desk.

"*Lu Yan, I hate to bother you, but there are some government thugs outside who are here for us, and if we don't escape, well, we might be the next bodies in your morgue. Is there any way you can hide us?*"

"Ai ya, Li Mei, *why do you keep getting yourself into so much trouble? And who is this handsome man?*"

"*My boyfriend.*"

Lu Yan walked toward Andrew and examined him. "*Couldn't you have found a taller man?*"

May winced and Andrew rolled his eyes. Lu Yan jumped back as if he'd bitten her. "*Does he understand Chinese?*"

May nodded grimly.

"A, bu hao yisi. Na wo zenme hui bang nimen?" *Oh, sorry. So how can I help you?*

May smiled and began to explain her plan.

***

Several minutes later the elevator doors opened on the ground floor of the hospital, and Andrew felt the wheels of the bed he was lying on bump through the elevator doorway and into the lobby. He couldn't see anything through the white sheet that Lu Yan had draped over him, and he practically held his breath, trying not to make the slightest movement. Slowly the beds moved across the lobby floor, the wheels squeaking here and there. The lobby seemed much bigger than Andrew remembered, judging by how long it was taking them to reach the front door. How close were they? It seemed to be taking hours.

The beds stopped moving and a gruff voice inquired in Chinese, *"Where are you taking these bodies?"*

"I'm about to deliver them to their family. It was a grandfather and grandmother who passed almost at the same time. Very tragic."

"We are sealing off the building to search for some criminals right now. You will have to wait until morning."

"The family requested their bodies be delivered immediately, I need to honor their wishes."

"Sorry, it's not possible."

Andrew heard Lu Yan raise her voice. *"Not possible? How would you feel if it was your parents, I wonder? Would you like to go with me later and explain to this family why they had to wait all night to receive their parents?"*

"Now, miss, be reasonable."

"Reasonable? You are talking about possible eternal damnation for these people. If they don't make it to the family house soon their spirits may not be able to find their way to the family ancestral graves."

Andrew could tell the guard was flustered. There was an awkward silence, and then the guard said, *"Very well, but let me just take a look at the bodies first."*

Andrew's heart began to beat faster. He could hear the guard moving closer to his bed, and almost thought he could feel the air move as the guard's arm extended toward his head, just seconds away from lifting back the sheet and exposing him. He clenched his teeth, ready to leap up and attack the guard.

Then he heard the sound of a hand slapping skin just above his head, and Lu Yan's voice, "Ai ya! *How stupid are you? Do you want to release the spirits by pulling that sheet back? The bodies need to be left as they are.*"

"*Very well, very well, move along,*" said the guard in an embarrassed and hurried voice. And to his relief, Andrew felt the beds begin moving again. Soon they began to rattle as the beds moved onto the pavement of the parking lot, and then Andrew had to stop himself from moving with surprise when the bed tilted and began moving up a steep incline, and then leveled off again a few seconds later. Lu Yan pulled back the sheet. Andrew looked around and saw that they were in the back of a van.

"*Ok, now I'm going to drive you to* Wudaokou, *and then you'll be safe. You just stay back here until we're clear, OK?*" She put the sheet back in place and started the van engine.

A few minutes later Lu Yan parked the van in an alleyway near the bustling college neighborhood of Wudaokou. Andrew and May hopped out, and May gave Lu Yan a big hug. "*Thank you so much, how will we ever repay you?*"

"*Don't worry about it dear, an invitation to your wedding would be plenty.*" She grinned at them, and then hopped back in the van and drove off.

"That was pretty amazing," Andrew said, turning to May.

May smiled, "I'm a pretty good spy, too, you know." But then her smile quickly faded, and she became unsteady. "I think I need to lie down again."

Andrew supported her. "I don't know where we can go, except to an old friend of my dad's, but he lives an hour and a half north of Beijing." He looked at May.

"We should go to the EJF headquarters. It's hidden underneath a factory. Actually they are also about an hour and a half north of Beijing."

"Under a factory?" And now Andrew remembered what Charlie had said about Jonah Wong's financials being funny. "You're not talking about the Blue Bull Porcelain Factory, are you?"

May stared at him. "Yes. How do you know about that?"

"Because the owner of that factory, Jonah Wong, is an old friend of my father."

May let out a small gasp. "And he's also the leader of the EJF."

CHAPTER 37:

PREPARING TO LAUNCH

Cheng's headache was improving, but his patience was not. For the first time since they'd begun the geoengineering project, a hostile party had gotten hold of documents revealing what they were doing. Of all the people involved in the project, he had been entrusted to oversee the execution of their work. Now he would lose face to the other executives because he'd failed to keep their secret secure. Not only that, but if those documents actually made it to the media or back to Howard Harrison, the loss of face for his country would be tremendous, and he would quite possibly lose his position and status, if not worse. And the geoengineering plans would certainly be killed.

He could not, under any circumstances, let those documents get any further.

It was time to draw on all the favors and connections he had. And he'd already put a few of them to good use. Now Andrew would not be able to get those documents out of China without someone physically carrying them. And neither Andrew nor any of his friends would be able to get past a border checkpoint.

But that was still not a guarantee that the documents wouldn't make it out somehow. He would have felt much better if the little American and his friends were locked up in one of his cells. The embarrassment of that morning was still haunting him. He'd regained consciousness lying on the pavement, with a squad of soldiers surrounding him, and Andrew and his friends nowhere in sight. They had slipped through his fingers again, and he could not afford another mistake.

There was, however, another way to make sure Andrew couldn't ruin their plans: launch the planes immediately.

There was a knock at his door. "*Enter,*" he commanded.

The door opened and Dr. Stone walked in. "*You called for me, sir.*"

"*Yes, come in please.*" Cheng's temporary office at the Geoengineering Center didn't have room for a chair beside his, something which continued to annoy him. So Dr. Stone had to stand awkwardly in front of him.

"*How are you feeling, boss?*"

Cheng would have preferred to pretend that the incident of that morning had never happened, so he decided to cut the usual pleasantries. "*Fine. How soon can we launch the planes?*"

"*Well, we are just finishing up the last synthesis batch of particle X, and we've already begun loading the payloads into the first few planes.*"

"*I asked how soon.*"

Dr. Stone shifted back and forth. "*I'd have to say 24 hours at the earliest.*"

"*Use all the manpower we have available. Take your scientists from their desks and get them hauling bags of material to those planes if that will make it go faster. I want to launch in less than 24 hours.*"

"*Boss, I understand the urgency, but I don't think that's going to help speed things up much. The procedure is pretty automated. At this point, more people will just get in the way.*"

Cheng stood up slowly, keeping his eyes fixed on Dr. Stone as he did so. "*You realize what this will mean for both of us if this gets out before we can launch.*"

"*Absolutely.*"

"*Then why are you telling me it can't go any faster?*"

"*It's just not possible. We need to load the particles into custom made cannons, a very delicate process that can only be done by robots. As soon as the particles are finished they are automatically loaded into carts that drive themselves straight to the planes...."*

"Why is everything done with robots these days?"

"It's really the most efficient way."

"Well, why don't you put some of that brainpower you and your scientists have together to come up with a faster way to do it."

"I, I'll see what I can do boss."

"Please do. We can't afford to let today's embarrassment turn into tomorrow's disaster."

"I really thought he was Mr. Ivanovich..."

"I brought you on board for your scientific mind, not your way with people, Dr. Stone. Never make a judgment call like that again without consulting me."

"Of course, boss."

Cheng's phone rang and he answered it. "Wei?"

"Sir, we've searched Peking University Hospital from top to bottom, and there's no sign of them."

"What do you mean there's no sign of them? We have a tracking device that pinpointed the American's location at that hospital, and a visual confirmation from one of my men that he entered the hospital. Did he just vanish?"

"I don't think that's possible, sir."

Cheng slapped his hand to his forehead, then winced as his head throbbed. *"Isn't someone watching the reading from the tracking device?"*

"We have a man back at base checking it now. We are standing by for an update, sir."

"Back at base? Why the hell don't you have a live feed with you in the field?"

"We didn't think it was necessary, sir. This was supposed to be a basic extraction."

"Basic? You think this is basic? How many times has this boy evaded your squadron's capture, Lieutenant?"

There was silence on the other end, then the lieutenant

responded slowly. *"A few too many times, sir."*

"You need to understand something, lieutenant. One time is too many. That's why I replaced your predecessor. Next time I will replace you too. And when I replace you, it doesn't mean you'll be transferred to another assignment."

"Yes, sir. I'm getting an update, sir. It appears he's now in Wudaokou."

"And how did he end up there if you had the hospital on lockdown?"

There was another pause. *"I really don't know, sir."*

Cheng gritted his teeth. *"Get after him, and make sure you have a live feed in the field from here on."* He hung up the phone and looked at Dr. Stone, who was looking at him expectantly. *"Why are you still standing here?"* he bellowed.

"No reason, boss." Dr. Stone turned and left his office in a hurry.

Cheng sat down, immediately regretting the outburst. Dr. Stone had been nothing but loyal to him, and he had a brilliant mind, even if he was rather easy to deceive. He needed to get control of himself and concentrate on finding the little American before it was too late. But he couldn't do that from Inner Mongolia. He picked up the phone. *"Get my plane ready to return to Beijing."*

CHAPTER 38:

THE ECONOMIC JUSTICE FRONT

Chu was already in Beijing when Andrew called him and came to pick them up immediately. A few hours later, Andrew and May arrived outside Jonah's house near the factory. Andrew hoped Jonah would be able to come up with a plan quickly. He'd spent time looking at the files with May during the car ride and realized they had less than 24 hours before the plans were scheduled to take off on their first geoengineering flight.

Jonah answered his door cautiously, but when he saw them he smiled and invited them into the house. He sat them down in his living room, which was quite modern looking and beautifully decorated with a wide assortment of porcelain from the factory. A short, plump Chinese woman soon entered to greet them.

"Welcome to our home Li Mei and Andrew Oxley. This is my wife Catherine," said Jonah.

"Can I offer you two some tea?" she asked, looking back and forth from Andrew to May. Then her eyes fell on May with a look of concern. "You don't look well, miss. Would you like to lie down and get some rest?"

"That would be nice," said May, as she tried to stifle a yawn, "But we don't have time. Andrew here has uncovered something that needs urgent action."

"Your health is more important than anything, my dear."

"Are you alright?" Jonah asked.

"I'm fine."

"Actually she has a relapsed case of malaria, so not exactly," interjected Andrew.

"Good God, where did you catch that?"

May glared at Andrew, then said, "In Florida several months ago."

"Ah, yes," said Jonah, with sudden understanding. "As the climate warms, malaria is making its way further north. It's already spreading to Hong Kong and southern China as well. I don't know if the government is prepared to deal with this when it becomes an epidemic."

"So all this extreme weather—the droughts, the floods, the hurricanes—you think they are all really just climate change?" asked Andrew cautiously.

"That's what the science has been telling us for about 50 years now. It still amazes me how much people complicate it, but the simple fact is that when you have more carbon dioxide in a given environment, it increases the temperature. The same thing happens in a greenhouse, right? That's why it was originally called the Greenhouse Effect. Today, there is more carbon dioxide in the atmosphere—because humans have been taking it from underground and releasing it—than at any point in at least the last million years. And when the temperature is warmer, you get more storms and more extreme weather."

Catherine came back into the living room with a tray carrying a teapot and three cups. She set them down on a small table, smiled at Andrew, and then left the room again. Andrew looked at the cups and realized that one of them was his father's teacup. It had been fully restored.

"Jonah, you're amazing, this cup looks just as good as new."

"Please, don't give me the credit. It was all Mr. Shao; he's extremely talented. Now drink. This is some of the finest tea in China, held in some of the finest porcelain you will ever see if

I do say so myself," he smiled at Andrew.

"Jonah, why didn't you tell me before that you were leading this Economic Justice Front?"

"A good question, young Oxley. Even though you're the son of Ray, I wasn't quite sure of your intentions. I'd gathered that you were posing as a teacher at NOCCOC, and working for someone else trying to collect information about Cheng's activities. But it wasn't until I realized you'd escaped from NOCCOC and Cheng was hunting you that I knew you'd be on our side. When you finally came here, I had intended for you to come alone, but when your friend Charlie showed up as well, I was still hesitant to share my work with you. I didn't know his intentions either."

"Well unfortunately my *friend* Charlie doesn't share my views. As we speak he's running away to hide with his parents in Wenzhou."

"Yes, well, not everyone is cut out to save the world."

"At this point, I don't know if I'm even cut out to save myself. I was hoping you would have a plan," Andrew reached into his bag and pulled out the files. "I got this from a secret facility way out in Inner Mongolia."

As Jonah skimmed through the report, Andrew watched his eyes get wider behind his spectacles. Finally, he looked up at Andrew.

"You've found what we were missing. Young Oxley, you really have brought good luck to the Blue Bull factory."

"But it doesn't make sense. Why would the oil industry be trying to reverse climate change? Aren't they the ones denying that it's even happening?"

"Actually, it makes perfect sense. Solar radiation management—that's what this type of geoengineering is called—is a cheap and relatively easy fix; the ultimate band-aid. They know that if they don't do something about climate change, the pressure to stop using fossil fuels will eventually run them out of business."

"So this would make it easier for them to justify not reducing carbon emissions because the problem would be

279

solved, at least sort of?"

"Effectively, yes. We've known for a while that Cheng was working with his counterparts in America, Russia, Canada and some of the OPEC countries to come up with a new way to muddle climate science. But this is far beyond anything I ever imagined."

"But to be honest, Jonah, in some ways it doesn't really sound that bad. I mean if whatever they're doing could reverse climate change, and at a cheap price, wouldn't that be a good thing?"

"That's why it's so dangerous. It seems comparatively cheap and easy in the beginning: flying a handful of planes around the stratosphere, versus changing the entire industrial structure of society to stop using fossil fuels. From a cost perspective, it seems like a no-brainer."

"But first, keep in mind, this involves dumping millions of tons of particles that we know little about into the upper atmosphere. This so-called particle X they've developed could have any number of unforeseen consequences. And consider that the alternative, a sulfur dioxide aerosol, is the same chemical that causes acid rain, and would cause the hole in the ozone layer to start expanding again."

"I guess that doesn't sound good."

"That's just the beginning. Then consider that once we start geoengineering, we may never be able to stop. At least, not for hundreds or maybe thousands of years."

"What? Why is that?"

Jonah paused. "First young Oxley, let me give you some context. You must know that at this point, the world has already warmed by about two degrees Fahrenheit, and is almost certain to experience at least a four-degree Fahrenheit temperature rise this century, just from the greenhouse gasses we've already released. If no drastic action is taken to reduce greenhouse gas emissions, the temperature rise could be much greater— as much as eight or nine degrees. That may not sound like a lot, but for the global climate, it's huge. It hasn't been that warm on earth for tens of millions of years."

"If we start geoengineering right now, we can prevent any further temperature increase, as long as we continue spraying those particles into the atmosphere, slowly increasing the amount each decade."

"But why do we have to increase them over time?"

"Because the concentration of greenhouse gasses in the atmosphere will still be increasing, and we would need to compensate for that."

"It's just like a drug addiction," May cut in. "Over time you need to use more and more to get the same effect, and at the same time your health is actually getting worse and worse."

"Yes, that's exactly right. So in this hypothetical scenario, if we want to stop geoengineering, we have to reduce greenhouse gas *concentrations* in the atmosphere, not just emissions. In other words, we have to start removing carbon dioxide. And then the big question arises: how do we do that? Well, no one really has a solution. So we would have to keep on geoengineering until, at some unknown point in the future, we not only have stopped using fossil fuels altogether but actually find a way to take all the greenhouse gasses we've emitted in the past two hundred years *out* of the atmosphere."

"But wouldn't stopping the geoengineering be just the same as if we had never done it in the first place?

"No, not at all. It would be far worse. At that point, geoengineering would be suppressing a global temperature increase of anywhere from four to nine degrees. As soon as we stopped geoengineering, the earth would very suddenly warm up by that amount. The rate of warming matters, you see. It would happen in the span of just a few years, instead of over decades or hundreds of years, as is happening now. Ecosystems around the world would have no time to adapt. Humanity would have no time to adapt."

"That kind of rapid temperature increase would likely kill off most life on earth. And that's not an exaggeration," May added. "It would be an even more dramatic event than the asteroid collision that killed off the dinosaurs sixty million years ago."

Andrew was silent, as he absorbed this information. Jonah and May stared back at him with grim expressions.

"So you're basically saying that, once we start geoengineering, we are locked in?"

"And the longer we do it, the worse the consequences of stopping."

"On top of that," Jonah continued, "once geoengineering is implemented, countries around the world will likely lose the will to reduce emissions because it will seem that the problem will have been solved, if only temporarily. This basically means that we are much more likely to keep burning fossil fuels like there's no tomorrow—just what the oil companies want—and push the potential temperature rise to the worst-case scenario."

"But the even scarier fact is," May jumped in, "the chances of us stopping prematurely are actually quite high."

"But if the consequences are that bad, why would we stop?"

"Consider this, young Oxley: who do you think would be responsible for conducting geoengineering and continuing to replenish the particles in the atmosphere? A corporation? An individual country? The United Nations? So then, what if there's a major war, or a major economic collapse and humanity can't agree on who will be responsible to continue geoengineering... or no one has the resources to continue it? It's hard to say where the world will be in 100 years. Will the oil companies that started this even be around still? Their senior executives certainly won't be."

"I can see now why oil companies would be eager to do this, especially because the real difficulties will come later. These are all long-term side effects that most people alive today won't be affected by."

"But there are also some potentially devastating side effects of geoengineering that will be felt right away. First, if we geoengineer the climate to reduce temperatures back to pre-industrial levels, rainfall worldwide would decrease significantly.

"Why is that?"

"It has to do with which part of the atmosphere the carbon dioxide ends up in. Essentially, greenhouse gasses have the effect of decreasing the difference in temperature between the upper and lower parts of the atmosphere. That temperature difference is what causes precipitation in the first place."

"But," May cut in again, "the overall increase in global temperature that is *also* caused by carbon dioxide is enough to offset this effect. Warmer temperatures mean that the atmosphere can hold more moisture. More water in the air will lead to more rainfall. *So* all else being equal, an increase in carbon dioxide levels doesn't really change the total amount of global rainfall."

Now Andrew was starting to see the problem. "But if we artificially reduce global temperatures, we lose the increase in precipitation that was caused by the temperature increase. And that will lead to overall less rainfall around the world."

"Exactly. Think about how scarce freshwater already is in some parts of the world, and how much conflict that is causing. A global decrease in rainfall could cause massive drought around the world. Models have shown that there would also be a disproportionate impact on certain regions. One of the most concerning is the potential to disrupt the South Asian monsoons, which bring seasonal rain to India and Southeast Asia. That would mean drought, decreased crop yields, and potentially starvation for nearly two billion people."

"So the kinds of disasters that climate change is already causing could continue to happen anyway if we use geoengineering," said Andrew.

"That's right," Jonah nodded, looking grave. "In addition, there is going to be a lot of disagreement between nations on how much we should reduce temperatures. Maybe the Arab countries would want to decrease it more, so that their countries become more temperate, while the Scandinavian countries wouldn't want to decrease it that much."

"But what if it's the global oil industry that gets to decide? And then, what if governments of the world decided to enact policies toward the oil companies that they don't like? If they are in control of the climate, they could threaten to adjust the level of geoengineering to negatively impact that country or region. They would be in control of the most powerful weapon known to man."

"Much more powerful than the ability to create a hurricane," May said quietly, looking at Andrew.

Andrew thought back once again to what his father had said to him on the boat, the day he died. "The day my father died, he told me the hurricane that killed him was manmade. And I always thought he meant someone had created it using weather control."

"I knew your father very well, young Oxley. He would have never suggested that."

"You're right, Jonah. Now I'm realizing that. I think he must have meant it was man-made by accident—through climate change—not intentional weather control. And all these years, I misinterpreted it."

"We always hang on to the last words of our loved ones, maybe more tightly than we should. And for someone that young, it would have been easy to misunderstand."

"And consider this too," May jumped in. "The atmosphere is very sensitive to small changes in solar radiation. Even a slight overdose of geoengineering particles could send the planet rapidly back into an ice age more destructive than the fallout from a nuclear war. How do we know these oil companies even got the calculations right?"

"Look at their timeline," Andrew said to Jonah. "We've only got another 24 hours before they begin flying those planes. We've got to find a way to stop them."

"I think it's time for you to see the base of our little operation," Jonah said. "We can share this information with the other leaders and come up with a plan." He got up and headed for the door, then turned to May. "You ought to stay here and take it easy while I show Andrew. Catherine will take good care of you."

"I'm coming with you."

"May, you really should rest."

"I'll be fine. I want to help come up with a plan."

"Well, as you wish." They followed Jonah out of the house and down the path that snaked between the other nearby homes toward the factory. The night was calm, and for the first time since he arrived in Beijing, Andrew heard birds singing.

When they arrived at the factory, instead of going in the main door, Jonah led them around to the backside of the building, toward the river. The ground began to slope downward, and soon it became evident that the factory had a basement level. When they reached the other side, Jonah walked up to the cement wall that stretched the back length of the factory and pressed his finger into a small hole. Suddenly a large section of the concrete began to move inward and then began to slide to the side. They followed Jonah into a hallway that seemed to stretch far back into the ground. As they walked Andrew began to hear the noise of voices chatting excitedly. As they came around a bend, the hallway opened up into a giant room.

Andrew stopped and stared. There were probably close to a hundred people rushing around, sorting what might have been gear for a small invasion. There were ropes, backpacks, boots, tarps, several small boats, weapons, and what looked like explosives.

"Welcome to the China headquarters of the Economic Justice Front," said Jonah. "We're a group of activists from around the world who are trying to stop the increasing income inequality gap. You know the Communist Party was originally supposed to be about the workers, right? But they've lost touch with that. And income inequalities have risen to higher levels here than even in America." Jonah looked around, with a smile on his face. "We aren't looking for regime change in China though, we just want to stop the growing power of the rich, at least the rich who exploit the poor, around the world, and of companies like NOCCOC that continue to line their pockets at the expense of the poor. You know, climate change will have the greatest impact on poor people around the world. Like the two billion people living in south and southeast Asia."

"Some of these big companies are so entrenched in the political system that we've given up on governments reining them in. So we've resorted to other means. We target key assets of these companies, especially those that are polluting the land and water of the poor. And we try to make the explosions seem like accidents. This sometimes galvanizes the local population into protest, forcing the government to reign in the companies. And we have allies in the central government who are looking for excuses to attack the power of the state-owned enterprises as well. I admit, it's not always the most effective method, and sometimes I do wonder if we're really doing the right thing," he paused. "But as the American saying goes, 'drastic times call for drastic measures.'"

"But why hide the operation in the basement of your factory?"

"Actually, this factory was built in order to conceal our organization. In fact, it was your father's idea. We needed a way to funnel money from our donors abroad into our China operation without it being detected. We also wanted to give them something in return for their support."

"So that's why you charge five times the normal price for your porcelain?"

Jonah turned and looked at him directly, "How did you know that?"

"Charlie broke into your accountant's office last time we were here."

"Ha, I knew that boy was a troublemaker. Well yes, we send the porcelain to our donors and they pay a very high premium in order to fund our operation. My family has actually been in the porcelain-making business for generations, so it wasn't difficult for me to start the business. And your father convinced the donors to go along with our scheme," Jonah sighed, "Unfortunately your father was a little too reckless. He didn't try hard enough to keep his leadership involvement in the movement a secret. He wrote threatening letters to powerful people, like his former classmate Will Rothschild…"

"Will Rothschild?" May seemed to have made the connection. "He spoke at our graduation ceremony. And he even admitted that climate change was a problem being caused by human activity."

"Hmmm, well, I'm actually not surprised. He tries to project a very affable public image, but behind the scenes, he runs a very sophisticated PR campaign for the oil industry, and they are ruthless. In fact, I suspect that if your father hadn't died in that sailing accident, they would have tried to... eliminate him." Jonah had a dark look on his face.

"In the years since the global recession, we've expanded our efforts to include cyber and financial attacks as well as physical ones. Of course, as we've become more successful, Cheng and others have stepped up their efforts to find us. At one point I had one of my workers sell him some porcelain vases with a wire planted inside so we could spy on him and try to get an idea of whether he was onto us."

"So that's what your vases were doing in his office."

Jonah smiled. "Yes. But regardless, we've been pretty good at keeping hidden here." He looked around at the people bustling to and fro.

Suddenly, all the lights in the room went out.

CHAPTER 39:

LIGHTS OUT

There was a collective sound of shock from the occupants, followed by a few moments of total darkness before lighters and candles began to light up around the room. Andrew looked around and noticed that the computers had gone out too.

"Looks like a power outage," said Jonah, and Andrew could hear the concern in his voice.

Just then, they heard screams from the factory floor above them, then the sound of smashing porcelain. Then they heard more screams and thudding sounds.

"*What's going on up there?*" Jonah shouted in Chinese across the room. A man ran across the room and up to Jonah.

"*Sir, I believe it's a raid.*"

"*By who?*"

"*I've been told two trucks of People's Liberation Army soldiers have pulled up outside.*"

"*What? Impossible.*"

"*Our man upstairs just told me over the radio.*"

Jonah turned to Andrew and May. "I can't believe it. After all these years, we've finally been discovered."

"You think it's the government?" May asked.

"I suspect the PLA soldiers are being controlled by Cheng."

"*Sir, I'm executing the evacuation plan.*"

"*Please do.*" Jonah turned back to Andrew and May. "You've got to get out of here with those documents. Find a computer, upload them and send them to as many people as you can back in the U.S. The more copies that exist out there in cyberspace, the harder it will be for them to contain it. This needs to become international news. That will at least put enough pressure on Cheng that he is likely to call this off. He has many enemies in the national government that would take advantage of the fact that he's collaborating with foreigners. He could lose a lot of his power."

"But will that happen quickly enough to stop them?"

"I don't know. But if I can't get some of my men out of here and out to Inner Mongolia to destroy that facility, this may be our only shot. Now you'd better get going."

"But what about you? What about your family?"

"I've got to stay and help with the evacuation. We've always had a contingency plan for this. My wife and daughter know where to hide. We'll be in touch."

"Come on," Andrew grabbed May's hand and they ran for the exit.

Outside, they could see the PLA soldiers converging on the front of the factory. So they ran in the opposite direction along the river, keeping low.

"I don't see any way to cross the river, do you?" said May, shivering.

"Doesn't look like it." And there was no way they were going to try and swim with May in her present condition. "We'll have to head back toward the town. If we go through the cluster of homes near the factory, we might be able to stay out of sight." They crept toward the homes, trying to keep as much distance between them and the factory as possible. But as they passed one of the homes, they heard a shout and turned to see that a group of PLA soldiers had come to search the homes, and had spotted them.

"Run," shouted Andrew.

They had a bit of a head start, but as they dodged between houses, the soldiers quickly began to catch up.

"Andrew, I can't keep this up, they're too fast."

"But we don't have anywhere else to go." They made it out into the open and headed down the road toward the town, but the soldiers were almost upon them. He would have to take on these soldiers by himself. But could he hold off half a dozen of them single-handedly? Just as he was preparing to turn and fight, he heard a car engine coming toward him and turned to see that a jeep was driving right at them. Had some other soldiers come to join the chase? Now they would have to surrender.

Then as the jeep neared them, it suddenly swerved and ran right into the group of soldiers, knocking them all to the ground. Andrew looked at who was driving, and to his surprise saw Charlie waving excitedly at them.

"Charlie," Andrew ran up to him. "What are you doing here? I thought you were going back to Wenzhou?"

Charlie grinned at him. "I told you before, we are brothers now. I realize I can't let my brother take on powerful criminals by himself."

"How did you find us?"

"I didn't. But when I decide to go back to the hospital and find you, I see PLA soldiers outside. So I wait, but I don't see you anywhere. Then I see them all get in their trucks and leave. So I follow them here."

Andrew shook his head, "I can't believe it." Then he heard a struggling noise and turned back to see that a soldier had somehow got past Charlie and was trying to grab May. Andrew was about to come to her aid when May delivered a punch right between the man's eyes, and he crumpled to the ground. She recoiled a bit, and then looked at Andrew. "I've never punched someone before."

"Well, I'm just glad you never tried to punch me. You're deadly."

May laughed and then shivered. Andrew went up to her and noticed that she was sweating profusely. He felt her forehead and it was quite warm. "You've got a fever."

"I know."

"We've got to get out of here." They climbed into the back of the jeep. Charlie put the jeep into gear and turned back to the road headed for Beijing. Along the way, Andrew took pictures of the documents. But when he tried to upload them to his email, he kept getting a loading sign.

"I'm not getting a good enough signal out here to upload the documents."

"The files might be too big. Let's try getting to a high speed wired connection."

An hour later they arrived at a new development on the outskirts of the city. Charlie drove around past clusters of stores and restaurants until they spotted an Internet café.

"We can upload here. Quickly though, I can see people already stare at us."

"They probably don't see two Chinese and a foreigner driving around in one of these jeeps every day."

They parked outside and descended the stairs into the underground café. When they entered, they realized that it was completely deserted.

"That is very strange. These places always packed. Well, no one is here to make us pay, I guess we can use the computers for free."

Charlie booted up one of the computers. He began squinting at it and typing furiously. Then he stopped and stared at the screen. "Oh no."

"What's wrong?"

"They shut the Internet down."

"What do you mean? The cafe?"

"No, the whole thing. It must be the censors."

"What? That's impossible, they can't just turn off the Internet."

"Yes, they can. This wouldn't be the first time. The government did this to Xinjiang many years ago after riots broke out there. And Internet is virtually shut down throughout the country for a few days during the leadership transition."

"What about using a VPN?"

"I just check. They shut them all down. There is no way

to get through."

"You think this is Lao Cheng's doing?"

"It's got to be," said May. "This can't just be a coincidence. This is unbelievable. He really doesn't want the information we've got to get out."

"How widespread do you think it is?"

"There's no way to know. It could just be Beijing and the surrounding areas, and it could be the whole country. Andrew, what are we going to do? This is serious. If he's this determined, we're never going to be able to escape him."

"We're going to think of something. What about conventional mail?"

"If Lao Cheng shut down Internet, I am sure he thinks of that too. Probably there is no mail going out of Beijing now. Hey, maybe we can give the documents to someone to take with them on a plane?"

"Like who? There isn't anyone we can trust that doesn't likely already have an exit control on them."

"Then we are screwed."

Andrew wracked his brain for another solution. Perhaps they would have to stow away on a boat. Andrew wondered if one of them could possibly survive inside a shipping container. That would be too dangerous, but maybe…

"Hey," said Andrew. "I've got an idea."

CHAPTER 40:

MESSAGE IN A BOTTLE

"Jonah? Are you alright?" Andrew heard the muffled sound of Jonah's voice on the other end of the phone. Finally, his voice came through clearly.

"Yes, some of us are, at least. I managed to get my wife and daughter into an underground hideout, along with a handful of others who escaped, but the rest were rounded up like cattle. Were you able to send the documents?"

"It looks like Lao Cheng has shut down the Internet. We can't send the documents back to America electronically."

Jonah was silent for a moment. "My God. It seems he'll stop at nothing."

"Jonah, I've got an idea. You must have some shipments of porcelain that have left your factory, but haven't been shipped out of China yet, right?"

"Ah, and you want to slip copies of the documents into those containers?"

"Not just into the containers. They could still be discovered that way during an inspection. Do you have any bottles or vases that would be big enough for the documents to fit inside?"

"That's quite an ingenious solution, young Oxley. Yes, I believe I do. Of course you'll have to make sure the shipment gets rerouted to a destination where it will fall into the right

293

hands. But it will still take the ship several days to reach the U.S. That's not enough time to stop their launch. And all our explosives were confiscated. We don't have the firepower to attack that facility."

"I think this is where I can help," Andrew and May looked at Charlie.

"Who is that?" asked Jonah.

"Uh, remember my friend Charlie I told you about? Well, he came back to help us. He's a pretty accomplished hacker."

"I am studying schematics of the planes," Charlie continued. "They have a remote-control function. And it looks like Lao Cheng wanted to be able to control them from the NOCCOC building because that's where one of the terminals is. And it has override capability, which means it can make the other terminal at the Geoengineering Center and the cockpit controls useless. So all we have to do is find that terminal and flip on the override, then destroy the terminal. It should permanently disable the planes. Or at least, it would take them weeks to fix."

"That is typical of Lao Cheng. He is obsessed with control. Of course he would want to have the master ability to control the planes from his building," said Jonah's voice over the phone.

"The NOCCOC building is like a fortress," said May. "Do you really think we can get in?"

"We've got to try," said Andrew. "And I bet we can get Fritz to help us get into the building without setting off the alarm."

"You really think you can trust him?" asked May.

"Ha, Fritz is harmless," said Charlie.

"And he's the one who gave me the files that Yang Fei stole from Lao Cheng which directed us to that research facility. He was in love with Yang Fei."

"Oh, big surprise there."

"I know, I know, but if it means avenging her, he will help," Andrew turned back to the phone. "Jonah, we might have a man on the inside. I'm going to try to get in touch with him."

"I will rally the troops here. Talk to you soon." Jonah hung up.

After a few tries, Fritz answered the phone with surprising cheerfulness for the middle of the night. "Drewster? So good to hear from you buddy. Whaz new?"

"Fritz, we're in some serious trouble. But you can help. I need you to sneak some of my friends into NOCCOC."

"Well, that's gonna be tough, dude."

"I know, but I just need you to get them into the building."

"No, I mean it's gonna be tough just getting into the building. Since earlier today, it's been crawling with PLA soldiers. Even employees have trouble getting in and out. It's like we're in the midst of a war or something.

"It must be in response to our raid of the geoengineering center."

"Geoengineering? Who's trying to do that?"

"Lao Cheng and a bunch of other oil companies. That's what Yang Fei's files led us to. They built a huge facility out in Inner Mongolia and they are trying to manipulate the global climate."

"Wow, dis spy movie plot keeps getting dicker. How'd you end up in the middle of all this anyway Drewster?"

"It's a long story, Fritz. I'll have to tell you later. Will you help us?"

"You know I would do anything to bring down that bastard."

"Good. I'm going to put you in touch with a man named Jonah Wong."

***

Charlie called a friend of his to drive them to Tianjin, since they knew that taking any official transportation might alert Lao Cheng about where they were going. They arrived at the docks just before dawn. A dense fog hung over them, but Andrew knew it would dissipate as soon as the sun began to rise. They didn't have much time. They could see rows and rows of crates stretching to the water's edge, where the ghostly figure of large cargo ships sat, waiting to ship the vast quantities of goods made in China out to the rest of the world.

They were all exhausted, and May had passed out almost as soon as they got in the car, but now she seemed to be getting a second wind. She consulted her phone with the instructions Jonah had sent her. As she did so, Andrew looked over her shoulder.

"What does it say?"

May looked up and down the wharf. "This way," she said, motioning for Andrew and Charlie to follow her.

"You still haven't told me what it says."

"No need, I can find it myself."

Andrew and Charlie followed her as she walked down the wharf. "I don't trust a woman's sense of direction. She probably get us lost," Charlie said to Andrew in a loud whisper.

"I heard that. Hey, here it is."

May turned down the next row of containers, and then finally came to a stop in front of one. "I think this is it."

Andrew began to pick the lock and soon was unwrapping the chain that held the big metal bolt in place across the container door. He and Charlie slid the bolt out and opened the door, which creaked as they did so. The sound echoed across the eerily quiet wharf.

"Charlie, you better stay outside to make sure no one sees us."

"Don't worry about it Drew, if anyone comes along, I kick their ass."

"I'm sure you could. But first priority: let's try not to be noticed."

Andrew and May crept into the container and began looking through the boxes that were stacked inside. It wasn't long before Andrew came across one that was labeled fragile. Andrew looked around at the labels and soon found the tell-tale blue bulls head. He opened the box and found it full of porcelain vases.

"Ok, I found one. Let's slip a copy of the documents into

each of these, and a few more boxes if we can find them. You have the new shipping label, right?"

"I thought you had it?"

"No, I have the copies of the documents, you were supposed to print the shipping label…"

"Oh, you mean this?" May pulled the labels out of her pocket, smiled, and winked at him.

"My God May, stop fooling around, you almost gave me a heart attack."

"You need to lighten up, Xiao Niu. Trying to save the world has made you too serious." She moved toward him and rested her hand on his shoulder playfully. Andrew realized how in all the excitement of the last forty-eight hours, they hadn't had any moments alone. He reached up and brushed his hand across her cheek. It was still clammy, but just as soft as ever. He realized how much he'd missed her touch during the time they'd been apart. He put his arm around her back, and pulled her in for a kiss.

Just then, Charlie came scrambling into the container. "I see someone pass by in the mist, but I am not able to see who. I think he see me though."

Andrew and May pulled apart and looked at him. Charlie seemed to realize a little late that he'd interrupted at a bad time. "Yeah, I think he see me," he repeated, looking away. "What we gonna do?"

"Did he say anything to you? Or seem interested in what you were doing?"

"No, but he looked fat and official. I think he might tell on us."

Andrew tried not to roll his eyes. "OK Charlie, we'll finish up quickly. Just stay out there and let us know if anyone else comes by."

"OK, but finish quick." He gave Andrew a sly look and then scampered back out to the pier.

"Is he always this excitable?" asked May, starring after him.

"Oh yeah, you should see him when he has a new business

297

idea." May giggled.

Andrew finished putting the copies of the report into the vases, as May placed the label on the boxes, and then they resealed them. Climbing out of the container and sliding the bolt back into place, Andrew looked around. Charlie was nowhere to be seen.

"Where has Kong Kong run off to now?"

"Right here," said Charlie's voice, as he appeared around the side of the container. Andrew jumped at the suddenness of his appearance. "Jesus Charlie, where did you go?"

"I go down to other end of container to look around. And I think we in trouble. I hear truck pull up and the sound of many voices."

"It's probably just another shipment being delivered."

Then through the fog Andrew heard the faint sound of boots pounding on concrete, and then voices shouting. And they didn't sound like the voices of workers.

"PLA soldiers. How did they track us here so quickly?"

"No time to ruminate, we need to get outta here. This way."

They ran down the wharf, past rows and rows of containers until the wharf suddenly ended with a cliff that dropped several feet down to the ocean.

"Dead end! Let's try this way." They ran along the edge until they came to a large warehouse. The soldiers' shouts and drumming boots were now coming toward them from all sides, closing in on them. Through the fog, Andrew could start to see their outlines.

"Quick, into the warehouse," said Charlie. He threw open the door, and they entered to find several long rows of wooden boxes stacked on top of each other in haphazard pyramids that made them look like small mountains. Andrew closed the door carefully behind them, then they ran down one of the rows to the other side, but there was no exit. They were trapped. Andrew looked around wildly, trying to find a way out.

"I think the best bet is to climb up on boxes and hide there. Then if soldiers come in we jump down and attack them."

"That sounds like a great way to get us killed." But Charlie was already scrambling up onto one of the mounds of boxes. Andrew looked at May.

"I don't think we have any other choice, do we?" Then the main door to the warehouse opened and soldiers began pouring in.

"I guess not," said Andrew, and they began climbing up the other side of the same aisle. Nearing the top of the stack, they pressed themselves up against the highest box, trying to blend in as best they could. As a group of soldiers came running down the aisle toward them, Andrew looked over at Charlie, who forced a grin and winked at him. Was he really planning to jump down on these soldiers?

But the soldiers stopped below them, and Charlie stayed where he was. The soldiers looked around, seeming confused. *"Where did they go?"* he heard one of them shout. All they had to do was look up and they would be spotted. Then Andrew saw movement out of the corner of his eye and realized that Charlie had begun pushing the top box on his stack toward the soldiers. Was he really doing what he thought? Andrew held his breath.

Suddenly one of the soldiers looked up and spotted him. As he called out to the others he pointed his gun in Andrew and May's direction. He heard May let out a small cry, and then there was a crashing sound, and Andrew saw Charlie's crate tumble down from its perch and smash into the group of soldiers, scattering them like bowling pins. A gun went off and the bullet went whizzing past Andrew's head. He stumbled, his ears ringing, and then vaguely heard May call out to him, "Help me,"

He looked and saw that she was also trying to push the top box on their stack toward the other soldiers who were now rushing toward them. Regaining his senses, Andrew pushed as well, and the box went tumbling down, hitting its mark and taking out several more of the men.

"Come on," Charlie was now jumping down from the stack and heading back toward the entrance. Andrew and May followed him. They sprinted down the aisle toward the main door. But when they were nearly there, more men appeared, blocking the entrance. Then some men came around the corner from another aisle and converged on them. Charlie delivered a kick to the stomach of the first one, who went tumbling backward into the others. Andrew joined him, disarming the next soldier and using his gun to deliver a blow to the head of the next two. But there were too many of them, and Andrew knew they couldn't hold them off forever.

Just then he heard a gun go off, and Charlie gave out a cry of pain. Andrew looked and saw that he was clutching his leg. Then he heard May begin screaming and looked to see that two soldiers had grabbed her. He delivered a blow to one of them, but then he felt hard steel on his neck and realized that someone had come up behind him and got him in a headlock with a gun. He kicked backward and made contact with a body, and it seemed he had hit his mark because the grip loosened. Then he felt a blow to his head, and everything went dark.

CHAPTER 41:

THE MAN BEHIND THE CURTAIN

When Andrew awoke, feeling dizzy and nauseated, he found himself lying on a leather couch. As he looked around, he realized he was in Lao Cheng's office. How had he gotten there? He was alone in the room, except for two armed soldiers standing at the door, and a man who was pacing back and forth off to the side. Andrew's vision was hazy, so he couldn't quite make out who it was, but it didn't look like Lao Cheng. Then the man turned toward him and Andrew saw a face that he recognized, but which had no place in that room.

"Mr. Harrison? What are you doing here?"

Mr. Harrison walked over and knelt down next to him. "I'm glad you're awake."

Andrew tried to sit up, but his head was spinning. "We shouldn't be here. This is Lao Cheng's office. He's probably going to come back any minute."

"I know, son," Mr. Harrison paused, and Andrew saw that he looked very uncomfortable.

Andrew was trying to remember how he ended up there. And slowly, the scene at the wharf in Tianjin began flooding back to him.

"Where are May and Charlie?"

Mr. Harrison stared at him blankly. "Who?"

"I was with a Chinese girl and guy at the wharf in Tianjin when Lao Cheng's men overwhelmed us. They must have been captured."

"Oh, I wouldn't worry about them right now."

"But the guy was hurt, and the girl is very sick. I need to make sure they're all right."

"I've been told they're fine. The boy is being treated at a clinic and the girl is with him. Now, Andrew, there's somethin' important I've got to discuss with you."

A clinic? Did Mr. Harrison really know what was going on? An intense feeling of unease began to creep over him. Mr. Harrison was here, in Lao Cheng's office, and he didn't seem the least bit worried that they might be discovered. Was he dreaming again? Andrew pinched himself and blinked several times, but there was no doubt, he was awake.

"What are you doing here, Mr. Harrison...." He repeated.

"It pains me, son. I never wanted to be associated with him, but everything was not as it seemed."

"I don't understand. What are you doing here, in his office? Why did his men leave me here... with you? Do you know how many times I've feared for my life in this room? What the hell is going on?"

"Calm down now, son, let me explain. It isn't what you think. Ya see, I really thought this Cheng fellow was operating a weather control program. But then you presented me with that information about a so-called geoengineering program with American collaborators. I thought the Chinese had set that up as a red herring to throw you off the trail, and that they must know about your mission. Well, when I relayed this information to the chairman of the Institute's board, he came back with a startling revelation."

Mr. Harrison took a deep breath as if bracing for a painful procedure, "Ya see, our board chairman was working with Cheng the whole time. They worked together to create false evidence of a weather warfare program. Now trust me, I had no idea this was goin' on. Threw me for a loop too when I found out. Their idea was for Cheng to plant the evidence for you to

302

discover, and then allow you to take it back to me in America, where we would reveal it to the media."

"Who is your board chairman? Why did he want to do that?"

Mr. Harrison signed. "You haven't met him, but you've seen him before. He's really a very wise man. And he has known who you are for a long time. In fact, it was he who suggested you might be a good candidate for the original mission." Mr. Harrison turned and called out, "Will, why don't you come in here and introduce yourself."

One of the back doors in Lao Cheng's office opened, and in stepped William Rothschild.

"It's good to finally meet you, Andrew," Rothschild's smile was disarming and genuine. Andrew hadn't gotten a close look at him during graduation, but now he could see wrinkles in his face and his graying hair, which together made him appear to be in his mid-fifties. His movements were slow and calculated, but his walk had a slight wobble.

"I apologize if Mr. Cheng's men were rough with you. I told them I wanted you and your friends brought here without a scratch, but I can see that wasn't exactly what happened. Please, come over here and let's sit down." Rothschild walked over to Lao Cheng's desk and sat down in his chair, motioning for Andrew to sit—as he had so many times during his classes—in the chair across the desk.

Andrew didn't move at first, but glanced at the security personnel near the door. They were armed with guns.

"I wouldn't suggest that, Andrew," said Rothschild. "Come sit and let's have a talk. There's a lot I want to discuss with you."

As Andrew sat down, the shock finally began to wear off, and he managed to speak. "What have you done with my friends, May and Charlie?"

"Andrew, don't worry, I've instructed Mr. Cheng to treat Charlie's wounds and not to harm May. They'll be fine."

"So you've been working with both Lao... Mr. Cheng and Mr. Harrison the whole time? And everything I went through was… planned?"

"Well, everything up until you began sleeping with Mr. Cheng's mistress."

"So all that time, Mr. Cheng knew I was a spy." Andrew blurted out, "I suppose you were the ones who put that camera in my apartment. You set me up to become his teacher. And he knew I would sneak into his office and find that report, and then go out and confirm the existence of the HAARP facility. That's why it wasn't very heavily guarded."

"That's right. The Chinese government built that facility back in the early 1990s with technology they stole from the Soviets," Rothschild began. His pace was slow, as if he were choosing each word with great care. "But when they weren't able to achieve the weather control and communications disruption capabilities they had hoped for with it, even after stealing and trying to apply the ARCO patents decades later, it was abandoned. Even the original HAARP in Alaska was never quite able to live up to its promise. Control of localized weather events is nearly impossible, even with the sophisticated modeling we have today. And it likely always will be, because weather, ultimately, is global."

"But you wanted the public to think that it *was* possible." Rothschild just nodded.

"So if you set all this up, how come Mr. Harrison didn't help me when I was switched from teaching Mr. Cheng to a group class?

Rothschild looked over at Mr. Harrison, who had been silently leaning against the wall, smoking his pipe. "He's going to find out eventually, Howard." Mr. Harrison gave him one short nod.

"Find out what?"

"Howard wasn't exactly counting on you to succeed at first, Andrew. In fact, he expected you to be discovered. You were a decoy. He believed that if Mr. Cheng suspected you to be a spy, it would draw his attention away from another agent—the real agent—who was supposed to complete the mission."

Andrew glared over at Mr. Harrison, anger burning down his throat and into his stomach. He got to his feet, but as he did, he saw the security guard make a move toward him.

"So you really were using me," Andrew's voice quivered as he spoke. "And I believed everything you told me." Mr. Harrison didn't look at him. It was hard to read his expression, but Andrew sensed that he was uncomfortable.

"Andrew, please sit down. There's no use holding grudges now. This was all just business. Besides, after the Chinese Ministry of State Security captured the other agent, Howard began to believe that you really could carry out the mission yourself. Of course, it was my intention the whole time that you should succeed. That's why Mr. Cheng and I set clues for you to find the old HAARP facility."

Andrew slowly sat back down and turned his attention again to Rothschild. "So if Mr. Cheng knew what was going on the whole time, why did he get so angry and kill Yang Fei when he found out she was helping me?"

"Andrew, what you must have come to realize is that Mr. Cheng likes to be in control, and when someone threatens his control, he gets very upset." Rothschild's expression was dark. Andrew got the feeling that he'd also experienced this firsthand. "It was the ultimate embarrassment and betrayal to see the woman he obsessed over reject him like that. I'm sure he couldn't take it. And then when his anger got the better of him and he killed her, he was likely to blame you for his uncontrollable rage, rather than taking responsibility, as people so often do."

"So that's when your plan began to fall apart."

"That's when Mr. Cheng stopped cooperating. He was intent on hunting you down. But you were surprisingly effective at avoiding his capture. Even after one of his soldiers shot and pinned a tracking device to your foot as you were escaping from the Geoengineering Center. When you have a minute, you ought to examine your shoes. It's amazing how small they've been able to make these devices now."

Andrew immediately looked down at his shoes. Sure

enough, there was a tiny device attached to his left shoe that was almost too small to see.

"And it was a good thing he listened, because in time you conveniently led us right to the EJF's China headquarters, which we'd been trying to find for years. What still baffles me, though, is how you discovered our Inner Mongolia facility in the first place."

Andrew felt a slight sense of pride that, for all his manipulating, Rothschild didn't know everything that had happened. "Yang Fei managed to access some of Mr. Cheng's emails before she died, and passed them to... me." Andrew stopped himself short of mentioning Fritz.

"Ah. Well, either she was smarter than he thought, or Mr. Cheng is much more incompetent than I thought," Rothschild had a sour look on his face. "Once Howard informed me that you'd managed to find our facility and escape with vital information about our little operation, I decided it was time to fill Howard in on what was going on, and for us to come out here and straighten things out."

"So you're going to lock me up so I won't tell anyone?"

To Andrew's surprise, Rothschild laughed a hardy, genuine laugh. "On the contrary Andrew, I've come to ask for your help. I'll admit, I had you figured wrong. I suggested to Howard that we find someone with no experience. I thought someone like that would be easily manipulated into finding the information we had planted. And at the same time, I thought you would be too incompetent to uncover what was really going on."

"But like your father, you're very single-minded at times. You also proved yourself surprisingly capable of improvising. We had expected that you would simply confirm the presence of the Chinese HAARP, not break into the old computer room nearby; that's why we posted soldiers there, but apparently they were no match for you and your friend Charlie. And seducing Mr. Cheng's mistress... well, I'm sure he wouldn't be happy if he heard me say this, but that was very innovative. Naturally, neither Mr. Cheng nor I had expected you to do something like that. And by doing the unexpected, you uncovered the real secret we had hoped to keep hidden. Now I see that you're capable of much more than I thought. So I want to ask you to join us."

"Join you? What do you mean?"

"You've got a natural talent for investigation, Andrew. We could use that talent in finding and destroying our enemies. There are still many people who don't agree with what we're trying to do, and will do anything to stop us."

"By 'we,' you mean the oil industry?"

"By we, I mean an international consortium of global business leaders, representing trillions of dollars in investor value. Oil and other energy interests are represented, as well as the world's biggest banks that invest in them."

"And what you're trying to do is mask the impacts of climate change in order to protect your company's profits."

"Before you start making accusations, Andrew, let's make sure you really understand what we stand for. There's no question that climate change is happening. We've known that for decades. But now we also know that geoengineering is the cheapest and quickest way to avoid the worst impacts of it. Most people have no idea how much of the world's assets are invested in fossil fuel assets and reserves. If ignorant people got to decide that we should stop using fossil fuels altogether, we'd be facing another financial crisis bigger than the last, because of all the value that the banks would lose. By watching out for our self-interest, we are in fact benefiting the whole world."

"So now the oil industry has finally decided to publicly admit that climate change is happening?"

"Our voice has been drowned out in recent years. Continuing to deny that climate change was happening was getting harder and harder as weather disasters became more frequent and the world's scientists got more and more bold about speaking out. We knew that we needed to take more drastic action to prevent the world from getting caught up in this sky-is-falling mentality and doing something that would permanently kill the fossil fuel business, and with it, the global economy."

"So a few years ago I convened a conference of the world's leading fossil fuel industry executives in Riyadh, Saudi Arabia, to come up with a new game plan. At the conference we decided that we would all contribute to a fund to develop the technology necessary to geoengineer the climate using sulfur aerosols. The price tag was surprisingly low: only several billion U.S. dollars. And the annual cost of constantly flying half a dozen planes around the stratosphere to spread the sulfate aerosol would only cost around 700 million dollars a year."

"But we knew that, despite this insanely low cost, the governments of the world would never be able to come to an agreement on whether or not geoengineering should be used. So we decided that we would begin implementing it in secret once the technology was developed. Since global temperatures fluctuate from year to year, it would take the scientific community many years to notice that the warming trend had been reversed. And as long as we kept what we were doing a secret for at least a decade, by the time they discovered us, the world would be locked into geoengineering for good."

"But locking the world into geoengineering means we will have to keep doing it for thousands of years to keep the climate stable," Andrew retorted.

"At least for the next few hundred years, until fossil fuels run out."

"But even after that, the concentration of carbon dioxide in the atmosphere would still be far too high. We would have to take all that carbon dioxide out of the atmosphere before we could stop."

"Well, that's something that people will have to figure out in a few hundred years. That's plenty of time for new technology to be developed that can extract carbon dioxide from the atmosphere. I'm more concerned with protecting the people alive today."

"But you don't know that that new technology will be

developed. And what about all the other negative side effects and risks of geoengineering? Have you taken those into account?"

"What side effects are you talking about?"

"I'm talking about the fact that just reducing the global temperature won't restore the climate to normal. There's a chance that worldwide rainfall will decrease, and some storm systems could completely collapse, like the Asian monsoon. Not to mention this doesn't solve ocean acidification, either."

"The risks of that happening are small, and we consider them to be acceptable."

"Oh, that's easy for you to say. How do you know the risks are small? No one has ever done this before. Didn't you say yourself that we can never truly predict local weather?"

"And if we do nothing, those same people will be doomed to poverty for decades to come, because another global financial collapse and the drastic rise in energy prices that would follow would hurt everyone."

"But how can a small group of people make a judgment like that for the entire world?"

"That's how the world works, Andrew. If we had true democracy all the time, the world would be in chaos. People don't really know what's best for them."

"OK, so if you had this plan to secretly geo-engineer the climate all along, why did you need me? Why did you need to make people think that China was manipulating the weather?"

"The key issue was how, in the meantime, could we stop the political momentum that has been growing around the world to limit greenhouse gas emissions. World governments are finally, after many decades of delay, very close to coming up with an enforceable, global agreement that would penalize the fossil fuel industry and significantly limit emissions. This might mean the beginning of a slow death for our industry, before our plan could be fully realized."

"We had been coming up with alternative narratives for decades, but each of those had one by one been discredited. We needed a new one; a story that would capture the public's attention with enough vigor that it would once again drown out the truth. The question was: what would our alternative narrative be? I discovered the answer when I met Howard Harrison."

Rothschild turned and looked at Mr. Harrison again, smiling this time. Mr. Harrison didn't return the smile. "Howard had this theory that the Chinese government had found a way to use weather manipulation as a weapon against America. This, as I quickly learned, was scientifically impossible, but it presented an intriguing new potential to influence public opinion. If only we could create some evidence to support this hypothesis, and get enough media coverage for it, we might be able to once again create enough plausible deniability that climate change was really happening. And additionally, we'd get China and America bickering again, delaying a new climate change treaty from being signed. Fear of the 'other,' after all, is one of the strongest, most basic emotional drivers of human behavior."

Rothschild had used that term —plausible deniability— that Mazken and Charlie had taught him. And suddenly, Andrew felt the guilt from Yang Fei's death come storming back. He'd seen himself as fighting for justice, for truth. But in the end, he'd used the same tactics as these powerful men to manipulate people. It wasn't just Yang Fei; he'd done the same thing to Charlie. He'd let the ends justify the means.

"So with the idea planted that China had been manipulating the weather in America for many years," Rothschild continued, "and everyone arguing again about whether or not extreme weather events were really being caused by climate change, we would secretly begin geoengineering. By the time our new narrative could be investigated and eventually discredited, our geoengineering operation would be far along enough that it would be too late to turn back. Then the world would see that there is in fact a quick and inexpensive way to solve the problem. And the global urgency to reduce carbon emissions would dissipate as quickly as tailpipe exhaust in an afternoon breeze."

"But why would Lao Cheng agree to that? He's very nationalistic. Your plan makes China look like the bad guy."

"If the oil industry declines, Mr. Cheng declines with it. And China is more dependent on oil and coal now than any country in the world. A treaty to drastically reduce fossil fuel use would have massive implications for China's economic growth. It was a sacrifice he was willing to make, and that ultimately, the Chinese government was likely to accept. Besides, once the Americans started accusing China of weather manipulation, China would be bound to start doing the same to America. It would only intensify the confusion. Some would believe America, and some would believe China."

Rothschild paused and looked at him. Andrew felt like he was giving him the same look Mazken always had when he seemed to be reading his mind. Would Rothschild be able to tell what he was thinking about all this?

Then Rothschild continued. "What nobody anticipated was the development of what our engineers are calling particle X. I'm sure you learned about it in those files you stole from us. It's designed to use latent energy from the air to stay in the stratosphere for up to fifty years, compared to the two-year life of the sulfur dioxide aerosol. Once we pull the trigger and particle X is up there, we can announce what we've to the world, without fearing that anyone would try to stop us— because they couldn't. Then we could sit back and let the scientists confirm the positive cooling effects, and proclaim that reducing carbon dioxide emissions was no longer necessary. In other words, we no longer needed the China front. But by the time particle X was developed and tested, and word reached me, you had already escaped from Lao Cheng. I tried to convince Howard to recall you, but he insisted on giving you more time. So I allowed it, thinking no harm would come, and that you might even prove useful in some other way. Little did I know that in a short time you'd discover our China-based facility."

"So why locate the geoengineering research centers in China and Russia? Why not in the U.S. where you could keep a closer eye on them?"

"I would have thought that was obvious. The chances of our operations being discovered and leaked were much higher in North America. Look what happened to the original HAARP. We needed to locate them in the most isolated areas of the world, under a less transparent government. Inner Mongolia and Siberia were ultimately the best options."

"But we found out what you were up to anyway. Documents detailing exactly what you planned to do are already on their way to the U.S."

"And I expect that you will tell me where you've sent those documents and how to intercept them before they reach their destination."

"And what will happen if I don't cooperate?"

A shadow passed across Rothschild's face. "You don't want to go down that path, Andrew."

"Will you just kill me, like you were going to do to my father if he had got in the way?"

Rothschild raised his eyebrows. "Your father was a nuisance, but I would never have tried to kill him, nor would I try to kill you. Your father and I used to be friends, before he started down the wrong path with Jonah Wong."

"Why should I believe you?"

"If I were in the business of killing people who occasionally get in my way, do you think you would still be standing here right now? I'll admit you've caused a lot of trouble for us so far, as have your friends. You ought to choose your friends more wisely, Andrew. Jonah Wong is not a good man. Once he's arrested, and I assure you that will be very soon, he will likely be sentenced to death for the violent crimes he's committed. And your friends May and Charlie are now also facing serious criminal charges, as would you if I hadn't intervened. But if you cooperate today, I will make sure that Mr. Cheng lets you and your friends go without punishment."

A sense of dread welled up inside Andrew. So Rothschild was prepared to use coercion after all. And yet, Rothschild's position on geoengineering made sense on some level. Would it really be so bad to cooperate with him?

Rothschild watched him. "In addition to saving your friends, the job I'm offering you comes with significant benefits. The pay will be considerable, and you will be joining an elite community of some of the world's most powerful businessmen. Your career future will be very bright. But most importantly, you'll be helping to preserve climate stability on this planet. Future generations will ultimately thank us for what we're about to do, Andrew. Geoengineering is the only viable solution to slow the effects of climate change on the scale that the world needs, in the short amount of time it has to act."

Andrew looked over at Mr. Harrison, who was still leaning against the wall with his arms crossed and pipe hanging from his mouth. Then he looked out the window at the cloud of smog covering Beijing.

And he knew what he had to do.

CHAPTER 42:

LIBERATION

The whole thing made Howard feel uneasy. Watching Will Rothschild try to coax Andrew into joining him, he reflected on the last twenty-four hours. He didn't like being in China, with its thick smog, nightmarishly congested traffic, people spitting everywhere and staring at him. Most of all, he didn't like being in the office of the man who until very recently he'd thought was his enemy. And as far as Howard was concerned, Cheng still was his enemy, whether Will was working with him or not.

When Will had first told him what was going on, he hadn't believed it. But then Will asked him to accompany him to China. First they had gone to the geoengineering center in Inner Mongolia, and Howard had seen the planes they were building there, and heard the researchers talk about geoengineering and how it would be carried out. And slowly, he'd realized that Will was serious about this. He still held on to the possibility that even Will was being deceived, and that Lao Cheng really was controlling the weather somehow. But what had been most startling was that one of the most powerful industrialists in the modern world really believed global warming was real. If that were the case, could it really be a liberal conspiracy like he'd always believed?

Or perhaps Will was *part* of the liberal conspiracy. After

all, he had talked about a small group of elite businessmen who seemed to be making most of the decisions that impacted key events throughout the world. And now he was part of this plan to engineer the earth's climate. If there was one thing Howard knew for certain, it was that man was not meant to play God like this. The climate and the weather were the dominion of the heavens. It made sense to him when he thought it was the Chinese. Godless communists had no respect for the boundaries between heaven and earth. But now that he knew it was really Will's plan, could he, Howard Harrison, really stand by and support such a project, even if it was ultimately to the benefit of America?

But he couldn't defy Will Rothschild. To do so would not only mean being cut off from what was by far his largest source of donations to run the Institute, but would also be political suicide. Rothschild probably had a third of the current U.S. Congress in his pocket. And even if he had been deceived, hadn't it been Rothschild who'd given his project life when he had very few supporters? He owed Rothschild a debt that could not easily be repaid. Still, he didn't like the way Rothschild had deceived him. He knew one thing for sure: he'd never be able to fully trust Will again.

And now, he felt uneasy about what might happen to Andrew. He knew that despite how conciliatory Will sounded, he was not as forgiving as he was letting on. And it was hard to imagine that here, in Cheng's country, Will could restrain Cheng from having his revenge. If Andrew decided to cooperate, things would not be as rosy as Will made them sound. Will was a salesman, and he needed to sell Andrew in order for them to follow through with their plan.

Then he heard Andrew speak. "You're right Mr. Rothschild. I know my father wouldn't agree, but it seems like controlling the climate may be in the greater interest of humanity. If you're really going to let my friends go, I'll help you."

Andrew's statement caught Howard off guard for a moment. Was Andrew really agreeing to work with him so

315

easily? But then again, Andrew had always acted rashly without really thinking things through. Well, perhaps things were better this way. It would save Andrew a lot of pain.

Rothschild smiled, "A very good choice, Andrew," he picked up his phone and began to make a call, "Mr. Cheng, Andrew has agreed to cooperate. Please come up to your office."

"Now, the first order of business: I need to get those documents back—every copy of them—that you took from the geoengineering center. We've already got the ones you and May had on you, but I'm assuming there are others."

"Well, I'll tell you where they are, but one of them will be difficult to get to."

"We have agents everywhere, Andrew. Nothing is outside our reach. Are you referring to the ones you hid at the port of Tianjin?"

"Yes, there are copies in one of Jonah's containers. They are rolled up inside some porcelain vases. But like I said, by now the container has already been loaded onto a ship and is on its way to America."

"Not a problem. We can intercept it when it reaches its destination port in the U.S."

The door to the office opened, and Mr. Cheng entered. Just looking at the man gave Howard a feeling of repulsion. Howard avoided his gaze. But Mr. Cheng seemed more interested in Andrew. He attempted a smile, but there was a fire in his eyes that made Howard think he hadn't forgiven Andrew for what had transpired.

"You make-a right choice. Now we crush-a Mista Wong and friends."

"Well, that's the other problem... see, there's another copy of the documents out there. Jonah has some friends who helped us hide them in a bank vault at the Bank of China... the branch on Chang'an Street in the Central Business District. It's heavily guarded, so it will be difficult to get in. But I'm sure they will stand down for a company of PLA soldiers."

"Yes, yes, we do that. No one can stop-a my men." Cheng

made a call and barked some orders in Chinese, then said. "They go now."

Rothschild continued to watch Andrew. "Now, about your friends, May and Charlie," He looked over at Cheng, "I told Andrew we could let his friends go if he cooperated. We will need to hold them until all this is wrapped up, but then we must let them go."

Lao Cheng's face began to turn red. "Then who pays for death of my mistress?"

"We will have Jonah Wong. I'm sure you'd be happy to have the man who's been destroying your infrastructure locked away."

"It not enough. I want-a him pay," Lao Cheng pointed at Andrew. "I no let he friends go."

"But you said you would let them go if I cooperated," said Andrew, turning back to Will.

Howard looked at Wills face, and to his surprise, the man who he'd always known to be so certain of everything looked conflicted. He decided he could no longer remain silent, given where things seemed to be headed. "Now see here Will," he interjected. "You did tell the boy that you'd let his friends go. Don't ya think we should hold to that?"

Just then, Cheng's phone rang. He picked it up, and after a few seconds a look of rage crossed his face. He shouted something in Chinese, and then hung up the phone.

"What's happened, Cheng?" asked Will slowly.

"EJF get-a inside NOCCOC."

CHAPTER 43:

BREAKING CHINA

Andrew was relieved that neither Rothschild, nor Mr. Harrison nor Lao Cheng had noticed him take out his phone underneath Lao Cheng's desk. Right before he'd made up the story about a copy of the documents being hidden at the Bank of China, he'd called Jonah under the table, with the volume on his speaker all the way down. He hoped Jonah would overhear the conversation and know that most of the PLA soldiers would soon leave NOCCOC. Then they would have much less resistance entering the building.

And it seemed his plan had worked. With any luck, they would be able to take over the eighth floor. Then they could find out where the control terminal was for the planes.

Rothschild turned on Andrew. "How did they get in?"

"I have no idea. Maybe they have someone working with them on the inside."

Rothschild narrowed his eyes, "And you have no idea who? You've been working with them. You must have had an idea of their plan."

"Getting into NOCCOC was never part of our plan. We were just trying to get the documents out of China."

Rothschild continued to stare suspiciously at Andrew. "Perhaps. Isn't it convenient for them that most of Mr. Cheng's soldiers just left the building based on your advice."

"They've probably been watching outside. Anyone could notice a large group of soldiers leaving and see an opportunity."

"An opportunity for what? A rescue mission?"

"I would imagine so."

"We must go to safe place," said Lao Cheng.

Rothschild stood up. "I saw the documents you stole and what they contained. If you read them too, you would know that our schedule would have us start geoengineering tomorrow. In that case, you should have known that documents sent on a ship would not make it to the U.S in time to stop us. So you must have had another plan. I'm guessing you planned to try and disable the planes from the terminal here."

Andrew just stared at him silently. He didn't know what to say.

Rothschild watched Andrew, and when he didn't reply, a smile began to form on Rothschild's face. He turned to Lao Cheng, "Call your men back. Sending them to Bank of China was just a distraction. Andrew is not really cooperating."

Without hesitating, Andrew turned and lunged at Lao Cheng, catching him off guard and knocking the phone out of his hand. It fell to the floor. Lao Cheng shouted at the security personnel, and they began to run over. Andrew looked around wildly, then grabbed a stone Buddha statue off a shelf, and brought it down on the phone with all his might.

The phone shattered. Lao Cheng screamed with rage. Then the security guards grabbed him.

They held his arms behind his back, pinning him to the wall, as Rothschild walked over.

"Quick thinking Andrew. You really had me fooled for a few minutes. That's another thing I like about you. It's unfortunate that you've chosen the wrong side."

"I won't let you go through with this. You're not really trying to make things better. This is just about holding on to your profits and power."

"You really are just as righteous as your father. You don't seem to understand that this is just how the world works.

There's no such thing as justice. There are only people with power, and people without."

Rothschild turned to Lao Cheng and Mr. Harrison. "We're going to launch the planes now before EJF has a chance to stop us."

"Will, shouldn't we think this through a little more?" Mr. Harrison interjected. "It seems like people are bound to find out about this. Do you really want the world to know that we are tryin' to control the climate?"

"I'm sorry you weren't involved earlier Howard," Andrew detected annoyance in Rothschild's voice, "but we've been planning this for years and don't have time to second guess it now."

"It's too late anyway. Jonah is going to be here soon. You'll be outnumbered."

To Andrew's surprise, Lao Cheng began to laugh. "He not-a find us."

Rothschild smiled again. "Mr. Cheng is right. We are about to head to a very secure place. But not with you, Andrew. You'll stay here with these two fine gentlemen," he looked back and forth at the security men, smiling. Then he turned and headed for the door. Lao Cheng followed, barking instructions to the security guards to lock Andrew in the back closet. Mr. Harrison paused for a moment, watching Andrew. "Come on Howard," Rothschild said.

Andrew finally made eye contact with Mr. Harrison, and to his surprise, he saw doubt. "You can't let them do this Mr. Harrison. You know it's not right."

"Howard," Rothschild barked again, more sharply.

Slowly, Mr. Harrison turned away and followed Rothschild, who closed the door behind them.

The men began dragging Andrew toward the back of the office. "Dung yixia," *Wait a moment*, Andrew said.

"Ni hui shuo Zhongwen?" *You can speak Chinese?* One of them said, surprised. Maybe he could distract them.

"Nimen weishenme ting ta de hua? Ta gen yige huai de laowai hezuo," *Why are you listening to him? He's cooperating*

320

with an evil foreigner." This caused them to stop for a second. It looked to Andrew like they were considering what he'd said. Could he find a way to break free?

Suddenly he heard shouts and the sound of fighting outside the door. The men turned toward the door, and as they did so Andrew quickly swung one of his feet up and kicked one of them in the stomach. The guard let go of Andrew and dropped to his knees. The other guard tried to grab Andrew's other arm, but Andrew swung it around and landed a blow to his head. Once both his arms were free, he grabbed their guns and pointed them at the guards, while moving toward the door.

Just then the door burst open and in came Jonah and Fritz, flanked by a dozen or so members of EJF.

"Took you long enough," Andrew said, grinning at them. "Did you see Lao Cheng and Rothschild? We've got to catch them. They just left to go launch the planes. It sounds like they're going to some secret location inside the building."

"Rothschild is here?"

"Yes, along with my former boss. They were working together the whole time. It's a long story. Come on."

Andrew ran out of the office into the hallway and looked in both directions. At the end of the hallway he saw an elevator door begin to close. Inside was Lao Cheng, who was crouched down looking at something, along with Rothschild and Harrison who were standing behind him. He began to run toward them. But the elevator door had already closed. He watched the numbers descending. But after the number five went dark, the number three didn't light up. It was as if the elevator had disappeared.

"Where did the elevator go?" asked Jonah, who had just caught up with him.

Then they heard the ding of the other elevator arriving. The door opened and out stepped a familiar figure.

"I-phone?" said Andrew in disbelief. She was followed by a young foreign woman, who was looking nervous.

"Teacha Osley?" I-phone looked surprised to see him. "What happen to you? You disappear suddenly and not teach class anymore. You so bad for business." Then she looked at Jonah, Fritz and all the EJF fighters. "You form your own English company Teacha Osley?"

"Not at all. I-phone, haven't you noticed that there's a fight going on here?"

I-phone shook her head, then she raised her eyebrows and clapped her hand to her mouth, "Teacha Osley, you work with the mafia?"

"No, no, I-phone. We're the good guys. Lao Cheng is the criminal. And he's about to commit a huge crime."

I-phone glared at him, "You trying to destroy my business by take away my key client?"

"Excuse me miss," Jonah interjected, "Lao Cheng is trying to carry out a vast international conspiracy. It's imperative that we expose him."

"Ok, well it have to wait until after class."

Andrew and Jonah looked at each other. "Is she for real?" Jonah said.

"Yes, I finally find a suitable replacement for you, and Lao Cheng want to meet her right away. I think Lao Cheng prefer a girl," I-phone grinned and pointed at the girl, who smiled meekly at them.

"He's not in his office, I-phone."

"What? How you know?"

"Because we just saw him get into this elevator. He started going down and then disappeared after the fifth floor."

I-phone stared at him, and then began to shake her head.

"Not disappear Teacha Osley, just go to fourth floor."

"What are you talking about? There is no fourth floor. You're the one who told me why Chinese elevators always skip four."

"You not so good at math, huh Teacha Osley? That's why you just English teacha," she giggled, "You count how many floors outside?"

Andrew tried to picture the outside of the NOCCOC building. "I'm not sure."

"There is eight."

"Ok…"

"And how many in elevator?"

"Eight…" and then Andrew realized what she meant, "The floor buttons go up to eight, and skip four…but there are still eight floors total…"

"My God, she's a genius," said Fritz, who was now staring at I-phone in a way that Andrew knew showed more than just plutonic interest.

I-phone shrugged. "I just notice it recently."

"Come on, we've got to find a way to get to that floor." They pressed the elevator button, and when it arrived he and Jonah stepped in. But Andrew noticed that Fritz wasn't moving. "Fritz, are you coming?"

"I'll join you in a bit, Drewster. First I need to ask Ms. I-phone here about…employment opportunities."

Andrew knew what was really going on, but he let Fritz be and got into the elevator.

"Now, there must be some way to trigger the elevator to go to this fourth floor," said Jonah. Andrew remembered seeing Lao Cheng crouch down, so he did so as well. Below the buttons, there was a panel with a keyhole. After some picking, Andrew got the panel open. Inside there was a lone button. Andrew pressed it, and the elevator doors began to close. They were headed down, until sure enough, they stopped between the third and fifth floor.

The door opened and two soldiers turned to look at who was coming out of the elevator. Andrew quickly delivered a kick to one, sending him sprawling on the ground. Andrew reached down and grabbed his gun, delivering another blow to the head, leaving the guard unconscious. He looked over and saw that Jonah was still wrestling with the other, but before he could intervene, Jonah had him in a headlock, and soon the man passed out.

"You're not a bad fighter for your age," Andrew said, then handed him the second gun he'd just picked up.

Jonah grinned. "I've kept in shape just for this occasion."

Andrew looked around and saw that they were in a

hallway that looked like the entrance to a karaoke club. The walls were lined with bright blinking lights, and down the hall, he could see a number of doors that were also lined with colorful flashing lights.

"This is amazing," said Jonah, looking around. "It looks like he's got his own private karaoke club here."

Andrew remembered what Charlie had told him about Lao Cheng taking all his enemies to his private karaoke club. So this was it.

Andrew and Jonah began to run down the hallway, peering into the doors through the windows. Some of them were empty karaoke or massage rooms, but soon they began finding rooms with people locked inside.

"This seems to be where they took the EJF fighters after they were captured. Well, now we've got our reinforcements in case the soldiers get back."

"I'll let them out, you keep going and try to find Lao Cheng," said Jonah.

As Andrew turned the corner at the end of the hallway, he heard a familiar voice calling his name from inside one of the rooms. He reached the door and opened it. Inside was Charlie, who was standing, clutching his side where Andrew could see a blood-stained bandage.

"Drew, they take May," he said. Before Andrew could respond, he heard footsteps behind him, and he turned around to see Lao Cheng, Rothschild and Mr. Harrison flanked by a group of soldiers. Rothschild was holding May with a gun to her head.

"We're going to launch the planes now," said Rothschild, with an unsettling air of calm. "You'd better not follow us again, or you can say goodbye to your girlfriend."

"Andrew, don't listen to him. You can't let them launch those planes," Andrew could tell May was afraid, but he could hear the resolve in her voice.

Just then Jonah and a crowd of EJF fighters rounded the corner. The soldiers turned their guns on the new arrivals, but only two shots went off before they had been overwhelmed.

Soon the soldier and EJF fighters were engaged in hand-to-hand combat.

"Andrew, we'll hold them off, you and Charlie have got to stop Rothschild," shouted Jonah. Andrew looked around and saw that Rothschild, Lao Cheng and Mr. Harrison were already down the hallway, with May still in tow. Andrew and Charlie pushed their way through the fight and took off after them.

They had a good head start, and Andrew just barely caught sight of them disappearing around another corner. They broke into a sprint, and when they rounded the corner they saw an open door and the face of Yu Mama peering through it, with Lao Cheng, Rothschild, May and Mr. Harrison behind her, already inside. She smiled triumphantly at him and began to close the door. Andrew ran toward it, but was too late. The door slammed shut, and he heard the sound of a large bolt being drawn across it.

"We gotta get inside," Charlie stepped backward and then rammed his whole body into the door. It didn't budge. "Drew, you must be able to break down this door. Come on, we do it together."

Both Andrew and Charlie slammed into the door as hard as they could, but still, it wouldn't budge.

"This isn't going to work, we need more help."

"We have no time. EJF still fighting soldiers. And all Lao Cheng has to do is flip some switches and the geoengineering will start."

And then, from behind the door, they heard the sound of breaking porcelain.

There was a thud, and then they heard Yu Mama screaming, and then one more smash. Then the door bolt slid back, and the door began to open. May appeared.

"Mr. Harrison just knocked out Lao Cheng and Yu Ma," she gasped

Andrew looked into the room and saw Mr. Harrison struggling with Rothschild, who seemed to be overwhelming him. Andrew ran up to Rothschild and delivered a kick to his side, sending him to the ground. Lying on his back, Rothschild turned to look at Andrew. "You've made the wrong choice, Andrew. You've just doomed this planet to…"

Andrew drove the butt of his gun into the side of Rothschild's head, and Rothschild passed out.

He looked around and saw Lao Cheng and Yu Ma lying unconscious, with pieces of porcelain scattered around them. Mr. Harrison was panting.

"I don't recall havin' this much excitement since the 90s," he gasped.

Andrew stared at Mr Harrison, with an urge to turn the gun on him, despite the fact that he had just helped them. Mr. Harrison looked back at him.

"I'm sorry for what I did, son." Mr. Harrison's voice had a different quality to it now. He wasn't speaking in his confident drawl anymore, but the voice also sounded more genuine. Somehow, Andrew began to feel sympathy for him. "I hope you can see that I'm on your side now," Mr. Harrison continued.

"Mr. Harrison… why did you decide to help us?"

"Well, I don't like the idea of someone controlling the climate any more than you do, son. And when Rothschild wouldn't hear my objections to his plan, and it seemed like he might hurt you, well, I decided I'd had enough of this."

Just then Jonah and the EJF fighters arrived. "You did it," he exclaimed. Then he looked at Mr. Harrison. "Who's he?"

"My former boss, Howard Harrison. He just knocked out Lao Cheng and his assistant. He's on our side now."

"That's good news," said Jonah, looking slightly confused. Suddenly they heard a gunshot. They all looked over to see Charlie pointing a gun at the control terminal. "I think it is disabled now," he grinned.

"Then let's get out of here," said Mr. Harrison. "This place gives me the creeps."

CHAPTER 44:

A PRESENT

Michael Harrison sat at his cubicle pondering a strange text message he'd received from Andrew Oxley. They hadn't been in touch since graduation, and yet Andrew had contacted him out of the blue, saying he was sending him a present from China.

Michael was touched that Andrew was still thinking of him. He still wondered why Andrew had taken the job with his father. The man was crazy—didn't Andrew see that? He wondered how they had been getting along. And he wondered how Andrew was doing in China. Hopefully, things were going well for him.

He looked up and saw his boss walking toward him. He was supposed to have finished proofreading that article half an hour ago. He quickly put his phone away and stared intently at the screen in front of him, as if he'd been concentrating hard. But his boss stopped beside his desk.

"You've got a lot of nerve, Harrison."

This was it, he was sure he was going to get fired this time. Better to go down fighting. Michael sighed, pulled his eyes away from the screen and looked up. "If you want me to do a quality editing job you've got to give me more time. I think I'd be embarrassing the paper if I let some of this stuff go out in the shape that it's in."

His boss stared blankly at him for a moment. Michael wondered which part of what he'd said hadn't computed. His boss had always seemed rather slow. Michael wondered how he'd gotten to be a senior editor in the first place.

"I'm not talking about the article. I'm talking about a half a dozen large boxes that arrived for you just now. I know people think they can get away with shopping online during working hours, but if you think you can have those things *delivered* here, that's crossing the line."

Now it was Michael's turn to stare blankly. Is this what Andrew had meant? "I have no idea what those are. I think my friend..." But he realized there was no use trying to explain. He got up and headed toward the front lobby.

"If you're going to ship things here, it's going to be public knowledge what you're ordering," his boss yelled after him. "So I told Angela to start opening them. Hope you didn't buy anything embarrassing."

Michael quickened his pace, and moments later emerged into the lobby to find a strange scene. The secretary, Angela, had opened two of the boxes and was now working on a third, looking quite perplexed. Each of the boxes so far contained a large porcelain vase with beautiful blue drawings on the outside. Was this the present Andrew had been talking about? And if so, why on earth would he send him such a gift?

Michael crossed the room to look more closely at one of the vases. They appeared to be hand pained and of very high quality. Then he looked around and noticed that several of his colleagues were peering over their desks at what was going on in the lobby. He was starting to feel very embarrassed and a little annoyed.

Michael's boss caught up with him and stopped when he saw the vases. "This is unbelievable," he said, shaking his head. "I'm going to have to tell Maria about this one."

He was going to tell the editor-in-chief. Any chance Michael had of advancing quickly here would be ruined. He lunged forward, "You can't, this is just a misunderstanding..." he stumbled over some packaging and bumped into the vase that Angela had placed on her desk. It crashed to the floor and shattered into pieces.

"Really, unbelievable," his boss said again. Michael was about to get up, but as he looked down, a small stack of papers that was visible among the pieces of the vase distracted him. He picked them up and began to read.

"Maria, you're not going to believe the scene down here. My new editorial assistant ordered..."

But Michael wasn't paying attention to his boss anymore. He was reading a note from Andrew saying that he'd uncovered a plot by a group of oil companies to geo-engineer the earth's climate. Now he was scanning through printouts of emails, schematics of what looked like a high altitude stealth plane, and a scientific paper describing a high tech nano-particle. Finally, there was a letter of intent signed by several major oil company executives saying how they would invest in research and implementation for geoengineering.

"Harrison, what are you staring at? Where did those papers come from?"

Michael looked up, his eyes wide. "We've got a new front-page story for tomorrow."

CHAPTER 45:

TIMES OF CHANGE

As Andrew strolled down a cobblestone street with May, their arms interlocked, he recalled how his father had taken him down to the docks to eat clam chowder as a boy. It had been his favorite food. Now he was taking her to try it.

"It's really beautiful here," she said. "I love the historic buildings. And I love how colorful the leaves are. They're even more brilliant than Boston."

"Maine is really beautiful in September."

"I suppose Washington D.C. will be beautiful in its own way, don't you think?"

"I'm sure it will be."

"What part of the government did you say Mr. Harrison got you a job in?"

"It's called the Federal Emergency Management Agency—FEMA. They're responsible for national disaster preparedness."

"Are you sure you don't want to work for the CIA anymore? You proved to be a pretty good spy after all."

"No, I'm done with that. I didn't like the person I had to become to be good at it. All the secrets and manipulation; it doesn't help to make the world a better place."

May smiled and put her head on his shoulder. "So now you'll work on climate change adaptation measures?"

"Hopefully, if I don't have to deal with too much bureaucracy in getting them to broaden their focus. You'd think we'd be better prepared to adapt to climate change given how long people have been talking about it, but surprisingly no one in the government is giving it much thought."

"Listen to you. And just weeks ago you were trying to convince me that the Chinese government could control the weather."

Andrew suddenly stopped and stared at a small vacant building by the waterside. "Where did it go?"

"Where did what go?"

"The chowder house I was going to take you to. Look, the building is empty."

"Oh, that's too bad. I guess they closed."

"I don't believe it."

"Why are you so surprised?"

"It was here for decades. I guess I just thought they'd be here forever."

"I see. I guess I'm just not that surprised because, you know, restaurants and stores in China close down all the time. One day you go for lunch and your favorite noodle place isn't there anymore, and so you just move on to the next one." May sighed and looked out over the water.

"Is something bothering you?" Andrew asked.

"Well, it's funny, you know I was so happy to get that job with the Washington Post, I mean it's what I always wanted. And I'm glad we're going to be together in DC," she smiled at Andrew and held his arm. "I guess I'm just going to miss China, and even my parents," she paused. "And I'm not sure if I can stay in America forever."

"Let's just take things one step at a time, alright?" Andrew smiled and pulled her closer to him. They were both silent for a minute. Andrew looked out across the Portland harbor, out toward the ocean. There wasn't a cloud in the sky. And yet he knew that as they stood there, another hurricane was building strength and was about to make landfall near Virginia.

Then May asked, "Does it bother you that the

geoengineering technology is in the hands of the Chinese government now? Would you feel safer if it was with the American government?"

Andrew laughed, "You'd think that I would, but to be honest I don't know if it really matters. Chinese government, American government, oil companies... I wouldn't trust anyone with this technology. Since it's not really that expensive to build—I mean, a few billion dollars is nothing for most major countries or corporations—practically anyone could duplicate it now and use it the wrong way. The important thing is that people know it's out there, and hopefully, the fear and stigma around using it will keep those planes on the ground. Just like with nuclear weapons."

"I think there's a lot more fear of nuclear weapons. I'm not sure if everyone is just as scared of geoengineering, even though using it incorrectly could damage the climate just as badly as a nuclear winter. Surely there's someone else just like Rothschild out there who thinks it would be a good idea for whatever reason."

"Speaking of Rothschild, you'd better keep an eye on him. I doubt he's going to be convicted of anything. I don't think there's any law in America against conspiring to manipulate the climate. And even if they find something to charge him with, I'm sure he'll have the best lawyers money can buy."

"I'm sure the Post will let me write any story I want about him. You know exposing billionaires' corruption is a hot topic these days."

"Don't forget, the Post is owned by one of those billionaires now."

"Right," May grimaced. "These are strange times. We'll see."

"Well, I'm sure Charlie would be happy to keep tabs on the Chinese billionaires for you at the same time."

"I thought he was going to be helping Mazken with his life-coaching business after he recovers?"

"Yes, but you know after he helped expose Lao Cheng, he's suddenly got a lot of political recognition in China. I wouldn't be surprised if the Chinese government started going to him every now and then to help them rein in rogue billionaires by leaking their activities to the western media."

"That's a good point."

They had been walking along the docks, and Andrew was keeping an eye out for another place to eat. As they approached a pier where several sailboats were docked, Andrew squinted at a figure near one of the boats. As they got closer he realized that he hadn't been mistaken.

It was his Uncle Cooper.

"Uncle Cooper, what are you doing out here?"

Cooper looked up and grinned. "I had wanted to surprise you. After all these years, I decided to get the sailboat seaworthy again and take you two and Rose and Mathias out for a sail sometime."

"It's a beautiful boat," May commented. Then she looked at Andrew. "But isn't this the one that your father..." she trailed off.

"Yeah," said Andrew. He looked at Cooper.

"I finally decided to stop letting the past prevent me from moving forward and enjoying these things," Cooper said.

"But is sailing really safe anymore? I mean, with the weather becoming so unpredictable, how do you know we won't get caught in a storm again?"

"The weather has always been unpredictable," said Andrew. "That's just how nature is. Storms will come and go; the climate will change. We've just got to be resilient enough to adapt."

The End